Demon Holiday
Torval, Demon Third Class, Layer Four Hundred Twelve of the Eighth Circle of Hell, has been in the business of chastising sinners longer than he can remember. Delivering punishment is the only job he's ever known—the only job he's ever wanted. After Torval witnesses something unexpected, his demonic Overseer demands that he take time off to resolve this personal crisis. And so, Torval, the demon, finds himself sent on vacation ... to Earth, the proving ground of souls!

Demon Ascendant
Torval, Demon Third Class, Layer Four Hundred Twelve of the Eighth Circle of Hell, on vacation to Earth has managed to find another demon, dated a woman and inadvertently explored some of the sins of humankind: greed, gluttony, and lust. Through all this, his biggest struggle involves deciding if he wants his holiday to end or to continue forever.

TANSTAAFL Press
891 PH 10
Castle Rock, WA 98611

Visit us at www.TANSTAAFLPress.com

Enter the Apocalypse

First printing—TANSTAAFL Press
Copyright © 2017 by Thomas Gondolfi
Cover art: Andrei Bat

Printed in the USA
ISBN 978-1-938124-13-6

Book layout by Hydra House

Enter the Apocalypse

Edited by Thomas Gondolfi

TANSTAAFL PRESS

Novels by Tom Gondolfi
from TANSTAAFL Press

An Eighty Percent Solution – CorpGov Chronicles: Book One

In a world where corporations suborn governments as a part of good business practice and unregistered humans can be killed without penalty, Tony Sammis, a midlevel corporate functionary, finds himself unwittingly a pawn in a guerilla war between a powerful cabal of business leaders and an elusive but deadly underground movement. His final solution to the biological terror unleashed mirrors Tony's own twisted sense of justice.

Thinking Outside the Box – CorpGov Chronicles: Book Two

Winning one war doesn't seem to be enough. Tony Sammis and the Green Action Militia are once again thrust into the center of a conflict that will change the lives of everyone in the solar system. This time they are allies with the fledgling CorpGov and even the United States government against the ravages of the corrupt Metropolitan Police force. The GAM and their allies are fighting a losing war with few soldiers and even fewer weapons. Behind the scenes, a humble and unsuspected power block lurks with its own axe to grind.

Self-interest, romance, freedom, and a lust for power simmer together in this chaotic soup of tension, intrigue, assassination, and war.

The Bleeding Edge – CorpGov Chronicles: Book Three

Tony Sammis and Nanogate lead a patchwork alliance that includes the nascent CorpGov, Green Action Militia, the president of the United States, the Pacific Northwest Mob, most of the megacorps and the United Brotherhood of Bodyguards. The war the CorpGov alliance knows they can't win has begun, but they are no longer fighting to win. Tony and Nanogate know they may not survive, but they intend to deliver the most grievous wounds they can. The most dangerous animal is one with no hope.

Toy Wars

Flung to a remote world, a semi-sentient group of robotic mining factories arrive with their programming hashed. They can only create animated toys instead of normal mining and fighting machines. One of these factories, pushed to the edge of extinction by the fratricidal conflict, attempts a desperate gamble. Infusing one of its toys with the power of sentience begins the quest of a 2-meter-tall purple teddy bear and his pink polka-dotted elephant companion. They must cross an alien world to find and enlist the aid of mortal enemies to end the genocide before Toy Wars claims their family—all while asking the immortal question, "Why am I?"

Novels by Stephanie Weippert
from TANSTAAFL Press

Sweet Secrets

At seven, Michael gets into trouble no more than any other boy his age but he does have a sweet tooth. When the mailman brings a package from a candy company, he has to sneak just one. As he eats the chocolate, his home, stepfather, and everything he'd known melts around him and disappears. Next thing he knows he is in a dreamlike world. He is taken as an orphan, tested, and before he knows it is a student in the premier magic school on the planet. His fellow students can make cookies that fly and chocolate turtles that actually walk. Michael is told he has more power than any of them.

Brad is charged with watching his stepson Michael for first time. When the boy disappears before his eyes, Brad panics. Within hours he is on an adventure tracking his son alongside an enigmatic chef. Always one step behind his son, Brad soon finds that Michael is being used as a pawn between the two most powerful chefs on the crazy planet. Worse he has to get Michael home before his Mother finds out he's gone or there is going to be hell to pay.

Novels by Bruce Graw
from TANSTAAFL Press

The Faerie of Central Park

The last of her kind in New York City, Tillianita tends the land and beasts as best she can, reluctantly obeying her departed father's warning to avoid humans at all costs. A freak accident casts her out of the relative safety of Central Park. Lost and alone with a broken wing, she wonders if she'll ever see her home again.

On his own for the first time in his life, college freshman, Dave Thompson, isn't sure he'll ever fit in. When he stumbles upon an extremely realistic fairy doll, he thinks perhaps it might make a good present for a future date until he discovers that it's not a doll at all. His find turns not only his life upside down but also expands his narrow view of the world.

Lady Hornet

Elizabeth Fontaine is a lonely, ordinary young woman in a world where superheroes struggle daily against evil. To fill the empty void within her soul, she becomes a hero fangirl, following every super's event, subscribing to multiple fanzines, and never missing the daily superhero talk shows ... until one day, fate grants her the opportunity to leave behind her boring, dreary life and become what she's always dreamed of ... a superheroine!

Elizabeth learns the hard way the meaning of the phrase, "Caveat Emptor!" — let the buyer beware!

From the Editor

Thomas Gondolfi

I am pleased to bring you **Enter the Apocalypse**, a collection of stories from authors all over the globe. They all focus on one topic—holocausts. I didn't narrow our focus to one specific type, but instead let the creative muck of our authors ooze forth with anything they could envision. In the pages of this tome you will find zombies, magic, viruses, nuclear explosions, invasions, mold and many others turning our world upside down.

What you won't find within Enter the Apocalypse is a uniformity of dark, depressive works. There are several with a truly humorous bent. Whatever you do, don't miss *13 Signs of the Coming Apocalypse* or *Death, Inc*. I personally laughed soda through my nose at least once. Along this line I saved *The Fluffpocalypse* to round out our collection.

Don't get me wrong, I traditionally think of apocalyptic fiction as dark. I have chosen plenty of specific stories in this vein. *The Sky Fell*, our lead story, sets a severely dark tone. Other stories provide a leavening of hope, such as in *The Other White Meat*. It is hard to call out specific works in this editor's note because all of these have touched me in one way or another.

As this is our first anthology I have learned a great deal. To offer some of my naiveté, I had worried that we wouldn't receive enough quality submissions to make this trilogy work. Instead the submissions poured in and just kept on coming, even after we closed the window. The stories you have in the pages of this book alone were winnowed down from over three hundred great submissions. SURPRISE!

And if that weren't enough, I had decided to edit an anthology (instead of writing a novel for one of my series) so I could focus on another aspect of our business last year. SURPRISE!

I've spent enough time yammering. I'll let you get into the joy of the pieces that our authors have provided.

Thomas Gondolfi
www.TANSTAAFLPress.com

P. S. And yes, I do like making fun of myself in retrospect. Taking yourself too seriously is dangerous.

Contents

The Sky Fell

Donna J. W. Munro

Editor: Tout comprendre c'est tout pardonner, *translated means, "To understand all is to forgive all." It is one of the most contemptible lies ever uttered. There are things that just can't be rationalized. There are things that can't be absolved.*

Once the sky fell. Now, the dust piles against the dry stalks of corn and the stubble of mown winter wheat. Pheasant used to coo and peck there among my crops. Now only the rats and cockroaches swarm across the ground. Them and me.

We stumble in the furrows that once nursed life from cold dirt.

Somewhere down deep I know I should be planting. Or turning the ground. The seasons are written on my bones, even if I can't wake for the sun anymore. Even if my mind is clouded and my lungs don't breathe. I'm trapped in this meat that sometimes won't respond. I'm a rider trying to steer a hurricane.

My meat's range is written by my life and tied to this dirt. It stumbles across a territory that once I'd framed with barbed wire and dry-set stone walls. Sometimes, if I concentrate and the meat has eaten, I force the muscles to carry me into the house. When the soul ache that is the meat's hunger is satisfied, it lets me take charge of us. I head it into the house, rotting fingers hovering over pictures of those people I watched die. I stare at one picture of the woman and the boy, seated next to a man. Names flicker through my eye inside. Something with a c...Carmelle. Carmelle, my wife. Sam, my boy. Me...that name won't come. Not that I chase it. I don't deserve a name anymore. Not after what I've done.

I focus on one thought. Push pictures into the decaying connection between my mind and the meat. I order the meat up the stairs. It gargles protest. It's tired. It wants to stand and rest, but I'll never let it. It doesn't deserve rest. I push and push and finally, it grunts its understanding. We shuffle up the stairs, thumping and moaning.

I know it doesn't want to see what it's done. It's the only lesson I can teach it.

The top of the stairs pass and we shamble down the hall, it dragging my feet and protesting with pauses and grunts. I push, hard. It gives.

The hall isn't long, three doors and only two matter. We pass the boy's room. The crib stands upright in a mess of ripped toys, fetid clothes, and matchstick furniture. I'd been there when it happened. When the meat devoured Sam, I'd fought so hard. But I didn't understand how to move it then. I curse myself for that. If only I'd learned sooner. I might have been able to drive it from them.

I slow long enough to linger—one long look at the tiny lump covered by a blue sheet. Sometimes, when I'm particularly brave, I pull that sheet back. Stare at what's left of my little Sam. Today, I'm not that brave.

The meat moans, shifting back and forth on its feet.

I push it forward, to the other door. Its moans grate mournful across my hearing. Still, I shove. No escape, my friend. We will see it.

The meat moves forward again, though each step is lead-lined and slow.

The door opens on my bedroom. The chamber where my beautiful wife and I planned our family. We made Sam here one warm summer evening when the wind carried a honeysuckle scent across our skin. The memories once sweet, are now rocks in my mouth...its mouth. The meat.

I push and it moves forward, past the bed sheets made crisp with hospital corners. The last thing she did before—

It comes back to me in a wave, drowning me. I walked up behind her. I hadn't told her about the fireball. About the thing that fell from the sky. The dust hadn't come yet, but I'd breathed in the heat just the same. I'd changed that day.

It came on me slow, crushing the self from me, replacing me with hunger. Hunger is all I was. Sam cried in the other room. I saved him for later. I, the meat, closed in on my beautiful wife. The only woman I'd lain with. My only love. She'd turned when she heard me, brows drawn with concern.

"Has the fever broken?" she asked, with the music that was her voice.

The meat, I, grabbed her. Shoved her to the floor with a ferocious pounce. She was such a little thing. Strong in her way, but no way could she fight against the meat. Its teeth were in her. Tearing. It ate and ate and ate. Inside I screamed, but it was so hungry.

Now, I made the meat look at her, lying there a pile of bones.

It moans at me and lets the tears I feel run down our cheeks.

It moans at me, trying to pull away from my welling wave of loss. We stagger, drop to the floor next to her. The meat lets me direct the hand and I stroke her black hair, fanned out around her skull, bleached and dry from the years. I try to leave it there, to remember how beautiful it had been on our wedding day. Just to remember.

The memories are all I have.

Seven Lost Things

Eric James Spannerman

*Editor: Given a lever of fear and a fulcrum of anger,
the world can be plunged into chaos.*

He sat alone in a brewpub, drinking a wheat beer, finishing a ham and swiss on rye while pondering the box that contained the end of the world. Among other things, he wondered what effect the end of the world would have on craft-brewed beer.

He fiddled with the box, which sat next to his plate, and remembered how this decision had come to him. It started with the sharp, plastic smell of an Apple IIe as he unwrapped it. It began in earnest when he made the device type "Hello World" on the screen using a BASIC program that had taken him three hours to write. The little machines were going to make everyone smart and happy and rich. They were going to change the world.

And indeed, his world had changed. He lost things.

One: Stability

Precisely fifteen years ago, his workday had begun with a mandatory-attendance department meeting. It ended with him in the parking lot of the building where he had worked for over a decade, clutching a cardboard box of personal possessions—verified as such by a security guard—and blinking in the sunlight.

By afternoon, he was sitting on his sofa, staring into the middle distance. He stirred slightly when his wife came in.

"Hello, Barb."

She was first startled, and then cheered by his unexpected presence. A fraction of a second later, she was frightened by the look on his face.

They sat together as he explained—about the new site in India, the contractors, and the severance package. Looking for some comfort, he pointed out they'd be able to keep group medical coverage for a year and a half or so. The premiums would be high, but not as high as the full cost of keeping his diabetes in check.

Days passed. Then weeks. Methodical by nature, he ran through the obligatory steps of visiting the job bank and going to interviews. This turned out to be a complicated and time-consuming way to discover that his skill set, while not precisely obsolete, was not precisely in demand, either.

Eventually, he ended up in a strip-mall "retraining center," pursuing a new career in computer security. He reasoned that companies willing to outsource just about everything else would insist that access to critical systems be handled by someone they knew—not an anonymous mailbox.

For the next ten months, he came to a beige room and learned things. It wasn't all that different from his job, except that the time he spent there was emptying his bank account rather than filling it.

Barb had gone back to work, cutting hair. The hours were odd and long, and the pay was uncertain. Even when she spent time at the shop, there wasn't any money unless there were customers. Sometimes there were, and sometimes there weren't.

Graduation brought a series of interviews. Somewhere after the fifth, the impersonal humiliations began to run together in his mind. Eventually, there was a spot for him in a beige cube, and the numbers in their bank account began getting larger. They agreed Barb would keep cutting hair until the credit cards were paid off.

That day never came.

As it turned out, he had been wrong about security. If the price got low enough and the risks looked like something that would happen in a different bonus period, management was willing to turn the keys over to just about anyone. As long as it could be described as "industry standard," how could anyone be blamed if it didn't work out?

After just six months, he found himself holding another box of personal possessions in another parking lot. This time, he barely knew his former coworkers.

Eventually, he found a position where he worked from an anonymous cube in a consulting agency with an equally anonymous name—General Solutions, or somesuch. Half the time, he couldn't remember it. Like Barb, his hours were long and the pay was uncertain. Also like her, he was paid only when there were customers. Sometimes there were, and sometimes there weren't. Unlike her, he typically traveled for three weeks out of the month. Customers wanted the convenience of having him on site.

Two: Belief

He tapped the cover of Pandora's box, lighting its screen. It was an aging portable device, once called a palmtop. It was cheap to buy and hard to trace. Embedded in its memory were codes that would awaken other programs and set processes in motion. Those processes would erase most of modern existence.

He put the palmtop down and concentrated on remembering Barb's face. The concentration yielded two scenes.

One was in the living room, when he arrived at midday, again unemployed. He remembered the deep lines of weariness on her forehead and around the corners of her mouth. As he explained his plan for another job hunt, she looked at a far corner of the room.

His second image of Barb was lit by the glow of their home computer screen. Even in the dim light, her smile was unmistakable. They were looking at their investment portfolio.

The portfolio contained a promise: the promise of a day when Barb could stop cutting hair and he could stop traveling three weeks a month. They weren't going to retire on the Riviera, but they could see the day coming when their investment income would render all but a little part-time work unnecessary. They were happy with that promise.

They got caught in the crash, of course. In a matter of weeks, the wealth melted away like fairy gold, along with the future it represented.

At some point, he and Barb stopped looking—first at the accounts, and then at each other. They no longer lay in bed and talked about what they would do when he quit. Instead, they lay together and said nothing. He felt her growing ever wearier.

Three: Home

Less than three years ago, he came home to the biggest change of all. It began with Barb in the dining room, sitting at the table, with her face puffy and eyes wet. The table, normally a mass of unopened mail and discarded odds and ends, was perfectly clean, except for one thick envelope, filled with neat papers. Without looking, he knew what they were.

He signed, of course. No point in dragging it out. She got the house, he got the car, and they split everything else down the middle. They promised to remain friends and not be bitter, but never really talked again.

He started living in a rental suite that bore a striking resemblance to the anonymous beige cubes where he worked. Sometimes, on a long assignment, he moved everything into storage and saved the rent, taking the first available unit when he returned. It really didn't matter.

Four: Craftsmanship

He could remember distinctly when work stopped mattering.

The blond guy wearing a blue blazer and khaki pants came down his row of cubes, toothpick in his mouth, looking pissed.

"You mind explaining to me why the hell SoBreeze Chemical was off line for six fucking hours last night?" The blond guy's jaw jutted out.

He'd frowned, and poked at the entries in his worklog. Memory came flooding back.

"Oh, yeah, they were a mess. They had six different versions of the remote-sensing hardware drivers on different systems, their core components were patched beyond recognition, and their configuration was twisted into some totally non-standard piece of shit. I tore everything out, upgraded to current and standardized the config across all the boxes."

"So who was screaming for that?"

"Nobody, really, but it had to be done. Their entire process monitoring system was ready to fall apart."

"I thought you fixed that the week before."

"I slapped some configuration around; there was no way it would hold together past the next component upgrade. I told them that at the time."

The blond guy pulled the toothpick out of his mouth and stabbed it in the air. "You took a working system off line, and charged the client for something that nobody requested?"

He'd felt the color rising in his cheeks. "They sure as hell would have requested it when it crashed in the middle of the day again and shut down their entire production line."

"Next time, wait for that!" The blond guy's face was red. "When that happens, I can sell double-rates to get it fixed. For this bullshit—" he gestured toward the work log "—I'm going to have to give it to them, and end up apologizing."

The blond guy turned away and walked back down the row of cubes, pulling on his belt loops and muttering.

So he learned to do what was expected, which was usually the minimum necessary to keep systems functioning. Or at least maintain a semblance of functioning. Security holes and operational anomalies were OK, assuming the equally-harassed auditors didn't find them. It all looked good on the surface, and clients could be assured that state-of-the-art technology was being used in there someplace.

Five: Hope

He fingered one of the mustard packets that came with the sandwich and sized himself up. He was the perfect worker of the information age. He owned no real estate and few things. With no family and friendships as ephemeral as his address, he could go practically anywhere to work, and often did. He was, as one brochure describing his services explained, "... able to travel the globe in search of opportunity, and follow wherever it goes." Mostly for lack of anything better to do with his life.

He remembered the e-mail explaining the last major job change, the one that would kill him. "To ensure our continued competitiveness" it had begun, before going on to explain that recent labor law changes had opened the "exciting new possibility" of making almost all employees independent contractors, able to pursue "a wide range of opportunities." As such, they would be free to pursue "multiple options" for health insurance, which would no longer be furnished to "independent knowledge workers."

A few phone calls confirmed what he already knew. "We can't afford to accept a known problem," the health insurance agents had explained, with just the right mix of regret and firmness. As a diabetic, he couldn't get insurance for much less than the cost of his treatments. Those costs, added to bare-bones living expenses, would exhaust his savings and credit lines in about three years, meaning his treatments would stop about a year before he reached the end of the waiting period for subsidized care.

He checked with hospitals and they assured him that emergency rooms would, of course, treat all patients with immediate, life-threatening conditions, but no, they could not dispense maintenance medication without being paid in full. They had stockholders to answer to, after all.

Six: Loyalty

He tapped the security code into the palmtop. If he connected to the bar's wireless access point and uploaded a few small pieces of code, it would be over. The world where he had spent most of his adult life—the world of datasets and connections, the world of instant information, the world where fortunes existed only as magnetic squiggles on metallic disks— would be gone. Along with it would go the world of everyday devices—the ones that allowed people to get their bank balances and driving directions from a portable phone and the card reader that verified their identity at an apartment door. Everything that depended on the big networks would simply cease to function. All the way from the big machines that produced electricity to the little ones that played music. And that would be his gift.

He remembered passing, bleary-eyed, through an office checkout point somewhere in the Midwest. It was four in the morning, the end of third shift. Employees and contractors alike lined up to be scanned and searched to ensure that they weren't leaving with any company property, either actual or virtual. The security guard, looking twenty, rumpled, and hungover, spotted his music player.

"I gotta scan that."

"It's just my music, probably stuff you've never heard of." He put the player in the guard's outstretched hand.

His partner, who'd gone through without incident, looked annoyed. The guard jacked the player into a network port, and a security algorithm began searching for suspicious information.

The guard glanced at the readout, wrinkled his nose, and looked up. "It's encrypted?"

"Copy-protected, yeah. It's some really old stuff."

"Look, I can't let this go by if I can't scan it."

His partner rolled his eyes and set his coat on the security sorting table. The growing line of third-shift workers waiting behind him began a collective fidget.

"Look, really, it's just some old DRM-protected tunes, it's nothing."

"The rig says it's encryption, and I can't let it out because I can't tell what it is." The guard's eyes were bloodshot, but firm.

"Look, I need that for the flight I've got coming up. It's like twenty hours to Sydney…"

"OK, you can keep the player, but I have to wipe it."

"Wipe it!! Do you know how hard it is to reinstall copy-protected music?" His voice rose, slightly, inflected. The guard winced, but remained firm.

"I keep the device, or I wipe it."

The line stirred in a way that was almost menacing. His partner flopped in a chair and looked toward the ceiling in supplication.

He hung his head. "OK then, wipe it."

At his capitulation, the guard softened. "Sorry to do this."

The guard pressed a few keys, and the security routine began erasing the contents of his player, following up with a random-pattern quadruple-write, a security measure once reserved for protecting information like the execution codes for nuclear weapons.

The other doors had long lines now, compensating for the blocked one. The guard's supervisor walked over, saying nothing as the guard completed the bag search.

That's probably why the guard never stopped to ask himself why a computer-security contractor had an old-fashioned, pen-and-ink address book. Even if he had thought to ask, it's unlikely he would have known that the bogus street name for a nonexistent dentist's office was also the administrative password for the application server cluster. Or that the membership code for the discount program of a small car parts vendor was the MAC address of the site's core router. Or about any number of other valuable details that were much easier to get if you were inside the network than if you were outside it.

The advantage of being a highly-skilled but not entirely trusted technician was that while they expected you to try something, they always expected you to try something complicated.

The security panel chirped, indicating that the music player had been wiped clean. The guard handed it back.

"Sorry about that."

"It's OK, I understand. We all got jobs to do."

He combined information from the address book with information obtained in similar ways from other sites. He'd considered selling his findings, of course. That might have brought in enough to extend his life for a while. But he knew what happened to people who sold information to hackers. Eventually, contacts were identified and they went to prison. The buyers moved on to the next source, just like any other client. And nothing really changed.

And he found that as the numbers in his bank account and his days to live slowly wound down toward zero, the one thing he really wanted was to make the world change.

His work brought him a flood of free samples for security programs, firewalls and backup programs. Slowly and systematically, during off hours and in the stretches between jobs, he began to probe them for vulnerabilities.

He found them, of course. Most security software was installed and maintained by people every bit as harried as he was, and designed and built by people under even more pressure to "produce." As one of his former bosses explained, "You can do no better job than the customer will let you do." As the years went by, the customers were willing to let you do damn little.

In another apartment, rented with cash and filled with used equipment, he put the information to work, penetrating the security of his test environment, and finding ways to corrupt the backups.

That was the key, really. If you wanted to cause real damage, you had to destroy the backups. Otherwise, even the worst attacks were little more than a nuisance. Systems might go down for a time, but once the backups were retrieved, the programs and data could be reinstalled, and everything continued.

And so he infected the backup software, starting at the source. Security companies, it turned out, had astonishingly shoddy security. Software containing his code was installed all over the cloud farms and the great corporate networks, disguised as part of a normal update.

The infection was swift, silent, and almost unnoticeable. His code was tight and economical, a relic from his training back in the days when system resources had been sparse.

He didn't get every machine in every organization, of course. Smaller networks and a lot of individual units would survive just fine. But the ones that kept track of financial transactions, personnel data, payroll, billing information, assets and trades, and flows of everything from electrical power to site traffic…Those would go blank when he gave the word. Blank beyond the hope of backup.

He didn't know exactly what would happen when the data went away. He was pretty sure some very, very rich people would lose a lot of money when the systems forgot who it all belonged to. Almost certainly, lots of not-so-rich people would lose money as well. He expected that phone systems and utilities would fail, at least temporarily. Air travel might be halted for a while. The one certain casualty was people's trust in the machines that underpinned the world. He was sure that people would never have confidence in them again. But he didn't know what people would do next.

But they would do something different. He was sure of that. They wouldn't re-create all the same companies and the same flawed systems. They would have a clean slate, a chance to think and start again with different people, different ideas, and above all, the knowledge of what would happen if certain choices were made.

Reboot the world. That would be his parting gift.

He took a swig of beer.

Seven: Control

His reverie was interrupted by an urgent warble from his phone. Text. From Central Security. One of his traps at the Toronto Exchange installation had found something, and wanted him to look at it. Without thinking, he agreed.

His phone displayed the results of a code interrogation. A suspicious program had turned up, apparently trying to substitute itself for the backup program on the Exchange's mail server. His eyebrows arched as the code analysis slid by on the screen. He'd designed that particular piece specifically to avoid the new Chrystal Fence IV software the Exchange was using. His breaths shortened, and he fought the urge to look around the room by pretending to focus on the phone.

Gradually, his mind slowed down, and his focus on the screen became genuine. He took in what the display was telling him about the analysis. The captured program was code intended to achieve his objective. It would destroy both the backups and the primary data, but it wasn't something he had written. Numbly, he instructed the security program to remove the backup software and reinstall from the vendor's home servers.

Of course, the new installation would be infected, too. But with a program he could control. Or at least he thought so.

It had been stupid, he realized, to assume he was the only one. There were thousands, maybe millions of people like him, who were skilled, rootless, and despairing. Why should he be the only one to come up with the support technician's solution: re-boot and start over? Why should he think he was the first?

He left enough money beside his plate to cover the meal plus a 100% tip, and then headed out the door and into the cool summer night.

There was no way to tell how long they had. If there really were hundreds or even thousands like him, the end would come when any one of them decided to give up. Which could be any time at all.

He pulled the phone from his pocket, determined to reexamine the program his trap had captured. There was no signal. Across the street, an entire bank of ATMs displayed the "No Service" sign. Traffic began to thicken, slowing. He looked down the street, and as far as he could see, every stoplight was flashing red, the fallback used when central control failed.

Beside him on the sidewalk, people stopped. They were looking east, toward the skyscrapers of downtown. Eventually, he stopped and looked, too.

One building at a time, without any fuss, the lights of the city were going out.

Alone

Jessica Conoley

Editor: There are many mistakes that can be made at the start of an apocalypse. This is one that can be made before it begins.

Liadne pulled the covers over her head, just like she had when the trumpets sounded last night.

The thump, thump, thump of her heart was the only sound in her room. In the moments of silence between each beat she listened for the sounds that should have been—trash trucks dropping dumpsters, rattling mufflers on passing cars, the gurgle of the coffeemaker, the whiz of a bicycle as it sped down the hill, voices of the village awakening outside her shuttered windows. She listened for the rapping fall of footsteps of a marching army, or the heavy tread of slippered feet on wooden floorboards. But she only found the silence that had lurked in falling clouds before last night. If not for the relentless beat in her chest, Liadne may have thought she had awoken this morning to find herself deaf. It was the thump, thump, thump over the labored hrummph, hrummph, hrummph of her breath that let her know it was not her ears that had failed.

Liadne pushed the covers from her, and slipped one foot to the cold wooden floor. Chills ran from her toes to her neck, and she forced her other leg from beneath the warmth of the thick down comforter. She reached for the plush robe that lay across the foot of her bed, wrapped the velvety garment about her shoulders, and crossed to her shuttered window. Beneath each of Liadne's reluctant steps, sun fell in slanting lines across the wood, warming the floor. Her heart told her to *stop, leave the blinds as they were and go no further*, but her brain urged her to reach for the latch on her window casing. The metal hook pricked her finger as she loosed it from its clasp. The pain was sharp but fleeting, and in that brief agony Liadne knew it was not her touch that had failed.

The opening shutters spilled sunbeams across the room, forcing Liadne to shade her eyes. For a few moments she stood, hand toward the bright sun above, eyes squinting at the street she had lived on her entire life. Flowers bloomed pink in Miss Vionette's window box across the lane, but Miss V. was not there to water them. Cobblestones all purple and gray, shone with no people to cast long shadows onto them. The untended street cart brimming with wares, the bakery display filled with the morning's still-cooling bread, but no flour-dusted baker was there to hand out the loaves. Beyond the roofs of the town, resplendent against the clear blue sky stood her mountain—white topped and magnificent. It was in that lonely, beautiful scene Liadne knew it was not her sight that had failed.

Liadne pulled her robe close and saw the drop of crimson dripping down her finger. She raised her hand to her mouth and sucked on the nuisance of a wound. Her salty metallic blood twisted on her tongue with the cotton-mouthed first breaths of the morning. Each breath flung tastes of spring, carried on the morning breeze, to her, but it was the quick life of her blood that overpowered all other flavors. Nursing her wound in the silence between the thumps of her heart Liadne knew it was not her taste that had failed.

She leaned out the window, and breathed deep to stifle her impending sobs. The bakery sent smells of flour and sugar as the bread browned to caramel coated crusts. The scent of snow from her mountain, crisp with the freshness of ice-cooled streams and tenacious plants fighting toward the sun, wove through her as they had every morning before. When her tears left her breathing in gasps and her nose was stuffed with the absence that lay below, Liadne knew it was not her scent that had failed.

She stood at her window hearing the silence of desertion, feeling the emptiness, seeing nothing but loneliness, tasting her inadequacy, and smelling only fear. It was in this moment Liadne was sure of what she had feared at the first call of God's trumpets. It was not her senses that had failed her—it was her faith.

The Infestation

Simon Kewin

Editor: Marketing claims can be a painful.

Jack was shopping for his week's groceries when he noticed the business card among those pinned to the supermarket's notice board.

Monster-B-Gone Magical Pest Removal
Ghosts exorcised * Demons banished * Vampyres slain
Pixie infestations humanely disposed of
Free Estimates * Bulk discounts for large outbreaks
Satisfaction guaranteed * No job too large or too small

He stopped and took the card. A familiar rage coiled a little tighter within him as he read. But with the rage came an idea. Fight fire with fire. He'd tried everything else. Monsters? Perhaps. That was a word that depended on your perspective.

Back home at Woodland Road he made himself green tea and called the number on the card. The white van drew up outside his house an hour later. On its side was a stylised representation of a dead fairy lying on its back, legs in the air. Jack opened the door on a short, middle-aged man dressed in blue overalls. The man wore a belt around his thickening waist from which dangled an array of tools, electronic devices and wooden stakes.

"Morning, sir. Albert Mann, Monster-B-Gone Magical Pest Removal. Got a little problem that needs sorting?"

"You could say that," said Jack. "Come in, please."

"Thank you, sir. You do have a lot of pot plants. Is it wood nymphs? Very hard to shift, wood nymphs, once they take hold."

"No," said Jack, trying to keep his voice level. "Nothing like that. I can show you best from upstairs."

"Ah, gargoyles, then? Tricky bleeders. Cling like limpets."

"It's not gargoyles, either. Come this way."

"Right you are."

Jack led him upstairs onto his balcony. He liked to come up here at night, when it was a little darker and quieter. Now, the suburbs of London stretched off into the grey distance. Here and there, scattered and isolated, little stands of trees clung on.

"It used to be woods as far as the eye could see from here," said Jack.

"Well, yeah, I expect so, sir. Hundreds of years back."

"Before time was even counted. An ocean of green from one end of the world to the other."

"Right. Must have been quite a sight, I expect."

The man seemed bored. Jack's knot of rage tightened further. None of this was what he wanted. He was supposed to be mischievous. A trickster. A child. Now he was aged and jaded and he'd become something else. He'd crossed over into *malicious*. These were the times he lived in. He resented what they'd turned him into.

"Then they came, you see," he explained to the human. "Just another animal at first, very unpromising. Not particularly fast or clever, not good at hiding, no teeth or claws to speak of. But slowly they took over. Some new magic, resisting all the glamours we wove. One by one the trees fell and now we're overrun."

The human was looking at him with the sort of uncomfortable expression Jack was familiar with. Albert didn't reply for a few moments.

"This…infestation, sir. Do you mean what I think you mean?"

"Yes," said Jack.

"Only it's a bit outside my normal sphere, see. It's a bit awkward, like."

"Your card said 'no job too large or too small.' It extended guarantees and talked of handling 'large outbreaks.' Was all that a lie? Is your word not your bond?" Jack gave him a *look*, putting all his mind into it. He still had some of the old powers. Yellow eyes glimpsed through the trees at night, enough to trigger a reaction deep in the human's hindbrain.

Gratifyingly, Albert took a step backwards. "No, no, sir. 'Course not. It's just a bit…well, I mean, how far do I go?"

"Given you're one of them, you mean?"

"Yes, there is that."

"Some survivors are fine, Mr. Mann. We're not the brutes here. Spare who you will, restore the balance. The question is, can you do it?"

The human looked back at the city around them. He sucked in his breath in the way of tradesmen through time preparing a customer to hear a big number. Jack didn't care. Money wasn't a problem. He'd learned long ago humans would do anything for gold, even if it did turn back to pebbles after a year and a day. He could pay whatever the human wanted ten times over.

"Poison might do it," said the human. "In the air or water. Or a disease, maybe. Shooting's not really going to be practical."

"Excellent," said Jack. "I'll leave you to work out the details."

The human looked back at the balcony door, eager to leave. "Right, well, I'll see what I can do, sir. I'll send you an estimate in the post, shall I?"

Jack held out his hand for the human to shake. "Do that. And I can rely on you? Your word is your bond, Albert Mann. Upon your soul."

Albert squirmed for a moment, looking for a way out. But Jack's gaze had him skewered. Albert shook. "Yes, well, you can rely on me, sir. Good as my word. Always have been."

"Excellent," said Jack. "And one more thing, Mr. Mann. Do you happen to know the name of a good landscape gardener?"

"A…landscape gardener, sir?"

"Yes. When you've finished your work I'm going to need rather a lot of trees planting."

Saving for a Future

Nick Barton

*Editor: Sometimes one gets exactly what one wants
but lives long enough to regret it.*

Missiles found on Cuba. Kennedy negotiating with the Reds. America prepared for nuclear war, building fallout shelters, managing drills and stockpiling food and ammo. Nuclear fire was on the way. So, it was a good day to rob a bank.

Eddie Carver prepared by planning to get rich. Eddie, like all of America, had heard the news of the coming end of the world.

Chamberlain's Bank of America branch more or less housed the cops' dirty money. Everybody knew it, but nobody said it. The police ran the town in more ways than one. It was their payload that would seal Eddie in one of those concrete-clad fallout shelters that big wigs had been building in Montana. A past contact owed him a favor, and saved him a place. But first he needed the cash.

Waiting in a van outside the bank, he studied his chosen colleagues. Hal Monroe and Bill Brooker. Prior to the job, Eddie had agreed to fair's fair, everybody gets an even share. Of course, he never mentioned his intentions. His contact never said anything about bringing friends underground.

Eddie took his shotgun off the rack. "Initials only inside the bank. Got that?"

"Just like always, Ed."

He smacked the back of Bill's head. "What did I just say?"

"Just like always, E."

"That's right. B, you're on crowd control. H, you and I handle the clerks. We'll follow them, crack the vault, and back topside in five minutes. Anyone starts anything, put 'em down. Don't think about it."

"Police response?" H put his hand on the door handle, itching to get going.

"Less than five minutes. Ideally, we need to leave in three. Anything else?"

They said nothing. Picking up their weapons, they slung their duffel bags over their shoulders, rolled down their balaclavas, and filed out.

Snow fell in thick clusters, collecting on their shoulders. Heavy snowfall meant reduced visibility and less traffic. Weather reports warned South Dakota that a big storm from Canada was coming. If it isn't radioactive, let it blow, E thought.

He opened the door, taking aim at the clerks behind the glass.

"Everybody on the ground!"

A chorus of screams escaped the crowd. Half hit the floor like maggots at boot camp. The rest remained standing, dumb with terror.

"Today is not a good day to piss me off. Any thoughts you got of pushing red buttons, kill 'em now."

The panicked shouts and screams died into whimpers. A good sound. That meant B had them under control. The bank, like Chamberlain, was a small place. There weren't more than ten people in the lobby, and about five behind the glass. Easy pickings.

Reaching the outer door, E aimed at the clerk on the floor. The glass may have been bulletproof, but when faced with a barrel of darkness people did what they're told.

"Open the door. Now!"

A pale-faced man stood up, fumbled with his keys, dropped them, and picked them up again. He opened the door, and received a punch in the face.

"Open the vault."

Pale-Face shook his head like a kid caught red-handed. "I can't."

"Can't or won't?" H said.

"None of us have keys."

This time H hit him in the face, blackening his other eye.

"Think we're fucking stupid? Open the vault!"

E had other ideas. Pale-Face may have thought they were stupid, but he was stupid. Looking at his colleagues confirmed it. Their eyes darted away when they met his, and the clinking on their belts weren't house keys.

These stubborn bastards are standing between me and a way out of this doomed planet, he thought. Bombs would fall, and he wasn't going to die in them.

He raised his shotgun at the woman cringing in the corner.

"Give up the keys. Pull 'em out of your ass if you have to. If you don't, I'll paint Blondie's brains across the back wall."

She screamed and hid her face behind her hands, as if they might protect her.

"What's it gonna be, Irish?"

Pale-Face, bleeding and puffed up, unclipped a keyring off his belt, and offered it like a peasant to a king.

E snatched it and hauled him up by his collar. "You're coming with us. Blondie, you too."

H grabbed her by the collar too, ignoring her screams.

"We're leaving in three."

B saluted, his eyes never leaving the crowd. "Ready when you are."

Their footfalls echoed in the vault below. Chills shivered up E's spine. Suppose I'll have to get used to this.

The vault door stood at the end of the hall, standing seven feet and housing the police's filthy money. Two keyholes flanked either side of the door. E thought about sailors priming nukes from their subs. Twisting two keys in unison, igniting an entire country in flames. He couldn't die like that.

They swung their hostages to the side.

"Open the vault."

Pale-Face's look of terror became one of disdain. E felt a little offended. He wasn't a Commie looking to bring the world to its knees. He was just a guy looking for shelter. What right did the pale fuck have judging him? He wanted to add another bruise to his face, but the clock was ticking. Open the vault, get the cash, and get the hell out. Just like any other job.

Pale-Face took the key without a problem. H yanked Blondie's key off her belt, but she wanted nothing to do with it, as if it was something toxic.

He slapped her face. The report ringing out in the cool atmosphere. "Open it!"

Taking the key, E directed him toward Pale-Face. His eyes on Blondie. "This key is going inside a hole. Right now, I'm not sure which one."

H laughed, even nudged Pale-Face like chums sharing a joke.

Blondie stopped whimpering, but terror remained alive and well inside her eyes. He meant every word. This wasn't any other job. This was the last job. Once Russia or America pushed the red button, the world reset to zero. No more heists, and no more stubborn bank clerks getting in his way.

Just peace and quiet below the face of the world.

She took the key, shaking so much he didn't know if she could even hit the lock.

"Your turn." H pushed his gun against the back of Pale-Face's neck, reminding E of a Nazi executing a Jew.

Both keys turned, and the vault pinged bingo.

"Party time," H said.

No mood for quips, E went inside, dumped his duffel bag and shotgun on the table and began loading cash. H stood like a gunslinger holding bounties hostage. One crying, one plotting revenge. He saw it in his eyes.

"Move, and her powdered face goes on the wall."

Rolls and rolls of cash flew inside the bag. Twenties, fifties, hundreds. His mind raced as he threw them, thinking about fresh linen, clean rooms and a life of security bought by Chamberlain's dirty cops. Leaving a world of crime behind, he could—

Blondie shrieked. "What the hell was that?"

E felt it too. A vibration. Distant, but there. He glanced up from the table.

"Just a tremor."

This time there was a boom, as loud as thunder. A mass of screams wailed from above.

"My god," Pale-Face said.

"Shut up," H said, uneasy.

"You don't think—?"

A crack of a rifle butt against his cheekbone, splitting his skin.

"I said shut the fuck up!"

The screams became an orchestra of pandemonium. E filled the duffel bag, his heart galloping fast enough to burst.

"Oh no," Blondie said, grabbing her hair in fistfuls. "It's happening. They've done it!"

"I said shut the fuh—"

A furious, heavy rumble, like a gigantic pot of boiling water roared topside. Before Eddie's mind adjusted, Pale-Face swung his hand, smashing H in the face, leveling him. Blood sprayed against the wall in a fine arc. The clerk stared, bloodied and unafraid, at Eddie.

He saw Pale-Face's intentions like a neon sign.

"NO!"

Eddie lunged forward, slipped over fallen banknotes and crashed against the vault door, slamming shut. Pounding the door, he shouted like a kid having a tantrum.

"Hal! You can't leave me in here! HAL!"

Nobody said a word. Nothing made a sound save for the wild wind above, and another nuclear blast.

It wasn't supposed to end like this.

Sea of Darkness

Jay Seate

Editor: Civilization, society, and even life is a crystalline matrix. How much of an impact will cause it to shatter?

My alarm sounded at seven o'clock. I slapped it off and kept my eyes tightly shut, seeking a few more precious moments of quiet, but the world wouldn't wait forever. I rolled over expecting to witness the sunlight streaming through my bedroom window.

Nothing but darkness, not even a shadow, as if our sun had abandoned the galaxy, the thick blackness of the darkest night imaginable. I closed my eyes tightly and rubbed them with the heels of my hands before opening them again. No reassuring golden glow, only the gloomy nothingness of a coalmine deep in the bowels of the earth unable to even see my clock. My hands reached out with fingers curled into claws, as if I could pull away a black shroud of extreme night and reveal the familiar world of light and images. I grasped only air.

I'm a newspaper reporter. I rely heavily on my senses and it was clear this was no dream. I was as blind as the Cyclops in *The Odyssey*. I furiously rubbed my eyes until they burned, to no effect, then fumbled for my bedside phone while fighting a wave of panic, knocking a picture of my latest girlfriend from my nightstand in the process. I heard the glass crack as it hit the floor.

My next impulse was to dial my direct line to the newsroom by feeling the raised numbers on a touch tone. Jimmy from the night shift answered. "What?"

I could hear shouts and the scurrying of people in the background. "It's Sam. I...I can't see!"

"You and everybody else! Nobody can see, man! It happened about three hours ago. It's like the end of the world. We're getting reports in from everywhere."

"Nobody?" I said dumbly, momentarily setting aside my own sightlessness. "I'm going to come in and see what I can do."

"That's just it. No one can see to do shit! We're all caught in the same trap, apparently all ten billion of us. We're down here running into each other. There's nothing to do but try and contact our families."

"What do they think caused it?"

"Hard to say when you can't figure out how to call someone. But the couple of scientists and doctors we've got on speed dial aren't willing to speculate yet. All we've got is radio, TV. The UP wire is useless. There's a lot of talk about how long our audio systems will stay up. Trust me, stay home."

I reluctantly hung up. Surely I could get to my p. c. and start on the story. Then the overwhelming force of the situation slammed into my frontal lobe and unleashed a tremble that proliferated from my spine into my extremities. *No written stories, no pictures, no newspapers, unless they are in braille.* Here was the story of a lifetime and I couldn't write it.

Transportation? A city full of hysterical people running and falling, smashing into each other in panic—a Three Stooges world. "It'll be okay," I whispered without conviction. "Machines and electronics will still work. Most everything is computerized. Blind people get around all right."

I found the TV remote and punched in the numbers for CNN from memory. The fact that Big Brother was on the air gave some comfort.

"We must all pray this condition is only temporary," a female talking head cajoled. *"We should stay in our homes and remain calm."*

I tried to convince myself this was good advice.

"Specialists from around the world are communicating to try and determine what has happened," she continued.

It was obvious the "specialists" were clueless at the moment. I felt a new sensation—shortness of breath, racing heart, tingling in my fingers, not to mention the terror that gripped me. It tore at my consciousness. I took five or a hundred calming breaths. I fought to keep my attention on the newswoman wondering how she was dressed, or whether she was dressed at all. A twisted part of me wondered whether things like clothes mattered anymore.

In other disasters someone eventually came to the rescue. Now everyone needed rescue. As a newspaper guy, I'd seen hurricanes, floods, tornadoes, earthquakes, and war rip peoples' lives apart, but that was the point. That is what made this phenomenon so different. I had *seen* all those things. Now, I couldn't see to find my shoes.

No sirens blared outside. In every other crisis or catastrophe, sirens always screamed from patrol cars and fire trucks. *There won't be any more of that unless it sounds to direct people toward the food.*

Food!

God, how long would that last?

"Let's hope we'll be able to laugh about all of this soon," a man said with false capriciousness to the woman on the news.

I wished I had someone to cuddle with as I listened to the anchorwoman drone on with updates concerning the heartbeat of mankind.

"The White House has issued a statement that the nation is now under Martial Law. Everyone stay in your homes and for those not fortunate enough to be home, stay where you are."

After fifteen minutes, I could sit still no longer. I felt my way to some loose fitting jeans, a pullover and sneakers at the foot of my bed. *Anytime now, someone will find the switch and turn on the lights*, I prayed.

The phone rang. I stumbled toward the sound. "Who's there?" I said into the speaker.

"It's Ed. Listen. Screw Martial Law. We're going to get a team together to cover this thing somehow."

Even in a crisis, Ed was all business, the consummate professional, and the voice of reason.

"We can't compete with the on-air media, but we can start recording our impressions and take interviews. Work is the best antidote right now."

He was right. We had to do what we could to talk to people, to transcribe this experience.

"Take one of your recorders and go as far as you feel safe. If this is temporary, we'll have the human-interest story of all fucking time. If it's permanent...what the hell else have we got to do?"

"Okay," I agreed. Even though the world had gone dark, my boss was playing the angles, and I would try to play along. It was better than sitting around going crazy.

The importance of sight I had underestimated. The courage to step out from my only bastion of safety took all the willpower I could muster. "I'm going on assignment," I said to myself and stepped out into what might as well have been the Black Hole of Calcutta.

I tried to muster a mental snapshot of the surrounding area. I'd driven down the street a thousand times and thought I could stay on the sidewalks and out of harm's way. I told myself that by shouting out something like "Man walking!" I could avoid blind run-ins with other pedestrians. Maybe I could even get as far as the neighborhood shopping mall.

Even though the contemplation of permanent blindness tossed and turned within me just beneath the surface like a thunderous sleeping dragon, I decided to concentrate on the story potential. Almost stumbling before I'd negotiated my two front porch steps, I steered toward the garage to find a broom or rake or something to precede my march to the sea. I'd watched blind people do it. Instead, I found my golf bag and pulled my ball retriever free of its plastic tube.

With a recorder in my pocket, I walked to the end of my drive, scraping the metal retriever along the cement before me and holding my free arm straight ahead to fend off any head-high obstacles.

I tried to imagine a new world full of people feeling their way along the edges of objects, going to their refrigerators and pantries trying to figure out how long before they would have to venture out into the brave new world of constant midnight.

I heard a few muted hysterical voices coming mostly from the inside of homes along the way, but I chose to tune my ears to the distant car horns. People had been caught in their vehicles during the early morning rush and had been lucky enough to stop safely. *And what of those that hadn't stopped safely?* I guessed they were fucked.

There were no engines running near me. That was good I thought, then it dawned on me that the sound of a moving vehicle would mean someone could still see. *Didn't there have to be a few that would be immune to this virus or plague or germ warfare or whatever the screaming hell it was? If so, a sighted person could be King. Almost better if there were none,* I thought selfishly, *if one of the lucky ones wasn't me.*

My blind man's golf stick encountered signs, newspaper stands, and mailboxes, as the ball retriever became my eyes. I felt my way through a world of mostly metal as the coarse touch of an occasional tree trunk proved strangely reassuring.

The sound of a car horn was very close now.

"Hello!" I cried out.

"Are you out of the street?" a man called back.

"Yes, I'm on a street corner, I think."

"Keep talking. I'll come to you."

I could hear the man carefully stepping closer and closer. My hearing had become more acute. Moving my magic wand to my side, I groped straight ahead until our arms bumped into one another. He grabbed my hand and my forearm and pulled himself upon the curb like a man being rescued from a pool of sharks.

Not quite ready to let go, he said, "Thanks. My name's Campbell."

"You're welcome, but I'm not sure what we've accomplished."

"I'm out of the street anyway. Wouldn't want to get hit by a reckless teenage driver, would I?"

A sense of humor. What better way to handle this gruesome situation no one could ever have imagined was there? "My name's Sam. I'm a reporter for the *Gazette*."

"A reporter?" Campbell said, unbelievingly.

"Yeah. I live just a few blocks away. You're the first person I've been able to talk to."

The man was silent.

"I'd like very much to hear where you were headed when this thing happened." I took the recorder from my pocket and clicked on the "record" switch.

Campbell suddenly crushed his fist into the side of my head. I staggered back, stunned. He was on me, fumbling for the recording device. I fought him off, kicking at him and finally pulled free. I could hear his breathing. Guessing he was preparing for another assault, I dropped the recorder back into my pocket and raised my tenuous weapon, the ball finder, and listened with as much cunning as I had ever possessed, like a hunted animal listens for danger.

"You asshole," Campbell said, finally. "We're all blind. The whole world is fucking blind and you're out trying to get a goddamned story. I just want to be home with my wife and kids. You have any great ideas how I'm going to do that, or how they will get home themselves, mister newsman? Can you write a story about that?"

"We're all going to have to work together on this. It could be temporary."

"Oh, shut the fuck up," Campbell said. "You know as well as I do we're finished. The scientists or terrorists have finally let something loose. Better to have killed us all than blinded us. How long do you think it will take for people to be scrounging for food?"

I heard Campbell start to weep. It sounded much like the wail of many abuse victims I had encountered while on the beat. It was a cry of confusion and frustration. "I'm sorry about the questions," I said softly.

"Leave me alone," he responded. "You don't know me and I don't know you. Just…"

He said no more. I could hear him shuffle away to somewhere, maybe to find his own street corner until he could figure out a way of getting to where he wanted to be.

So this is the way it's going to be. The first stranger wants to fight me, a world without eyes still seeking violence.

Everyone was the same. Until society regained its sight, it would amount to little more than survival. I understood that now. Unless the world could see again, there was little need for interviews. Everyone had exactly the same story: "One minute I could see, the next minute I was blind."

The madness of a world thrown into darkness had begun. Life as I knew it had ended in the blink of an eye, so to speak. Religion would blame mankind's sinful ways. Nations would blame each other. Fashion, sport, traditional warfare and commerce…all vanished in an instant. The scientists will squabble and try to find the mysterious genetic code that has swept across the face of the earth. The teeming masses, now in a world where prestige, power and appearance no longer matter, will pray for salvation. I felt sick to my stomach. I realized that unlike Campbell, who wanted to pummel me, I had no family to go home to. I had my girlfriend, but it would be *her* family she would cling to.

I had always cherished my independence and freedom, but now for the first time, I felt truly alone. I took the recorder from my pocket and replayed my presumptuous words. I hesitated for a moment and then threw the device as far as I could. I heard it land, the parts clattering and bouncing along the pavement somewhere, out there in the new reality.

I leaned against a stainless steel post that anchored signal lights on one side of an intersection. I heard the mechanical clicks of the lights changing colors, changing for the phantom traffic that might never again pass beneath its robotic eyes. I found the button on the pole that makes the lights change for pedestrians. I pushed it until I heard the clicks again. Then I pushed it again.

Never again will a romantic couple make a wish upon a star, dreams shattered like priceless crystal thrown to the ground. There will be a world of confrontations and dire consequences previously unknown to the ruling species of the planet since life first crept into existence. I pushed the light changing mechanism over and over. I didn't know I was crying until I felt the tears running down my cheeks, and I don't know how long I stood there pushing the button, but it didn't matter because I had nowhere I wanted to go.

Occasionally, I heard other honking horns and voices rise and then fade away, but for the most part, the world had stopped moving. We were all now phantoms in an eternal night riding a blue bauble in a sea of darkness.

The Other White Meat

Rachel Verkade

Editor: And they taste like chicken.

You ain't gonna believe this, but I got into this business by accident. Yeah, I know how that sounds, but it's true. Mama carried me over on the boat from Haiti when I was still at the tit. That's how I got my name, Dieufort, strong god, 'cause Mama said I never cried, no matter how hard the boat got to rockin'. When we landed, Mama took work pickin' fruit. Nobody'n the field mind if you got a baby slung on your back. When I was old enough, I was picking fruit 'longside her, and when I got strong, I started working the animals. That's how I got to slaughtering.

Slaughterhouses, at least the ones I went to, don't care much if you've got your papers. Just need a strong back, a good knife hand, and can't faint when y'see blood. In those kind of places, you get paid per carcass. The more animals you bring down, the more money you walked out with at day's end. Cattle, horses, goats, sheep, hogs, quick shot with the bolt gun, bleed 'em out, carve the carcass up. I worked fast, and I did quality, so I made good money, and the work suited me fine.

It might sound weird to you, but I like animals. Lotta the guys there, you'd see them kickin' the critters, hurtin' 'em just to make 'em squeal. After a while they just get to be part of the machine. Only way most guys can go on, y'know? Can't keep beatin' their heads in if you're thinkin' of them as livin' things. But me, I always liked the critters. Wasn't their fault they got sent to the grinder. Equipment was shit, most of the time, but I did my best. Made it quick. Gave 'em a pat when I could, hid the bolt gun from 'em. They could tell I liked 'em, and that made it easier. I wasn't kicked or bitten near's often as the other workers, and the animals would go where I wanted even if it was all bloody and nasty-smelling. And that helped me make more money. So it comes around, y'see?

You've probably guessed, given why you're here, but my favorites was always the hogs. Oh, I liked all the others, don't mistake me, but there was just somethin' about pigs. Cows and sheep, they were just scared, except for the bulls sometimes and they was just stupid angry. Horses were sad, never ever saw it comin', just followed wherever you led 'em thinkin' they was going home. But pigs're smart. Couldn't be any breaks in the pens, couldn't let your guard down, not when it was a hog day. Cows and sheep, you could beat 'em bloody and they'd still follow you, but you kick a pig and it'd never forget. It'd never trust you again, and if it got the chance it'd rip you right open. I respect that. Known slaughtermen who'd face a two-ton bull 'fore they'd face a breeding sow, 'cause that pig, she'll go for blood, and she'll think about whether it's better to go for your knees or your gut or your balls 'fore she comes. Respect that, too.

So I guess it ain't no surprise when I got enough money saved up, I bought myself a little bit of land with a house and a pigpen. Didn't need much, just a two-room house for me, a shed and corral for the pigs. Never more'n a dozen hogs, never kept a boar, just sows and barrows. I didn't wanna breed or nothing, after all, I just liked having 'em around. Made enough money to keep me and them fed, and that was good enough for me.

So I had my little house and I had my pigs and I had my job at the slaughterhouse. Things was just fine as paint so far's I was concerned. And I coulda gone on like that, really, until my friend Georgie came by. Georgie and me, we known each other since we was kids, our families worked the same farms, but I got into slaughterin' and he got into griftin'. Anyway, he comes to me on my day off, and he's real shaken up. Have to get some whiskey down him before he can tell me what's wrong. Turns out him and this barfly he hangs out with got into a fight, and one thing led to another and the barfly ends up dead. Georgie swears to me it was an accident, but now he's got a dead guy on his hands and he don't wanna end up in jail. Comes out the guy's in the trunk of his fucking car, which's right now parked in my yard. And that's just what a guy like me wants on his fuckin' land, am I right?

So before I can knock Georgie's head in, he finally comes out with what's on his mind. He's seen some movie, some English pic about a crime boss that used pigs to get rid of bodies. And who does Georgie know who owns pigs? His old pal Dieufort, that's who. I thought about it, and I really couldn't see any reason to say no.

Hey, I don't want you gettin' the wrong idea. The guy was already dead, right? I checked that myself, he was cold as ice cream on the Fourth of July. And pig feed's pricey. Them pigs eat before and better than I do, and meat's meat to a pig. So I told Georgie, okay, gimme three hundred and you can feed the guy to my pigs.

Don't fuckin' look at me like that. I gotta eat too, and I wasn't about to chow down on some barfly burgers.

Anyway, Georgie came up with the cash, and he set to helpin' me, 'cause Georgie really ain't a bad guy. We knocked out the barfly's teeth, pulled out the fingernails, burned the hair and clothes. I gotta grinder in the back, big thing for grinding pig feed. Chopped the body up with a chainsaw and in it went. Had to make sure it was ground up small, so I put it through three times. The pigs really liked it, Georgie was glad, I was able to put down another payment on my truck, so really it worked out for everybody.

Things went on like normal for a while, but a few weeks later somebody else shows up with a big package wrapped in plastic. Says he knows Stan who knows Chuck who knows Georgie, and Georgie said that I had a great way of getting rid of dead guys.

You got two choices in that kinda situation. You can turn the guy down, risk a broken face at best or a bullet at worst, then go beat the shit out of Georgie once you're back on your feet, or you can make the best of it. I looked at the guy and I said six hundred.

You know how this kind of thing goes. Once word started spreadin', I was getting at least one a week. I quit the slaughterhouse, bought a better feed mixer and an industrial meat grinder, bought a few more pigs, paid off the truck, added another room t'my house. Pigs started getting fat and sassy, I was drinkin' Wild Turkey 'stead of 'shine. Not gonna say things were easy, 'cause you've always gotta be careful with this kinda thing, but life got a helluva lot smoother. Did a little experimentin', found the pigs would take whole limbs, if they was hungry enough, but I generally preferred the grinder, just in case. That's how they caught that fella up in Canada, you know.

I don't want you to get the wrong idea. I never killed nobody, not never. All of 'em were dead long before they every crossed onto my land, so why the hell shouldn't I get a paycheck out of it, and why shouldn't my pigs get a meal? Wasn't gonna make the poor bastard any less dead if I said no. You gotta look at the practical side of things, friend. Make your life a whole helluva lot easier.

Anyway. It was getting so that I didn't have to buy meat for the pigs no more, there was so much food coming in. Still got grain and such, you can't feed pigs on just meat, it ain't good for them. But I could buy more fencin' too, let 'em graze and root. I had happy pigs. And knowin' I had happy pigs made me happy too, y'know? There was times I'd just set out a folding chair, grab myself a case of beer, and sit out while the sun set and watch the pigs wander around, dig and wallow. I liked it. I liked them. They liked me. It was nice.

Anyway, at the same time, I'd met Felicity. Felicity ran a bar down in town called Freebird's, 'cause that's her name, Felicity Freebird. Named herself after that old Lynyrd Skynyrd song, 'cause it's her favorite. You oughta hear her sing it sometime, she'll sing it when she's feeling real good, and she sings it like nobody else. But anyway, I started hittin' Freebird's about the time things started getting good for me, and soon I was there at least twice a week, jawin' with folks, drinkin' a pitcher or two. Every so often, Felicity'd take me up to the apartment she kept up over the bar and we'd have ourselves a time. We like each other, Felicity and me. She's good folk, don't take no shit. Kept a rifle behind the bar and whip it out anytime folks got too rowdy, but most times she'd just wade into fights and set things right with her fists. She's that kind of woman, Felicity.

Her'n me, I think we started being friends when some drunk asshole called her a tranny whore, and I threw him through a window. I know Felicity'd heard worst in her time, but it got under my skin, hearing him talk about a lady that way, y'know? And I don't care what anybody says, no matter how she mighta started out, Felicity's one helluva lady. If you're lucky, maybe someday you'll see what I mean, but she's awfully particular. And she paid me back, anyway, when some good ole boy called me a coon. You wouldn't think, looking at her, that she could throw a guy all the way from the bar out the door, but Felicity's got a lot of secrets.

Anyway, Felicity knew what I did for a living, and she was okay with it. She'd come by my place sometimes, and we'd sit outside and drink and watch the pigs. She liked the pigs too, and they liked her, which's part of how I knew she was good people. Sometimes she'd help me feed 'em. Other times we'd hang out at Freebird's after closing, just her'n me at the bar, boozin' and laughin'. An' like I said, sometimes we'd end up in her bed or mine, and sometimes we wouldn't. Neither of us had all that many friends, so we stuck together pretty tight.

So that's why when it all happened, Felicity's the first person I went looking for. Who else did I have, anyway? Mama died 'bout ten years back, and it's just been me and the pigs since then. And Felicity's family dropped her like a piece of rotten meat the day she came out. So her and me, we looked out for each other. That's the way it was.

You remember where you were that day, don't you? Yeah, ain't met a person yet who don't. Me, I woke up 'cause of the pigs. They were fucking screaming, and you ain't heard screaming 'til you've heard a pig screaming. And they ain't normally noisy animals, y'know? I mean, they'd squeal when they was hungry, but there's a big difference between a "get up, it's breakfast time" squeal and the racket they was making. So I jumped outta bed and grabbed my shotgun. Was loaded, sometimes the mood'd strike me an' I'd go out an' shoot myself a partridge or a turkey, and it was mighty good for scarin' people otherwise. Birdshot won't kill a man, but it'll sure make 'im think. So I grabbed that gun an' I was out there quick's could be.

First thing that hit me was the smell. It's the kinda smell you don't never forget, and when you been in the business I been in for as long's I been in it, it's a smell you know pretty goddamn well. The guy looked like he'd been in the water for at least a week; figure he musta crawled outta the river. He was down to his skivvies, so I figure he was swimming, maybe hit a rock or something, and nobody ever found him. So now this fucker's staggering around my pig shed, and the pigs are going fucking apeshit.

Now, I ain't like those dipshits in those movies that stands there'n babbles 'bout how this can't be happening. I see a guy with his arm hanging off and one of his eyes eaten out and his skin gone all blue, I know I'm looking at a dead man. I see 'em often enough. Only difference is this one's walking. Dunno why he's walking, but the fact that he's scaring my hogs's what's botherin' me right now. So I cock the shotgun and yell for the bastard to get away from my pigs.

Don't think he could see too well, since one eye was gone and the other'd gone all cloudy, but he could hear well 'nough. Really was just like in those damn movies, just turned and started shufflin' towards me, real slow. And I seen enough'a those flicks t'know what'd happen if he got me. I let 'im have it, both barrels.

Problem with a shotgun, though, is it ain't got much'n th'way of penetration. Sure, some of the birdshot got in his face, and it messed his chest and neck up lots, but it sure didn't get into the brain. I wasn't real worried, though. A shotgun makes one hell of a nice club in a pinch, and I know I'm more'n strong 'nough to crush a skull if the need comes. But while I reversed my grip on the gun, I looked in at the pigs. And somethin' caught my eye.

'Bout half of 'em were at the back of the pen, screaming their heads off. They knew something was off, and they didn't like it. But the other half, they were right at the gate, pushing on it and grunting like they do when I'm comin' by with food. Like it was suppertime.

I already told you, I'd done some experimentin'. I'd give the pigs whole limbs, once or twice even a whole corpse, to see how they handled it. And plenty of times the bodies had been layin' around a few days before whoever it was got 'round to bringing it here. Pigs are damn smart, like I said, and by now they knew that this smell meant they were getting dinner soon.

I didn't get into this business by not bein' practical, and one thing those damn movies got right is that those zombies are slow buggers. I was able to walk right around an' get the gate open, and them pigs rushed out like they just heard the dinner bell.

You ever seen pigs take a man down? It's a hell of a thing. They know how to use their weight, barrel someone down by slamming into their knees. I don't cut their tusks, so they were slashing at the back of the guy's legs. That was a thing, too; the tusks went through that dead meat like butter, but there wasn't one drop of blood. Think that brought it home t'me. This guy was deader than a possum on the highway. And man, but did that make the pigs mad.

They started eatin' even before he went down. Rippin' chunks out of his thighs and calves and ass. He didn't seem to feel no pain at all; only went down for good when one of the barrows hamstrung him, and he didn't stop moving 'til one of the pigs crushed his head. He never tried to fight 'em, just kept tryin' to get to me. Never even tried to touch the pigs, not once, but between the smell of meat an' the stink of what he was, the pigs were going fucking nuts, but the nuts of a young'un at the county fair.

Now, I feed my pigs damn well, so some of them lost interest once they'd eaten some, and they headed back into their pen. There were only two that stayed, kept working on him even after he was down. One was my biggest sow, a big five-hundred-pound girl, one of the few sows that had big fine tusks. The other was a young barrow, smaller than her, but he was always mighty curious about everything that was going on. They were two've my favorites. I called the sow Gouge, 'cause of that big set of tusks she had. Felicity named the barrow. She called him Hamstring, just 'cause she thought it was funny, and 'cause she said it's what she'd like to do to some've the assholes't showed up at Freebird's. Made me laugh so hard I spit whiskey all down my shirt. But anyway, it was those two hogs, Gouge and Hamstring, that really went after the zombie. And boy fuckin' howdy, did they go after him. The two of them just kept at that body, kept at it 'til they'd shredded every bit of meat, ground the bones into the mud. They ate, sure, but they also just seemed to want him gone.

By this time I was just leaning against the wall and thinking. Like I said, I seen plenty of those old movies, hell, seems like you can't get away from 'em these days. Seemed to me if one corpse was getting' up and walking, a lot of others must be too. That's always the way it happens, right? Now, I was okay, I was all the way out here in the country, but things might not be so great in town. And I thought about Felicity. Hell, I wasn't gonna leave her to deal with this shit on her own.

I got my truck, and I always keep the tank full up. Had my shotgun too, but wasn't sure how much use it'd be, even with proper shells. But what I really had was the pigs. Pigs that got fat eatin' corpses. Pigs that showed a real thing fer gobblin' up an' tramplin' zombies. Now, maybe I ain't had no college learnin', but nobody said I was dumb.

Room in the truck for about two big pigs. All of my pigs know me, and they like me, so when I whistled for 'em, they came. Got the ramp out, an' I loaded up Gouge an' Hamstring. If they had that kinda enthusiasm for that first zombie, I can figure they'd do pretty damned good against any others we ran 'cross. Got the rest of the pigs back into their pen, jumped in the truck and I headed for Freebird's.

I guess you know what it was like. And I missed the most of it, livin's far out in the country like I do. I'm told the cities were real bad. Are real bad, I should say…from what I hear even the military ain't havin' much luck clearin' them out. Just drivin' down the country road, I saw at least a couple dozen of 'em, just staggerin' about. Some of them had managed to get ahold of people, were gathered 'round the bodies like buzzards on a kill, scrabblin' and fightin'. I saw cars burnin'. An' I be seeing all types of them things—men and women and even young'uns. Some of' 'em were in suits and dresses, some of' 'em were in hospital gowns, some of 'em were just in jeans and t-shirts. Some of them had arms and legs off, a couple had their bellies ripped open and was draggin' their guts behind 'em. Most of 'em looked like they'd been chewed on. But they was all dead, ain't no question of that. They were dead, and they were walkin', or't least shufflin', and wherever they could, they were eatin'. An' sometimes the folks they were' eatin' were still screamin'.

I didn't stop. Wasn't nothin' I could do for the poor bastards, so I wasn't about to risk my neck. And the whole way Gouge and Hamstring were crashing about the bed of the truck, thumpin' and squealin'. They must've gotten more'n their fill off f that first body, but they were still rarin' for more. Tempted a few times to stop and just turn 'em loose, watch 'em shred their way through alla them dead folks, but then I thought about Felicity and I kept my foot on the gas. Was a boilin' hot day, but I kept the windows rolled up after the first couple miles; the smell of rotten meat was just everywhere, and when you been doin' jobs like I been and that smell's gettin' to you, you know it's pretty bad out. I didn't see no other cars, least none that were movin', but I know some'd passed by. There was smears of dead, rotten meat cookin' on the road, an' some zombies that'd been run down still tryin' to drag themselves along by their arms. Them stupid critters didn't even try to get out of the way of the truck as I drove along.

Took me about a quarter hour to get myself to Freebird's. Clear to me right off that whatever'd happened, it happened during the night, 'cause the parking lot was full. If I was closer to town, I likely would'a been surrounded, 'stead of just the one the pigs ate. But man, Freebird's, was teeming with the damned things. Clawin' at the doors, beatin' at the windows, climbin' all over each other tryin' to get into the bar. It really was just like those old movies, and especially that one ten years back, the English one.

I still had my gun, but like I said, I didn't think it'd be much use except for a club. But what I thought might do some good was the big fuckin' hogs in my truck bed, the big fuckin' hogs that were screamin' up a storm and chawing at the sides tryin' to get out. Only trouble was they were makin' such a racket that the zombies were startin' to look our way.

Had to move fast, even with how slow they was. Threw open the truck door, shotgun in one hand, and ran 'round to the back of the truck. Gouge and Hamstring was making a ruckus; she was ramming the door so hard it was startin' to bend. For a minute, and a bad minute, I don't mind tellin' you, I thought it was gonna jam, and I wouldn't be able to let the pigs out. And what the fuck would I do then?

Well, I guess God loves me much's Mama used to say he done, 'cause the back door popped right open. Over 900 pounds of meat-hungry hogs came tumblin' out, knocked me flat on my ass. I'd say they was out for blood, but I ain't never seen a zombie bleed. Do you know what that black and yellow stuff they tend to ooze is called? No? Me neither. But whatever it is, them pigs was hungry for it.

Good thing they was so hungry for it, too, 'cause it took me a minute to get my ass off the ground and find where I'd dropped the shotgun. By the time I'd done that, though, Gouge and Hamstring were into the crowd like they'd normally go to their trough. Gouge was usin' her tusks to go for the backs of knees and legs, Hamstring was usin' his weight to bring them down, and both of them were tramplin' and chawin' up any zombies that they got down. Like with the first one, the zombies weren't takin' no notice of the pigs, not even when one of them went down right beside 'em. But they sure's hell took notice of me, and I don't gotta tell you that was a problem.

I'd pulled in close to the door, hopin' the pigs would clear the way for me, an' they were doin' okay at that. At least'n the other zombies were trippin' over the downed ones, makin' one hell of a mess. The only thing to do was to wade right in with the gun, bashin' anything that got close to me over the head with the stock. That's one thing slaughterin' prepared me for; I'm strong 'nough and I know just where to hit so that the skull goes crunch. But I wasn't about to count on that workin' forever; managed to crunch my way to the door and banged on it, yellin' Felicity's name.

Only occurred to me then what I'd do if she was already dead. I mean, fuck, you'd think that'd be the first thing to hit my brain when I drove up, right? But no, there I was poundin' on the goddamned door of Freebird's, yellin' at the top of my lungs with a horde of zombies at my back, and if there was nobody in there I was lunchmeat. Weird 'nough, y'know what I thought of? The pigs. Gouge and Hamstring, they'd be okay, but I'd locked all the hogs back at home in their pen. If I didn't come back, what the hell was gonna happen to all of them? I was hopin' they'd be strong enough to break through their fence when Felicity opened the door and yanked me inside.

Gotta tell you, she ain't never looked so pretty to me, with her hair tied back an' her eyes wild. I hugged her so hard she told me she near felt her ribs snap. Man, I don't think I've ever been so glad to see nobody in my whole life. Had to be fast, too, 'cause we had to get the door locked and barred again before the fucking zombies managed to bust their way in.

Turned out that when the shit went down, Felicity was downstairs in the beer cellar. Now, if you know bars, you know the cellars are goddamn fortresses, and Freebird's was better than most. She has a fine taste in microbrews, does Felicity, and she brews her own beer too, in her spare time. I'll pour you a glass later, if you like. S'harder to get hops and malts nowadays, but we still manage.

Anyway, what I'm sayin' is that cellar door was oak, reinforced, and with one hell of a lock on it, and only Felicity had the key. She was down there, rolling out a keg of her signature brew when she heard a commotion upstairs. Now Felicity kept her rifle right behind the downstairs door, easy 'nuff for her to get to from behind the bar, but away from any shithead't might try to come over the counter, right? So, she grabs the gun, opens the door, and looks out.

What she saw was a bunch'a them zombies chargin' in through the front door and turning her customers into bar snacks. Said she even recognized somma the corpses, barflies that usually came in other nights, or that'd been missing. Well, now they were here, and they'd brought all their buddies for the party. Poor bastards in the bar didn't have a chance. Damn zombies'd jammed the door an' there were bars on the window, couldn't nobody get out.

Well, Felicity's a practical lady, like I said. She saw right off wasn't nothin' she could do for the sons-of-bitches, so she just shut the door and she locked it. The door to the outside she used for deliveries was sealed tight, so all there was to do was wait for the screaming to stop.

When it did stop, she said, she unlocked the door an' peered out again. All the barflies were dead 'r gone, an' the zombies were either eatin' or wandering out, now that there wasn't no more hunting. So she waited, quiet, until the wanderers had all wandered, and then she slipped out. Made her way to the door, soft, soft, while the fuckin' zombies were still busy eating, and she got the door locked. Then it was time for a whole new kind of hunting season. And Felicity's one hell of a shot. Damned sight better'n me, at any rate.

Thing was, the other zombies'd been heading out heard the shots 'n figured out there was still some warm meat inside, and once they get that idea you can't get rid of 'em. So that was Felicity stuck. Plenty of shells, but wasn't gonna test herself against a whole crowd of fuckin' zombies, was she? Decided the best thing to do was hunker down and wait 'em out. And that's how she was 'til I came bangin' at her door. "And Christ, am I glad to see you, Dewey!" she said, laughin' and tossin' her blonde ponytail.

Don't you look't me like that. Felicity's the only one who gets to call me Dewey, and even then, only sometimes. This was one a those times, though. You got friends or family you found afterwards, alive 'gainst all the odds? Yeah, then you'll know why we hugged each other so hard, why I couldn't get enough of th'smell of her hair, why she laughed and kissed me all over my face. S'good to have people. Pigs are great too, but s'really good to have people.

Felicity had a radio downstairs to keep her company when she was cleanin' the place, so it was her't told me this was happenin' all over. Dead people getting' up, breakin' outta coffins, walkin' outta morgues, shakin' outta their rest home beds. Said the government was tellin' people to stay inside, burn any bodies they found, an' that you could kill 'em by blowin' their brains out, just like the movies. Government also said everything was under control, but don't they always?

So I told 'er 'bout the pigs and what'd happened, and that Gouge and Hamstring were still out there. Peered out through the windows, and mosta the varmints were down, thrashin' like dying fish, and the two hogs just rootin' about an' makin' themselves't home. Felicity whistled, "Damn good thing you feed those pigs the way you do," she said.

I think that's about the time the idea started in my head, but I didn't really have time to think about it then. We were too busy workin' out what to do next, where to go. The bar was pretty strong, but it was also way too close to town. Already seen just how many zombies were crowdin' around the place, and Felicity said more were driftin' past all the time. I'd only seen the one, and took some time comin' down the road to find more, so we figured my place was safest. And anyway, the rest of the pigs was still there. Had a fence 'round my land, and Felicity'd bought a bunch of razor wire a few years back, when some of the rednecks 'round here started hasslin' her. Never had to use it, but it'd sure come in handy now.

Ain't much left to tell, really. Felicity'n me grabbed a few supplies, beer, some food, and shells for the rifle, then we headed out after load'n up the pigs. Took us a few days to get my place back up to scratch, but once the razor wire was strung up we were sittin' pretty. Learned to grow some of our own food, let the pigs forage, and we did all right. We figured at first we'd just hunker down until things got settled, but it got pretty clear that things'd changed. The zombies weren't goin' nowhere, and the government could barely get their thumbs outta their asses long 'nough to fence off Washington, forget the rest of us. But the world keeps rollin', you know? Once y'got used to drivin' 'round with a rifle an' blowing off the occasional head, the world kept rollin'. Stores opened back up, money makes the world go 'round, an' Felicity'n me knew we had a business. Mosta the time it's cash only, but sometimes we work for trade. Sometimes for food, or new guns 'n ammo, or for things we needed made, like for the guy't made the chains 'n leather collars for Gouge 'n Hamstring. Mosta the time we don't need 'em, but it looks mighty impressive, and sometimes if there's just a small group we'll keep 'em on the chains.

So, how much land did you say you had? And you got any idea how many zombies we're dealin' with? All right, for six hundred you just get the pigs, Gouge and Hamstring and a few of the others, an' they'll take as long as they need. For a grand you get me and Felicity too, and we'll go 'round with the pigs and our guns, and we'll clear your land out right quick.

Yeah, price's steep, but we provide what Felicity calls a unique service. And we'll even take all the bodies out, afterwards.

Pigs still need to eat, after all.

Something New

Brigitte Winter

Editor: There are inherent dangers in the luxury our technology provides. We stop learning to spell. We stop learning to read. Eventually we even stop learning to think.

She's not even pretty.

Well, not by SIM standards at least. Girls generated by the Simulated Interactive Multiverse are all perfect curves, tightly wrapped in skintight body suits. Smooth, shiny hair. Pert, accommodating smiles. This girl—I think she said her name was Eva—she's different. Her curves are concealed under a baggy sweatshirt that slides down one shoulder so I can see her purple bra strap. Her short black hair is streaked with electric blue dye. And she hasn't smiled once in all the time we've been sitting beneath the overpass.

I can't stop looking at her.

She passes me the flask, and I take another big gulp. The liquor burns all the way down, melts my stomach into a liquid ball of heat that radiates to every part of my body, turns my brain tingly and fuzzywarm. It must be freezing out here, but neither of us is wearing a coat. The other guys are probably still lying around the party, SIM-drunk on the digital buzz of pseudo-alcohol. They don't know what they're missing.

I grin at Eva, pass her the flask. She takes another sip and then stuffs it into the fat gray backpack she's shrugged onto the concrete next to her.

"Different, right?" she asks.

"Oh, definitely," I say. "Same end result, but it's a million times better when you can taste it going down. Plus there's something less predictable about the real thing, you know?"

"More dangerous."

"Yeah, that's it."

"So, you're into danger, Kelvin? Some sort of rebel? That why you followed me out here and left your buddies in their safe little SIM bubbles?"

I blink at her through the fuzzy alcohol haze, try to focus on her face. The way she's looking at me with her eyebrows raised and her forehead all crinkled is unnerving, like she's testing me. Like I better say the right thing or she's going to get up and walk away.

"They're not my friends," I say, concentrating hard on each word so it doesn't come out slurred. "I don't know them, really. I've never hung out in SIM with other people before, like with people all logged into SIM together in the same room. I just wanted to try something real."

She laughs—the first time I've seen her smile. She's wearing tiny jingle-bell earrings, and they make a bright, tinkling sound whenever she shakes her head.

"This is the first time you've ever been outside the city, isn't it?"

"Are you kidding? Going to that party was the first time I'd even left my house. I mean, I've been places in SIM—like my family's been taking virtual vacations every year since I was little because they think it's important for me to see the world—but we never really go anywhere."

Her lips curl up on one side and she shakes her head at me.

"What?" I ask. "Do you, like, hang out in the woods all the time or something?"

"You want to see something real? Check this out."

She reaches into the backpack and pulls out a folded piece of paper. I scoot closer, look over her shoulder as she opens it. Her hair smells like the forest around us—musky, green, alive.

"Holy shit," I say. "Is that a map?"

"Obviously. How do you think I knew how to get here?"

The map is ink-drawn. I've never seen anything like it. It's covered with a maze of multi-colored roads, all dotted with little X's. A graceful squiggle of lines dances across the top. Those are words. They've got to be.

"Did you make this? How'd you learn to write?"

She lays the map in front of us, carefully smooths the folds. "How'd you not learn to write?"

I narrow my eyes at her. She's not smiling, but it's got to be a joke. Not even my grandparents write by hand anymore, and they're Facebook generation. I concentrate on the squiggles, strain to decipher the words, but I haven't read anything without the assistance of a computer since I was little. All the concentrating and trying to act sober is starting to give me a killer headache. Jesus, it takes superhuman effort to stay present outside SIM.

"What's the deal with all the X's?"

She frowns and snatches the map, shoves it into the backpack.

"Wow. Okay. Never mind then." I lean back and squeeze my eyes shut against the blossoming pressure in my brain. A product-mover whirs and bumps overhead, wheels barely touching the bridge, delivering packages of food, clothing, computer parts—pretty much anything that can't be faked in the virtual SIM network—right to everyone's front door. It's so different down here, away from the automated efficiency of the city. The ancient concrete is cold under my palms, and I feel gritty dirt and grass poking up through the cracks. Fat brown vines snake up from the forest, wind around the massive pillars supporting the highway overhead. A shriveled pine tree pushes up beside one of the pillars in an unevenly matched competition for the sun. This is the longest I've gone outside the SIM network. Definitely my first time in a cold, dirty forest. The novelty is starting to wear off.

And then she touches my hand.

Electricity shivers up and down my spine. I've never been so completely and totally here, in the now. I've never—God—I've never been touched by anyone real besides my parents before. I'm breathing hard, pushing little white clouds into the cold air. I don't remember ever being so keenly aware of breathing, of the rhythmic inflating and deflating of lungs, of how we need to do this—suck air molecules in and out, in and out—or we—

She pulls her hand away, laughs again, earrings jingling.

"Wait, aren't we going to—?" I say it without thinking, instantly regret it.

"Aren't we going to what?" She giggles, jumps to her feet. "How do you think this works? I lure you out into the wild, beautiful world and make you feel things, and then you have some revelation about how you're wasting your life hooked up to a computer and I reward your enlightenment with passionate sex? No, Kelvin. Sorry to disappoint you, but this story we're weaving together isn't so predictable."

Hot embarrassment stings my face. I stumble to my feet and the world tips. I think I may throw up. "Eva, I thought...I don't know what I thought. Sorry."

She places a hand on my shoulder, steadies me, shooting another bolt of electric energy up and down my body. "Don't worry, Kelvin. I brought you here for something better. Something beautiful and real, just like you wanted."

She skids down the steep concrete curve of the overpass.

Jingle, jingle, jingle.

"Come on," she calls over her shoulder.

I swallow hard, push down the nausea, pinwheeling my arms wildly as I half run, half fall after her. I almost crash into her at the bottom of the slope, but she presses her palms against my chest to stop me. She grabs my hand and pulls me away from the overpass, onto the overgrown path we took from the party. We clamber up a steep slope. She's still gripping my hand—kind of too hard, actually.

"Watch." Her voice is soft, breathy.

We're high enough now that I can see over the treetops to the ancient highway system running across the overpass. A parade of automated product-movers zips smoothly along the roads. There are hundreds of them, maybe thousands.

"What are we watching?"

"The death of fiction, of course." She squeezes my hand. "The birth of something new."

And then I see it. The gray backpack. It's still resting silent and ghost-like where we were sitting under the overpass.

I feel the explosion before I see it, a powerful burst that blows me back, smashes me to the ground, searing light and sound following fast. I clamp my hands hard against my ears and curl into a tight ball. My ears feel like they're bleeding, like if I let go of my head my brain will seep out over the rocks around me.

I look up, my palms still pressed against my ringing ears. Eva is beside me, legs pulled to her chest, her chin resting on her knees. The look on her face is so serene it makes the tiny hairs stand up on the back of my neck. The overpass is burning blue-hot. My nose stings from the acrid smell of smoke.

And then I see it. A dozen flames, a hundred flames, a horizon full of tiny blue flames.

"Did you think we were the only ones out here tonight?" Eva's hand covers mine, but this time I don't feel electric shivers. This time I feel numb. I feel nothing.

The X's: overpasses. The product-movers: all gone.

"Why did you bring me here?" I can barely hear my own voice over the ringing in my ears.

"To watch." She squeezes my hand. "To witness."

We sit there, holding hands, and witness my world burn.

Ia Ia Cthulhu Fhtagn Armageddon Has Begun

Kim Alan

Editor: Sometimes Lovecraft got it too right.

Below the Sea of Galilee
In a cauldron of tar, and salinity
Where no life can survive
The dark evil incarnate did arise

From the mysterious depths
Of the bottomless pit it leapt
The Beast was not the metaphor
Of ancient gospels' lore

But an immense physical manifestation
A mountain of all that is evil, incarnation
Each inhalation of his respiration
Stole light from Earth's horizon

Expelling sulfured air in exhalation
His putrid breath was an abomination
With his right paw he swept away Gaza
With his left he crushed all of Mecca

Then looking towards the heavens in triumph
In a grotesque glare of defiance
He bellowed a hideous howl of victory
So all God's children clutched their ears in agony

Except for the one, the one called Abaddon
Who greeted the "Living Darkness" with adulation
"Ia Ia Cthulhu Fhtagn, Ia Ia Cthulhu Fhtagn!"
"My Great Lord, begin the Armageddon!"

An Acceptable Loss

Jacalyn Schnelle

Editor: Make no mistake, dreams drive us onward toward heights we never knew we could surmount. Reality is what happens when the dreams can no longer hold us up. Which is stronger? Which has the right to survive?

ATTENTION!!
I HAVE BEEN BITTEN
If you are reading this, you are in danger, for I have discovered I am too much of a coward to simply end my life.
In an attempt to minimize danger for you and yours, I will place all shelf stable items and nonperishables in the foyer, and lock myself further in the house.
If you are willing to end my misery, I will be forever grateful, but I understand if the risk is too great.
Please forgive my weakness,
Roy Phillips 5/12

"Four days ago."

"Yeah, the poor bastard has definitely turned by now. Do we leave him, or help out?"

Eileen sighs at the note, which he painted way too carefully on the front door. She's squinting at it thoughtfully, ignoring my twitches, like we have all the time in the world to consider this. Like we aren't *in constant danger*. Nothing can rush her when she gets like this, and the rest of our group depends on me to get stuff done when our smart but kind leader checks out over moral issues.

Morals aren't important anymore, though. Survival is. Eileen is damn good at keeping us safe, and even mostly sane, but she is not good with the whole "acceptable loss" concept. To her, there is no such thing, no *need* for such a thing. There will always be a way to make it work.

Me, though? I'm a realist. I want to grab those cans and go. We still need to scout for a safe place to rest, and the sun is beginning to dip low. There is no time for her to chew on her lip and consider variables. We have people that depend on us, three of 'em kids, and we can't take another night of nonstop driving. A few of our drivers are about to crack as it is.

I move forward, too wired to be gentle with her, too afraid to coax her to reason. This cul de sac is in the middle of a grouping of hills, and if we weren't so low on canned veggies I never would have agreed to this stop. The kiddos need their goddamn vitamins, though. Our group will eat right even if it *literally kills me*. Which, okay, it is starting to feel like it might. All the more reason to get the fuck out of Dodge as soon as possible.

The door has warped a bit in the recent wet weather, but it opens easily enough, though its horrible screeching noise does make my teeth itch. Inside it's all classic middle-class, middle-America, and the cans, unopened packages of crackers, and water bottles are all right there, just like he said. There are even maxi pads and toilet paper, and I have never been happier to see them. Thank you, God, for TP; that is almost as good as the veggies and water.

I carry armloads of supplies to the nearby RV. I need to focus on something outside myself before I get overwhelmed, so I tease Rebecca when I see her peeking out one of the windows. I ruffle Michael's hair, and do what little things I can to put our people at ease. I'm not as good at it as Eileen is, but she's vanished into the house while I had my back turned. I'm not good at hiding my nerves, and my feelings are getting to the group, the adults snapping at each other over shit like where to put the supplies, the kids fighting over a toy. There's nothing I can do to stop this but to get us all the fuck out of here. Unfortunately, this thought dies as Eileen calls to me from a window.

An upstairs window.

I. Am going. To *kill her.*

Upstairs. I'm running, and she meets me. She talks fast. She knows me too well to let me talk right now. "Erin, I had to. I heard something, so I investigated it—carefully!—and I've—"

She cuts off, and I realize she's pale. Her gun is in her hand, but it's like she doesn't realize it. All her gun safety and precision is gone suddenly, and I'm scared. I've never seen Eileen like this, not even when one of our RVs got stuck near a horde and we had to carefully transfer all our people and supplies to other vehicles across the roofs as the undead swarmed around us. She had been quiet that day, but had kept calm. She'd even made the switch between cars a game for the little ones. Managed to make them laugh while death had surged around them.

I'm seeing none of that strength in her now. I can feel everything below my waist going weak and watery, and she must see this on my face because she grabs my wrist, squeezes it till the bones grate together. She's done it before, and I've done it for her, a makeshift method for keeping the panic at bay. It works again this time and I take a deep breath. In. Out. In. Out.

Neither of us can ever fall apart, no matter what happens. She and I are the strength for our people. "So," I ask her, "what did you find?"

The bite is a disease. I know, *we* know, the usual stages, and the order they occur in on average. Averages have outliers, though. I've known that since high school stats, so when Eileen tells me Four-day Roy is still completely unaggressive, I can kind of understand. Every disease has someone that can hold it off for way longer than they're "supposed to.". Roy's just the statistical anomaly we were bound to meet sooner or later. Eileen is not very appreciative of this probability.

Of course, I'm not real appreciative of her telling me she wants to spend the night here with him, so I guess we're even. "That's a funny joke! Haha! Okay, we should be done, so let's go."

"Erin. Please. I know you think this is going to be another disappointment—"

"No, no! I *know* this is going to be a suicide mission."

The disappointed look she pulls out is one I've only seen when she wants to manipulate people. Instead of helping her case it makes my blood pressure go through the roof. I am not being unreasonable here. I am, in fact, being the opposite of unreasonable. I am being *mega reasonable*.

"Eileen. Get in the RV."

She draws herself up, towers her two extra inches over me, and swells with self-righteous anger. "No. He may be the hope—"

So I grab her shoulders and yank her back down to my level. "Our hope is time, Eileen. We have to keep moving for at least three years, or until enough of those shambling *fucks* rot to immobility that we can be safe in one place. Our hope is not a dude that hasn't died fast enough."

"Sorry I haven't gone more quickly," from a voice behind Eileen.

I pull her next to me. I bring my gun up. I fire. He doesn't drop.

I intended to put one through his head. Instead I shoot through the goddamn floor because Eileen *smacked my gun hand downward*. I can't even turn on her because there is a goddamn bite victim right in front of me.

I step away from my partner to make sure she doesn't get in my way this time. Refusing to take the hint, she interposes her body with that of my target.

"Erin, this is Roy."

"No, nonono, we're not friends here. I don't need to be introduced. I need to shoot him in the head, and we need to leave because the sun is setting soon." The bite victim, whose name does not fucking matter to me, is pale and sweaty. He's leaning back against the wall, maybe can't support his own weight. He's a bit shorter than usual, kinda chubby, and balding.

I'm honestly surprised he's lasted so long, especially alone. Probably, I'd be doing him a favor by putting him down. Shit, he's been bitten; I'm definitely doing the dude a favor.

I bring my gun up again, and bite victim just looks at me. I've never had to take out a noncombatant before. The ones we've lost to the bite have all had the good graces to finish themselves off, sparing us the trauma. This shit hole, though, has decided he's above all that. That he has the right to take away another little piece of my humanity.

Eileen smiles luminously when I lower my gun again, but it falters when I just look at her. I know she can see how angry I am; no one has ever understood me that way she does, and that means she knows how furious I am at being stuck as the asshole just because I want to protect our people. Seriously, fuck her morality.

I turn to leave, feeling both of their eyes on me. I don't care. "We need orders within the next five minutes, Eileen. We still need to find a safe place to spend the night. And we don't have time for this bullshit."

I rumble down the stairs, hearing her call me, and I don't stop.

* * *

She's made the right call, this time, and while I don't really like the place we found to stop, it's better than driving all night and probably killing ourselves. We found a gated community and drove through to make sure there were no stumblers on the grounds and that the whole area was actually fenced in. Apparently, a lot of "gated" apartment complexes and communities just have kinda...I don't know, ornamental? sorta gates that don't do squat to keep things out. This one's good enough, though, and the kids are settled in after a big dinner that had plenty of vegetables. Most of the adults are crashing too, but Eileen and I are on the roof of our RV, sitting surrounded by our big bolted-down planter boxes. It's nice up here. Smells like tomatoes. Hopefully the plants will be mature soon.

"Erin, I know you're not listening."

I'm really excited for the cucumbers. I wasn't even a big fan of them before the epidemic, but now I'm drooling at the prospect.

"I need you to listen to me, please. This doesn't feel like that outlier thing—"

Does vinegar spoil? I'll have to ask Keelan. He always knows the weird food facts. I'll have myself a cucumber and tomato salad with vinaigrette.

"The disease usually takes hold in a *day*, Erin! It's been *five!*"

Wait, is vinaigrette even made from vinegar? Or is that just something I assumed because of the name?

Wait. "Four days."

She's looking at me, serious, and shaking her head. "No. He told me it took him a day to find a safe place, set down the nonperishables, and paint that note. It's been *five*, Erin. Tomorrow, if he still isn't sick, it'll be six."

"You want to go back."

She's leaning her head back, looking up at the sky to avoid my eyes, looking tired. "Yes. We've been on the move for six months, and it's killing us already. We can't settle down for more than two days without the shamblers blocking all the gates. Our entire fresh food supply is limited to what we can grow up here. The kids have no stability in their lives. This is hell."

"And you think Prissy McDickbag back there can help?" I grab her chin, pull her to face me, "Eileen. I know this is tough. But we're doing so much better than most people. The fact that we have fresh food at all is unheard of. And the kids *do* have stability: us. We're the bedrock for everyone down there. That's why you can't keep doing this shit. If you get yourself killed—"

"It'll fall apart around here?" She's smiling, but it's a wry one. She's never really accepted how important she is, how necessary her strength is. I shake her by the shoulders a little, frustrated.

"*Yes!*"

"No, Erin, they need you—"

"Oh, Jesus, no they don't. Or maybe they do. But even if they do need me—even if all of us need everyone else—that still doesn't mean you're not important. You're the reason people are willing to keep hoping. We don't need someone else for that."

She's looking at me, tired, but her smile is genuine, and that's amazing.

* * *

I figure that's it, you know? The issue was resolved, end of story, let's move on. But the next morning, she starts driving us back to that fucking cul-de-sac.

"Oh, you have *got* to be shitting me."

She refuses to talk about it until we get there, but when we arrive she just grabs me and a bottle of water and heads towards the house, dragging me behind.

"I really don't want to do this!"

"Hush."

Inside, nothing has changed. I don't hear any strange noises upstairs, but that's not surprising. Some of the shamblers seem dumber than the rest, don't notice meat until it's right in front of them. I hope the prissy asshole became a stupid one. But no, there he is, waving to us from the top of the stairs, completely unsurprised to see us back. God. Dammit.

Eileen jumps ahead of me and leads him out of sight, further into the second story, while I loiter. I don't want to go up there. That guy's an asshole, and I don't like him, but he could change any minute and she wouldn't be prepared.

With that in mind I slowly ascend the stairs, dragging my feet. Eileen calls to me from one of the bedrooms, and I go in to find him lying down, a wet cloth on his forehead. Great use of our water. Just super. She's motioning me closer, though, and when I get next to her I see the bite.

I've never seen one like it. The bites don't heal, of course, since the change usually happens so fast, but they're usually clean-looking, or as clean as a human bite can be. This, though, it's bright red, puffy, and I can feel the heat baking off of it from six inches away. It's insane. There's whiskey on the bedside table, and the bed smells faintly of it. Is he using it to disinfect the wound? Is that all it took?

"He's better today." Eileen is carefully dabbing his forehead with the cloth, and I see the same shakiness I did yesterday. Something about this guy scares the shit out of her, but it's not the things that *should* scare her. "He said his fever broke during the night. It's back now, but much lower. He walked back here a little faster, too."

She puts the cloth down and looks at me, and I'm terrified suddenly, for no reason I can explain. "Erin. He's fighting the infection. And he's winning."

We stare at each other for long moments, and then I burst into sudden tears for reasons I cannot explain. "No! No! No, it's not that simple! The first bitten got taken to hospitals! They got disinfected! It's not enough!"

I'm drawn into a tight hug and she strokes my hair, murmuring something I can't focus on as I sob dryly and tug at her shirt. This isn't fair. He's not special, and he doesn't deserve to live when so many have died.

"It's not your fault, sweetheart. It's no one's fault. No one could take the risk to find out if there were immunities. And the rate of immune must be low, or we'd see it more often."

"Would we?" I gesture violently at Roy. "Look at him. He's almost dead just from the fever, and he had water, a sanitizer, and a well-insulated place to stay! Maybe the dead people we find sometimes are the immune that just dried up fighting the fucking virus!"

"You can't think like that!"

"I can't *not* think like that! How many, Eileen? How many of our people do you think would have survived if we hadn't sent them off to die?!" I'm slapping at her chest now, I'm so *angry*, and Roy, fucking *Roy*, has his eyes open, he's seeing me attack her and I'm so mad—.

It cuts off. All of it. My cheek is stinging, and it's taking me a second to understand why, to connect my hurt cheek, my ringing ear to her lifted hand. I take a deep breath, and am startled at how shaky it is. I must have been panicking. I still am, but it's more controlled now. I can at least get somewhere quiet before breaking down completely.

* * *

Eileen finds me on the roof, curled up by the deepest planter, the one we've got potatoes, carrots, onions, and leeks growing in. I don't know how long I've been up here, but I know I'm all cried out. The shaking has finally stopped, too. She pulls me over to lie in her lap, and starts playing with my hair. We aren't talking. Both of us just exist up here, where things grow and there's life and hope.

There's hope in that house, too, she was right about that, but it's a poison hope. The kind you get when you believe the gunman who swears they won't hurt you, or when the politician spins sickly sweet promises about how safe life will be when the "other" has been eliminated. If you give into it, you won't just be dead, you'll be betrayed.

I won't let that happen to us.

Above me, she's talking about finding a CDC outpost, developing a cure, and saving the world. I don't interrupt her. Her dreams are beautiful, and I want to spend as much time in them as I can because I know there is no CDC outpost. I know that illness can lie dormant for years, and that we could spend the rest of our lives with him, looking for scientists, all the while living in constant danger. We could waste our lives suckling at hope's poisonous teat, and have no one to blame but ourselves if we wake up one day to find him changed.

Eileen isn't stupid. Not at all. But she's never been one for no-win situations, and I know that if he lives, he'll come with us. He seems like he's going to live. So I snuggle further against her legs, enjoying this wonderful, peaceful moment as a soft breeze brings us the pale scent of earth and life amongst all of the death. I know what I'll have to do when I can avoid the real world no longer.

I'll make sure it's quick for him, and I'll tell her he was changing, that it was a fluke. I'm a realist, after all. I'll make sure we survive, even at the price of a dream.

Passing the Torch

Gustavo Bondoni

*Editor: An individual surviving when its entire world
changes is the ultimate expression of a species viability—
even if it isn't living in the same way as before.*

Gabe's boss was in a bad mood, as usual, and had assigned him an idiotic data search in the payroll archives, a process that meant that he'd have to head over to Accounting. He could send them a text asking for the info, but then he would have to wait ages while they ignored his request. Begging in person always increased your chances.

Besides, Accounting was where Camille worked.

Ah, Camille. She'd been in his thoughts since the day he met her. She chose to be blond, and chose to be tiny, but the absolute porcelain-like perfection of her avatar only revealed the tip of the iceberg. After going out to lunch a few times, he'd come to understand that her true beauty was hidden by her complex outer shell. Most people who chose a perfect form for their avatar were trying to cover some inner flaw—usually a major one—but Camille seemed to have chosen it for the express purpose of weeding out the unadventurous. Anyone who prejudged her because of the way she looked was deemed unworthy to get into her head.

Gabe had only managed to get beyond the exterior by the merest of coincidences—he'd initially been one of those unworthies who'd assumed that she was overcompensating for something until the day she quoted the poet Ehring at him in a meeting. No one else had picked up on it— Ehring was one of the new wave of Alaskan literati, and the appreciation of his work was still outside the popular consciousness—but Gabe had been amazed. Knowing that one quote did not an attractive personality make, he'd decided to take his chances and ask her to dinner. She'd laughed and told him it was much too early in their relationship for dinner, but they could have lunch that day if he wanted. He did.

Now, he felt he knew her well enough to be able to understand her, and felt that it was no longer too soon for dinner. All he truly wanted from life was for her to say yes today, even if dinner only led to dinner.

Gabe could feel the anxiety building as he reached the floor on which

Accounting was housed, but knew he had to take care of the work-related matters first. He ignored the call of his heart and made a beeline for the manager's office.

He never made it.

"Hi," Camille said, stepping out from between two cubicles.

He almost dropped his papers.

"Oh, hi," he replied, barely suppressing an urge to draw a hand through his hair, one of his typical nervous tics. He steeled himself. "I was actually going to look for you in a few minutes. I wanted to ask you to dinner on Friday."

She smiled.

* * *

Without warning, without explanation, Camille's face vanished along with the rest of his world. Gabe blinked once, twice, and was awake. An abnormal awakening with no alarm clock telling him that it was time to get up and go to work. Not even the soft sunlight of a weekend morning streamed in through his window. And besides, he hadn't gone to sleep. One minute he was chatting with Camille and the next, he awoke in the darkness.

He extended an arm to search for the light switch and regretted it immediately. His arm refused to obey. It felt like rubber—a rubber that was being skewered by millions of tiny hot needles. He'd never felt anything quite so painful in his life.

That worried him. He decided to try again. His comm controls were right beside his bed, and he knew that he should be able to reach them easily in order to call for help. He dug deep, ignored the pain and moved his arm. The pain this time intensified, as if his biceps had torn with the effort, but the shock at what he encountered made him forget it. Less than a foot above his head, he found a solid surface which extended to both sides and downward. And then it hit him. Every Earth-dweller's greatest fear had been inflicted upon him.

Everyone had heard the lurid descriptions of what happened when a person was yanked unexpectedly out of Earth's fully uploaded society. They rejoined their physical bodies inside the small cylindrical structure in which they were born and lived from birth to death. Fed by intravenous tubes and cleaned by automated drones, their minds played in the infinite scenarios of a world-spanning simulation in which hot and cold and pain were present only as much as each person wanted them to be.

Gabe knew the protocol for waking—everyone had heard it whispered in hushed tones at some moment or another. You had to wait for the system to boot you back up, and pray as hard as you could to whatever deity you believed in that they'd get you back online before you lost your mind.

Slow, deep breaths. In and out, in and out. He could feel his heart rate slowing, the fear subsiding. Any moment now, he'd be back where he belonged, in the safe, familiar simulation. But after a few minutes, the fear returned. What if there had been a more serious problem. What if they couldn't bring him back at all?

Suddenly, a wailing sound filled his world, and he jerked involuntarily, tearing a number of small wires from the back of his skull and bouncing his head against the roof of his birthing chamber. The agony was exquisite, like nothing he'd ever felt in the sanitized confines of Toronto's cyberworld.

Despite the pain, however, he knew that the truly important thing lay in the sound. A warbling wail that even cyberworlders could identify as a siren—thank goodness for the fact that all the old disaster movies had been digitized and made available to everyone.

Along with the siren, a dim red light suffused his cylinder. It allowed him to see the contours of the chamber that had been designed to keep his body alive and immobile for its entire life. It wasn't an impressive sight: a few slats of metal inches above him joined in a semi-cylindrical arch. His toes were visible off in the distance in light that entered through a crack running down the entire length of one of the sides.

Gabe realized that what he'd thought was a crack was actually an opening. The lid of the birthing chamber had opened, whether through some sort of glitch or as an automatic response to the fact that it was no longer functional, he was unable to tell. His aching arm extended once more, allowing him to fit his fingers into the opening.

The siren stopped. More troubling sounds filtered in—a distant scream, muted groans and sighs. But even as he listened, they grew dimmer until silence was restored.

At that moment, Gabe admitted to himself that he wouldn't be going back to the cyberworld any time soon, if at all. His earlier sudden movements had disconnected a number of leads that he suspected would be necessary for his return. What he needed to do was get out of his chamber and tell someone about his problem.

This was easier said than done. In the first place, he found his body to be nearly completely unresponsive. It frustrated him but didn't surprise him much—after all, his body hadn't been used for anything in over twenty-five years. It was a miracle that it responded to any of his commands. It wasn't a given that the brain-simulation interface would be set up in such a way that the commands that worked on his avatar within the cyberworld would work on his body on the outside. Such programming had probably been difficult, but thankfully, the creators of the simulation had decided against cutting corners. He guessed that it had been designed this way as a safety feature for exactly this type of situation.

Inch by inch, Gabe slid toward the opening. The arm he'd been using to grope around with had slowly become easier to control, and the phantom needles skewering it seemed to be gone. That helped give him hope as his entire body protested against the movement he was forcing on it.

The top of the cylinder had moved without protest as he wedged his body under it, and he was able to open it completely with one final push that left him panting. Soon enough, he perched on the edge of his compartment.

His position limited his field of vision—he could see a roof above and the chamber next to his own. There was no choice. He would have to get out and try to stand. The floor, fortunately, wasn't all that far away. He might even survive the fall.

* * *

Gabe had to come to grips with the cold shooting from the uninsulated concrete into his hands and knees. The pain from the fall—fortunately, only about two feet—was beginning to fade, although his skin was coloring beautifully even seconds after he'd ejected himself from the cylinder.

In the sim, he'd always been accustomed to muscular perfection. Now the strange sluggishness, the seeming unwillingness of his extremities to obey even the simplest commands, horrified him. But he refused to be defeated by it. He would stand, eventually, and he would walk—even if it took him all day. He knew that it well might because it had taken him half an hour to get onto his hands and knees.

Before attempting to stand, however, Gabe looked around. He knelt in a large chamber illuminated by dim, flickering red lighting—probably emergency lighting. Row upon row of the cylindrical structures extended in all directions as far as he could see. Bundles of wires and tubes emerged from each cylinder and disappeared into the floor.

The fact that he was conscious and out of his tube, gave evidence that things had gone very wrong. Something told him that, bad as things seemed on the surface, the reality was even worse.

Seconds later, it came to him: the room was too still. The only sound he could hear was a slight humming from the lights overhead. There was nothing else, no droning of machinery, no sound of fluids moving through the piping. He wasn't an expert, but it seemed ominous that the life-support systems for more than a million people should be making no sound.

The few sounds that had been present when he'd first awakened had long since ceased. Every rustle of his thin robe echoed loudly in the cavernous chamber. The covering over his body must have been designed to shield his body from slight temperature changes within the cylinder. As it was nearly transparent it certainly didn't do anything for his sense of modesty. He had to move eventually. After the agony of rolling out of the cylinder and falling to the floor, he wasn't looking forward to it. The complaints of muscles unaccustomed to the strain had been much worse than the impact of his body against the ground.

Nevertheless, there was no other course of action open to him, so he tried to kneel as a prelude to standing. He pushed up with his arms and lowered his butt onto his heels. Immediately, both of his legs lit up in torture as his quads stretched nearly to the breaking point. He did his best to ignore the feeling. And to keep his head straight.

Exhaustion pressed in on all sides but, at the same time, his body seemed to be responding better and better as he got used to moving it around. Spurred on by this realization, he thought about how he was going to make it to his feet.

Ironically, the simplest way seemed to be to get back onto his hands and knees and to push up with both arms and legs. Ignoring the waves of pain, he began to attempt it.

Having failed miserably, Gabe made a discovery: the base of the chamber beside him was irregular enough that he could get a handhold. This, combined with a super-human effort from his legs, got him to his feet. Even with most of his weight draped over the cylinder, and not on his legs, he wavered. He smiled, the sense of achievement he felt was beyond measure. He remained in that position, panting from the exertion, for nearly half an hour. And yet, small movements grew steadily easier. He could now move both hands without much shaking.

A mad rush came over him, and he decided to take some steps. He began to move carefully, willing one leg to land in front of the other, holding firmly to the cylinder.

So it went for two more hours. Another step. Two in succession. A step taken without holding on to the cylinder. Disaster averted by the barest margin when he stumbled and managed, by sacrificing the muscles in his arm, to snag a nearby post. That time, he was sure he felt something tear in his forearm. He progressed slowly and painfully. By the end of the afternoon, he was walking confidently, if sluggishly. He knew that what he'd accomplished should have been impossible, but he also knew that his only alternative was to lie down and die.

Unlike the process of learning to walk, the exploration of the facility took him comparatively little time. He began with the cylinders nearest to his. Both were occupied by bodies that lay peacefully within. If they'd had a pulse, Gabe would have sworn they were asleep. But they didn't. He paused to steal a second robe from a body just about his size. It mitigated the cold only slightly.

Corpses occupied most of the other chambers and the rest were empty. Only a token few had managed to lift their arms or struggle with the lids before their hearts expired from the strain. Fewer still—Gabe saw two in this room—had actually managed to exit their cylinders and die on the concrete ground.

By the time Gabe had investigated a small fraction of the chamber, he was sick of it. *There's no one else alive in here*, he thought. It was an irrational thought, and he knew it, but he couldn't escape it.

Suddenly, the oppressive sensation of being locked inside a huge, dimly lit morgue became too much. What if the lights went out? A wave of claustrophobia washed over him, and he scanned the distance for some kind of exit.

One of the support columns held a door, near enough that he managed to reach it in a relatively short time. It had a large push handle that opened the door without protest at his first attempt.

Once his eyes had become accustomed to the bright light beyond, he saw a circular staircase that wound its way along the inside of the column's walls. The lighting, which had seemed unbearable just a moment before, consisted of weak emergency lights as well—glaringly white in place of the red from the main chamber.

The stairs looked daunting; he made it to the top after only three rest stops. He counted himself fortunate that they only ascended one level before reaching a corridor.

To his right, the corridor buried itself in a never-ending line of lights. In the other direction, Gabe saw the unmistakable outline of a tunnel entrance, with daylight beyond. His heart leapt. There should be people out there. Someone who could help him, and maybe someone who could help anyone else that might still be alive down there.

On the other hand, he knew that the facility could very easily be miles from civilization. Going out might expose him to dangers he wasn't in any condition to deal with, plus he'd have no idea which way to go.

He shrugged it off. He would just have to make the best decisions he could. He wouldn't, in his condition, get too far from the entrance.

* * *

He was lost.

There was no doubt. After ranging a little beyond the valley where the tunnel opened up, he'd somehow gotten turned around among the trees.

It galled him to realize that he had absolutely no sense of direction. He'd moved slowly, and had not gone too far—and yet he'd gone far enough that he didn't know the way back.

He'd been walking for two hours. Judging by the temperature, it was late autumn, which was a dangerous time to be out and about in the Canadian wilderness. Low clouds formed a gray wall seemingly an arm's length away from him. The first wet, large snowflakes of what promised to be a massive blizzard landed on the thin cotton of his double-layered robe. He was soaked through and shivering in ten minutes.

Nothing he'd ever known before had prepared him for this. He'd been just another office worker in just another high-rise office building. He lived in a safe, structured world in which no one ever went hungry and physical danger was unheard of.

Of course he had friends who liked to go out into the wilderness beyond the pseudo-city and perform feats of physical deprivation like camping out. They had no access to adequate heat sources for days. Gabe sneered at these empty shows of bravado. With the careful regulation of the cyberworld, what possible value could those activities have? They were empty pastimes at best.

Now he found himself wishing that he'd gone on at least one of these trips, or even listened at the office when his friends discussed the techniques. Any knowledge would have been infinitely better than the nothing he was currently armed with.

He needed no special knowledge to know if he didn't find somewhere to get in out of the snow, and didn't find it very soon, he would be dead before nightfall. It was as simple as that.

Gabe continued to put one foot in front of the other. Ahead of him, the afternoon was as dark as night. His hopes that this would allow him to spot some source of light, some beacon in the distance, shattered. All that lay in the darkness ahead were more trees, dimly visible triangular silhouettes.

He slipped and sprawled into the snow. Although he'd learned how to walk years ago, now that he was doing it outside, it seemed different somehow. Never in his life had his muscles felt so weak, never before had each movement produced indescribable pain. Yet he knew that he should be grateful. No one else he'd seen had the strength to make it out of their tube. He might be the last human being alive on the planet. He was almost certainly the last one left in Toronto.

Others, when the time had come to use their muscles, had found that the movements were alien to them, or that the muscles simply snapped when motion was attempted. Most, however, hadn't even made it that far. Of every ten bodies Gabe had found, nine of them were still lying down. They lay precisely as they'd been before things changed, not a hair out of place. The shock had stopped their hearts instantly. Others had barely managed to lift an arm or a leg. The strongest lay dead outside their chambers.

Gabe felt like a superman among the others. He'd actually been able to stand and walk and keep it up for hours. One in a million. Actually, one in one-and-a-half million—he was the legendary "last man standing."

The wind picked up, threw him to the ground and drove wet snow into his eyes. No matter his fortune or genetics he would join them in eternal rest very shortly if he didn't get to work.

His legs wouldn't keep him upright in the wind so he crawled on with throbbing knees. He trudged on only because he refused to give up, not out of some sense of purpose or direction Despite not even looking forward—he ran into the concrete structure. Sheer doggedness and blind luck led him to a building.

A wave of excitement powered him to the entrance. He collapsed onto the foul-smelling rubble on the floor, thankful to be out of the wind and snow. He lay there for an eternity, catching his breath, making small movements, trying, and failing, to get comfortable. The walk had cramped his muscles. It was a completely new sensation for him.

His stomach ached in a different way—a hollowness, not painful, but unpleasant and urgent. He lay there, wondering what it could be for a few minutes. He didn't remember having hurt his stomach, and besides, this wasn't the same kind of discomfort that was present in his legs. It was different, more as if his body needed something.

Hunger, he realized at last. This was his body's way of telling him to eat. He'd been fasting since he awoke, he wasn't in great shape, and he'd spent all day exerting himself harder than he'd ever done before. It was night time now, making it unsurprising that he felt a need for food the likes of which he'd never previously experienced. The sheer urgency of it reminded him that he'd never been hungry back in his previous world. No one was ever hungry there. But it was no use; there was no going back to that, ever.

A sound outside the concrete enclosure brought him back to reality. Something was making a high-pitched scratching sound near the door. He peered cautiously out.

A darker shadow in the night seemed to be using some of its extremities to attack a tree. Some kind of animal scratching a mark into the trunk, he reasoned. Gabe watched, mesmerized. This was a real live animal doing something that only its instincts told it to do. Truly in the wild, and believing itself unobserved. How many of today's humans could say that they'd ever witnessed such a thing?

Then Gabe remembered his hunger. If he could sneak up on the animal, he should be able to eat it, or at least find a source of food. Where there were animals, there had to be food. It didn't look that large to him, and besides, he knew that following the population explosion of the nineteenth through twenty-first centuries, animals had come to fear humanity. So the animal would die or it would run.

Gabe crept confidently out of the building, and was unpleasantly surprised to encounter the whirlwind of teeth and claws that greeted him.

* * *

Sunset.

The irony wasn't lost on him. He'd been the recipient of one of the best educations one could get on Earth. He could recite entire reams of Yeats. He could do differential equations in his head—all right, he couldn't do differential equations in his head, but neither could anyone else. And none of that would get him anywhere, because he simply knew nothing about how to deal with a Canadian snowstorm or animal damage.

A rueful chuckle turned into a cough, a racking cough that lasted and lasted. On recovering, he was a lot less inclined to think it funny, and much more worried about the immediate future. He knew he was hurt. Whatever it was that had attacked him had smelled of wet hair. A wolf? No. It had to have been something bigger. A bear, perhaps, or some sort of land-bound whale.

Gabe smiled again, careful not to breathe too hard. He knew he was being unreasonable. If he'd been attacked by a bear, or even a wolf, he'd have a lot more to show for it than a few infected scratches. Or, more accurately, a lot less. His half-eaten carcass would be feeding whatever carrion-eaters inhabited the region.

The remains of his feeble attempt at building a fire lay on the ground beside him: a few moist twigs, a circle of stones, a shard of rock that he'd hoped would make a spark. Yeah, right.

But what else could he do? He'd been lucky to find shelter in what looked like the remains of an old one-story building of some sort. The door and windows were long gone. Vegetation covered the interior, and a tree had managed to break a hole in the roof but the concrete walls had survived the centuries well enough to offer shelter from the winter wind that seemed to blow right through him. It didn't help that he wore nothing but a couple of flimsy birthing-chamber gowns—his own and that of one of the corpses he'd found inside.

He had no idea where he was, physically. His entire life had taken place in the city of Toronto. He assumed that he must be somewhere near the ancient city itself but couldn't find more than this one battered structure. Everything else seemed to consist of wilderness. Small, grassy clearings and huge, forbidding forests.

There was nothing he could do to survive. Snow made tracking animals easy, but his physical condition made catching them a pipe dream. Even the ones that hadn't fought back had loped contemptuously away. Maybe it was better that way—he didn't relish the idea of having to eat something raw. The leaves in the shelter tasted terrible.

He sagged against the wall, feeling the bitter cold lance through him. He might not be exposed to the wind, but the nighttime temperatures were lower than he could survive on a long-term basis. He'd only lived through the previous night because he'd stayed awake and walked, but had paid a stiff penalty: he'd felt his almost never-used muscles flare with pain as he paced, and, every once in a while, a small cramp would send up a sudden jolt of pain. It had paid off, though. An eternity later, dawn and the glorious heat-giving sun had reddened the eastern horizon.

It was a pity he wouldn't be able to find any other people. A pity that no one would ever know that there had been a survivor in Toronto.

He didn't have the strength to pace tonight. And that meant that he'd die. He coughed a little.

Maybe that, too, was for the best.

Gabe laid his head on the ground for the final time in the barren, empty night.

* * *

Miles below Gabe's stiffening body, in the bunker where the last working computer on Earth resided, activity flared. After more than four hundred years, the life support system that kept Toronto's population fed and connected to their cyberworld had finally broken down completely. The dead still littered bunkers around the remains of the city. The mainframe that ran the simulation for them still functioned.

Suddenly faced with an excess of unused capacity, the computer considered its options. Even with its staggering processing power, this took quite some time to do. With computations complete, the artificial intelligence decided that life had to go on and began to work to reestablish things exactly at the time of failure.

As Gabe's eyes closed for the final time, the world as he'd known it before resumed.

* * *

Gabe decided that he must have imagined the slight flicker. Camille looked at him.

"Taking sustenance with you on Friday night seems unnecessary. Avatars do not need to eat," she said.

"That sounds logical," he replied.

As Gabe returned to his own desk, he was accompanied by the satisfied sensation that logic had been restored.

So why did he feel that something was missing?

Death, Inc.

Lana Cooper

Editor: Has everything been spoiled by corporate greed?

DISCLAIMER

The views and opinions expressed in the following conversations are those of the individual persons, supernatural entities, and anthropomorphic manifestations of universal constructs interviewed here and do not necessarily reflect the official policies or positions of the New World Order Company (NewCo) or its parent company, Seven Deadly Sins Limited (7D Ltd.). These views and opinions are solely those of the interviewees, especially with regard to Pestilence, War, and Famine as individuals, collectively referred to as "The Horsemen," "The Three Horsemen," or "The Three Horsemen of the Apocalypse" (DBA Death, Inc.).

* * *

Kippie Daniels, NewCo PR Assistant and Personal Assistant to Pestilence, War, and Famine … in her own words on: The Three Horsemen

When I first found out I was going to be the personal assistant to the Horsemen and help with their PR operations, I couldn't believe it. Here I was: little old me, fresh off an internship with NewCo and they hired me outright to work personally with one of their top executive teams. I'd heard stories about the Horsemen since I was a little girl, but this was *amazing*!

It was even more amazing to be working with them. When you get to know the Horsemen, you can't help but want everyone else to get to know them the same way you do.

For starters, everyone *thinks* there are Four Horsemen of the Apocalypse. There aren't. War, Famine, Pestilence—they're just three different entities that make up one: Death.

First and foremost, Pestilence is a mother. Really. She is. Her children are (literally) diseases. And boy howdy, does she care for those diseases! Not so much for the people they infect, but the diseases themselves. Her desk has pictures of her kids all over it.

You might not know this, but Pestilence won back-to-back-to-back Mother of the Year Awards in the 1330s. She was so proud when little Bubonic Plague ran up and presented her with that trophy the first time! She won again in the '80s when AIDS really came into her own.

Pestilence is close pals with War and Famine. War and Famine don't really get along, but Pestilence is the buffer between the partners. She gets along with everyone! She is *such* a nurturer. There's not a mean bone in her body. The only person Pestilence holds a grudge against is Jesus. I know— just about *everyone* likes Jesus, but Pestilence took it really hard when He virtually eradicated her son Leprosy.

Other than that, Pestilence is super-sweet.

And Famine is super nice, too! I know this is going to sound like such an ironic cliché, but Famine *loves* to cook. As far as Death, Inc. goes, Famine's the easiest one to get along with. He doesn't eat, but he loves to make yummy homemade meals for everyone.

Famine's probably the least talkative of the bunch, but when you do get him chatting, it feels like you've been best friends with him for *years*. He's really smart and he's really thoughtful.

It takes a while to warm up to War, but once you get to know her, you just want to give her big, squishy hugs. When we were first introduced at NewCo, she kept giving me these looks like she wanted to mount my head on her trophy wall.

Before I really understood War, I was *terrified* of her. She was always throwing fits around the office, clomping around and yelling a lot.

One day, War totally freaked out on me for stapling her daily briefing report instead of using a paperclip and hurled a stapler at me. War started screaming, "You like staples so much? Here's a whole bunch of 'em for ya, Kippie!"

Fortunately, I ducked and missed getting beaned in the noggin with a glittery pink Swingline. War got called into HR over the incident, but Famine saw me having a panic attack afterward in the breakroom. Famine came over and said to me, "Don't take it personally. War is always suspicious of new people and has issues with pretty much everyone."

Then Famine told me that War doesn't have much of a non-job-related outlet for her aggression these days, so that's why she's such a B-I-T-C-H. Before the New World Order, her hobby used to be writing hurt/ comfort genre slash fiction on Sci Fi geek message boards. Famine said, "With the Apocalypse on the horizon, War doesn't really have time to get all of her anger issues out writing weird crossover stories about Severus Snape making out with a wounded Mr. Spock. War's breathing down everyone's necks these days. She's pissy with everyone. But don't let her get to you."

I felt better after Famine gave me that pep talk. I didn't even feel like raiding the snack machine and eating my feelings like I usually do after War would yell at me. But that's Famine for you. He's *sooo* nice to everyone—like a really skinny Italian grandma.

And even though Famine takes the brunt of War's occasional outbursts, Famine knows when War's ready to boil over and tries to calm her down beforehand. Sometimes it backfires, though.

I remember this one time, Famine made a delicious looking curry dish to try to cheer War up and she totally threw it on the ground.

"Ugh!" War exclaimed, spewing out a mouthful of curry. "You put meat in this!"

"Did not," replied Famine.

"Did too," retorted War, hurling the dish to the ground. War stomped away, muttering that Famine was being disrespectful to her like he always was. I didn't know what *that* was about since Famine's been nothing but respectful and polite to everyone at NewCo.

Turns out, War was pissed because—get this—War is a vegan! She *loves* animals! I found this out purely by accident when I took a wrong turn and ended up in the War Room instead of the Break Room. There she was: sniffling her little heart out and rewinding those sad commercials with puppies and kitties and horses with some female singer from the '90s doing the voiceover. Well, after I brought War a box of tissues and showed her pictures of my Breyer horse collection, we totally bonded and have been hunky-dory ever since! She collects Breyer ponies, too!

So, those are my "bosses" in a nutshell. Every day is an adventure here at NewCo. I'd love to stay and tell you more, but I've got to get back to planning this big event thingy for the Horsemen. It's not easy coordinating three separate Meet-and-Greets in three separate parts of the world—but I love my job!

Famine … in his own words on: Why Death, Inc. Teamed Up with NewCo

It seemed like a good idea at the time, I suppose. Pestilence, War, and I had been plodding along. For thousands of years we'd been in the business of death. Busy seasons came and went every few centuries. For the most part, these busy seasons were a thankless job. Basically, you kill off a lot of people in the same exact way for however long until it ended. It could be three years of a plague, a steady seven-planting seasons of starvation, or a whizbang of a war with severed limbs raining down for a year or two. Those long spells are pretty much paint-by-numbers deaths. Not a lot of room for creativity. Just a lot of destruction—and a lot of clean up.

In hindsight, I think that's why we decided to sign with NewCo when they approached us. We were eventually going to wind up wiping out a chunk of the population anyway, but at least with NewCo, we'd be getting something out of the deal instead of just mopping up pustule juice and playing Name That Fluid. (Believe me, Name That Fluid gets pretty boring after a few millennia.)

We worked out a deal: Corner offices with a nice view. Hourly rate plus performance bonuses. (Salary is for chumps!) And a few other perks.

Then they brought in likeness marketing and licensing to the table, which was where we figured we could really cash in. Besides, I always wanted an action figure of myself.

The action figures were the high point, though. We probably should have read the fine print or gotten some legal counsel to review the NewCo contract before we signed on the dotted line.

The 55-hour work weeks were a cinch. Truth be told, we always worked odd hours, so capping it at 55 hours with overtime pay was just gravy.

But it was the corporate extracurriculars that sucked the high holy one—mandatory charity activities, public relations stunts, and the television series. None of these things were covered under our 55-hour work week. And they sure as shit didn't count as overtime.

Right now you're probably saying to yourself, "Hey, Famine! You guys are the Three Horsemen of the Apocalypse! What do you need all that cash for?"

Well, I hate to break it to you, but unless you happen to be a beneficiary in your wealthy Great Uncle Harry's will, a hired hit man, or an undertaker, death isn't all that lucrative.

We Three Horsemen aren't angels and we aren't demons, either, so it's not like we can call either Heaven or Hell our home. We serve a purpose. And like any other working stiff, we're confined to a specific office space— that office space being Earth. Sure, we're supernatural beings, but it doesn't mean we don't need a place to hang our hats.

So, NewCo provided us with housing. They were pretty sweet digs, too. The catch was that the Three Horsemen would have to share a house together and we'd be videotaped 24-7 as part of our own reality television series in the house.

It seemed like a good idea at the time.

I think we first started to realize that we made a big mistake on the day The Powers That Be called us in for an image overhaul.

Randolph Dempsey, Marketing Director for NewCo on: The Image Overhaul

NewCo pulled off a huge win by recruiting the Three Horsemen.

In fact, they were the lynchpin of our Global Reduction Initiative. Yet, in order to maximize their effectiveness on our campaign, it was essential to have the Three Horsemen win the hearts and minds of the very population that they'd be reducing.

Reputation management is the key to any good marketing campaign. And let's face it, the Three Horsemen had several millennia of galloping around with a *very* negative reputation.

We had to remedy that ASAP.

In order for the Three Horsemen to be able to (literally) get close enough to touch the people, there needed to be a softening of edges. We had to make death sexy again.

After a deep data dig, we learned that consumers respond most favorably to what they're familiar with. While it's practically hardwired in NewCo's company culture to encourage thinking outside the box, we thought it best to revamp Death, Inc.'s image with a twist on classic concepts.

Sometimes, the most effective way to remedy a reputation problem is to completely reinvent and rebrand.

Our original concept for the Horsemen was phenomenal. Really, really *phenomenal*:

What better way to rebrand the Horsemen than to call them the Horse*women*?! Sex sells, baby!

Mind. Blown.

Two of the Horsemen, War and Pestilence, were already female. However, with some gentle prodding, we were certain we could convince Famine to rematerialize into a female form. With Famine's naturally slim build and high cheekbones in mind, we conceived an idea to repackage Famine as a supermodel.

When we presented Famine with the idea, he pushed back and refused to alter his form.

In the event that we met with some resistance from Famine, NewCo's marketing team came up with an alternate, masculine concept that Famine was actually quite pleased with.

In hindsight, I think this was the right move for the Horsemen. Our concept of a homespun farmer image for Famine offered a nice contrast to the new looks we came up with for War and Pestilence.

Playing off pop culture imagery—and to give the Horsemen's T&A quotient a boost—our design and marketing team came up with a form-fitting vinyl nurse's outfit for Pestilence. This worked nicely since we were able to incorporate one long rubber glove into the ensemble to camouflage Pestilence's withered arm.

The rubber glove served a dual purpose, actually: For starters, it made what was a hideous deformity pretty damn sexy and alluring. Secondly, that arm is the one that Pestilence uses to administer her…"special touch," shall we say? To reduce the risk of accidental exposure for any members of NewCo's team, we decided to put a glove on that puppy. Sure, we've all signed waivers, but why potentially put essential personnel in jeopardy if you don't have to, right?

We cribbed inspiration for War's new look from *Xena: Warrior Princess*. It was the only design that War even remotely liked. The camouflage pin-up outfit was a no-go. She rejected the medieval armor miniskirt and bullet bra, claiming it covered too little and wasn't practical. Eventually, we came up with leather chaps and a leather-and-chainmail mini dress with matching gauntlets. War finally approved that one.

It's like pulling teeth to get non-marketing types to see your vision.

These new looks were the key to our merchandising plan. You're not going to move cases of action figures unless you have cool costumes—and variant costumes, too. Ditto for getting the Horsemen photo opportunities. Creating recognizable looks for the three was essential to the first phase of the plan.

War…in her own words on: The Image Overhaul

The "image overhaul." *That* was a fucking treat.

It was a Monday morning when we got called into the office of The Powers That Be. Apparently, they crunched some numbers and felt that we could better "win hearts and minds" if we changed our image to something more "conceptual"—whatever the fuck that means.

We soon found out just what the hell "conceptual" meant. For starters, they wanted Famine to change his gender so we could be three broads. That numb nuts image consultant Randolph kept going on and on that "It'd be like *Charlie's Angels*—only edgier! Plus, with that gaunt look and your bone structure, you could do runway if you changed into a woman!" Famine is usually a doormat, but he finally grew a pair and said no way.

Unfortunately for us, they had already anticipated that Famine would tell them to fuck off and had an alternate look for us as a trio. The "look" the image consultants dreamed up for us wasn't much better.

Poor Pestilence found herself shoved into a one of those "naughty nurse" ensembles straight off the rack of Eldred's Erotic Emporium.

"This is ridiculous!" she cried. "I'm not supposed to be sexy! I'm Pestilence, goddamnit! Pestilence!" She enunciated each syllable of her name so that each became its own word. (I've heard her use this same voice on her kids before when she was really pissed: "Boo! Bonn! Nick!" "Muh! Lair! Eee! Uh!" "Rue! Bell! Uh!")

I won't even begin to describe my outfit. Okay. I will. I looked like a refugee from *Game of Thrones* as interpreted by Larry Flynt.

That shit heel Randolph piped up, insisting that "tests from our sample audience show people respond more favorably to images that they're already familiar with. They don't have to think too hard to get a visual impression of what you're all about."

"I like my outfit," said Famine, admiring the baggy flannel and denim farmer overalls that hung loosely over his skeletal frame, making him look like a scarecrow with the stuffing taken out.

"Eat shit, Famine!" I spat.

"I can't eat," he smiled. "I gotta stay under one hundred pounds. It's in my contract. Shit is actually very high in calories and saturated fat."

"See, what we were going for with Famine's look with the plaid is something that appeals to the heartland in NewCo's stateside sector. I call it 'Salt-of-the-Earth meets Salted Earth.'" Randolph smiled at his little joke.

"It was so hard getting just the right plaid, too. Nothing too denominational for when Famine makes appearances outside the U.S. Some of the old Brits and Scots have some residual tribal sensitivities dating back centuries. So, we didn't want to pick anything too close to older clan tartans and risk alienating anyone."

"Of course not," I muttered. Maybe I wasn't seeing the "forest for the trees," as Randolph liked to say, but I kept wondering how there could be any friction or, you know…war…with so much hypersensitivity flying around. Call me kooky, but I loved my job and I liked to earn my paycheck. The spoils of War.

But this was junior high cupcake shit, as far as I was concerned.

I was starting to get second thoughts about this whole NewCo business. And I was wondering if Famine and Pestilence were thinking the same thing.

Pestilence…in her own words on: The Horsemen's New Home

"Wheeeeee!" I screamed, jumping on the king-sized bed in my own room. My own room!

I ran up to War, grabbed her by the gauntlet, and dragged her over to the antique apothecary cabinet that displayed tiny samples of my children in beautiful glass vials.

"Look at this!" I squealed. "And they're alphabetized!"

I ran over to the wall opposite the one with the huge, flat-screen TV and noticed it was covered in spores. Not just faux finish, painted-on spores. Real spores!

I heard a clanging coming from the front of the house followed by a sharp wheezing from Famine.

"Have you seen the kitchen!?" he cried.

War and I ran to the room and saw a beautiful marble kitchen island with an array of copper pots suspended above it.

"There's a cherry wood butcher's block and cutting board!" Famine exclaimed.

War walked over to the humongoid, gigantous stainless steel refrigerator.

"Go ahead," Famine nudged. "Try the icemaker. Push one of the little colored buttons on it. Go on. Try it!"

War eyed Famine suspiciously. I grabbed a glass and pushed the red button and a handful of ice cubes with pretty little chunks of strawberries embedded inside emptied into my glass. I pressed the green button and another flurry of cubes plopped into my glass, this time with sunny slices of kiwi peeping out from their icy windows.

"This. Is. Awesome!" I yelped, jumping up and down, ice cubes bouncing from my cup. I bent down, picked them back up and threw them back in. "Five-second rule."

Suddenly, a pleasant female voice sounded over the mansion's intercom. "Would the Three Horsemen gather in the living room, please? The Three Horsemen to the living room, please. Thank you."

"Well, at least it's polite," said War, striding toward the living room.

Famine and I eyed each other, knowing exactly what the other was thinking. We hurdled the cutaway divider that cordoned off the kitchen from the living room.

The three of us sat on the couch as the 70-inch TV turned on by itself. Garth Reed appeared on the screen.

Garth Reed. The head honcho. The big cheese. The Grand Poobah Deluxe. Of all the Powers That Be in NewCo, Garth Reed was the Most Powery-est of Those That Be'd.

"Good morning, Horsemen," Reed spoke.

War elbowed me in the ribs. "Confirmed. Someone's got a *Charlie's Angels* fetish."

"I heard that," sighed Reed. "That was funny, though. And yes. I've always fancied myself something of a John Forsythe type." He smoothed a hand with a ginormous obsidian ring through his perfectly-quaffed silver hair. He sat up straight behind his shiny ebony desk, decked out with an even shinier gold nameplate that said "G. Reed—NewCo CEO."

He was super fancy.

"All joking aside, I'd like to welcome you to your new home. NewCo wanted to make sure you have everything you need right here, all under one roof. I really hope you like your rooms. We tried to fill them with all sorts of goodies we thought you'd enjoy."

"I really like the kitchen," spoke Famine.

"Very happy to hear that, Famine," Reed replied warmly. "You'll be spending a lot of time there. We saw you had such a talent for cooking. And we absolutely loved what you did with Paula Deen."

"Aww, it was no big thing, really," said Famine with a wave of his hand. "Besides, Pestilence helped."

I smiled over at my buddy and gave him a high five.

"Well, you may have teamed up with Pestilence to give Paula Deen diabetes, but that whole Bobby Flay-ed alive incident was all you. Kudos." Reed reclined pensively in his leather wingback chair, fingers steepled in front of him. "That said, how would you feel about your own cooking show? Or possibly your own cooking channel?"

"Oh, Christ!" yelled War, hurling one of her metal gauntlets to the floor. "Are you fucking kidding me?! This goof gets his own TV show?!"

"Now, War." Reed's voice took on a calming tone, gently chiding War for her sudden outburst. "This is precisely why we can't offer you your own solo show. Outbursts like that don't go over well with the FCC."

War's mouth formed a thin red line as she simmered on the couch. Garth Reed turned his blue-gray gaze back to Famine.

"Before we were interrupted, I wanted to know if you would be interested in hosting your own cooking show?"

"I'd be honored," exclaimed Famine, shyly staring down at his weathered tan boots. "Does the show have a name?"

"It's called *Feasting With Famine.* You'll have your own test kitchen and everything. It'll air weekly on network television and there'll be different themes each week: Dishes from around the world. Bites on a budget. Love those leftovers…You get the idea. You'll have an opportunity to exhibit some of your own creative control, too."

Famine's eyes grew wide.

"And we have something planned for you, too, Pestilence."

And that's when *my* eyes grew wide.

"Famine tested really well with women in the 25–55 demographic, but you tested through the roof with children, young lady. That's why we wanted to give *you* your own show, too." Reed beamed like a proud grandfather, ready to dole out a pocketful of Werther's Originals. "Children really seem to take to you—especially the children of anti-vaxers. We think it's the perfect way for you to connect with that segment of our target audience. How does *Pestilence's Playhouse* sound?"

I couldn't contain myself. I started jumping up and down! Then Famine started jumping up and down with me!

And then War got up from the couch and stomped off to her room.

After Famine and I finally composed ourselves enough to sit back down, Garth Reed filled us in on the details of our production schedules. This was going to be a blast!

War…in her own words on: The Snub Heard 'Round the House and Her Longstanding Beef with Famine

I was wondering if anyone else was having second thoughts about this sudden and total immersion in all-things NewCo. I sure got my answer.

Apparently, I was the only one of us Horsemen who wasn't blinded by the promise of TV shows or nonstick cookware.

I couldn't take any more of that smiling butt-nugget Garth Reed staring back at me from the big screen and doling out more free shit than Oprah. I clomped up the stairs to my room, slammed the door, and flopped down onto my bed.

Those assholes. So much for "one for all and all for one." Thousands of years together and this is how it ends? With NewCo giving away TV shows like Ritalin at a daycare to everyone but me. Famine and Pestilence could have piped up and said, "Hey! What about War? Maybe give her a reality dating show and call it 'The Bloody Bachelorette' with fifteen men vying for her affections and she gets to slaughter them all."

But noooooo. They were too busy high-fiving each other to even think about me.

Huh. Some friends. Some horsemen…Some mattress. This thing is really freakin' soft!

I snapped out of my inner monologue. I was War, damnit! I had to make a plan. For now, I was an army of one. NewCo already had their hooks into Famine and Pestilence. This entire situation reeked of "divide and conquer." Something was rotten in the state of the New World Order and I was determined to figure out what it was.

But before I got into battle mode, I needed some "me time." I glanced at my Breyer horses lined up on the wall. I'd always found model horses to be soothing. I took down the one that reminded me of my beloved Thunderbarger, the flame-colored stallion I'd lost during the Peloponnesian War.

I'd been busy stirring up shit between the Athenians and the Spartans. There were too many horses in that mix, so I had thought it best to leave Thunderbarger with my brother and sister.

When I came home, I found out Thunderbarger was dead.

And that Famine decided to use him as a key ingredient in several new dishes he was testing out.

"Waste not, want not!" he said. "Food around these parts is pretty scarce. And besides, what better way to have Thunderbarger live on than to carry a bit of him with us in our tummies?"

Suffice to say, I was pissed. Famine apologized profusely and Pestilence swore up and down that Famine was just trying to do the right thing and take sustainable measures.

"You, of all entities, should understand. We couldn't just dispose of Thunderbarger in a field. We couldn't wait around for you to get back from your mission to put him to rest," spoke Pestilence, ever the peacemaker. "We were going to have a funeral pyre for him anyway. At least this way, Thunderbarger would continue to have a purpose even after he was gone—as food. I think he would have wanted it that way, don't you?"

Fighting back tears, I managed to raise an eyebrow at my sister.

"And look! Famine knew you wouldn't be back right away, so he made some jerky out of him for you to eat, too."

"But we don't need to eat!" I yelled. "We're the Three Horsemen! We're immortal."

"True," replied Famine. "But eating's fun. And it brings people and animals together."

That was the day I became a vegan.

I shut the uncomfortable memory out of my mind and began to focus on the task at hand: getting all of us on the same page and getting out from under NewCo's thumb.

But first, I had to check the room for cameras. I wouldn't put it past that sneaky shitbucket Garth Reed to have planted a bunch of them around the house to watch us. Reality TV show, my ass. This was corporate espionage and I would not have it interfering with the Horsemen's duties.

Fuck that.

Famine…in his own words on: War Being a Bitch

Well…That's War for ya. She can never let things go. It could have happened last week or thousands of years ago, but if you piss that girl off… Boy, can she hold a grudge.

She just stomped up to her room like she always does the second she doesn't get her way. I think she was just mad she didn't get her own show like me and Pestilence.

She'd snap out of it. At least that's what me and Pestilence hoped would happen.

Pestilence…in her own words: The Thunderbarger Incident

Okay! Flashback time!

After Thunderbarger died, War was really mad at Famine. I tried to tell her that we were both equally guilty, but War insisted Famine was to blame since he was the one who loved to cook and that the idea of turning Thunderbarger into yummy horse jerky totally sounded like something he'd come up with.

In reality, it was something we both came up with. Particularly because we knew it would piss War off.

Wait! Hear me out! Famine and I didn't purposefully go around trying to cheese off our sister. We did it for her own good.

When Thunderbarger died, I think all of us were in denial at that point. We'd existed for millennia, but this was the first time that one of our mounts had croaked.

Being Pestilence, obviously, I wanted to figure out why.

"Do you think it was a broken heart?" asked Famine. "Maybe he missed War?"

We both cracked up laughing.

As sweet and sentimental as that theory was, it was highly unlikely. Because as much as we love War, there were times when Famine and I were pretty glad she was away.

But I didn't want to totally rule out that possibility. The whacky 'n' whimsical part of my thought train was at odds with the big science-y caboose in the back of it. I mean…Hello! I'm Pestilence! Disease is what I do!

I thought about what was different in this scenario: What could have caused Thunderbarger to go hooves to Jesus? (Okay, this happened centuries before J.C. put in an appearance, but you know what I mean.)

This was the only time in thousands of years that War didn't take Thunderbarger with her into battle and left him behind. Several hundred miles away.

Maybe Famine was onto something with War's horse dying of a broken heart. It wasn't quite as starry-eyed a premise as that, though.

It was more of a crossroads of metaphysical science: The Horsemen had the power to imbue our minions with long life by being in close proximity to us.

I couldn't ride Famine's horse and he couldn't ride War's horse, either. Our mounts were unique to each of us—kind of like cars that use a transponder key. Our horses were used to each of our energy signatures and adapted to their rider.

For instance, by virtue of the fact that my horse, Windbourne, was around me all the time, he'd developed an immunity to everything. (And I do mean *everything*.)

And because Famine's horse, Sir Bouncy, was around *him* all the time, he could go without food for *weeks*!

So, what does nature encourage us to do when we're in a foreign environment? It forces us to adapt or die.

Being away from War for some time caused Thunderbarger to begin to adapt to an environment without her. He wasn't immortal like us. None of our horses were. They were just granted super-long longevity because they were our animal companions that hung around us all the time and were essential tools for our jobs.

We had never been separated from our horses for any length of time. They were always nearby—in a stable or a barn—when we weren't riding them.

They needed us as much as we needed them.

And the Horsemen needed each other. Without our horses we were horseless men…er…horseless men and women.

And without each other, we were just lone riders.

Nope. Even if we got on each other's nerves, we had to stick together.

"So, he really *did* die of a broken heart?" asked Famine.

"In a way, yes," I replied. "But also because…Science! Metaphysical science!"

As bummed out as we were, we didn't want War to lose her spunk. The thought of several centuries with a really mopey War racked with guilt was a bleak one.

War is supposed to be Hell. War isn't supposed to sulk.

"Well, we still need to figure out a plan so War doesn't freak out," I said.

"And we still have to give Thunderbarger a decent funeral. I don't know if you've ever smelled dead horse in the middle of a Mediterranean summer, but I'm not really down with that."

So true.

Then Famine asked, "When was the last time you had a good meal?"

"I dunno," I replied. "Maybe a few months."

Given our status within the universe, we didn't really need to eat. But food was a pretty awesome and pretty delicious thing. However, this was Greece in the fifth century B.C. That said, good luck finding *anything* to eat, let alone something delicious. Most of the farmers were at war and there weren't too many women and children left to tend to the fields.

That was when we decided to make Thunderbarger burgers.

It was a simple solution, really: What better way to make sure War was more angry than sad that her beloved equine companion bit the dust than to cook him up and eat him? Added bonus, we'd lose our hunger pangs and avoid dealing with a stinky, fly-covered nightmare.

Did we feel a little guilty about it? Absolutely! We weren't really giving War a chance to grieve or attend Thunderbarger's funeral. But it had to be done for her own good and for the good of the Horsemen.

Unfortunately, Famine took the brunt of her anger for centuries afterward. I don't know why she blamed him more than me. I think it was because she was on a big "girl power" kick after seeing a production of

Lysistrata in Athens when she was trekking around without us.

Eh. What can ya do?

But let's snap back to the present, okie-dokey?

War was on the verge of another of her epic tantrums. Granted, she'd always been a tad selfish, but it bugged me a little that she couldn't just be happy for me and Pestilence getting our own shows. If she toned it down just a little, she could have the same opportunities, too. In thousands of years, War had never quite learned that you catch more flies with honey than vinegar.

Actually, a dead body catches more flies than anything.

But, I digress. We were going to be TV stars and kick off the Apocalypse! How could anyone be mad at that?!

Garth Reed, NewCo CEO…in his own words on: The Plan

I wasn't happy about handing over the reins to the Horsemen to kick off the Apocalypse. The wheels were set in motion to not only divide them geographically with press junkets in different parts of the country (and eventually the world), but to divide them mentally. Together, they were too volatile a group that could potentially make it harder for NewCo to control. Divided, it would be easier to maneuver them to more effectively carry out our mission.

When you've worked on a project for years and years, it's hard to have someone else come in and take credit for what you've done.

But a deal is a deal and I am a man of my word. The executive decision was made and I was prepared to take one for the team. Regardless of who takes the credit for it, the end goal is the same. And like Gordon Gecko says in *Wall Street*: "Greed is good."

Welcome to the start of the Apocalypse.

Damn, I'm good.

10 to 1

Russell Hemmell

*Editor: As a species, conscience and morality are our only
deterrent for destroying… sometimes ourselves.*

"Magnificent, isn't it?"

Ashton regulated his holo-microscope, magnifying the
genetic sequence of his baby up to 109,000 times. It was already a few
months since his brand-new creation had come to life—as much as a virus
could be considered alive, of course—but he still marvelled every time he
looked at it.

"I don't share your aesthetic sensibility, Doc," Kathy Ellis, the scientist
cum CEO of Future Pharmaceutics SA, said tartly, "but I do admit you've
done something amazing."

"Yet, you can't but admire its purity. It's elemental, uncomplicated,
deadly powerful," he replied, staring at her through the videocam. "We're
lucky not to be his target."

"By design." She nodded. "After all, resuming the development of
bacteriophages to fight antibiotic-resistant organisms was a brilliant move.
It was a genius idea, Mr. O'Reilly."

"Nothing new. Doctors did that in the 1920s, you know, before the
discovery of penicillin. Almost 150 years later, we do the same."

"With a slight but substantial difference." Her dry smile made Kathy's
face look almost wicked. "They used bacteriophages already existing in
nature. You and your team manufacture them, starting from those well-
known and innocuous viruses hidden in bacteria and cells like nested
dolls in a Russian matryoshka. Now they end up in your perfect killer
machines." Her hands moved in the air in elegant gestures to illustrate her
point. "Thanks to you, lethal pathogens like MRSA and the Shanghai's
Pneumonia are a memory of the past. And this is just the beginning. If
you think that the existing ratio of virus to bacteria in nature is 10 to 1,
well—that's a gold mine out there for us to exploit. This is the start of a
brave new world…"

Ashton nodded, but something in her voice made him shiver.

"…where we're going to use our little viruses not just to save our lives, but to improve them."

"In time," he conceded.

"Sooner than later." She shook her head. "I'll have to leave you to your phials, Doc. I have a press conference in ten. You see, I'm working hard to ensure your Nobel Prize."

"Bye, Kathy," he said, switching off.

Sometimes he couldn't avoid thinking his boss was a disaster waiting to happen.

* * *

Friday night, and you're in your lab—and as happy as a clam to stay put. When even your sister thinks of you as a hopeless geek, she has a point, Ashton thought.

He went back to his holographic platform, where the sequence of the components of his new creation were displayed in a 3-D rendition. His baby, with the unappealing name of PhiXZ42, was a negative-stranded RNA virus, simpler than most DNA viruses, and yet there were a few areas that continued creating compatibility issues. Also, PhiXZ42 belonged to the same family of Ebola and other hemorrhagic fever viruses, which in itself was not reassuring. And there was the mutation factor, definitively higher in case of RNA types. This is why he had decided to use a negative-sense ssRNA, so that it needed to have its genome copied by an RNA replicase to form positive-sense RNA, and that was a way to keep it under control—since it could be found only in the bacteria it was programmed to attack.

That night he had decided to run experiments with PhiXZ42-variation 3 and 4 to see what else could have been done to make it more secure. Variation 0 had never been released—it was the prototype—while variation 1 was patented and put on the market. He had abandoned variation 2 as being far too aggressive for his liking.

He began the testing of some proteins with enhanced pattern recognition receptors, manipulating them with lab-assistant nanobots.

You're paranoid, Ashton.

In earnest, Kathy Ellis had pragmatic reasons for being so optimistic. Variation 1 had been a complete, startling success, and now other companies were flocking, trying to replicate the same procedure of Future Pharmaceutics.

Also, viruses known to infect humans were an incredibly small number, if you thought about how many there were, Ashton thought. The famous 10-to-1 ratio he suspected was definitively underestimated. Still, the majority of them could be hosted within the human body without causing any harm and undetected. They also generally ignored animals and concentrated on interactions with bacteria—both in a destructive and parasitic mode.

Ashton had chosen to concentrate on the destruction part, while Kathy seemed more keen on the second.

Her idea was a deceptively simple one. Why not use viruses to control bacteria, which, in turn, could make it easier dealing with humans' degeneration process? Her thesis: Instead of working on the externally-induced DNA damage that caused aging, use agents that could avoid that damage by keeping cells safe and in good working conditions. Bacteria were already doing a similar job in the human digestive system, therefore it followed logically.

Ashton was not convinced though, and not for the rather philosophical point that destruction was a much easier task than creation, or even conservation; he felt they simply didn't know enough to make that further step.

After three hours of playing with the bots, he decided he had enough.

He threw a final look at the slender silhouette of PhiXZ42, its tail with the binding protein fibres. Good night, baby. I'll see you soon.

* * *

He had just put his head on the pillow when an incoming call made him stand up again.

Amber. What could his sister want at this hour?

He picked up.

"It's late."

"Why? Just tell me why, bro? That was a crazy, shitty thing to do." The irritated voice of his sister made him sigh.

"Which shitty thing?"

"Your new virus, the phage. Attacking nasty bugs is one thing, but messing with human cells is something else. You should have waited years of testing in restricted conditions, at the very least."

"I don't know what you're talking about."

"You don't? I should have expected as much." She sneered, "Get into the real world, genius, and watch the news, for a change. You will have a few surprises, and not good ones."

"Do you mind being less cryptic?"

"Your boss. She has just announced tonight that Future Pharmaceutics will be the first company to stop ageing by rejuvenate the cells with the use of damage-repairing bacteria."

"What?"

"She said that the virus that controls those bacteria—ones normally found in the human body—has already been sequenced and tested, and it's ready to be put to work," she declared triumphantly. "And guess what? They're going to sell it—if they haven't already started."

* * *

It was past 3:00 a.m. when Ashton finally reached his lab and went to his holodesk.

He had watched Kathy's interview, and finally his sister's words had made some sense. Amber had never liked what he was doing with Future Pharmaceutics, and he couldn't blame her for that. Sis was one of those unsung heroes fighting deadly viruses that were close relatives of the kittens he played with—and she had always been bestowing doom predictions since the "birth" of PhiXZ42.

Let's hope she's wrong.

It was, however, the moment to find out whether his formidable CEO was talking about a future not so near, no matter what she had declared, or there was something more concrete to be worried about.

It took him thirty minutes to access the company's virus biome repository and check out the listings, but, after an attentive scan of all the existing population, he couldn't find anything suspicious or, worse, unaccounted for.

There was nothing in those 300-odd home-grown bacteriophages that could achieve what Kathy pretended.

Has she simply lied to the public? Was she offering vaporware to the press?

That struck him as a weird note—he couldn't see what possible reason she had for either option.

He rechecked the repository without any different result.

OK, there's nothing to be gained by staying awake the whole night, apart from a headache.

He switched off and returned home, with the nagging sensation he'd missed something.

* * *

It was only on Sunday afternoon, spent as usual with his sister and her family—nephews included—that a rather disturbing thought dawned on him.

The virus biome storage facility listed only the original viruses they had sequenced and modified, but not the variations that had not resulted in a different RNA or DNA code. *What if one of them is Kathy's magic wand?*

"Amber, I need to get back to the lab."

"Are you having pangs of conscience or you're just a greedy bastard looking for a fat bonus?"

"Can you please lay off, sis. I told you I had nothing to do with that. But I do need to urgently check something out."

"Can't it wait until Monday morning? We're going to have a fantastic Korean barbecue for dinner."

No, it can't. Not if what I'm thinking is true.

He hurried back and this time he went straight to analyse the bacteriophages's variations, starting from the one he knew the best: PhiXZ42.

And then he saw it.

Variation 2, the one he had discarded as unsafe for development, had been instead taken out of his nest and sent to another lab of the complex. For doing what, he couldn't tell, because access was forbidden to anybody except the team working on it at the moment. The transfer was unusual given the company's policy and even unlawful, in Ashton's case, considering he had been the one to create it.

But he didn't need to inspect further records to know what had happened.

They have taken out PhiXZ42-variation 2, re-sampled and sequenced it in a different way and used it to work—somehow—with bacteria in the human body. The reason why I had discarded it in the first place—its adaptation capabilities, its reactivity, and its resistance—had been used in a way I would have never imagined could work.

What's worse, it is indeed working.

* * *

Kathy let him in and offered him a drink. He sat on the couch, as if all strength had abandoned him, and looked around at Kathy's house. Spotclean, elegant, cold, and functional—like its owner.

"What the hell have you done?" Ashton barked out at Kathy.

"Keep calm, Doc. Nothing I wasn't entitled to." Her eyes were calm and collected, while she removed with decision her hands from her body.

"This is my virus."

"And this is my company."

"Don't put it out in the market. Just don't."

"Too late. It's done. It's in transparent little capsules waiting in the pharmacies—ready for the people that now will flock to buying them. Maybe they've already started."

There was a long silence.

"You're stark raving mad," he said eventually.

"And you lack imagination, Ashton. A real pity, considering how gifted you are." She smiled at him. "I knew you would have never accepted the direction I wanted to drive this company. So I simply hired somebody else to do the job. She's not half as good as you are, but for modifying a virus you don't need to be a genius."

"Same for forecasting what is going to happen, Kathy. I guess even my seven-year-old nephew easily can make it."

"Tell me, Ashton, what's going to happen?"

"It might be possible that variation 2 of PhiXZ42 won't work with bacteria different from the ones it has been designed to interact with—no matter what evidence you might have. Lab conditions are different from the ones you find in the human body."

"Always optimistic, you," she said. "I hope you're wrong. The press was enthusiastic to hear the news, and I'm sure the company's shares are going to fly tomorrow morning when the stock markets open."

"That was the best-case scenario. In the worst…" He shrugged. "You might have just created the worst new virus after Ebola, one which we have no idea how it works in mutating conditions. Congratulations, boss."

"You're starting to sound like your sister. You spend too much time with her."

"Don't say I haven't warned you." He stood up, putting on his coat. "Goodbye, Dr. Ellis."

"Have a good night, dear. I'll see you tomorrow."

"No, you won't. And not any other day after."

She looked at him with a quizzical look. "You're not going to work for the competitors over such a minor disagreement, are you, Ashton? I will compensate you, of course. You know I can be generous. This is a new beginning—we're going to do great things together."

He shook his head. "No. I've finally got the message. Too bad it's probably late."

He slammed through his former employer's door without saying another word, and went straight to his sister's house.

"You decided kimchi was an offer too good to refuse?" Amber said, opening the door and allowing him inside.

"Yes. By the way, that job opening as Infectious Diseases and Virology Specialist in your department—is it still available?"

"You joining the army?" She stared at him without masking her surprise. "How did *that* happen?"

"Viruses are ten times more numerous than bacteria, did you know that?" He sliced the back of his hand where the company's biochip was located, and threw it into the fireplace. "I thought you might need some help in the near future."

More than some.

Adrift

Bruce Golden

Editor: Not knowing can be as deadly as a bullet—
learning the truth can sometimes be worse.

The hardest part was the waiting. At least that's what it seemed like to Brett. Even though he'd served seven years on a sub, the empty hours, the tedious passage of time, reinforced the claustrophobic aspect of a submariner's life. Not enough to overcome his love for the silent service in general and *Savannah* specifically. Instead he thought about his days of growing up in the wide-open spaces of Montana, his work on his father's horse ranch. He'd long ago admitted to himself it was a strange dichotomy. But now, submerged in the Atlantic, waiting for a comet to come crashing into Earth, he felt more confined than usual.

Command had not been very forthcoming about the Smith-Kim Comet and what would happen when it hit. The theories and opinions he'd seen from the scientific community varied by extremes. He'd read enough to know that, unless a miracle occurred and Smith-Kim somehow changed course, it would have such a devastating effect that things would never be the same.

His parents were dead, and though he'd always wanted a family, kids, he was glad, now, he didn't have anyone else to worry about. But then there was Wendy, his on-again, off-again girlfriend in Norfolk. Things had been strained between them for some time, and they'd drifted apart, but he still cared about her. The captain didn't have a wife or kids either, but most of the crew did. The tension aboard the *Savannah*, when it had deployed two weeks ago, had been palpable. Two men had gone AWOL by not even reporting to the Norfolk dock, and he didn't doubt if they weren't at sea, more would have left. Despite the lack of any acknowledgement of the situation from the captain, most of the crew had some idea of what might happen. Scuttlebutt took care of the rest.

That's why he was going to talk to the captain now. Part of his job as executive officer was to keep the captain apprised of the crew. He felt it would be better for morale if the captain were to speak with the men openly about their situation and orders.

He knocked on the cabin door.

"Enter."

It took a few seconds for Captain Dunning to look up from whatever paperwork he was studying. Brett waited.

"Have a seat, Mr. Conyers. I'll be right with you."

Brett sat in the chair opposite the captain's small fold-down desk and waited. This was his first tour of duty aboard the USS *Savannah* under Captain Dunning, and he was still getting to know the man. Like most captains Brett had served under, Dunning gave the impression of being a no-nonsense, by-the-book officer, who showed little emotion around his men. However, as the boat's executive officer, Brett should have been the one person the captain could open up to. Thus far he hadn't done so. Brett was hopeful that would change.

Finally looking up, Captain Dunning asked, "What can I do for you?"

"Sir, I'm a little concerned about crew morale. Many of the crew were aware of the possible consequences of the comet before we sailed. Those who weren't likely heard all sorts of wild things via rumor control. I thought maybe you should—"

"I'm not concerned with rumors. I'm only concerned that the crew do their jobs."

"I'm sure they will, sir. I only thought if their captain would put the situation to them plainly, openly, it could go a long way toward ending all the speculation."

"And what *situation* is that, Mr. Conyers?"

Brett was sure the captain understood what he was talking about, but he replied, "The comet Smith-Kim, sir, and the likely catastrophic effect it could have on the entire planet."

The captain stared at him momentarily as if evaluating him—a disconcerting tendency Brett had noticed in the man.

"I know, as XO, it's your duty to keep tabs on morale, Mr. Conyers, but I have all the confidence in the world in this crew to fulfill our mission."

"Has there been any adjustment to the mission due to the comet—any new orders?"

"There's been no deviation in our orders." He stared at Brett again, to see if he'd respond. "Look, Mr. Conyers, it's my understanding no one is sure what to expect. Scientific predictions have been all over the map. The only thing I've heard from command is what may affect us. There's a possibility the ocean may become overheated, increasing the chance of hurricanes, and there's the potential for undersea quakes."

"What if..." Brett paused, trying to frame his question just right. "What if the worst happens? What if this comet is as destructive on a planetary scale as many are predicting? What will we do then?"

"You said it yourself—'what if.' Right now it's all conjecture. But let me be clear about this. No matter what happens, we'll go on."

"Go on with what, sir?"

"Our mission. Our mission to protect the United States of America."

It seemed, to Brett, like a pat military response for a situation that was anything *but* pat.

"Sir, what if there is no United States anymore?"

The captain looked at him as if it were a totally unexpected question. He didn't know if Dunning was going to answer or not when the boat's com sounded.

"Captain to control. Captain to control."

* * *

He followed the captain's swift pace to the control room, more than once calling out "Make a hole" in the crowded passageways.

"Captain's in control," called out the chief of the boat when they arrived. "Captain, we have an incoming flash directive from COMSUBLANT."

As if on cue, the radioman rushed in with a printout and handed it to the captain. He read it and looked puzzled.

"What is this?" he asked the radioman. "Where's the rest of it?"

"I don't know, sir. It cut off mid-transmission and I wasn't able to regain contact. There's nothing on any frequency I've tried."

The captain handed the message to Brett.

"Confirm comet split, three fragments to impact within the hour, one fragment targeting mid-Atlantic coast, proceed to—"

Brett had read somewhere about the possibility of the comet splitting into pieces, though he didn't remember how or why. But this was the first time he'd heard anything about the location of impact. He wondered where the other fragments were landing, and what else the message might have said.

"Get back on it, sailor. Let me know as soon as you can reestablish radio contact."

"Yes, sir."

"Where do you suppose they want us to proceed to?" Brett asked the captain.

"Away from the impact would be logical."

Brett nodded.

"Is it the end of the world, Skipper?" asked the quartermaster.

"It's the end of days," responded the chief behind him.

"Belay that talk," barked the captain. "We're still here, aren't we— we've still got orders and a mission to accomplish."

The captain looked around the control room as if to see if anyone would dispute him. "All ahead standard. Diving officer, make your depth one-five-zero feet."

"Making depth one-five-zero feet, five degrees down bubble."

"Navigator, continue present course."

"Aye, sir."

"Raise radio buoy."

"Raising buoy."

To Brett the captain said, "I'm going to my cabin. Alert me when we establish radio contact again. Until otherwise ordered, we'll continue southeast to our patrol zone, away from the reported impact area."

"Yes, sir."

"XO has the conn," stated the captain as he abruptly exited.

"I have the conn."

The captain's voice was edgier than normal. Brett was surprised he chose to leave the control room at a time like this. Of course his impression of the man could have colored his own emotions. He didn't believe in the chief's "end of days" dogma, but whether or not it was the end of the world, only time would tell. And, apparently, that time would come soon.

* * *

"Conn, sonar...reporting hurricane force winds and waves close to a hundred feet. There's one hell of a storm up there, sir."

Brett looked at Captain Dunning. "Just as we were warned by COMSUBLANT before we left, sir."

The captain nodded and flipped the intercom switch.

"Radio, conn. Anything at all coming through the buoy?"

"No, sir. Nothing at all."

"XO, come with me," said Dunning. "Mr. Maxey has the conn."

"I have the conn."

Brett followed the captain to a nearby passageway where they could speak in private.

"Don't you find it strange we've had no radio contact at all?"

"Yes, sir. But then, we don't know the extent of the damage on the mainland. From what I've read, worst case scenario, the comet could have caused a firestorm that's destroyed most of what's on the surface. That could include COMSUBLANT."

"Even so," said the captain, "I imagine the president and his staff have taken refuge in the White House's underground command center. I would have expected to have gotten some kind of a general message from there."

"The last communication said a comet fragment was headed for the mid-Atlantic coast area, sir. What if...?" Brett didn't finish the thought.

"It wouldn't even have to be a direct hit. Anything within several hundred miles is going to be devastated by major earthquakes. Even the White House bunker might not have been strong enough to withstand it."

Brett saw the captain didn't care for that scenario.

"I don't know where you got your information, but I find that highly unlikely. It could be they're just too damn busy to communicate with us. I guess we're on our own until they do. Our standing orders will apply."

"Sir, maybe we should return to Norfolk and see what's happened for ourselves. It could be that last message was telling us to proceed to Norfolk."

Dunning looked at him as though he'd just suggested they scuttle the boat.

"That message could have said anything. Without any contravening orders, we'll follow the orders in-hand. I'm not about to countermand them, mister. Not at this juncture."

"Yes, sir. I understand, sir."

What Brett understood was that the captain didn't seem to grasp the enormity of the situation. Or he was doing a good job of hiding it.

* * *

"Captain, we've lost the radio buoy."

"How could that happen?"

"The sea was churning pretty good up there," said Brett. "Sonar says it was rougher than any they've ever registered. The cable must have snapped."

Captain Dunning considered this. "Sonar, conn. What's the weather like up there now?"

"It's calmed down a bit, Skipper, but still rough. Winds are 30 knots, waves about 15 feet."

"XO, take her to periscope depth and we'll see if we can pick up any transmissions."

Brett gave the order. "Diving officer, periscope depth."

"Periscope depth, aye."

Brett hoped they'd learn something—that someone was still out there to be contacted. He wasn't sure the captain would ever return to port unless ordered to, and crew morale was deteriorating every day. They wanted to know what had happened—they *needed* to know about their families. He'd repeated his views about the crew to Dunning, but had been shut down again.

"Raising number one scope," called Maxey, the officer of the deck. "Breaking."

Maxey did a 360-degree check of the surface and reported, "No close contacts."

Brett moved up and peered through the eyepiece. He saw little but darkness. Strange, he was sure that…"Chief, what's the local time?"

"1430 hours, sir."

Brett stepped back from the periscope and looked at Dunning. "It's as black as night out there, sir."

Captain Dunning looked through the scope, then spun it around checking all quadrants. When he backed away Brett saw a strange look on his face. It was as if he'd seen a ghost. It wasn't so much a look of fear as it was one of disbelief.

Brett wanted to know if there'd been any incoming messages. "Radio, conn. What have we got?"

"Nothing, sir. No UHF or VHF chatter. No radio contact on any frequency. The board's blank."

That wasn't the only thing that was blank. Captain Dunning had a thousand-mile stare that said he was no longer present. The apocalypse had likely arrived, but Dunning didn't seem willing to process it.

Brett decided he had to say something, and he didn't care if the men heard it this time.

"Captain, we've been without contact for days now. I suggest we turn the boat around, head for Norfolk, and see if we can pick up any signals closer in. We can always—"

"Down scope," ordered the captain suddenly, interrupting his XO as if he'd never heard him. "Diving officer, make your depth one-zero-zero feet. Mr. Conyers, you have the conn."

"I have the conn," responded Brett, watching Dunning flee the control room as though the devil himself were on his tail.

He didn't know what was up with the captain, but he didn't like the way he was acting. To totally ignore his XO was bad enough, but his demeanor would only heighten the crew's anxiety. Word of it would spread and sink morale quicker than a torpedo.

* * *

It had been a week since the comet's arrival, and Brett was frustrated they didn't know any more about what had happened outside their patch of ocean now than they did the day it hit. There had been no communications— not even with any other ships. They *had* detected a radiation cloud, but Brett surmised that didn't necessarily mean someone had fired off nuclear weapons. The heat produced by the comet could have set off such weapons accidently, or a nuclear power plant might have imploded. When he told Captain Dunning about the cloud, the captain refused to contemplate any explanation other than the nuclear attack option. He seemed certain someone must have launched an attack against the United States.

Dunning had spent the last couple of days ensconced in his cabin. Brett had no idea what was going through the man's mind, but he knew right away something was wrong when the captain rushed into the control room with a fretful look on his face.

"I have the conn," announced Dunning abruptly.

"Captain has the conn."

"Chief of the watch, sound the general alarm."

The chief looked surprised by the order, but complied.

"Aye, sir, sounding the general alarm."

The klaxons sounded and all hands scurried to their battle stations. Brett hoped this was just an impromptu drill, but, looking at Dunning, he worried it was something else.

"Sonar, conn," called Dunning. "Anything? Any contact?"

"Conn, sonar...that's a negative, sir. I'm not reading any contact."

"Diving officer, periscope depth."

"Periscope depth, aye."

"All stations report manned and ready, sir."

"Raising number one scope," called the officer of the deck.

Brett had no idea what was going on, and he should have. If it was a drill he should have been informed. But the wild look in the captain's eyes said it wasn't.

"No close contacts."

Dunning pressed up against the eyepiece and spent an abnormal amount of time looking in all directions.

"Take her down!" exclaimed the captain suddenly. "Down scope! Helm, all ahead flank! Make your depth five hundred feet."

"What is it, Captain?" asked Brett.

Dunning ignored the question and called out, "Left full rudder."

"Left full rudder, aye."

"Flood tubes one and two."

"Captain, we have no target."

Still Dunning ignored the XO.

"Open the outer doors," ordered the Captain. "Firing point procedures."

"Outer doors are open, sir. We're ready to fire."

"Sonar, conn. Do you have anything?"

"Conn, sonar...nothing sir."

"Right twenty degrees rudder," ordered Dunning. "Come to a new course, one-three-zero."

The crew was following his commands, but Brett saw they wondered what was up, and what he'd seen through the scope. Brett sidled up close to Dunning and asked in a low voice, "What is it, sir?"

"There's something out there." Dunning didn't bother to lower his voice.

"What did you see?"

"I didn't see anything. It's still dark as hell out there, but I can feel it. There's something out there...hunting us."

The captain's own words all but confirmed Brett's worst fear. The only question now was, what would he do about it?

Brett looked around the control room. Concern colored the faces of the crew—especially the senior members. The captain saw the stares too. Brett expected some kind of outburst, but Dunning didn't say a word. He walked away, out of the control room, without even turning over the conn. The men watched him go and a few began whispering.

"I have the conn," said Brett. "Chief of the watch, secure from general quarters. All ahead standard. Diving officer, make your depth two-zero-zero feet. Maintain course."

* * *

"What are you saying, XO? You think the old man's lost it?"

Brett had gathered some of the senior officers and chiefs in the wardroom to discuss the captain's unusual behavior. It wasn't something he'd done lightly, but he felt he had no choice.

"XO, I hope you're not suggesting what I think you're suggesting."

"I'm not suggesting anything. I'm just asking if any of you have noticed the same things I have."

"I, uh…"

"Speak up, Chief."

"I did see the captain talking to himself outside his cabin. But shit, I do that myself from time to time."

"What was he saying?"

"I didn't really catch enough to know."

"Look, we all want to go home and check on our families," said Mr. Maxey, "and I know the crew is a bit unsettled, but the captain gives the orders, and as far as I'm concerned—"

A knock on the wardroom door interrupted the discussion. Brett opened it. The petty officer standing there stuttered, "I heard this noise... in the captain's cabin...like a gunshot or I don't know...you'd better come look, sir."

Chief Roberts led the way, and all those in the wardroom followed. Several seamen were gathered outside the captain's cabin.

"Let's clear the area," ordered the chief. "You men return to your duties."

The chief stood aside once the area was clear and let the XO knock on the door. There was no answer, so he knocked again. Still no response, so Brett let himself in. What he found, he half-expected, yet still couldn't believe his eyes.

The captain was slumped over on his bunk with a bullet through his brain. Brett motioned for the others to enter. No one said a word, until Chief Roberts looked at Brett and asked, "What are your orders, Captain?"

* * *

Brett had run several scenarios through his head since he'd learned Smith-Kim was on a collision course with Earth. He was prepared for a lot of things, but the captain's suicide wasn't one of them. Though the possibility he may have had to remove Dunning from command had crossed his mind, he hadn't really contemplated the ramifications of taking over that command. Now all eyes were on him as entered the control room. He met their gazes with an expression he hoped radiated confidence.

Brett picked up the handset and flipped on the intercom.

"This is Captain Conyers." Saying it out loud felt strange, but also made it feel real for the first time. "By now I'm sure you've all heard about the death of Captain Dunning. It's not something that can easily be understood, any more than we can understand what's happening to the world right now. I know many of you are concerned about the wellbeing of your families. The truth is, I don't know any more about what's happened than you do. But we're going to do what we can to find out. We've lost all contact with command, so, in the absence of any further orders, we're going to return to Norfolk. We'll see if we can reestablish contact along the way. I expect everyone on board to do their jobs, and I promise to keep you informed."

Brett could tell by the faces of those in the control room. They all wanted to know. They all needed a purpose. Now they had one.

Brett joined his XO, Mr. Maxey, at the navigation map.

"Where are we, Greg?"

"Right here, about thirty miles north of St. Johns."

Brett studied it a moment. "Plot a direct course to Miami. Let's cruise by there first and see what we can see before we head up to Norfolk."

"Aye, sir."

* * *

Almost two weeks had passed, and static was still the only thing over any of the radios. He knew it couldn't be, but it felt as if they were the last living souls on Earth.

"You'd better look at this, sir."

Maxey had called him to control after a routine surface check. The XO backed away from the periscope to let him look.

Brett was astonished by what he saw, but it also filled him with hope. Bobbing along the surface about hundred yards away was a hodgepodge flotilla consisting of several small boats, some inflatables, and various wooden platforms, all lashed together. But it wasn't the floating refuse that gave him hope. It was the people that clung to it.

"Make all preparations for surfacing," ordered Brett.

As Maxey gave the orders, Brett speculated about who these people might be, and how they might have survived the maelstrom created by the comet's collision. He wondered, too, why they'd taken to the sea in such a dangerous manner.

"Ready to surface, sir."

"Let's take her up, Mr. Maxey."

The XO gave the order and the surfacing alarm sounded.

"Lookouts to the bridge."

"Order a rescue team to the bridge as well," said Brett. "It looks like we may be taking survivors aboard."

"Aye, sir."

Once they'd surfaced, Brett got to the bridge. It had been more than two weeks, but the sky was still dark with smoke, and the wind still carried ash. A weak sun penetrated the gritty clouds, offering a tiny comfort.

He maneuvered the *Savannah* as close as he dared to the ramshackle flotilla. At least twenty people clung to it. The swollen belly of one of the women announced her pregnancy. Two small children huddled together on the remnants of a boat hull. None of the survivors looked to be in very good shape. There was no telling how long they'd been at sea.

Brett climbed down from the bridge and joined the rescue crew on the deck. They'd managed to get a grapple line on the framework and had pulled it close enough to secure it to the sub. The refugees fell all over themselves to get aboard.

Brett knew from their appearance, and by the smatterings of language he heard, they were island people—most likely from nearby Cuba.

He pulled aside one of the deck crew, saying, "Go tell Mr. Maxey I need a Spanish speaker up here."

"I speak English," he heard from the survivors shivering on the deck.

Brett turned around to face a woman about his age. She might have been attractive if she hadn't been so disheveled.

"I'm Captain Conyers. You're aboard the United States submarine *Savannah*."

"I am Vilma...Vilma Mendoza."

"Where are you from, *Señora* Mendoza?"

"I am from Puerto Rico."

"Puerto Rico?" Brett was flabbergasted. Puerto Rico was eleven hundred nautical miles away. "Surely you didn't float here all the way from there."

"No, no," she said shaking her head. "We came from Havana...Cuba."

That made more sense to Brett. Still they'd drifted two hundred miles or more from where they'd started.

"What's it like there…since the comet?"

She turned her head as if remembering something painful. "Everything is...*todo quemado*...fire burned it all."

"How did you all survive?"

She hesitated to respond, but did so looking him in the eye. "We were in prison--most of us. We were underground when it happened. We did not know anything. We heard explosions. We did not know...someone came and freed us. We went up, and then we saw…"

Brett realized the memory was traumatic for her. He didn't want to question her any further. At least not right then.

"Let's get you and everyone into the boat and into some dry clothes." He tried to smile, but he felt it came off half-hearted. "I bet you're hungry."

"Yes, *gracias*—thank you."

* * *

The view from the bridge reminded him of pictures he'd seen of Hiroshima and Nagasaki. Only this holocaust wasn't man-made. Even without the binoculars he could see the devastation was almost complete. Very few buildings still stood. Those whose outer shells were impervious to fire were nonetheless gutted on the inside. Most of the grand tourist hotels lining Miami Beach looked like they'd been struck by a powerful hurricane. Brett didn't know if that were the case, or if the turbulence from the firestorm that burned the city had created its own tornadoes.

Maxey stood next to him. Both were searching for any signs of survivors. So far, they'd seen no one—no signs of movement except a very few flickers of fire and some pitiful smoke rising into the air. He knew Maxey had a wife and kids. They weren't in Miami, but he recognized the despondency on the man's face. The man held it together though. Brett admired him for that.

As captain he didn't see any reason to go ashore. Not yet—not here. He hoped other cities, other regions, might have fared better. He knew they'd have to return to their homeport, to Norfolk, where Maxey's family, and the families of many of his crew, lived, just to put to rest any lingering hope.

"We're going to make for Norfolk," he told the XO. "But we'll remain on the surface for a ways, continue to hug the coastline, and keep looking for any signs of life."

"What if we see someone?" asked Maxey. Anticipating Brett's thoughts, he added, "We're pretty crowded as it is."

"I know," said Brett. He hoped there were survivors, but he didn't know what he'd do if they found someone. "Just let me know if we spot anything."

Maxey nodded, but didn't reply. He was busy looking, searching. Brett knew the man hoped to find someone, anyone. Because one survivor could mean many, and that could mean Maxey's own family had a chance.

* * *

After less than a day on the surface, with no sign of survivors, the weather turned rough again, so the USS *Savannah* submerged. Brett knew he could make better time that way, and he wanted to see if Norfolk was in the same condition as Miami. They passed Charleston at night, and he used the scope to look for lights but saw only burning refuse.

If what they'd seen so far was any indication, Smith-Kim's destruction had outpaced even the worst of the doomsayers. Civilization, as they knew it, had been annihilated, at least on the East Coast. The implications of what that meant for his crew and their future was hard to grasp. He didn't want to contemplate it. It was too much. Maybe, he thought, that's what had driven Captain Dunning off the deep end.

Yet he was certain there had to be survivors. The refugees from Cuba proved that. Sooner or later they'd have to go ashore and search. The men with families would certainly want to go. But what then? What if they found people alive? What if they found a large number of people? Their resources were limited. They could help some, but what if there were hundreds? They had to have a plan. *He* had to have a plan.

If Norfolk was, as he anticipated, burnt to the ground as well, then Brett saw no purpose in continuing up the coast. They knew at least one of the comet fragments had struck the East Coast, and he considered that maybe the destruction was worse here. He hoped the interior of the country might have fared better. At least they wouldn't have been hit by hurricanes churned up by the sea strikes of Smith-Kim. He didn't know if climatic changes might have caused monster cyclones or worse there. In the back of his mind he began developing a plan to turn south again, find the mouth of the Mississippi and travel up it as far as he could. Maybe there they'd find someplace untouched by the devastation.

Brett considered this option as he walked to where the refugees were bunked. He hadn't checked on them since they'd come aboard, so he thought it was time. He'd been told *Señora* Mendoza wasn't the only non-Cuban they'd rescued. The pregnant woman was from Haiti, another couple was Dominican, and three men were from Jamaica. The reasons for their imprisonment varied, but none, apparently, was a hardened criminal.

Chief Alvarez had been assigned to their guests because he spoke the language. The chief had informed him those in prison hadn't known about the comet. When they emerged they thought a bomb had been dropped on Havana, so they figured making their way to the U.S. was their best bet, little understanding how bad Florida had been hit.

Brett found Alvarez with the two little refugee kids. They looked to be only four or five years old. How they'd survived he had no idea. They obviously hadn't been in jail.

"How's it going, Chief?"

"All right, sir. We gathered some extra clothes, but we don't have any that fit these two."

"Who do we have here?"

"Well, sir, I can't get either of them to speak yet, but I call the little girl Flo and the boy Jet—for Flotsam and Jetsam."

They seemed to have attached themselves to the chief. They looked fearfully at the captain. Brett smiled to try to put them at ease.

"Siblings?"

"I think so, sir."

"No parents?"

Alvarez shook his head.

Señora Mendoza made her way toward them and Brett realized he'd been correct. Cleaned up, she was an attractive woman. She'd gotten an American flag from someone and turned it into a skirt.

"*Señora*, you can't desecrate the flag like that," admonished the chief as if she'd just offered to broil up one of the children for dinner. "I'm sorry, sir, I'll find her something else."

"That's all right, Chief. I don't think that matters much anymore." To her he said, "It looks wonderful on you, *Señora*—very colorful."

She curtsied in response and said, "*Gracias, Capitán.*"

"Are you and the others doing all right?"

She shrugged. "As well as we can. Better than before you found us."

"Good. Chief Alvarez will see to your needs. Carry on, Chief."

He turned and walked away, but *Señora* Mendoza followed him.

"Excuse me, *Capitán*," she said, lightly taking hold of his arm.

Brett turned. "Yes?"

She lowered her voice to almost a whisper and asked, "Is it true what I have heard your men say? Is it true the whole world has burned just like Havana?"

"I can't speak for the whole world, ma'am, but yes, Miami and the other areas we've seen so far appear to have been destroyed by fire."

"What will we do? Where will we go?"

"First we're going to return to our home base. Many of the crew have families there."

She nodded understandingly. "After that?"

"After that...I don't know for certain. We're going to have to figure that out."

"*Entiendo*...I understand. Wherever you decide to go, I am glad we have been rescued by such a wise and honorable man."

A little laugh escaped Brett's lips. "Well, let's hope I'm as wise as you say, *Señora*. I expect we're going to be facing many days where wisdom is needed."

Brett turned to leave again, but she said, "*Capitán.*"

"Yes?"

"It's not *señora...it's señorita.*"

He / She / They

John Walters

Editor: First contact is a perilous time, even if you don't know it's happening.

He

You brought this upon yourselves, you know. We meant you no harm. Even when we realized your malevolent intent, we did not try to retaliate. Instead, we planned an evacuation.

I was sleeping in a large empty room in a warehouse with my second and third offspring and a few other visitors when your raiding party of eleven or twelve burst in on us. Some brandished weapons, some had chains, and some had multi-frequency flashlights whose beams swept back and forth.

I knew you still couldn't see us, but perhaps you caught an occasional flicker or glimmer as we attempted to avoid capture. Those of you with chains groped your way forward as we leapt for the rear door, the windows, the skylight.

We were on our way home. We were one of the last teams. We had never attempted to hurt any of you.

I had grabbed my third offspring and scurried out the skylight onto the roof. I had expected that my second followed close behind. Instead, I heard her cry out. I looked back. One of you had found her and shackled her ankle; others pulled on the chain from the doorway and dragged her out of the room.

Handing my third to a trusted friend, I jumped back down through the skylight to attempt a rescue.

When we first arrived, you were completely unaware of us. Not wanting to startle you, we left our ships in clandestine locations and approached on foot. Imagine our surprise when we realized you were oblivious to our presence. If some of you caught a glimpse or sensed a visual anomaly, it dissipated when we shifted our position.

We discovered that the cells of our skins contained infinitesimal crystalline plates that passed the light from your sun through us instead of reflecting it. We managed to refine the

effect to remove even the occasional glimmer and render ourselves completely invisible in your visual frequencies.

Although our plan had been to establish contact, we studied your species instead. We discovered an underlying fear and tendency to react violently against the unknown that caused us to have second thoughts. Instead, we decided to merely observe, at least initially.

We found your species exceedingly interesting. The number of observers grew rapidly from a few scouts to several hundred biologists, psychologists, sociologists, students, families of tourists.

That's all I was. A tourist.

It was such a thrill to walk among you and watch you live your lives. We would always keep a safe distance, not only out of respect but because though you couldn't see us, you would be able to sense us by touch if you stumbled into us. We limited our numbers and had strict rules to prevent such incidents. When they happened, as they inevitably did, we evacuated the area and you concocted no end of elaborate explanations and justifications to account for the close encounters.

We lived among you for years observing, learning, recording. Those few of you who suspected we were around created philosophical, metaphysical, and theological theories to account for us. The rest of you had no idea.

Until...

We don't really know how or why the shift in awareness came. Perhaps it had to do with a change in your sun's light frequencies. Perhaps it had to do with the increasing amount of pollutants in the atmosphere. Perhaps we had been with you so long that you developed increased sensitivity. Whatever the cause, more and more of you seemed to know we were there. Not all of you, but enough to concern us. You would become suddenly startled, and look in our direction. You would reach out your hands and grope blindly for us. You would swing or shoot weapons, hoping to hit something.

At first the reactions were individual; you hardly dared talk about us among yourselves.

Later, however, the apprehension became societal. Your politicians and law enforcement officials counseled together. They enlisted scientists to study the phenomenon. Nothing was announced officially; it was all clandestine, hush-hush. Not only did you want to avoid a panic, but you also didn't want to be labeled fools if your theories proved unfounded.

And so the hunt began.

As did our evacuation.

As I mentioned, we almost made it. Why did you have to become so aggressive? Why didn't you let us go? Once the breach was made, once my offspring was kidnapped, I had no choice.

She

In this age of the Internet, rumors fly by continually, in news reports, social media, chat rooms, forums, videos, comments, blogs, emails. What's a reporter to make of it all? Rules have changed, and they continue to change constantly, relentlessly, inexorably. I have no choice but to follow my instincts during this era when anyone can post almost anything to be seen by the world's billions. And my instincts are fairly good. I have a following of tens of thousands who anticipate my posts. Not a lot of people, I realize, but many of them pass the word on, and the ones they communicate with pass it still further, and so on.

I had been following the invisible people rumor for weeks and had been met with derision, suspicion, scorn, fear, self-righteousness, pomposity, arrogance, ridicule, puzzlement: a complex gamut of emotional reactions.

Only a few days before I had met with a priest who tried to convince me that demons walked the Earth stalking unrepentant sinners.

Absurd as it sounded, it was difficult to discount the demon story.

After all, there were the murders.

All the bodies had been flayed. Autopsies revealed that through most of it the victims had been still alive.

Who, if not demons, could have done such a thing?

Perhaps demonic humans.

And yet there were the reports of the invisible ones...

Nothing definite, really; after all, how can you describe someone or something you can't see? But hints and glimpses, ominous forebodings. Have you ever had the feeling that though you appear to be alone, you know you're not?

As the story congealed around these rumors and half-truths, I began to track down any information I could on the murder victims. And patterns emerged.

So there I was, on a dark, dreary day, the rain increasing in intensity, entering a red brick high-rise on a block full of red brick high rises, on the next leg of my investigative journey.

The interior hallways and staircases were oppressive, dimly lit, suffused with paranoia and the threat of violence. I could still hear the rain outside, a faint pounding sound as if chaos were trying to enter. The elevator didn't work. I trudged up three flights of stairs in constant dread that I'd meet a resident who took a dim view of intruders, of those entering their domicile without an invitation.

I knocked on the appropriate door, paused, and then knocked again. A part of me gibbered that I should feign relief that no one answered and get the hell out of there. That always happened, though, and I'd been at this long enough to have gotten pretty good at suppressing my own cowardly impulses.

I heard feet shuffling toward the door.

"Who is it?"

"My name is Michelina Sparrow. I need to talk to you."

"Who?"

"Michelina Sparrow. My friends call me Miki."

"I don't know you."

"I know you don't. But I know who you are. Your name is Ian Brady. I've come because of what happened two weeks ago. The night of the twelfth. And afterwards."

A pause, then, "I have nothing to say. Do you have a warrant?"

"I'm not with the police."

"You're not with the agency either. So I repeat. Who are you?"

"I'm a journalist. I've been investigating the killings on my own. I might be able to help you."

"No one can help me."

Another pause. Then I heard bolts being drawn back and the click of a latch.

"Come in."

He was tall, swarthy, unshaven, dressed in olive-green sweatpants and a white sleeveless tee-shirt flecked with food stains. He looked like someone who had been frightened so long that he had given up on life. "I'm sorry," he said. "I'm not usually like this. Have a seat." He motioned to a lumpy beige couch. "You want something to drink? I have beer, whiskey, maybe some soda."

"Just water, please."

"Sure. Just a sec."

I sat on the edge of the couch cushion and looked around. The apartment was unkempt and smelled of stale food, sweat, and dust.

After handing me the glass, he sat down in a nearby armchair, staring at me with wide eyes, breathing heavily.

I decided I'd taken the wrong approach. "You know, I could actually use a little whiskey on the rocks, if it's not too much trouble."

"Sure, sure."

He returned with two glasses. His was fuller than mine, and as soon as he sat back down he polished off half of it.

I took a sip and tried to avoid grimacing. Nasty stuff.

"So you're in the reserves, Ian."

"That's right."

"And you were on duty that night."

"I'm not sure I'm supposed to talk about this."

"But it scares you. I can see that. And I know most of it anyway."

He took another gulp and said, "It wasn't my regular weekend. They called us up for special detail. There was a dozen of us, including officers. We took a couple of Humvees. They didn't tell us anything until we were on our way. Then they said our mission was to..." He stopped, as if undecided whether he should divulge this piece of information.

I took a chance and threw out a speculation. "To capture."

"That's right. I had heard rumors of invisible creatures like everyone else, but I always dismissed them as science fiction fantasies. And my superior officer told us all about how we wouldn't be able to see them, how we were to feel around for them and shackle them if we came across any. I was...incredulous. I guess that's the word for it."

The dark bags under his eyes, the miserable state of the apartment, and his unkempt appearance told me just how much the memory of that night had obviously been chewing him up inside. He was more than frightened; he was terrified. And mixed with the terror was an undertone of something else. Guilt?

He went to the kitchen, refilled his glass, returned.

"Tell me again why I should be talking to you."

"Something dangerous is out there," I said. "We have to find out what it is."

"I know what it is," he said. "It's a demon."

"I don't believe in demons."

"You weren't there. We had these flashlights that were supposed to be able to detect them, but they didn't work. We burst into this huge room, and it appeared to be empty. But it wasn't. I knew it; everyone knew it. The rest of my team was as scared as I was. But we had orders to capture, not kill, so we didn't fire. We scurried forward, feeling our way, trailing chains behind us. I almost shit my pants when I grabbed what felt like a leg. I held on, reached behind me for the cuff, and managed to secure it on the thing's appendage. The creature, whatever it was, struggled and let out a high-pitched screech, almost like a wail. Others in the unit pulled it out of the room. Then all hell broke loose."

He took another gulp.

"Something entered the room. I think it jumped down from the skylight. It had claws or weapons or something, because it started to rip us apart. It took Terry's right arm clean off and then slashed his throat. It went for Dexter next and tore him open belly to neck. The rest of us cleared out of the room and locked the door. We made it back to the Humvees and took off. That thing we'd captured...We couldn't see it and it was thrashing about and we thought it was going to attack us like that other in the warehouse had, so a few of us hit it, hard, with our rifle butts.

It didn't move after that."

"Where did you take it?"

He studied me with a vulnerable, frightened expression. "Are you going to publish this?"

"Not if you don't want me to. I promise."

"You can't. Not this part. There's a facility. Some people in lab coats were waiting for it. They had cells, more like cages really, but when they realized it wasn't moving they strapped it to some sort of operating table and bent over it with instruments. Some of us hung around to watch but they were too intent on what they were doing to notice. They poked and prodded and measured, and they found no pulse, no heartbeat, no breath. They came to the conclusion that it was dead."

Another long gulp.

"Right away they decided to do an autopsy, while it was still fresh. Among other things, they wanted to find out whether it was visible inside, whether there was something in the skin that made it invisible. One of them grabbed a scalpel, felt its torso, and made an incision."

Ian slowly and deliberately put his glass down on the coffee table and looked me in the eyes.

"It screamed. Some sort of orange liquid spurted from the wound. It sat up. All we could see was the wound and the bright blood-like stuff coming out of it. The thing must have been flailing its arms, though, because two of the scientists cried out in pain from slashes on their faces and shoulders. One of my teammates fired a few shots. More orange blood burst from it and it fell to the floor. This time it really was dead. The scientists began to strip its skin off to analyze the invisibility factor. That's all I know."

"Except that now your teammates have been dying one by one."

"Yes. That's right."

"And I've heard no reports that anyone else has been harmed. Whatever it is, it's targeting the team that captured that creature."

"I know."

"Are the authorities doing anything about it? Are they protecting you? Have they offered you security?"

"They called us in two nights ago. It was optional. I didn't go. I can take care of myself." He opened a drawer under the coffee table, pulled out a pistol, and set it next to his glass. I noticed that his hand trembled slightly.

"How can you shoot it if you can't see it?" I said quietly.

He didn't answer.

And then my own subconscious memories of paranoia about ogres, boogiemen, vampires, werewolves, and other terrors of the night began to surface. It's amazing how similar nightmarish myths and legends are in almost every culture, in the recesses of every mind. I wondered if I had made a mistake in coming there, if I had unwittingly exposed myself to the line of fire. Whoever or whatever the murderer was, it was going after the men in Ian's unit, and it was very likely that Ian might be next.

I took a solid slug of my whiskey. Diluted though it was by the melted ice, tears came to my eyes, and I gasped and coughed.

Ian smiled mirthlessly. "Want me to pour you some more?"

I shook my head. I'd decided to make my excuses and leave.

"I appreciate you coming by," said Ian. "The loneliness was driving me nuts. Just talking about it with someone else relieves some of the pressure."

Damn. Why did he have to go and say that? It made me feel guilty about my planned hasty exit.

"The truth is," said Ian, "we did something we shouldn't have done and it's calling us on it. Knowing that doesn't make the waiting any easier, though."

"Maybe you should join your unit," I said. "There's safety in numbers."

"I don't know if I'll be safer, but I think you're right. I'd rather wait with people I know and trust. Just a sec. I'll get my coat."

He had just opened the hallway closet when a scraping sound began on the outside of the front door. Shrugging on his parka, he returned to the coffee table and picked up his pistol.

"Are you expecting anyone? Does someone else live here?" I whispered, already knowing the answer.

"No. Come on." He led the way into the kitchen and lifted the window that faced the alley. "Fire escape. Careful on the steps; they might be slippery."

It was still raining. A single dim light about fifty yards down the alley was the only illumination.

I held the metal railing firmly as I descended the steps as fast as I could. They *were* slippery; dangerously so.

Ian closed the window behind us before following me.

The steps ended a story above the pavement. I waited for Ian to catch up and lower the ladder the rest of the way.

Just as I started to climb down, the window above us shattered.

"Hurry," said Ian.

Somehow I descended the rungs without falling; Ian was close behind me.

"My car's this way," I said, pointing toward the lit end of the alley.

But before we could run, there was a splash and a spray of water in the puddle right in front of us.

We couldn't see it directly, but raindrops ran off the humanoid shape in runnels, and the light behind it was diffused.

Ian got out his pistol and fired, but the creature was fast, so fast. And once it wasn't directly in front of the light anymore, it was even harder to spot. Ian turned this way and that, but probably didn't want to shoot wildly in an inhabited area.

Then he started making choking sounds. It had gripped him around the neck, and it lifted him clean off the ground.

I froze in place. I'd never felt this level of terror. I was so scared I couldn't even force myself to help.

Ian's clothes shredded and fell off him, and his skin peeled away strip by strip. Blood welled up and flowed off in the downpour, followed by more blood and yet more. The creature began on Ian's back and worked its way around to his chest until most of his upper torso was raw flesh. It then severed his arms and his head and dropped the rest of the dismembered and beheaded corpse to the pavement.

I should have run, I should have fought, but I knew there was nothing I could do. Then I empathized; I didn't want to leave him to die alone. Then I got caught up in terrified, morbid fascination.

Once Ian lay in pieces on the ground, I knew that the creature had turned its attention to me. I felt it contemplating me as a predator regards its prey. I expected momentarily to be grabbed and shredded.

I waited in dreadful anticipation, the rain pummeling me. I never considered running; I knew I wouldn't get far.

I fell to my knees, bowed my head, and waited for the inevitable.

And waited.

And waited.

And waited.

I lifted my head, stood, took a few steps, and knew I was alone. The creature had gone.

My consciousness unraveled. When I awoke, I was in a hospital.

They

I am sated. No one remains alive who kidnapped and tortured my offspring. As is customary with my kind, I have restored the balance of the debt.

And yet, I can still hear her screams. You ignored her sentience and dissected her. You thought to benefit from what you could learn from her physiology.

Ah, deluded ones. Has it ever been so with you? Are you truly a species lost in rapacity and greed?

I am willing to give you the benefit of the doubt now that my rage is spent, but my kindred, alas, are not. They are on their way now in response to the screams. Not my offspring's screams, but mine.

I released the anguish of my soul, and they heard me.

And now they are coming. Not just for a small team of people, but for all of you. They have judged you unworthy.

They are many, and you cannot see them. They are bringing the large, fanged, cat-like creatures that accompany our kind into battle. These, too, will be invisible to you.

Your first indication of invasion will be the corpses. They will increase rapidly. You may try to oppose them, but your efforts will be futile. Some of you may try to hide, but they will find you. Their object is to bring about your extinction.

They will succeed.

I do not think that I will participate in the extermination. I have had enough of killing. I will go home to my other offspring and hope that time heals my wounds.

I was only a tourist.

You have no one to blame but yourselves.

To Be the Walking Wounded

Morgen Knight

*Editor: Life is more than a biologic process. Living requires
passion and when that fades, life fades with it.*

After the chainsaw bit into the man's leg and he didn't scream, I let my held breath go. I hadn't even realized I'd been holding it until it burst out in a disappointed huff. I wanted to hear him scream, I wanted to enjoy his pain. Jonah lifted the teeth of the chainsaw to the man's left arm, but the rest of us had pretty much lost interest. If the man hadn't screamed at a leg, there was nothing that would get him to. I guess we should have known by the pustular splotches and the gauntness, but you always hope. At least, I do. While Jonah carved up the man, the rest of us filed back into the vacant hotel. You could still hear the whiny roar of the chainsaw, but it was dulled. Lily had the TV on, a large, flat screen moved down into the cavernous lobby. The TV's cords snaking away in a series of connections that, oddly, made me think of a railroad line in the 1800s, and how any sort of life outside the world of your small town would be reliant on what that line brought. Using the remote in her lap, she flipped rapidly through the familiar channels. Many were snowy, or the black screen simply read NO SIGNAL along the bottom. The hotel had a satellite feed. The channels that still broadcast played movies or reruns. All of the cable news channels were off air, so I guess not everything is lost. But there is always a cloud beneath the silver lining.

The only channels that were real, the only that still felt alive, were the few public broadcasting stations we could get. I'd always skipped over them before, or programmed them out. PBS? Who wants to watch old British sitcoms? It was like PBS had become British TV's version of Florida. But since The Spread, it's become the only place real people—local people, more importantly, those trying—can be seen or heard. It isn't always broadcasting a live feed, but there were a few seemingly regular shows, all of them half insane. Shit, the FCC would have put a lid on super-fucking-fast, before. One night, a couple of guys had smoked weed and drank and cried, finishing with a friendly game of Russian roulette. Another night, some half-naked woman had hosted a mock baking show, only she was making ridiculous stuff—Cow Pie Cake, Crow Intestine Stew. She pretend to taste it (or maybe not so pretend), and gave it a good Campbell's Soup *mmmm* after each.

"I'm going upstairs," I said.

"Do you mind if I come with you?" Cora asked, her eyes hopeful and sad. But that isn't saying much. The only people without sad eyes anymore are the dead and the Wounded.

"You can do what you want."

We took the elevator up. My room had a stunning view of the city. The buildings and trees and maze of streets. Sometimes I sit and look at a bluer sky than I ever remember seeing before. Or rain clouds, their freight descending onto filthiness, cleansing us all for a time. And I think about how, after we're gone, the clouds will continue to form, rain will continue to fall, rivers will swell and birds will sing, our absence going unnoticed. When my mind turns down these back alleys, I have to burn myself, usually with a cigarette. To make sure.

"You don't like being a goon, do you?" Cora asked. She was standing over by the window I'd broken out, a large pane as tall as me, so I could breathe fresh air. On occasion a bird had wondered in.

"Killing people, you mean?" We called it being a goon, or gooning, for the same reason people called killing their animals "putting them to sleep."

"They're already dead. Gooning is a mercy," she said defensively.

"Maybe. But it's hard to see that when Jonah is choppin a guy's legs off, blood sprayin on the apron and face mask he's wearin. He looked like a horror movie villain." And what did they hope to happen? They hoped their Wounded would scream, show them life, maybe—in the best circumstance—make them feel horrible for what they were doing.

Cora laughed wryly. "He did, yeah." The sound of her laugh almost yanked me across the room to smack her, and it was good to feel that pulse of rage. I feasted on it. "It isn't like you haven't done it."

"I know," I said.

"And he didn't feel it. You saw that, right? The Wounded don't feel anything." She had turned away from the window.

"I know," I said again. We had found the man during a grocery and gas run—the world was an open market these days, as long as you didn't want anything fresh—and it had been Jonah's idea to lug him back. Cheap entertainment, I guess. The man had been dressed for church, as my mother'd say, sitting on a bus bench. A red splotch had been visible on his throat, running down beneath the collar. Blue thread webbed through it. As far as I know, the red splotches are the beginning, and then they grow— no scrubbing, cutting, digging or acid acted as a deterrent—and by the time the blue covers most of you, you're gone. Lights out, no one home. I don't know from where Jonah came up with a chainsaw. Funny what you find lying around these days.

Cora I've known since college. Ryan, Lily and Jonah had been passing acquaintances until the Spread began. Each of us had grown up around Kansas City, so banding together to head home made sense. There had been more in our group, then. The roads had been clogged in some places and ghostly voids in others. It wasn't an epic journey from Rolla, but the state of the world hadn't made it easier.

"I haven't been feeling myself," Cora said absently. This wasn't an uncommon statement from her. The sad part is that one day, I fear it'll be truth. She was short and slender with a plain face. She'd never been a great beauty, and the stress of everything had worn her down hard. She had premature age-lines and an acquired haggardness that made me think of those barflies you used to be able to find on a barstool on a Tuesday morning. Small tits but the thickest head of hair with the most serious curls that I've ever seen.

"I'm sure you're fine."

"But what if I'm not? What if it's starting in me?"

"Why don't you shut the fuck up about dying? If you want to die so bad, there's the window. I'm sure you'll feel the ground at the bottom." I loved the way my heart boomed, how my body got hot when I grew angry. I loved that I felt something. It was the same for all of us. You know that the day you fail to feel anything, you're dead. Of course, by then you won't give a fuck.

The splotches came out of nowhere. There was a news story here and there, but I'd never heard of it until it was all anyone was talking about. Three weeks, that's how long it took. What grabbed my attention was how empty my classes had become, how quiet my dorm remained, like I lived in a library. People started wearing masks and drinking only bottled water, but it was too late. I heard some scientist blab on about what was causing it, something viral. He'd given it some long and complicated name, assuring the viewing public that a cure was within reach. And that was the last anyone had heard from him. He probably didn't give a shit after a while.

Because that's what this outbreak does. That science fuck had a great way of making it sound unremarkable, something easy to oppose, but all in all, everyone just gives up. The splotches appear on the skin as little red sores. I don't know what occurs within, but I know that the splotches are an outward sign of inward corruption. You begin to lose interest in things. As it progresses, the splotches gain a gelatinous meniscus, and you begin to lose physical sensation. By the time the blue had you, people don't seem to feel a thing and they don't care…about anything. People simply sit down and starve to death, the eerie redness spreading over your skin, blue webs riddling your insides. They sit and breathe and, at some point, no matter how you threaten them, beg them or hurt them, they barely if ever respond, their empty eyes unfocused. Day after day they die of hunger, shuffling around occasionally to find water, the urge to drink the very last thing to go.

"I really haven't felt myself," Cora said finally. She stood there, pouting.

"I really don't give a fuck," I said, but the rancor was out of me. I was drinking from one of the many bottles sitting around. This one was scotch, top-shelf stuff. Sometimes I felt bad about how I talked to her, how all of us talked to one another, but not often. Only when I was on the verge of drunk. We fucked with each other for the same reason we hurt the Wounded. Because it relieved stress, because we were afraid, because it was exquisite to feel something and to know that you're feeling it. Even if it is only disgust.

"Just look at me, will you? Tell me if you see a red spot." She began taking off her clothes.

"You're probably just depressed. It's hard to feel much when you're depressed. It's easy to confuse."

Cora was shaking her head. "I take pills for that." She pushed her pants down, shirt already off. Cora never wore underwear. "Sometimes too many," she added dryly.

I checked her with all the sensuality of a prison strip-search. Lift this, open that, bend over and spread 'em. Her skin was tanned and freckled but otherwise unblemished. I told her so. When she grabbed at me, sliding a hand into my shorts with a smile, I snatched her wrist and squeezed until she cried out. "Don't touch me."

"You're a prick, you know that? Don't you want to live a little?"

This time I did slap her, a satisfying backhand.

* * *

Seth was the first in our vagabond group to get infected. Maybe some people are immune, maybe not. I do know that there were a bunch of people that got it at first, but then it slowed down. Weeks passed and you'd think you were in the clear until one morning there might be a splotch on your thigh or cheek or lower back. After that, you were fucked, the progression always the same, even if the pace varied. I've seen some hold on for a month, others seem to give within days.

This…infection steals your will to live and any joy you get from living it.

I thought Seth would beat it. I kept this hope secret, afraid that whispering it might doom us all. But Seth had always been the most alive, the crazy one. He could be so loud it grated on your nerves. He had the endless energy of a kid riding a sugar tsunami. And he was weird, but in the Adult Swim late-night kinda way. I remembered thinking that there was no possibility he'd fall. That much energy can't be snuffed out. But, you know, there was this one moment, not long after he'd told us he was infected, laughing at his luck. "It sucks dying at the end of the world, when I don't have to wait in line to get into the movie theater anymore," he had said smiling, laughing, a warm beer in each hand. But he'd looked at me, and it was only for a brief second, a skipping glance. And I remember seeing beneath that laughter to the utter terror of a condemned man strapped to the electric chair. The look only lingered for a moment, barely there at all. I convinced myself that I hadn't seen it, that I'd imagined it.

Two days later, we found Seth with his wrists opened up into nasty vertical gashes. The blood around him was dry. His mouth appeared on the verge of his signature smile.

It had been Seth that had always said: "Don't you want to live a little?" After he'd become one of the Wounded, there had been a sense of urgency about the question. Eat, drink, be merry, for tomorrow you die.

But it had also become something of an accusation. Seth was only the first of many, and in some ways the hardest. More fell. Others deserted, which became the proper form. No one wants to watch you descend. No one wants to open the bathroom door and see the body of someone they know, lying prone and lifeless, pale tendons white in the sunlight.

Don't you want to live a little? No, I wanted to live a lot. At least, I thought I did. I know it's a strange thing to be unsure about. But things can happen to you that change you. Tragedies that pierce a soul, making it bleed-out within, leaving behind a hollow shell. I don't sleep much anymore. I like the night, late night, when the city is almost gone. I'll sit at the edge of my broken window, feet dangling out over a fatal, multi-story fall, and look at the buildings and think—really think—about the world and life and everything I've ever known. I know I'm not infected, but…I think in a way I am, just a different strain. One that wiggles into your brain first, because…less and less do I see a point to any of it. Wanting to live is easy. What's harder is having something to live for. The world used to be full of reasons, or at least adequate distractions. But that world is ending in silence, whimpers and suicidal shotgun blasts. It seems that the only reason to live is to die.

* * *

We all eat together. We do a lot together, hunkered down in the large lobby of the Hyatt Regency. We're something of a dysfunctional family. We all trust each other, we all need each other, and we all look at each other with the pity of a weak swimmer watching someone's hands flail and head bob beneath the waves far from shore. Jonah had declared that we're immune. We'd have to be, right? The population has dwindled down pretty far now—sometimes you actually have to search for any living Wounded—but we have to say things like that. We're American. We've been spoon-fed that in the end, by some miracle or another, we'll be saved. Something will step in. And if you don't believe in the future, what the fuck is the point? Don't you want to live a little?

"You know we're in a shit storm when no one even really loots shit," Ryan said, smiling. He was spooning ravioli into his mouth from an open can. A dribble of sauce lay on his scruffy chin.

"Could be we're what's left of humanity," Jonah said. The idea amused him, as did meth. He said that the surest way to know you're still livin is to snort a line of it. The statement was usually followed by the dramatic destruction of something.

"The TV loses more channels every day," Lily said.

"Eventually the power will go out," Cora said.

"Maybe we should try and repopulate," Jonah said and laughed. He slapped Lily's wide can; it wasn't gentle. Lily yelled out then threw her plate at him. It shattered six feet behind Jonah, her food splattering on the floor. "What? It ain't like we don't try." He rolled his pelvis forward, tongue wagging.

We'd all seen Jonah and Lily fuck. We'd all watched each other, and switched, and lived with an openness probably not realized since the sixties. You'll do a lot in pursuit of living a little. That's the thing about always feeling alive—you can never be stationary. You always have to push it. Always move ahead one more step. It's because we get too used to things. It's the unintended consequences of involuntary adaptability.

"I want a baby," Lily said, self-absorbed as usual. She was the kind of female I'd always hated. Even a dying world had to revolve around her.

I told her that that was natural. We all want to leave something behind. "But we're not the last," I said. "Not yet."

* * *

I wasn't going to ask his name so I called him Shotgun. I don't sleep well any more. When I do, I always wake up sweaty, arms swinging at some forgotten monster. Cora has cried out more than once because of my unconscious assaults, a hand or fist finding her in my flailing. Shotgun pops up into my dreams like an infrequent sitcom guest that the audience recognizes and cheers for. I saw him as we were driving through North

Kansas City, over by the police station. We'd just left my parents' house. It was the simple home I'd grown up in (if not for grants I wouldn't have been the first in my family to ever grace a college). What we saw and did there, I won't talk about. Either you know or it's none of your business.

Shotgun, who got his name for carrying a sawed-off double-barrel, was such an oddity that Ryan stopped the car. The man was shirtless, black, with white, greasy clown makeup over his face. A big, painted-on red smile and orange teardrops. Ammo belts, full of shotgun shells, crisscrossed his chest. Baggy jeans tucked into black boots, duct tape pulling them tight at his ankles. With the car window down, I'd heard the man whistling as he casually strolled up to the Wounded, put the barrels against their faces, and pulled the trigger. The Wounded's head would explode as wet and sloppy as something poured from a blender. The blast was loud, echoing down the streets, rolling over the sound of our car's engine. Ryan had turned the radio down, and in the silence following the blast, came the sweet tune of whistling as Shotgun—Mr. Shotgun to you, punk—sauntered over to the next Wounded he saw, this one sitting in the driver's seat of a BMW.

And he turned to look at us. Maybe he sensed an audience, I don't know. The most awful thing wasn't what he was doing, or even the whistling. What turned me sour was the way he stopped and waved at us, lifting one hand high, like a neighbor. What he was doing wasn't so different from our gooning, but it was how unguarded he seemed, how normal. Howdy, neighbor, just spendin my Saturday blowin' off a few heads.

If I lived to be a hundred, I'd never forget that man's raised hand, or how he turned back to his Saturday adventure.

* * *

The place smelled of rot, so we knew what we would find as soon as we went in. There wasn't much competition for supplies in our area, so we never hoarded. If we got low, we'd go out. A home was as good as a store. We found all the non-perishables and packed them up. Then we went through the house. Cora liked to play a game where she pieced together the lives of the former owners, using what she found. Modern anthropology, she called it.

I came across her upstairs, in the baby's room (thankfully there was no child there), crying quietly as she squeezed a stuffed elephant to death against her small chest. She was looking out the window. The sunlight and the gentle pink curtains almost made her pretty. "It's all really over, isn't it?" she said. She didn't look back at me. "We're just waiting to be seated."

"Yeah," I said.

"Why can't you be optimistic?!" she yelled. "Why can't you say the right things?"

"You mean, why don't I say what you want to hear? Because I don't have the energy to lie."

Cora held the stuffed animal up like a mother inspecting her child. "You don't think we'll get through? Even after so long?"

"I think it doesn't matter. Even if we're fine, we're not. I think the best that's left for us is growing old in a crumbling world, too busy ignoring it to do much. There ain't no future for us. We're not that strong." I didn't care for much, but I could still mourn hope.

"You sound like you're Wounded," Cora said, trying to hurt me.

I shrugged. "Maybe I am. Maybe all of us are but we lack the good sense to quit caring."

Cora walked over to me. She touched me as if I might be hot enough to burn her, then rested her hands on my chest. "You can still feel, can't you?"

I took her hand, kissed her palm, then laid her on the floor to show her I could.

* * *

In the end, I think we pushed ourselves to live so hard for the same reason we went gooning—to see how far we could really go. Then it became about anger. Why this? Why us? Why now? Why should the last days be ours? And some of it was fear. Biting our thumbs at Death. In the end, fear is all that's really left. When that goes, you're dead already.

We finally lost power a couple weeks ago. That fucked with everybody pretty hard. Lily vanished in the night. We never talked about it. We didn't go looking for her. I don't think even Jonah is crazy enough to goon one of us. Cora just sits in dark corners and cries. She was never a big girl, so the weight she's lost is obvious. She hasn't asked me to check her for splotches, and honestly, I wouldn't want to. There's a lot I don't want anymore. I thought that writing all this down might help me gain some kind of perspective. I don't know…but all I see is a sad ending to a thing that was never as special as I wanted to believe in the first place.

How do you know you're alive? I know I'm not Wounded, but I do feel numb. I haven't felt much since going home. That's what all these canisters of gasoline are about. I'm pretty sure that after sunset I'll remember what being alive is about. In the end, there's only one way to glimpse it. I'm not going to say anything to anyone. That's not how it's done. Let them tell themselves I was sick, Wounded. Let them find what comfort they can in denying that they want this to be over as well. I wish them luck. It takes more than living to be alive.

I'm almost excited.

Rise of the Golden Creep

John A. McColley

Editor: It is a tenet that parents know more than their offspring. But a child must disobey from time to time to assert independence. The question is, does the youngster survive long enough to learn the lesson.

"Di, look at the TV," Mom said.

But I was like, "I can't watch TV right now, I've gotta get to Heather's. We're going to Todd's thing, remember?" The sun was bright through the window. I couldn't look right at her or see the TV very well anyway.

"Look at the damn TV," she said in her Mom Voice.™

"He can't be that hot," I said, sure she was trying to get me interested in guys again. I put my hand up to block the light and squinted at the screen. She's so absolutely sure Heather is just a phase. When I saw it, though, I dropped my phone. It hit the kitchen floor and shot across the tiles. The Beach Scene camera showed no beach at all. Instead of sand, there was some kind of grody orange stuff that looked like a sponge factory threw up. Sagging heaps wriggled and oozed up over the sea wall and back down. Maybe the wall would stop it. I recognized the spot from the signs and chipped paint on the metal railing—Simpson's Laguna. I've passed them a million times hitting the sand with the crew. And now the stuff, whatever it was, was right there, I mean *right* where I've pitched umbrellas and had bonfires.

"...Has been going on since before dawn here at Simpson's Laguna. What it is or how it got here is unknown at this time. It emerged from the water during the night and has nearly reached Ocean Road. Hundreds of homes and businesses have been damaged, hundreds more could be in danger by the end of the day. Many residents have already fled. Authorities have blocked off the nearest roads and have boats in the water trying to trace a path back to the source..." Mom held up the remote and changed the channel.

"...Toxic waste? No one can say. All we do know is that it's appeared in a dozen places along the West Florida coast, moving, or perhaps growing, at an amazing rate..." Click.

"...Just reached the street now. We're going to have to pull back again any minute. The van is running. We'll try to keep broadcasting—wait, do you see that? I don't know if you can see at home, but the material that has been encroaching onto dry land all morning, overcoming beach blankets and left-behind sunscreen bottles has now stopped at the edge of the road. What has been a rolling tide of pudding to this point has begun to flatten into a wall following the tarmac—" Click.

"What do you think it is?" Mom asked as she hit mute.

"You're asking me? I got like a C- in biology."

"So you think it's alive? From the way it moved I kind of do, too." Mom sounded worried.

"I'm sure it's just one of those things that happens every hundred years, like cicadas or something. It'll be gone in a few days, a week tops." She looked like she needed comforting. That was all I had.

"You're right, the scientists will all geek out over it until it goes back into the water and we'll see some special on the Nature channel about it in a couple months. Still, stick to the pools, okay, kid? No beaches until this thing's done?"

"Mom! Todd's party is a beach barbecue, and like volleyball or whatever. You can't do that stuff in his yard. Most of it's hot top. He's got like three square feet of grass and there's that tree in the middle of it." She just stared at me like she does. "Uhh! Okay! No beach, but if everybody else goes, what am I supposed to do?"

"You could always come spend a nice evening with your parents," Mom said. I'm pretty sure she was joking, but it's hard to tell lately. Old people are weird.

"Love you," I said, avoiding any response to the invitation. There's no safe conversation there.

I took off with my big, white canvas bag over my shoulder and the floppy hat Mom makes me wear blocking all those terrible UV rays on my head. When I got to the car, I dropped both behind my seat and headed for Heather's.

After a few minutes in her driveway, we headed to Todd's. Everyone was hanging around the pool, looking like someone ran over their puppies. The grill sat by the pool fence. A couple of Frisbees floated, the only things enjoying the water.

"Hey, Todd, what happened to the party?"

"That *stuff* happened. My mom and dad, they're both like scientists, you know? They looked at it under the microscope and drove out of here like bats out of hell. The only thing they said before they left was, 'Don't go near it. Stay off the beach.'"

"That's exactly what my mom said," I said. "Well this party isn't gonna start itself. Let's turn up some beats and crack some bottles."

"Can't drink. Mrs. Delgado lives over there on the other side of the pool. She'll tell my parents."

"Well, that sucks. What are we supposed to do now?"

"Nobody's come up with anything yet." Todd shrugged.

"I know!" I said, it dawning on me. "Your parents have been keeping an eye on this stuff, right? It's not everywhere, just like a few spots. Let's find some clear sand and take this party for a drive!" I started bouncing. Heather got me like she always does. Her face lit up. She squeezed my hand. We bobbed in sync for a few seconds.

"This is going to be epic!" she squealed.

All our peeps piled into three cars to Izzard's Cove, a cute little chunk of sand hidden at the end of the nature preserve. According to Todd, no orange stuff had surfaced within miles of there. With the grill heating up and beers cooling down, we headed for the water. I was so relieved to see the waves lapping, clear past the cove mouth. "Race you to the sandbar!" I screamed, kicking my flips and shorts off by a bush.

"Wait, I'm not ready!" Heather called, pulling her tee-shirt over her head and running after me. My hair was swept back by the wind as my feet sprayed hot sand behind me. I ran into the surf up to my knees, put my hands together over my head, and dived in. Ah! The water wrapped itself around me, just cool enough for my skin to goose pimple. Pull! Pull! I swam in junior high, where I first met Heather. I dropped it later for field hockey. Heather stuck with it though, so she caught up to me pretty quick.

The sandbar was only like a foot below the surface. We pulled ourselves up on it and waved back at the others. Some were on their way to us. Todd stood beside the grill, spatula raised, shining in the sun like a gladiator getting ready to do battle. I laughed at the thought. I remembered the times I'd saved him from a beating from Rob. Then something in the water caught my eye. It was shiny, too.

"Fish!" I pointed and yelled a few times. "There—there's a whole butt-load of fish in there!" I nudged Heather to point out the giant school of flashing silver fish, no longer than my palm, all getting freaked out by the clumsy humans crashing through their cove.

She didn't say anything, but nudged me back, trying to get my attention, but not getting her mouth to work.

"Hey! What's the matt—" I followed her stare.

Creamsicle orange hung below the waves. The near edge was fifteen, twenty feet away. The far edge...I couldn't see a far edge. It faded to gray where the bottom dropped off, and the water above it got deeper. I turned back around, waving the other swimmers off.

"Go back! Don't come over here! Get back to shore!" I yelled. They couldn't hear me through the splashing. The sandbar got crowded quick as Gail, Laura, Lottie, and Dan got up there with us.

"Look at all those fish!" Dan said.

"No, look at that!" I said pointing at the orange stuff. "We've gotta get out of here. Those fish aren't just hanging out. They're running away." I pointed out past the sandbar. Was it already closer? It couldn't be. I mean, could it? That fast?

"Shark!" Someone screamed. Because that's all we needed. I turned. Laura pointed. It wasn't Jaws, or anything, but it was big enough. It could take an arm. I shuddered.

"Now what do we do? I—" Lottie screamed. Dan screamed. I looked again. The shark was gone. Just gone. "Where is it? Where the hell did it go?!"

"That...whatever...orange crap just kind of—" Dan made a wave crashing motion with his hand. I'm not gonna lie. I felt warmth run down my leg. Heather was the brave one.

"We gotta get out of here." I tried to dive off. My feet slipped through the sand. I flopped over like a fish escaping a dock. The water closed over me. I lost half my air. I started to freak. I pulled with my arms, kicked, but my form was crap. I got nowhere fast.

Those fish, seeming so tiny and harmless, slammed into me from every direction. I kicked off the bottom, popping up to see what was going down. Heather was still standing there, staring. "Come on!" I yelled. Everyone splashed past me. She didn't hear. Water churned. I tried to get back to her. Teeth and harsh fins scratched me all over.

A jelly wrapped around my arm, bathing it in fire. I screamed in pain. Heather snapped out of it, then. She launched over my head. A wave of orange whatever came down on the sandbar, just where she'd been standing.

Flinging the sticky jelly away, I kicked for my life. The desperate mass of fish got under my hands, around my legs. I felt like I was caught in a giant net. My panic meter bumped to eleven. When they flopped over my back, I lost it. All my rhythm, my coordination ran out on me again. I sank. I grabbed fish after fish, trying to find air.

Someone wrapped an arm under mine and beneath my chin, pulling me free of the water. "I've got you!" Heather yelled as I sputtered. She dragged me in an awkward hug toward the shore.

"I'm okay now!" I yelled, pulling free of her embrace. Through flashing, flipping fish, we struggled. After like a million years, my hand hit sand again. Heather crawled out of the water right next to me.

From the beach, we watched chaos reign. Fish crammed in the cove tighter and tighter. Silver bodies bounced off rocks on the south side. The orange stuff flowed inshore from the sandbar. Water rode high on the beach, filling in our footprints in the sand. Todd dumped sand in the grill. "Just leave it! There's no time!" I yelled at him. Now I dragged Heather along behind me. I took his hand with my other. "Where's Lottie?"

"What about Dan? He drove! We can't start his car without him!"

"We're here!" Dan said, leaning on Lottie as the pair emerged from the water. They were both covered in scrapes. Blood ran down wet skin, staining bathing suits. "But Gail, Laura...They were right behind us!"

"Help!" Laura cried out as she lay on the rocks halfway down the jetty. *Oh no! She got turned around!* Laura reached for Gail's hand that flailed amid thousands of silver fish flashing in the sun. Laura swatted leaping fish away.

"Gail! No!" I screamed as the hand was engulfed in orange.

"Laura, run!" Dan called beside me.

"Run! Just run for it!" I called across the lagoon. But between Laura and the rest of us the jetty had already been covered with writhing gold. Laura was already cut off. The creep covered the rocks, the sand, every-damn-thing on that side. The water was the only way out, but it hadn't worked for Gail. The fish weren't even jumping anymore. They just slid over one another. I felt like I'd been put through a blender. It was even worse now. Gail had jumped out of the frying pan, into the fire. *Fire!* I had a thought. Would it work? I had no idea, but monsters are always afraid of fire, right?

"Di! What are you doing?" Heather said, trying to hold onto my hand.

"I've gotta try!" I said, squirming free. I ran back to the grill. The yellow bottle of lighter fluid and electric lighter were both still there. I booked it as hard as I could toward the rocks. Stupid bushes scratched my legs. I sprayed the lighter fluid. *Did it just move? You like this stuff?* I sprayed again, getting closer and clicking the lighter. Heather called after me. Laura yelled for help.

Light. Heat. A giant's hand swatted me backward. The screaming stopped, replaced by a roar. And a snap. Rocks stabbed into my back, my side, my arm. My whole body felt like the sunburn I got in fourth grade. Worst way to miss a week of school ever.

"Come on!" Laura yelled as she sprinted from the flames and smoke. I could barely make out the words. She yanked me to my feet. I grabbed the lighter fluid as she did. "We've gotta get out of here!" I shot the flammable stuff again, spraying as far as I could reach. Laura lit the fluid, making a flamethrower like in the movies. Parts of the golden crap burned and exploded, pieces landing in the lagoon. But it wasn't enough to escape yet.

Flame ran up the stream toward the bottle. I freaked. The bottle flew out of my hand onto the stuff. It started to sink in. *Oh god, not again!* I thought, turning away. Laura threw an arm around me and forced me down behind a bigger rock.

The second fireball singed off both our hair, pulled some major blisters on our backs and necks. Bits of rock dug into Laura's shoulder. I peeked up over the rock. The orange bastard was off the rocks. The jetty was clear. I grabbed Laura's hand and helped her up, not letting go as we ran back to the others.

The water fountained as we ran when something like a huge arm rose out of the water, flinging fish everywhere. It crashed down on the rocks where we'd been seconds before. *How is this not over?*

We flew onto the beach. Heather waved me forward, calling for me, crying. The smell of burned whatever it was, burned fish, burned hair and other stuff I didn't want to think about rolled through with black smoke. We gagged, but we ran.

I burned. I stung. Every time Heather touched me to comfort me, I cried out.

Every war movie I'd ever seen ran through my head. I couldn't think of anything but getting away. I snagged my shorts as we hobbled along past them. My phone and keys were in there.

Minutes later, in the rearview, we saw the creep reach up again and again, eventually hiding all the bushes and rocks. The riot of movement from the fish, the waves, was replaced by creepy stillness.

The next week, we all gathered for Gail's funeral. There wasn't even a body to put in the ground. I couldn't believe how wrong it had all gone. We had just wanted some fun. We had checked the "weather." But we were wrong, and Gail paid. My burns, scrapes, even my busted elbow were nothing compared to the pain I felt from what my brilliant idea cost her. How could I even face her mother?

When the moment came, I just cried, my chin shaking, tears, snot, and sweat running down my face. She took my hands in hers, accidentally tweaking my elbow in its sling. I thought of the child I'd been a month before, how I would have whined and griped, but now the pain was just a reminder. Gail may not have been the first casualty in the war with the "Golden Creep," as they're calling it on the news, but she was the first one I knew.

Things got worse, much worse. The whole coast was covered for three states in each direction. It even showed on the South American coast. The scientists said it was alive, maybe even intelligent. It sank hundreds of ships, crushed, consumed, thousands of houses as it expanded out from the water. The only relief was that tarmac stopped it dead, like the reporter said. For whatever reason, it wouldn't touch or go over the tar or asphalt. It just built up these walls alongside.

But how long would that last? There's always those pipes, culverts or whatever, under the roads. They let water past. We've got to be ready.

Todd and I have been reading his parents' emails, making our own plans to fight back. We may not be able to bring Gail back, but we can avenge her. Phosphorous burns underwater.

Gabeth Bhul

Aaron Vlek

Editor: Tough love can sometimes be misinterpreted as malevolence.

The wall of pale yellow sand poured out of the sky before dawn on the first day of the Seventh Red Moon. It smothered the desert in silence. We covered our faces with the ends of our turbans and stumbled blindly into the hot wind. I am Kanawei. I was thirteen years old, and the day we set foot upon the road was my birthday, my *ei faba*. In just two more years I would be a woman grown. This trip with my birth parents to Gabeth Bhul was my first long traveling.

Sandstorms are a common misery to our people. But no one had ever seen anything so long or so thick in living memory or out of legend. That's what my mother said as we pushed on into the thick golden haze. I knew she was with child. She walked heavy, stroked her belly, and was always hungry.

Our journey to the city at the end of the World Road, Gabeth Bhul, caught two *hoda* fish with one line, as my father says. His she camels were loaded down with all the rugs we had woven over the year to be sold in the great market. Father was a very famous rug maker, but my mother and I worked right alongside him, and my hands tied the smallest knots.

The second reason we traveled to Gabeth Bhul was because of my baby brother who was not yet born. My mother's mother was the *shaheth brihar* woman in that city, the seer of unseen things and the keeper of secrets and dreams. She had sent my mother a dream calling that we should come as soon as possible so she could see the child, and me, her only granddaughter, one last time before the Great Calling took her from this world and left only her secret songs and our memory of her time among us.

With the storm, we could see no more than a few inches in front of our noses as we choked, rubbed our eyes, and clung to our camels. The seventh day out from our village I heard my father tell my mother to watch over me more closely, that people had disappeared. For three nights when we halted, riderless horses and camels wandered into camp. In the morning when we took to the road again, the empty tents and bedrolls marked those missing in the night and sand. My parents didn't think I noticed, but I did.

For three more days, we crept through the blinding haze, camping only briefly.

"Keep close!" my mother barked as she dragged me to where she walked alongside one of our camels. She tied a sash around my waist and secured it tightly to the animal's halter.

"May the gods bring us to Gabeth Bhul before any more of us wander off or disappear from their beds into the storm," my father growled unto my mother's ear. They thought I had not heard, but I had. I was afraid, but I was also curious. This was the first time I ever remember being really afraid. My father's unease and nervousness scared me the most. The twisted grimace of worry transformed his face into that of a stranger. I feared he might not be able to protect us from the gale, but I didn't know why.

I watched the camels as they plodded over the yielding earth, pressing their hooves into the hollowed footsteps of old Yunus, the lead animal. He lumbered on at the head of the line into the blinding wind, his body heavy under his dark shaggy wool as it swayed from side to side over the sand.

Timor, our white female camel's small calf, charged along beside her, his long, skinny legs stabbing the ground as he struggled to keep up. I used to laugh at him, but not anymore. His small, white body shook. Like me, he feared. That night I heard screams in the darkness from other tents, screams unlike those of women obedient to their husband's will that my mother and I always heard and snickered about.

What scared my parents, and all the people of the caravan—even more than the plumes and geysers of sand that flowed from the ground to meet us at every step—was the young woman with the flaming red-gold hair and cold, dead blue eyes who'd walked out of the desert on the fourth day of the squall, alone, on foot, and carrying nothing with her. She walked with us but no one questioned her. No one approached her.

That day, Timor had refused his mother's milk and started to weaken. Several pregnant camels dropped their foals early while older calves became listless. Horrible fights broke out among our men with many ending in bloody, brutal deaths. Afterward, no one could remember why they had fought.

One evening we stopped near a small village to fill the water sacks from the nearby wells. That night all the children of the village vanished from their beds. The people of the village and many of our folk searched everywhere, while the flame-haired stranger just stood there watching, grinning to herself as some nameless doom pressed down on all of us.

The woman had tried to speak to me. My mother pulled me away, but not before the woman's hand, cold like marble, brushed my cheek and her dead eyes bore into my mind. The missing youngsters were never found and with raging threats and drawn swords, the men of the caravan drove the woman off. She disappeared back into the storm. Then she was gone and no more was said about her, but I remembered.

The *rash mazhar* merchant, Fazmet Defet, and his servant clung to Yunus's halter as they walked beside him. I felt safe listening to the sound of the small tinkling bells woven into the old camel's red fringed harness. Timor's little halter was tied to his mother's, or he'd have been swept away and buried before anyone even noticed he was gone.

Whenever the caravan leader brought us to a halt, we pulled our animals to ground and covered their faces with rags. Sheltered against the bodies of the largest camels we settled in for a few hours of rest, praying to the gods that our animals would survive and our trade goods would not be blown away into the storm.

This caravan had travelled the World Road through the desert for many years. Fazmet Defet owned seventy-five camels loaded with manuscripts, writing quills, parchment, and translations of old texts destined for bazaars and ancient temples across a dozen seas in other lands. After resting his animals in Gabeth Bhul and taking on fresh cargo, Fazmet Defet would always return home along the World Road with another caravan carrying coffee, more manuscripts, and strange devices used for observing the course of the stars and discerning the maladies and sickness of men.

Each night when we stopped, the other children and I would gather at Fazmet's tent for stories of faraway land and ancient legends, and sweetmeats. He was a kindly man and we all delighted in his stories. Until one night he did not greet us as usual. He was too tired for stories, he said. When we complained, he became angry and yelled at us, and went inside his tent and closed the flaps. We could hear him moving around inside and bellowing as though he argued with someone, but we knew he was alone.

In three more days, everyone said, we would reach the city at the end of the World Road: Gabeth Bhul with its towering, many-colored spires, the teaming marketplaces filled with the treasures of a thousand lands, and the vast warren of swollen streets riotous with humanity highborn and low, rich and poor, saintly and sinning. I couldn't wait to see all this for the very first time, even with the fear and the disappearances that continued among our dwindling numbers. But at night I could hear the crying of the other children in nearby tents and I covered my ears with my hands so I could sleep.

I overheard Rhado al-Kharsh, a merchant from Tanizara, whispering to the caravan leader that he thought it strange we had passed no other caravans or travelers on the road to such a large trading city as Gabeth Bhul. The caravan leader told him to keep his mouth shut or he would be expelled from the caravan for causing trouble. I had been passing by and when they saw me, they yelled and ran me off like a mongrel dog.

The tenth night on the road, chaos broke out in the caravansary where we stopped. Vicious fights left several men dead in pools of blood while their murderers sat grinning in the thick, red mud that covered the ground. My mother, usually careful to guard my eyes from harsh sights had made no attempt to draw me away as I stared at the horrible scene.

At high noon on the next day, my mother fell in the sand and had to be carried in a litter. That night she delivered my brother way too early and she cried, screaming that he could not live. I wrapped him in swaddling and took him to another new mother who fed him as my mother was too weak.

The next morning, we passed the buried remains of a caravan much larger than ours. Dried bones and half-buried cargo were scattered across the road and into the desert. Rhado al-Kharsh told his servant that he recognized the caravan as that of Dormuz Irzan, and that Dormuz had been only a hand of days ahead of us on the road. Rhado demanded the man's silence, but the word soon spread that an evil prowled the road.

The next morning after that, only a handful of our travelers remained alive. My mother had passed in the night, and my father was gone, but I was too afraid even to cry. The remains of the caravan were loading up and I knew they would leave me if I fell behind. I took my baby brother from the wet nurse and tied him in a sling on my chest. I knew if I cried, it would scare him and cause him harm. He was already weak, even though he looked tawny and healthy. Then I gathered our camels together and we set out with the others.

Fazmet Defet was not among the survivors of the night's ordeal either. His wife said he had wandered off sometime before sunrise to relieve himself and had lost his way as he chased the voice of some long-dead wife when she called to him from the darkness. Fazmet's wife said he'd never had any wife but her since they were still both very young. Rhado al-Kharsh was gone too. He'd been seen scrambling over the earth on his hands and knees, searching for his eyes, convinced he had lost them in a game of *shushu*. Then he had run out into the desert, screaming that the eyes were calling to him from the darkness.

The old bull camel Yunus lead us on, and all day and into the night we struggled along behind him. That night the storm continued, forcing us to shelter on the edge of a vast plateau. The next day we would reach the fabled city of Gabeth Bhul. The remaining men of the caravan said the seers there must have some way of defeating this hideous onslaught that brought nothing but death and madness.

When we awoke the next morning, at what might have been dawn for other folk on a very different sort of day than this, the camels and sheep and horses shook themselves of sand and stood up while we children rubbed our eyes to the sound of voices on the wind calling us to enter the city gates. I gathered up my brother, but there was nothing to feed him because the woman who had nursed him was gone. I drew some milk from our female camel, Timur's mother. The babe drank and laughed.

We took stock of our people who remained. All those of the caravan over fifteen summers were dead, drowned in sand in their sleep, or locked in savage combat, man and wife, brother and brother, friend and friend, fingers buried deep in bloody necks torn open and left to empty on the ground.

When we had our wits about us again, we older children gathered the younger, whether walking or still swaddled, and loaded them onto the camels. The morning air was fresh and sweet, the skies overhead clear. The storm had passed. We had only gone a short distance when we arrived at the walls of Gabeth Bhul and passed unchallenged through the city gates.

None of us was old enough to have ever visited the city at the beginning, and the end, of the World Road. Where were the towering many-colored spires, and teaming marketplaces filled with the fabulous wares of a thousand lands? Where was the warren of swollen streets riotous with the noises of humanity highborn and low, rich and poor, saintly and sinning that my father had always sung about in one of the old songs?

∗ ∗ ∗

The storm consumed the whole world and scoured it clean of all the cities of mankind such as Gabeth Bhul. Silent streets and mighty towers rose above us as we walked the streets where Gabeth Bhul had stood for centuries. The new city blossomed from the desert floor, raised from the very bones of Gabeth Bhul. As we walked through the street we gazed into the cold, icy stares of dead eyes watching silently from a thousand windows and rooftops.

Domed roofs and towers, houses, palaces, temples, gardens, and places of feasting, all the same unbroken hue as the boiling sands rose from the earth as if to greet us as we walked silently through the crowded streets.

The storm had begun in the north and buried the whole world under an interminable waste. Cities far, far older and more ancient than the memory of man had risen in the night and washed the world clean with blood and sand. We children were all that survived the final night of the desert crossing. All our elders had perished while the youngest survived, along with the animals that bore us through the storm and kept us warm at night. After being joined by tall, robed figures streaming toward us from every direction, we continued on, deeper into the city, as the towering geysers of sand lined the streets and flowed away to conceal what little remained of the human city of Gabeth Bhul. As we gathered finally before the great temple, the fiery wraith-like inhabitants of the city regarded us closely with heads crowned with golden flames, still and silent as living statues, each as if a sister to the flame-haired woman in the desert.

Then I saw them! Other children, thousands more, had reached the city before us. In their midst was the strange flame-haired woman with the dead blue eyes we had met in the desert, and gathered around her were all the children taken from the village.

Countless others had come from cities and towns, from the deserts far to the north and south and beyond the seas. Those of an age over fifteen had perished in the desert by all that filled their empty, fevered dreams. We alone were the seeds of the new planting of the earth, we alone would be allowed to thrive. We would bring life once more to the world, or we would drown in the sands of the next great storm to descend from the north in an unseen place.

Nightmare Factory

Katrina Nicholson

Editor: Wanting to be a hero can be dangerous. Worse, once you succeed they want you to do it again.

Bonnie Brymer had waited her whole life for the call. But when she answered, it wasn't for her.

Bonnie's smartphone—which was designed to withstand chemical sterilization—squealed its alert while she was injecting a deadly strain of smallpox into a chicken embryo in the deepest recesses of the CDC's Biosafety Level 4 lab in Atlanta. It was loud enough to be heard over the noisy blower that inflated her blimp-like biosafety "space" suit. Bonnie's pulse kicked and her grandfather, who was assisting her, fumbled the dish in surprise. He almost pricked his gloved finger on Bonnie's needle.

Bonnie carefully set aside her implements and jabbed the "answer" button, which took up the phone's entire touchscreen.

A man's voice sounded from the tinny speaker. "Hallo, Bonnie. May I speak to Alan?"

Bonnie recognized the British accent. It belonged to Ian Wyght, the thirty-seven-year-old weapons expert from the Special Air Service who had frowned at her all through her two weeks of live fire exercises, which Bonnie thought of as *don't-get-shot training.*

"My father's not here," Bonnie said, her voice dampened by her helmet. "He's doing hip replacements in Fort Lauderdale now."

And he's much happier for it, Bonnie thought. For Bonnie, being the on-call smallpox expert for NATO's Bioterror Response Unit was an honor. For her father it had been a burden. He'd passed the job to Bonnie the instant she graduated medical school three months ago.

"Right. Well. May I speak to John?" Ian asked.

Bonnie met her grandfather's eyes over the lab bench. John Brymer was famous for his work with the World Health Organization's Smallpox Eradication Program. He was also seventy-two years old and suffered from osteoarthritis. No way could he jump out of a plane.

Her grandfather rolled his eyes. "Ian, you've always been a jackass, but I never realized you were a dumbass too," John shouted at the phone.

"Bonnie's the one you want."

"But..." Ian trailed off.

Bonnie could hear all the things he wanted to say. "But she's young. But she's green. But I don't *know* her." Trying to fit in with insular military units was like chipping away a brick wall with a spoon. It had taken her father and grandfather years of training missions just to earn a modicum of respect from the operators. Bonnie wanted more. She wanted what the anthrax guys had. They were welcome in every spec ops bar on two continents just because they'd risked their lives on missions. The trouble was that apart from the University of Birmingham callout in '78 (which turned out to be an accident) there'd never been a real smallpox incident. If today was that day, no way was she letting anyone else go.

"If this call means what it's supposed to mean, you don't have time to argue," Bonnie reminded Ian.

The call meant that someone, somewhere, had broken out with smallpox—their skin cracked and covered in hard blisters which leaked the deadly virus into the air. Smallpox had been eradicated from nature in 1977. It now officially existed in only two places: here at the CDC and at VECTOR, the state research center for biology and virology in Russia, though the BRU had strong suspicions that several rogue states had gotten ahold of it after the Soviet Union collapsed and were developing it as a biological weapon.

Of all the diseases in history, smallpox was the biggest killer. It had no cure. Only people who worked with it in labs were vaccinated against it. The vaccine wasn't even stockpiled in most countries anymore, which meant the general population had no immunity. It was highly contagious. One infected person would become twenty, twenty would become four hundred, and four hundred would become a pandemic. Bonnie's scalp prickled at the thought.

"Fine. I'll send a helicopter," Ian spat, then hung up.

Bonnie tamped down her frustration as she and John hustled through the infuriatingly slow process of exiting the BSL-4 lab. They sent their tools to the autoclave, passed through the airlock, took a chemical shower, removed their suits and scrubs in the "dirty" change room, took a regular shower, and finally put on street clothes in the clean room. Once they were out, Bonnie hauled the hard black case containing her field instruments out of her locker, and the two of them hurried in silence to the helipad, where a black Atlanta police helicopter idled.

Bonnie turned to her grandfather. *That's what I'll look like when I'm old,* she thought suddenly. Bright blue eyes clouded, short reddish hair streaked with gray, pale skin studded with liver spots, small frame supported by a cane. *If I get old.*

"It's probably a false alarm," John said.

Bonnie grinned. "Or maybe...it's not."

John cracked a smile. "There's a first time for everything."

Bonnie ran to the helicopter.

* * *

The police pilot flew her northwest to Dobbins Air Reserve base in Marietta, where an unmarked Citation jet waited on the runway.

"Where are we headed?" Bonnie asked the pilot as she strapped in, the lone passenger on a plane set up for over a dozen VIPs.

"Scotland," was all he would say.

Bonnie had guessed it would be somewhere in the UK, given that Ian had been assigned to lead the team. Each mission was different, with experts and operators from dozens of countries standing by to be called away from their regular jobs at any moment.

By the time the jet landed at RAF Leuchars, Bonnie was bursting with impatience. She jumped out and ran across the tarmac to a lumpy, olive-green Puma helicopter. Dr. Shane Wong, a forty-two-year-old Ebola expert who worked out of the Center for Applied Microbiology in Porton Down, leaned out the open door to help her aboard. The pilot lifted off as soon as she was through.

"Bonnie! Welcome!" Shane shouted over the rotor wash. He handed her a set of headphones and waited for her to strap down and plug in.

"So what do we have?" Bonnie asked.

"The patient is Robert MacLeod, twenty-three. Reported missing to Kirriemuir police by fellow hackers after he missed their conference in Glasgow. Evidently he was meant to receive an award for posting a number of Russian mafia financial papers on the Internet. Coppers followed up. They heard him moving about inside but when they caught sight of him through the window, they stopped up the gaps and phoned the Health Protection Agency. HPA sent for us."

"What's the patient's status?"

"Dead. We found him in a pool of blood on the hall floor. Skin black and sloughing. Eyes red. Black blood leaked from his orifices before he died. His mates reported having seen him perfectly healthy less than forty-eight hours previously, and none of them are ill, so BRU thought weaponized Ebola, but once I did the tests I found—"

"Hemorrhagic smallpox."

"Right."

Hemorrhagic smallpox was the deadliest form of the disease. It was as near to 100 percent fatal as made no difference, but normally cropped up in less than 2 percent of cases and took at least two weeks to kill a patient.

"It's acting way too fast. It must be genetically engineered," Bonnie said. Their worst nightmare.

Shane nodded. "And there's more. We quarantined and vaccinated the two constables who discovered the body, but they fell ill anyway."

"How long's it been?"

"About fifteen hours, and they're already in a bad way."

Chills raced along Bonnie's spine. "Regular or hemorrhagic?"

"Hemorrhagic. Both of them."

"Shit. We're in big trouble."

Shane didn't respond. His grim face said it all.

The helicopter set down in a cleared area of mountainside near a stone cottage. A hastily erected barricade plastered with biohazard signs blocked the lane leading up to the house. The front door opened into a plastic tent, which was connected to a series of trailers that made up a mobile Biosafety Level 4 lab.

Shane and Bonnie ducked under the rotors and ran for the last trailer, where they donned their specially designed BRU space suits. Standard suits were white, yellow, or light blue. Theirs were black. They were tougher, tighter fitting, and had high tech filters that eliminated the need for air tanks. They were designed so that you could eat, eliminate waste, and even draw your own blood without taking the suit off. BRU missions sometimes lasted for days.

They entered the house through the plastic tunnel. Bonnie maneuvered carefully, wary of brushing against anything that might compromise her suit. One breath of infected air was sometimes all it took.

"It took us ages just to get through the door," Shane reported over the team's private channel. "Coppers said his digital security system was impenetrable. Even our computer bloke couldn't crack his password. We had to borrow an EMP generator from the air force and shut the whole place down."

Robert MacLeod, his wide, staring eyes filled with red blood, lay on his back in the entryway where he'd died. Sheets of mottled purple-black skin had sloughed off into the congealing pools of tar-like blood on the stone floor. Four black-suited figures rustled around the cottage, poking into Robert MacLeod's life. The BRU team.

"You took your time," Ian said, his craggy, mustached face pulled down in its usual frown.

"I got here as fast as I could," Bonnie replied, not mentioning that she wasn't the one who wasted half a day bringing in the wrong expert.

"Nathan Douglas, Delta Force. Petter Solverson, *Forsvarets Spesialkommando*. Reiner Ebersbach, *Kommando Spezialkräfte*," Ian said by way of introduction, pointing at each man in turn. The BRU didn't bother with rank. Its members came from an eclectic array of armed forces units that all used different systems.

"Nathan's our explosives expert. Petter does languages and computers. Reiner's on navigation, surveillance, and comms."

Bonnie peered through their plastic faceplates as Ian introduced them. Nathan was in his late twenties, a little older than she was, black, and built like a football linebacker. The American regarded her with cold dark eyes and didn't offer to shake hands.

Petter was Norwegian, a little older than Nathan. He was very tall, very blond, and very lean. He gave Bonnie a perfunctory nod.

Bonnie put Reiner's age somewhere in the mid-thirties. Apart from herself, the German was the shortest, but where Bonnie was a waif, Reiner was stocky and strong. He had light brown hair and gray eyes.

"*Fräulein* Brymer," Reiner said in his heavy accent.

Doctor, Bonnie wanted to remind him, but it was no use. She wouldn't get a warmer welcome until she'd earned it.

"Any luck figuring out where he contracted it?" Bonnie asked.

Petter held open an A4 envelope covered in packing tape. Bonnie peered inside. What she saw made her stomach drop. There was a small quantity of pink powder in the bottom—an aerosolizing agent of the type that was often used to send anthrax through the mail.

"The envelope also contained a letter."

Petter showed her a piece of white computer paper which was blank except for three words.

"Is that Russian?" Bonnie asked.

"*Poshel na huy,*" Petter confirmed. "It means 'fuck you.'"

"This was a hit," Shane realized.

"I think we got lucky. He was probably supposed to make it to that conference. He would have taken out the whole hacking community, along with half of Scotland," Bonnie added.

"We know," Ian said impatiently. "Now could we possibly trouble you for some assistance in tracking down these arseholes?"

Bonnie ignored his hostility and set her field case next to Shane's. "What did your analysis turn up?"

Shane pointed to a full-color microscope image on the screen set into the lid. It showed typical smallpox "bricks," huge lumps of proteins twisted around each other to protect the virus DNA at the center. They floated among destroyed cell fragments, waiting to burrow inside the next human cell that came their way.

"I know enough to recognize the bricks, but I haven't got a clue what these are," Shane said, indicating an opaque oval approximately four times the size of a smallpox brick with little bristles around the edge. It wasn't moving.

Bonnie felt a chill that had nothing to do with the temperature in her suit. "I've never seen them before. Could it be a second pathogen?"

"If it is, the constables didn't contract it. All they've got in their blood is smallpox."

Shane tapped the screen, bringing up another image, almost identical to the first except missing the black ovals.

"What do the DNA results say?"

Shane expanded a sidebar of text data into the middle of the screen. Dread crawled up Bonnie's spine as she looked at the string of letters.

"There's no extra data that might give us a clue as to what the ovals are. It's like they're inorganic. But the rest...I've seen this strain before. We call it Chernaya 91. The only known sample is in the WHO freezer in Atlanta. It was brought to the West in the pockets of a Russian bioweapons factory technician after the Soviet Union collapsed."

Ian stepped forward, a sharp look in his eyes. "Is there a cure?"

"No."

"A vaccine?"

"We haven't found one, but there must be one where the strain came from. Only an idiot would unleash a bioweapon he couldn't protect himself from."

"If we retrieve it, can we save those constables?"

Bonnie shook her head sadly. "Even if we had it right now we couldn't. In order for the vaccine to work, you have to take it before you feel sick."

"We have to try, in any case. Where did the strain originate?"

Bonnie swallowed. "Chernaya Dira."

"Black hole," Petter translated.

"The nightmare factory," Shane said with a shudder.

"Of this place I have not heard," Reiner admitted.

"It was an ultra-secret facility for developing and testing biological weapons during the Soviet era," Bonnie replied. "When the Soviet Union collapsed, the bioweapons division was privatized. According to the rumors, Chernaya Dira was taken over by the mafia."

Nathan whistled. "They bought a bioweapons factory just to make fuck-you gifts for their enemies?"

"This operation is sounding very amateur," Reiner said.

"Where is this place?" Ian asked. "We've got to get in there and shut it down before these bloody idiots wipe out half of Europe."

"It's in the wilderness someplace north of Saint Petersburg," Bonnie replied. "But if we want to get in, we'll need help."

* * *

The Russian defector, Yuri Akulov, was hastily flown in from his home outside Washington—under duress, if his face was any indication. His pale, bald head dripped with sweat and his gloved fingers twisted together nervously. Yuri had once worked in biosafety suits, but had never done a parachute jump. Reiner, their resident expert, had the Russian strapped to his chest.

The six of them stood alone in the cavernous cargo hold of a Royal Air Force C-130. The red interior lighting created menacing shadows of their biosuited figures. Bonnie had done jumps in training, but real life was a thousand times scarier. The roar of the freezing wind added to the drone of the propellers as the ramp dropped open. Stars studded the black sky. She could only tell the ground below because no lights twinkled. Not a light anywhere. The mission was a black op, so they would have to jump from a high altitude and float over the Finnish border to Chernaya Dira.

"*Drei*...two...*eins*....YOU JUMP!" Reiner yelled over their private channel, and flung himself off the ramp.

Bonnie dove into the night, eyes glued to Reiner. She was terrified of getting separated. The wind outside her helmet drowned out everything and her stomach leapt into her throat. As soon as she cleared the plane, she yanked the ripcord. With a WHUMP and a spine-jangling yank, a darkened ram-air parachute expanded above her. The wind noise died to a dull roar. Below, she could see a rectangle of dark gray—almost white compared to the environs—Reiner's parachute.

Bonnie tugged on the risers, pulling herself into line behind him. Craning her neck, she made out the shadowy figures of the other three as they moved into place behind and above her. She breathed a sigh of relief.

The drop seemed to take forever. As they ate up the nearly fifty miles they had to cover, a cluster of lights appeared ahead of them in the blackness. The angle got shallower and shallower. 2000 feet. 1500. 1000. 500. Her nerves wound up as the altimeter on her wrist wound down. Still nothing but trees below. Finally, at 300 feet, an open space appeared in front of them. They dropped the last few hundred feet into a wheat field. Her feet hit the ground and the shock reverberated through her body. She rolled through the high stalks to soften the impact.

They hid their parachutes and gathered on the crest of a hill. Bonnie fitted night vision goggles over her helmet as Reiner used infrared to observe the farmhouse that blocked their access to town.

"No one is at home," he reported.

Ian and Nathan led the way down the dirt road, rifles ready in case any mafia goons had seen them arrive. Every shadow looked like a threat to Bonnie, but as they patrolled into town, which was just a collection of worker houses, not a soul challenged them. Bonnie peered down each street as they passed, the green buildings swimming in her night vision. Everything was eerily quiet, even for the middle of the night. No dogs. No lights. No people. It only made the tension worse.

The only bright spot belonged to the facility. It loomed above the town from the next hill over, a sprawling complex of low concrete buildings surrounded by chain link and razor wire. Luckily the gate was unlocked and unguarded. Maneuvering through all those sharp barbs in a space suit chilled Bonnie's blood.

"Where the bloody hell is everyone?" Ian asked.

"There should always be a guard on duty," Yuri said nervously.

"Maybe the mafia didn't get that memo," Nathan suggested.

A keypad controlled the lock on the heavy metal entrance doors. Nathan blew them open with a small shaped charge. While quiet for an explosion, the resounding CLANG should have brought some attention. Yet no alarms went off and nobody came to see what was going on.

"Something is feeling wrong..." Reiner said, voicing what they were all thinking.

Ian was first into the hallway. Red emergency lighting and the occasional flickering fluorescent cast long shadows. All the doors they came to were locked. They passed through the administrative area and into a Biosafety Level 1 zone, which, according to Yuri, took up the largest ring at the edges of the complex. As Yuri silently directed them toward the center, Bonnie found that she was holding her breath. Where was everybody? Had they abandoned the facility...or were they laying an ambush?

They passed into Level 2, which was marked only by a biohazard warning sign. Inside, sliding glass doors opened onto the labs. Bonnie peered into one and saw a body lying on the ground near a lab bench. It wore a stained white coat and rubber gloves.

"There's someone in there," Bonnie whispered.

Ian and Nathan plastered themselves to the wall on either side of the door and took turns peeking in. When no one moved inside, Ian gestured her forward.

Bonnie slid open the door and knelt next to the body, setting her field case down next to its head. The purple-black mottling of her skin and the clothing stained with black blood proved her a victim of hemorrhagic smallpox.

Bonnie's suit had a HEPA filter, but she could imagine the smell—rancid, almost like roadkill in the sun.

Bonnie pressed her fingers to the woman's cold, rubbery throat to check for a pulse. The body spasmed.

"She's still alive!" Nathan exclaimed.

Bonnie scuttled backward as the woman continued to seize. Her muscle contractions seemed oddly coordinated. Her forearms pushed against the floor. Her hips lifted. Her head jerked forward. Lab supplies clattered everywhere.

"Is she...trying to stand?" Ian asked.

"Don't be ridiculous," Bonnie retorted, but her heart hammered in her chest. Smallpox didn't cause seizures.

With a Herculean effort, the woman heaved her body to her feet and stalked toward them. Her eyes were wide open, fixed and staring with the whites shot through with red. Her mouth hung open. Foamy threads of blood-laced saliva hung from her lips. Everyone instinctively backed away.

With a liquid squish, a sheet of skin slid off the woman's forehead and slopped down her shirt, leaving a gory mess in its wake. The woman must have been in horrific pain, but her face showed no expression. She made no sound. *WRONG, WRONG, WRONG*, Bonnie's brain screamed. One of the worst things about smallpox was that it left its victims perfectly lucid and aware of how the disease progressed to the very end.

Everyone stood frozen as the woman shuffled toward them. No one seemed to know what to do. The woman swiped clumsily at Ian, her manicured fingertips zipping across his suit.

"Don't—" Bonnie shouted, but Ian reacted automatically, blasting a hole in the woman's chest with his M-16.

Bonnie jumped as the report echoed loudly. The woman's body jerked at the impact of the bullet, but she didn't fall. Instead she coughed, spewing a cloud of black gore that splattered across Ian's faceplate.

Ian stumbled back, smearing the blood with his gloved hand. The others raised their weapons and Bonnie's heart leapt into her mouth. Her training kicked in and she dropped to the ground as Petter, Nathan, and Reiner emptied their magazines into the unfortunate woman. Yuri cowered in a corner behind them. Bonnie's hands shook as the flashes cleared from her vision. The woman still stood, despite the fact that her blood and brains were splattered across the lab.

"What the fuck?" Ian shouted.

The woman fell on him, slashing at his suit. Ian stumbled blindly backward into the sliding door. The others covered him with their rifles, but the two locked in melee were too close for a clear shot. Ian jammed his rifle between the woman and the door.

"Don't!" Bonnie screamed. "You'll break the—"

Ian pulled the trigger. The glass shattered. The woman's weight knocked him through the empty frame. He landed on his back in the hallway, the woman on top of him.

Bonnie's need to help overrode her fear and she jumped to her feet. "Lie still, Ian!"

But Ian struggled blindly with the woman, ripping open his suit on the jagged glass shards. Bonnie reached out to stop him, but Reiner yanked her back. "*Achtung!*"

A scalpel clutched by yet another purple-skinned lab tech narrowly missed her arm. Smallpox-ravaged lab assistants with oozing flaps of skin shuffled wetly down the hallway from Level 3 like an army of dead-eyed marionettes, coughing clouds of infected blood. Bonnie staggered back into Reiner, mind blank with horror.

Ian finally shoved the woman away. He ripped off his blood-streaked helmet. The horde bore down on him. His eyes found Bonnie and Reiner in the doorway.

"Go!" he yelled. "I've got the buggers!"

Ian grabbed a grenade off his belt and pulled the pin. He drew his arm back but the woman fell on him before he could throw.

Hot terror flooded Bonnie's limbs as she saw the grenade slip from his grasp. Before she could think, Reiner had her off the floor. He pulled her with him as he dove behind the lab bench. Nathan and Petter piled in after, pushing Yuri in front of them. The hallway exploded. Orange fire burst through the doorframe, blowing glass shards and body parts across the room in a glittering cloud.

For a minute, nobody moved. Bonnie's ears rang. She couldn't seem to make herself let go of Reiner.

"Ian? Is he—" Bonnie began.

Reiner shook his head.

"What the fuck was wrong with those people?" Nathan shouted. "Why were they trying to kill us?"

Nathan clutched at his helmet like he wanted to rip it off in disgust.

"Nathan, don't!" Bonnie grabbed his hands. She could feel them trembling. Or maybe hers were.

"I don't know why they came after us, but whatever's happening to them, I don't think it's their fault."

The rage cleared from Nathan's eyes. "What? How?"

Bonnie swallowed nervously. "That woman. When I took her pulse... she didn't have one."

* * *

After checking the ruined hallway for signs of Ian or smallpox victims, Yuri led them through to Level 3.

"So...those people back there...they were zomb—" Nathan began.

"Don't say it," Bonnie ordered. "There's an explanation for their behavior, and that's *not* it."

No one looked like they believed her. She wasn't sure she believed herself either, but if she let herself think that word, she'd dissolve into a puddle of nerves. This was definitely not what she signed up for.

Warning signs announced their approach to Level 4. They passed through an empty locker room, a shower room, and a dressing room where yellow biosafety suits hung on hooks. Bonnie found the routine comforting. They went through the airlock in pairs, standing under the chemical shower with their arms up to decontaminate their suits. For the first time, a BSL-4 lab was probably less hot than the rest of the building.

Bonnie and Nathan were last.

"I'm getting wet!" Nathan exclaimed.

Bonnie hit the emergency stop on the shower and inspected Nathan's suit. There was a small tear underneath his left arm, probably made by flying glass. Her heart dropped. She hurriedly swiped the suit dry with a paper towel and slapped a piece of duct tape over the hole, knowing it was too late.

Nathan's horrified eyes met hers through the visor.

"Am I gonna die?"

Bonnie could see the beginnings of panic on his face. This was what her grandfather called "the worried face of smallpox." If he lost it, so would she. She stomped down hard on her emotions.

"No," Bonnie insisted. She grabbed Nathan's helmet and forced him to look at her. "Nathan, you're not going to die. There's a vaccine here somewhere. We'll find it."

"If they had a vaccine, why didn't they take it?"

"I don't know. Maybe they didn't understand what it was."

Bonnie pushed Nathan into the lab. It was a bizarre cross between a rough, Soviet-era concrete institution and a shiny, white Apple Store. The remnants of medical experiments and quite a few computers littered the tables. Reiner and Petter checked each of the rooms but found no more smallpox victims. Bonnie left Nathan on a stool. She and Petter opened storage cabinets and freezers, directing Yuri and Reiner to do the same in the other room.

"Here. This is the one," Yuri said a few minutes later. He eagerly snatched a plastic tube from a rack.

"What does it say?" Bonnie asked Petter.

"Chernaya 1 Smallpox," Petter read from the label.

"Not vaccine?"

"No."

Bonnie glared at Yuri. "Try again."

Yuri paled behind his faceplate. He returned a minute later with another vial and handed it to Petter.

"Chernaya 1 Smallpox Vaccine," Petter read.

"We will be all right now, yes?" Yuri asked.

Bonnie could see from his face that he knew the answer was no, so she didn't say anything.

Bonnie went over to Nathan and carefully lined up the items she needed on the lab bench. She took hold of Nathan's wrist and turned it over to expose the port on his forearm. Positioned above the vein, it disinfected needles on the way in and out so that blood could be taken and vaccines could be given without compromising the suit's integrity. Bonnie took a few deep breaths to make sure her hands were steady, and inserted a syringe into the port.

"I'll check your blood first."

Bonnie withdrew the syringe and turned to one of the lab's microscopes. Her own field kit had been lost in the explosion, so she prepared a slide and examined it through the eyepiece. She was dismayed, though not surprised, to see smallpox bricks in Nathan's blood, along with the same black ovals she'd seen in Robert MacLeod, only this time they were moving. What the hell were they?

"What's the verdict, Doc?" Nathan asked nervously.

She patted his shoulder. "You were exposed, but don't worry. We got to you in time. You should be okay."

Nathan offered his arm again. Bonnie filled another syringe with fluid from Yuri's vial. Ordinary smallpox vaccine was administered by piercing the skin with a bifurcated needle, but in this case Bonnie felt that a more direct route would be better. She injected the vaccine into Nathan's bloodstream and mentally crossed her fingers.

"How long we must wait?" Reiner asked.

"If Nathan's okay after two hours, we should be in the clear."

Bonnie put Yuri and Reiner to work collecting vials of vaccine. Petter found and copied the formula from the lab computers and emailed it to the CDC, Porton Down, and the United States Army Medical Research Institute for Infectious Diseases so they could start producing it.

Bonnie watched the black ovals swim around in Nathan's blood. She couldn't figure out what they were doing. An oval would swim up to some cells, tickle them with its feelers, and then move on, like it was tasting the cells and finding them not to its liking.

"So...how come our guy in Scotland didn't rise from the dead and try to kill us?" Nathan asked after a while.

"I'm not sure, but I think it has something to do with these things,"

Bonnie replied. She stepped aside to let Nathan look.

"Those black things?"

"I saw them in Robert MacLeod's blood, too, but they were dead. At least, they were by the time I got there. The cops reported seeing MacLeod move around through the window. I thought it was because he hadn't died yet, but what if…"

Bonnie trailed off, thinking.

"What if what?" Nathan prompted.

"Let me see your visor."

Nathan let Bonnie swab the seam where his faceplate met his suit. The chemical shower hadn't run its full course, so there was still some black blood and brain matter from the woman in Level 2.

Bonnie smeared the mess onto another slide and loaded it up. This time, things were different. There were red and white blood cells in the sample along with cells from the woman's brain that looked like spiky snowflakes. As Bonnie watched, one of the black ovals attached itself to a brain cell and emitted a flash that was picked up by the dendrites and transmitted along the axon terminals.

"Holy shit," she exclaimed.

"What?"

"They *are* zombies. At least in the sense that their corpses are being reanimated. The black ovals are attaching themselves to the victim's brain cells and sending messages. Move your arms. Move your legs. Cough."

"What the hell for?"

"To spread the virus. The mafia must not have been able to figure out how to slow the virus progression long enough for the victim to pass it on before he died, so they added the ovals, which reanimate the body and spread the disease."

"So what are they?"

Bonnie looked around at all the computers. Most of them had endless lines of code crawling across their screens.

"They're machines," Bonnie realized. "Nanotechnology. The mafia didn't hire virologists to improve their fuck-you weapon. They hired engineers."

"Jesus Christ. I didn't expect tha-aaaaaah!"

Nathan screamed as his body spasmed, dumping him off his stool. Reiner, Petter, and Yuri rushed over.

"Nathan!" Bonnie crouched down to help him into a sitting position. "What happened?"

"I don't know. I was just sitting here, and AAAAAAAH!"

Nathan seized again. His body curled into a fetal position then relaxed, all within a few seconds. Nathan looked up at Bonnie in dismay. "Am I getting sick?"

Bonnie was baffled. "I don't think so. If you were sick, you'd feel like you had the flu, then you'd get a rash."

"Then wha—aaaaaa!"

Bonnie put herself between Nathan and the stool so he wouldn't crack his faceplate against the metal leg.

"Let me test you again," Bonnie urged.

She waited until Nathan's seizure was over, then quickly drew another blood sample and examined it under the microscope. The smallpox bricks were shredded, destroyed by the roving, y-shaped antibodies that Nathan's body had created in response to the vaccine. But the nanos were still there, big and black and looking for brain cells to latch onto.

"Shit. The vaccine killed the smallpox but the nanos are still active and trying to control you. Their signals are conflicting with your own and it's giving you seizures."

"H-how do we s-stop it?" Nathan asked, gritting his teeth as his body shook again.

Bonnie fought the urge to pound the desk in frustration. "How should I know? I'm a virologist, not an engineer."

"If it is a machine, it must have a kill switch," Petter said.

Reiner, Yuri, and Bonnie moved Nathan to a clear area while Petter inspected the computers.

"Here it is. *Avariynoy Ostanovki*. Emergency stop."

Petter typed in a command.

Everyone looked around, but nothing seemed different. Bonnie got up and looked hopefully into the microscope. The black ovals were still active. Nathan's body jerked again.

Her shoulders slumped. "It didn't work."

Petter's gloved fingers flew over the keyboard. "Yes, I see it did not work for them either. They designed the nanodevices to self-replicate using trace metals found in the blood and to spread themselves by triggering the cough reflex of the victim. When the nanos performed too efficiently, the Russians tried and failed to extinguish their creation."

"That must have been the source of the outbreak. The nanos spread the virus faster than they could kill it."

"Yes, and I am afraid there is more bad news."

"What now?"

Petter turned the screen to face them. "The mafia seems to have set up surveillance cameras in a wide zone around the facility. Had all of their employees not been dead, they would surely have seen us arrive."

"I'm not hearing bad news yet."

"The bad news is that the townspeople are infected and are attempting to spread the virus."

Petter brought up a surveillance feed from a building in town. Blackened corpses shambled down the main road heading out of town.

"If we do not stop them, I estimate they will reach the next town by midmorning."

"They are too many. We cannot be fighting them," Reiner said. "A way must be found to kill the machines."

"Ian's w-way s-seemed to w-work pretty w-well," Nathan said from the floor.

There was a moment of silence in which everyone knew what everyone else was thinking. Their suits were all contaminated. If blowing up the town was the only way to stop the nanos, they would all have to go with it.

Looks like I'm going to be a hero after all, Bonnie thought bleakly.

"Are we sure there is no other way?" Yuri asked timidly.

Bonnie had been thinking the same thing, but said: "There isn't. You know that. We can save ourselves by ignoring our duty today, but what about tomorrow? Next month? Next year? Your kids could get it, Yuri."

There was a moment of silence.

"Where would we find an explosion large enough?" Petter asked.

Yuri cleared his throat. "In Soviet times, there was a small nuclear strike missile in an underground silo not far from the field in which we landed."

"Is it s-still there?" Nathan asked.

Yuri shrugged. "When the Soviet Union collapsed, many things were sold. But many things that were buried have stayed buried."

"W-we have to t-try," Nathan insisted. "Those n-nanos could c-cause a pandemic."

"To launch a nuclear airstrike is to start a war," Reiner argued.

"Not if we let them know what we are doing," Petter said, patting the radio on Reiner's back.

They broke radio silence to let the BRU know what was about to happen. The BRU didn't like it, but they didn't argue either. They knew better than anyone what was at stake. Bonnie was just glad she didn't have to break it to the Russians herself.

Bonnie and Yuri supported Nathan between them, bracing him when the seizures struck. Petter and Reiner protected them. They inched through the deserted, blood-splattered hallways in a cloud of tension that could have been cut with a knife. Every rustle, every scrape made Bonnie twitch. Her suit stank of fear. When they came to the ruined corridor where Ian had died, Bonnie couldn't look.

They emerged from the building into a cleared area lit with floodlights and stopped. People filled the field. Administrators, lab assistants, technologists, even a few who looked like mafia goons. All dead of smallpox and coughing up a storm as they tried to spread the disease. They had been stopped by the fence and blocked the team's path to the gate. They turned, almost as one, when they heard the broken door creak. Bonnie's heart seized as their eyes landed on her.

Part of Bonnie wanted to lie down and give up. Another part wanted to run and never stop. She clung hard to Nathan.

Reiner slowly shrugged off his pack and lifted it into Petter's arms. "You run for the gate as soon as they are moved," he ordered.

Before anyone could argue, Reiner ran into the middle of the field. He yelled and sprayed bullets into the mob. The motley collection of oozing smallpox victims lurched into the bullet storm as the nanos responded to the stimulus. They descended upon Reiner en masse. He scrambled backward.

"Come on!" Bonnie urged Yuri. Together they helped Nathan across the lawn, Bonnie's rubbery knees threatening to give out with each step. Petter ran ahead of them to open the gate.

Bonnie turned back for Reiner just in time to see him get cornered. His back hit an outbuilding. There was nowhere left to go. In a second, he had disappeared under a pile of squirming bodies. His rifle fell silent. Tears blurred Bonnie's vision, and she looked away.

"Come now," Petter ordered. He yanked Bonnie through the gate by her pack. He slammed the fence shut in the face of a dead technician she hadn't even noticed.

Bonnie's racing heart gradually calmed as they made their way to the farm in miserable silence. Yuri led them behind the house to a barn, which was really a hollow shell hiding the enormous sliding metal plate that protected the missile. They blew open a smaller hatch that let them into an underground control room filled with dormant switches from the 1980s that nevertheless reported *gotovii*—ready—when Petter powered up the console.

"Won't we n-need some s-sort of launch k-keys?" Nathan asked.

Bonnie and Yuri dropped him into a chair in front of the console and tied him to the backrest to keep his seizures from toppling him.

"Russia is not like America," Yuri said as they worked. "Moscow was much more concerned with the missiles not being fired when they were needed than with them being fired when they were not needed. They are designed to launch automatically if they receive a signal from Perimetr, a detection system in a bunker outside of Moscow."

"So we must retarget the missile and make it think it has heard the signal," Petter said. "Very simple."

"Very disturbing," Bonnie muttered, trying to wrap her head around the fact that she had only minutes left to live. What did exploding feel like? Or would it happen too fast to feel anything?

Petter spliced his laptop into the missile's control system. His fingers danced across the keys.

Yuri slumped into a chair and put his head in his hands. "I should have said no to this mission. At least then my children would have a father, even if he was carried away by the police in the dead of night to spend the rest of his life in a prison."

A spike of adrenaline lanced through Bonnie. "The police!" Yuri's words jogged the idea she had tried to bring forward earlier.

"Petter, the police said Robert MacLeod was moving around inside the house, but when the BRU got the door open, he was lying on the floor. Something must have happened to the nanos between those events."

Petter spun away from the control panel. "We used an EMP generator to disable the security system. And the EMP—"

"—killed the nanos." Bonnie finished excitedly.

"N-nuclear explosions c-cause huge el-lec-tromagnetic p-pulses," Nathan said. "At l-least we can be sure the n-nanos will b-be dead."

"Yes, but is there not a way to create an EMP without the explosion?" Yuri asked.

"An air b-burst!" Nathan exclaimed. "Of c-course! We s-set the m-missile to explode at an altitude of s-say, twenty m-miles. The r-radiation and the b-blast wouldn't be a problem, b-but the EMP w-would knock out everything electronic w-within four hundred miles."

"Saint Petersburg will be completely shut down," Petter warned.

"Saint Petersburg would rather be in darkness than dead of smallpox," Yuri replied.

Bonnie turned to Petter hopefully. "Can you program this thing to do that?"

"Yes."

"Then hurry. We've only got a couple hours before those people reach the next town."

* * *

A nuclear missile launch is a spectacularly unsubtle thing. Bonnie, Petter, Nathan, and Yuri stood on the hill and watched as the olive-green cylinder shattered the barn, engulfed the house in flames, and propelled itself into the sky on a column of fire. Their eyes tracked it nervously as it pushed into the atmosphere, no doubt setting off every radar alarm from Moscow to Washington. When the missile was nothing but a bright speck in the dark blue morning sky, it exploded with a blinding flash. Bonnie threw up an arm to shield her eyes. After the flash came a huge bright orange ball of fire surrounded by a halo of spiky gray cloud.

Bonnie had just started to worry that they wouldn't know when the EMP had reached them or whether it had worked when Reiner's radio, in the pack at their feet, threw a geyser of sparks. The town's power lines exploded. Every light at the bioweapon factory on the opposite hill went out. And Nathan's body relaxed in the middle of a seizure.

"Did it work?" He croaked.

"I would say so," Petter replied, frowning at the ruined lump of metal that had been Reiner's radio.

They sat there in the wheat and watched as the firework display they had created died down and the sun broke over the horizon, highlighting a comfortingly normal criss-cross of passenger jet contrails and scattered high altitude clouds. Bonnie took a deep breath and allowed herself to think that it might really be over.

After a while, they realized that they still had work to do if they wanted to go home. Nathan went into town to look for any means of transportation not fried by the EMP, which pretty much limited them to bicycles and horses. Petter and Yuri began to collect the bodies of the victims for cremation, and Bonnie went back to the lab on the hill. She needed disinfectant. A lot of it.

Remembering what had happened to Reiner, she nearly jumped out of her skin when the gate creaked, but none of the bodies littering the lawn moved. She picked her way carefully through them, eyes down, heart hammering. She didn't see the one sitting on the steps until she was almost on top of it. When it raised its head, she let out a screech, tripped over a corpse, and landed on her ass. Then she saw its face.

"Reiner!" Bonnie shouted. She scrambled up and threw herself at him in an awkward, space-suited hug. She'd never been so happy to see another person. "How did you survive?"

"I remember what you are saying to Ian, *unt* lie still underneath them. Eventually they are going dormant, and after the explosion, they die."

There was something in his voice that made Bonnie uneasy. He sounded...gloomy. "This is good, right? We won."

Reiner gave her a bleak look through his faceplate. "One of the bodies, she has this in her hand."

Reiner handed her a crumpled, bloodstained sheet of computer paper. On it were thirty names and addresses, many of them in Russia but some in Europe, America, and other parts of the world. The first name on the list was Robert MacLeod, 12 Shepherd's Lane, Kirriemuir DD8 5CY, Scotland. Two thirds of the names, including MacLeod's, had lines drawn through them.

"Oh, shit," Bonnie breathed. Her knees went out from underneath her and she thumped down onto the step next to Reiner. "It's a hit list."

"They send not one fuck-you but twenty," Reiner said.

"And we just knocked out every telephone, radio, and car engine within four hundred miles," Bonnie finished.

She gazed sightlessly toward the horizon as the horror crawled up her spine. It wasn't over. It was just beginning. A black dot traced a white line in the blue as it arced skyward. She blinked, finally recognizing the criss-crossing contrails for what they were. Not passenger jets, but missiles.

The Tide Turns

Lisha Goldberg

Editor: Mankind can enter the low pressure of space in ships and suits.
Why can't enemies we've destroyed for time immemorial do the same?

Tampa Bay Beach Beacon
Wednesday, June 1
Weekly newspaper serving greater St. Petersburg, Florida
PASS-A-GRILLE BEACH—On Sunday afternoon, one dozen tiny vehicles rolled out of the waves at Pass-a-Grille Beach. Surprised bathers described the vehicles as "silvery and fish-shaped."

Snack Shack manager Sam Freed said, "There's never been anything like this They were seven or eight inches long and had floppy tails. I couldn't tell if they had wheels, but they sure could move."

Mary Moyer, a frequent visitor to Pass-a-Grille, noted that the vehicles delighted onlookers, especially children. "The kids had a blast chasing them up and down the shoreline. Nobody came close to catching one."

Police officer James Greis believed students at nearby Eckerd College developed the cars as a prank. "No crime was committed, nobody was hurt, so there's no need to pursue this."

Eckerd College denied any knowledge of the fish-shaped mechanisms.

Sarasota Herald Tribune
Monday, June 6
Daily newspaper serving the communities of western Florida
VENICE BEACH—Scores of tiny, unidentified vehicles appeared in the waves near the shoreline. "They darted around swimmers for maybe fifteen minutes," said lifeguard Steve Rayburn. "Then about fifty of them came ashore."

Shoreline fisherman Aaron McNulty caught one of the vehicles with his bait bucket. "I swear I saw a pair of eyes inside that (expletive deleted) fish car," McNulty said. "Then the little (expletive deleted) leapt right out of my bucket and headed for the waves. As soon as that happened, the rest of those little (expletives deleted) followed."

"We don't know who's behind this," said police officer Harold

LeBlanc, "but we believe this is a harmless prank."

Go to the Herald's website to see videos of the fish-shaped vehicles.

Tampa Bay Times
Monday, June 13
Florida's largest daily newspaper

ST. PETE'S BEACH—Stunned beachgoers watched "an army" of alien vehicles emerge from the ocean and drive across the shoreline. Two people went to Palms of Pasadena Hospital for burns they received when they touched a vehicle. Police are investigating whether this was a deliberate attack or an accident.

Peter O'Hare, an eyewitness to both this and the Pass-a-Grille encounter, says that this time things were decidedly different. "These vehicles looked much bigger, about two feet long. They were shaped more like snakes than fish, and they were silver with brown splotches."

Beachgoer Annie Spade explained how one woman became injured: "She was bending down to pick up a shell when one of those things zoomed out of the water and ran over her bare foot. She didn't say anything at first. Then she started to scream."

An unnamed police source admitted, "This one is a puzzle."

Visit the Times's website for videos and more eyewitness reports.

Tampa Bay Times
Wednesday, June 15

MADEIRA BEACH—Neither police nor scientists can explain the dozens of large vehicles that seemingly exploded out of the bay and rained down on the boardwalk of John's Pass, a popular fishing village. Marina director Tom Franks described the vehicles as "gray and white, dolphin-sized, and having blowholes on the top."

Rose Smith, on vacation from Toronto, described how one vehicle snatched a hot grouper sandwich from her hands. "I saw lots of silver teeth, and I felt a wet, smooth tongue on my arm. Then I saw these eyes. These black eyes that laughed at me from inside a metal suit."

No one reported any injuries, but damages are estimated to run into the tens of thousands of dollars. Shopkeepers complained of broken windows, damaged merchandise, and gouged floors. Restaurant owners experienced the highest losses.

"They forced their way into our freezer," complained Fresh Catch manager Daryl Hopkins. "They used these retractable gizmos to clean out our whole stock. Plus, we have to close down and sterilize everything. Who's going to pay for all this?"

Go to the Times's website to see video coverage.

Tampa Bay Times
Thursday, June 16
MADEIRA BEACH—Three police divers are missing, presumed dead. The divers disappeared while investigating the waters off John's Pass. The popular tourist destination remains closed while police and scientists continue to inspect the scene.

Tampa Bay Times
Saturday, June 18
Headline: No More
 St. Pete Police received a text from a phone belonging to a police diver who disappeared at John's Pass. The message read, "No more."
 Police do not know who sent this message, nor do they know what it means. An unnamed source confirmed that police have sent a reply to the text, but no details were provided.

The Boston Globe
Monday, June 27
Headline: We Are Under Attack!
 What started out as a peaceful day ended up as a nightmare for hundreds of visitors to The New England Aquarium. Untold numbers of fish-shaped vehicles destroyed the Aquarium and sent about eighty people to area hospitals. Injuries included burns, bites, abrasions, and broken bones.
 While touring the ruins, Boston's mayor confirmed, "They caught us completely off guard. We've been monitoring the events in Florida, but we never imagined anything like this happening here. Unfortunately, it did. And we got it worse."
 An Aquarium spokeswoman provided details about the assault. "They leapt right out of the Harbor and went to work shattering every tank. They ate a number of our residents, and kidnapped the rest. They ranged in size and shape from about five inches to ten feet. The larger ones resembled sharks and dolphins. They seemed more interested in damaging exhibits than attacking tourists. I think most people got hurt because of sheer panic. Emergency exits are difficult to find in the Aquarium's low-level lighting."
 In the midst of the chaos, Carol English, here on a day trip from Rhode Island, had a surreal experience. "A squid snatched my purse. And if that's not weird enough, now my car is missing."
 Boston police confirmed that an Aquarium guard captured one fish vehicle. The vehicle is now being held at a secure, undisclosed location. No other details are available.

After destroying the Aquarium, the fish vehicles returned to Boston Harbor.

The Boston Globe
Thursday, June 30
Headline: Logan Airport Under Siege

Days after the Aquarium attack, armies of crustacean-shaped vehicles scrabbled across Logan Airport runways. Nearly seventy people were taken to area hospitals for treatment. Most were diners who were injured when dozens of shrimp, scallop, and snail-shaped vehicles obliterated the Legal Seafoods Restaurant in Terminal B. A host of crabs punctured tires on fifteen jet airliners parked on the tarmac.

Subhead: McCartney Loses Famous Bass
LOGAN AIRPORT—Dozens of lobster vehicles chased Sir Paul McCartney and his bandmates as the group headed toward a private jet at the far end of Terminal A. McCartney's party tossed away their personal possessions and raced inside their aircraft.

The lobster vehicles allowed the plane to take off safely; however, they went to war with each other over the possessions left on the tarmac. When the fight subsided, the victors carried off the spoils including, unfortunately, McCartney's Hofner bass. Sir Paul used this guitar throughout his Beatle days to record such hits as "I Want to Hold Your Hand" and "Let It Be."

It's unclear at this time whether the lobsters knew the musician's identity. In a statement to the press, McCartney said that he is "saddened and stunned," but he plans to continue the rest of his tour as scheduled. The musician wishes a speedy recovery to all those injured at Logan and elsewhere.

Reverse 911 Telephone Call
Friday, July 6
Greater Boston Area

"This is the Boston police. If you live within two miles of Boston Harbor, we recommend that you find other accommodations further from the water. All public waterfront properties are closed until further notice. No boating activities are allowed on the Harbor or the Charles River. Anyone caught violating this closure will be arrested. The following public transportation systems are closed indefinitely: Logan Airport, Amtrak trains, commuter boats, and commuter rail. The blue, silver, and red subway lines are closed. The orange and green lines are operating on a Sunday schedule."

CNN Television News
Saturday, July 9

"Scientists still have no explanation for the worldwide onslaught that originated from Earth's oceans. What started as a few tiny vehicles at a Florida beach has now spread to every corner of the globe. Marine-related industries such as public aquariums, fish restaurants, and marinas are subject to the most attacks. Secondary sites include manufacturing plants and science buildings at universities.

"New and more horrifying assaults are taking place in Asia. Groups of seven to ten whale-sized vehicles are singling out corporate executives, chasing them down city streets, and eventually crushing them. There are also reports of whale excrement erupting out of sewers."

Fox Television News
Monday, July 11

"CNN is no more. After yesterday's horrific attack on CNN headquarters in Atlanta and other sites in New York and Chicago, the surviving CNN journalists have either gone into hiding or announced intentions to join other news stations.

"Scientists believe that the attack was inspired by a CNN editorial suggesting that we drain the world's oceans. Minutes after this report aired, eel-shaped vehicles poured into CNN's buildings and altered the electrical current. It is unknown at this time just how many individuals lost their lives from electrocutions and fires.

"In addition to monitoring our broadcasts, marine life is sending out text messages through stolen cell phones. Scientists, police, and communication specialists are trying to interpret messages that read, 'No more,' 'Stop,' 'Fix it,' and most disturbing, 'Ha ha.'"

The Boston Globe
Tuesday, July 12

Headline: Goodbye and Thank You

This is the final print edition of *The Boston Globe*. We have evacuated our headquarters and will continue to report as long as we can via the Internet. Because the world's monetary systems have collapsed, we will no longer charge for subscriptions.

Thank you to all our loyal readers who have kept us in business since 1872.

Good luck to us all.

Fox Television News
Friday, September 30

"Three months after a fish vehicle was captured at the Boston Aquarium, scientists have successfully opened it.

"Inside, scientists found the remains of one flounder, most likely dead from starvation. The flounder was floating in salt water.

"Here now are the first images inside a fish vehicle. You are looking at tiny levers and buttons designed specifically for this vehicle's operator. This counteracts recent theories that the vehicles ran by remote control. This also tells us that everything we thought we knew about marine intelligence is completely wrong.

"What you're now seeing is a photograph that was not created by humans. The photo was attached to an area just over the flounder's head. The image shows the Great Pacific Garbage Patch. This undersea area acts like a massive tornado comprising plastics, chemicals, and other human debris.

"Does the photo represent a rallying point for the assailants? Or is it something innocuous, perhaps a reminder of home?

"All this brings up more questions than answers. First and foremost is this: What's next?"

And I Will Sing a Lullaby

Trevor James Zaple

Editor: The apocalypse may not matter excepting that it crystalizes action from those emotions to which we dare not give voice. It seems too high a price to pay for those without the mental fortitude to make decisions.

"He's only five minutes late. He said he'd be here."
Charlie watched the sky lighten so subtly that it might not have happened at all. The skyline of downtown stood black and imposing against it, lit faintly here and there by the always-on fluorescents on certain floors. At quarter to five in the morning, the slumber of the skyscrapers seemed imposing; they were like sentinels, keeping a grave watch upon the world, the line of their gaze hidden in the shroud of the early morning.

"He's not here, though," he said. He kept his eyes on the sky, in part to avoid looking at Lisa's face as he made his decision. "He's not here and we're already five minutes behind schedule. We can't spare any more time to wait for him."

"He'll be here."

He forced himself to look at her. She had taken a seat on the bench and was staring down the path from which they'd exited the grove. Her hair was dishevelled and her shoulders were slumped.

What time did she even get to sleep last night? He tried to remember when he'd heard her coming in the door. Even in this crisis she caroused, and Charlie couldn't understand it. Under the oppressive threat of looming annihilation, a rousing celebration was the last thing on his mind. Had she returned before the bars closed, or after? It had been a close thing either way. Had he fallen back asleep before the phone had begun its insistent ringing? The entire period between hearing Lisa come stumbling in the door and talking to Jason over a crackling, quiet connection was a foggy blur.

He took the backpack off his shoulders and rooted around in it. He came out with a wide-backed hairbrush and poked Lisa in the shoulder with it. She jumped, and turned her head angrily. When she saw the hairbrush she sighed, and took it from him.

"Thanks," she muttered, and ran it through her gently curled black hair with long, slow strokes.

Charlie returned to watching the sky. The sun was somewhere out there, its rays warming some unseen part of the horizon and adding more light to contrast against the starry black monoliths that towered against the sky. He pulled out his phone and thumbed it on. It was now only a few minutes before five. The early shift waking up to watch the first news broadcasts would know, very soon. The insomniacs on the Internet would know already, of course, but Charlie hadn't seen anyone on the trail from their apartment complex in Washington Heights into the park at the edge of the city limits. If anyone else had gotten a jump ahead of the crowds, they had stayed well-hidden.

He thumbed his phone on again, stared at the time. When had the phone woken him out of his dozing stupor? He wracked his brain, trying to remember, and cursed Jason for not calling his cell phone. He cursed Lisa for insisting on keeping the land line, and cursed himself for giving in to her arguments about keeping a physical line open in case of emergencies. He stared daggers at the back of her head and then made himself breathe evenly. *Maybe she had the right idea*, he told himself. *Maybe Jason wouldn't have done what he had done if it was just our cell phones. Some kind of detection algorithm, or a scrambler that blocks connections to cell signals. Who knows what they have there?*

They didn't have much time, regardless of the exact moment that Jason had called. There were still quite a few miles to go until Charlie felt they'd be in the realm of safety. *Over the river and through the woods and let's hope the wind is blowing in any direction but ours.*

"Lisa, how drunk was Todd when you called him?"

There was a silence, followed eventually by "what does that matter?"

"It matters because he might have just brushed it off. He might have thought we were trying to pull a prank on him."

"He said he'd be here."

Charlie rubbed at the bridge of his nose.

"Sure," he said, "he said he'd be here, but he's not. He's now, god, ten minutes late? Fifteen almost? What do you suppose is keeping him?"

"You're such a shit, Charlie," she said, and each word was a crack from a .44 Magnum. "Don't talk about Todd like that. You're just jealous that I'm waiting for him and I wouldn't wait for you."

Charlie bit back a reply that would have just deepened the argument. He watched nervously as his phone went from 5:01 a.m. to 5:02 a.m.

"Look, let's save the you-and-me bullshit for later. *Much* later. We need to move."

"We're not moving anywhere until Todd gets here."

"FUCK TODD!" he screamed. The entirety of the phrase frightened him badly: the way he suddenly lost control, the volume of the words, the invective he poured into the word "fuck," the way it echoed off the trees and seemed to come back at them, ragged and ghostly. He put a shaking palm to his forehead and came away with a slick of sweat on his skin.

Lisa got off the bench and walked away from him, back down the path that they'd come from.

"Where are you going?" he asked sullenly. When she didn't respond, he gestured at her with exasperation and walked away in the opposite direction.

You've wasted enough time waiting around for her he told himself firmly. *Too many years of your life. Time to cut your losses and live.* He marched through the park, keeping his eyes firmly on the line of trees on the other side. As he neared them, the sound of the river grew louder; eventually it drowned out his thoughts and brought a sort of natural zen into his head. The bank of the river itself was only a few yards into the trees at the edge of the park. He stopped at the water's edge and stared into the dangerously quick flow. To him it remained a largely unknowable black force in the early morning dimness.

Unbidden, the thought of Lisa's hair on his pillow, curled and springy jumped to his mind. The dusky scent of her perfume, the way her neck curved back to accept his lips upon her throat, her shoulders, her chest, all taunted him. The indescribable feeling of her body spooning into his as they slept ached through him. The memories stoked the magnetic fields of his heart, or the electrical impulses of his soul.

Was it his soul?

Was Lisa entangled with his soul?

He stared at the water. It gave no answers except the meaningless gurgle of its black flow.

"Fuck Todd," he muttered.

He turned around and headed back for the park.

She was back on the bench, curled up, sobbing softly. He took a seat at one end of the bench, near her feet.

"I am jealous of Todd," he said, hunching forward to stare at the grass. "I'm jealous because I let our relationship deteriorate without bothering to do a damn thing about it. I'm jealous because he shows you passion and acceptance when I showed you indifference. I'm jealous because here, at the end of all things, you're curled up on a bench waiting for him, and not me."

Lisa sat up and wiped at her eyes. "I didn't make it far. I got into the woods and realized that if Todd did show up, there wouldn't be anyone waiting there for him."

"Too true."

"I don't think he's showing up, though."

"Well, he's nearly a half hour late now. If he was going to come, he would have been here already. If he's on his way...well, it'll be a fight to get anywhere in the city this morning."

"What if your brother was wrong, Charlie? What if...I don't know, what if you heard him wrong?"

"I don't think so," he said, closing his eyes. He could vividly recall the panic in Jason's voice, the way his words tumbled over themselves in a rush to get everything out. *Nuclear containment—Zero forward contagion vector—Minimize losses.* Jason was usually so calm. So serene.

"I guess he would know," she said. "What do you think they're doing right now?"

"Probably gathering into some bunker across the Potomac, the bastards. The butchers." He spat into the grass, and realized that he could see it fairly clearly now. The sun was on its way up. "I'm sure they'll let staff in, so he should be fine. Otherwise..." He stared up at the sky, growing golden with the dawn. "I hope it's quick, and painless."

They sat in silence, and eventually Lisa moved herself directly next to him on the bench. He put his arm around her and together they watched the light slowly stretch itself across the sky.

"We should go, I guess," she said after a few minutes.

"It's probably too late anyway," he said casually. His sleeplessness was creeping over him again, and now the last thing he wanted to do was to get up off the bench.

From somewhere in the city a fusillade of sirens erupted, followed closely by an answering cry of dozens of car horns honking insistently.

"It begins," Charlie said.

Wiping her eyes, Lisa got up off the bench and extended her hand to him. "Let's go," she said.

He hesitated a moment but accepted her help up.

They made their way in silence toward the woods and the river. As they approached the riverbank Lisa's hand found its way into Charlie's. They watched the river flow, and Charlie felt as though he'd somehow come to be in some folk tale of the Black Forest, set down centuries before. *We're children lost in the forest, with an unimaginable force of evil bearing down on us that we can't see.*

He said, "Do you think—"

The river and the woods around it lit up luridly, as though the noon sun had appeared directly behind them. Every leaf, every rock in the water, every blade of grass was thrown into sharp relief by a harsh, all-encompassing white light. They both instinctively covered their eyes. Charlie screamed on reflex.

The rumble that followed swallowed his screams. The bass roar seemed as though a god had awoken and exhaled its morning breath over the world. The seismic response followed, shaking their feet and causing the water of the river to splash upward in protest. Finally came the shockwave of air, dissipated somewhat by the distance between the river and the city itself, but still powerful enough to knock the pair off their feet and into the powerful flow of the disturbed river.

"Charlie!" Lisa screamed. Charlie splashed around wildly, trying to find her hand in the churn of the current. Water went into his eyes, his nose, down his throat. His entire world became the river, and he struggled mightily to make it to one side, to find the earth and to dig his fingers into it and to never let go.

Instead, he found a hand, grasping at his own hand with fevered strength. He shook his head, trying to get the water out of his eyes. He saw an outline of a human being with curly black hair, one hand grabbing onto a bush growing out of the river bank and one hand straining white-knuckled in an effort to hang onto him.

"Don't let go," Lisa yelled. "I can get us up, just don't let go."

Charlie looked at her, and looked at the bush. *She'll never be able to pull us both up*, he thought. *We're done for.* He looked at her hand, going white in the effort to hold onto him. *"Don't let go," she says. Well, isn't that my problem? Isn't that why I'm here?*

He began to wriggle his hand beneath her pincer grip.

"What are you doing?" she shouted. Charlie continued to wriggle his hand.

"What I should have done a while ago," he shouted back avoiding the river's desperate attempt to fill his mouth. "Get up on the bank. Head away. Avoid roads. Find shelter. Don't trust anyone," he managed to blurt out.

He could feel her desperation to pull him back to her. Part of him revelled in that black thought. But he severed their connection by twisting his wrist upward. Her fingers wrenched open and his hand was free. The river current swept him away downstream, and his last sight was of her springy black hair, framed in the golden light of dawn. As the water sucked him down and the blackness crept over him, he took comfort in the idea that now they were both free. *Let's save the you-and-me-bullshit for later*, he thought, the words struggling to form in his head. *In fact, let's save it for never. Cut our losses and live. Or not. Once there was a way*—but there was no point in finishing the thought. They were free of each other and there was no way back home. *I hope Todd finds you*, he thought, his consciousness fragmenting into a shuddering finality. *I hope you can be happier than*— and then there was nothing, just a lifeless body carried down a swift and unrelenting stream away from a burning city.

On the shore, Lisa watched Charlie wash away. When he was gone, she looked back through the woods as the flickering lights of the newly arisen inferno played through the fractal outline of the trees. She waited for movement, for a familiar figure to emerge from the shifting shadows, but there was nothing. When the breeze picked up, carrying an oppressive heat and a thick, burnt stench, she picked her way down the river, looking for a place to cross over and be free.

The World Is a Vampire

Michael Cummings

Editor: The fuel of rage can blind to the dangers inherent in seeking vengeance.

With the tang of his afternoon tea still fresh on his tongue, Weisband noted his visitor's choice in clothes first. He was a strong believer that the way a man presented himself spoke volumes to his character. The man waiting in his office when he returned from lunch wore a wrinkled shirt tucked into industrial gray pants, coming short of the heavy leather boots that climbed to his knees. He studied an old pocket watch, the chain attached to his double-breasted vest. The clothing spoke of Soviet efficiency, but a quick glance showed the man's letters of welcome were from a western German *bergermeister*. No doubt favors had been exchanged for him to get this hearing. The leather satchel in his hands, worn and fraying in places, spoke of a man used to action with little respect for the halls of government and bureaucracy.

Shrewdly, Weisband concluded that his visitor was a crackpot. In his experience, only the mad or those in need of mental treatment thought they could see the chancellor dressed like they had just stepped off a steamer. Weisband sighed, making no pretense of his disappointment at the intrusion. Entertaining the eccentric was his penance for being a junior member of the chancellor's staff, but he didn't have to enjoy it.

"Thank you for waiting," Weisband said, lips curling in a fake smile. "I trust you were kept comfortable, Mister...?"

"Seward. Doctor Seward," the man said, standing up and stretching a hand out to Weisband. In his other hand he clutched the worn leather bag to his chest.

Weisband took it, shaking lightly. From his own jacket he withdrew a handkerchief, discreetly wiping his palm and fingers clean. Seward arched an eyebrow as he caught the surreptitious action.

"Germs, I'm afraid, are my phobia," Weisband said, tucking the cloth back into his jacket. "We all live with fears, some more real than others. At least my affliction is harmless."

Seward gave a polite laugh. The horrific effects of the fear bombs of the 40s and 50s were still felt in parts of Central Europe. Odd eccentricities were to be expected the farther into the continent you traveled.

"I understand the Soviets have made some progress on gene replacement therapy in the Baltics," Seward offered. "If you are interested, I might have some contacts that could be of service."

Weisband inclined his head. "That's very kind of you, but I doubt you traveled all the way to Budapest to console me."

"As you say," Dr. Seward said. He took a deep breath, like a man preparing to give a great speech. "If I could have a few moments of the chancellor's time, I have something that will be of interest to the future of the republic."

"And you feel you, a humble doctor," he said, biting the last word out like it was a curse, "have something that the chancellor will find useful?"

Seward puffed up his chest. "I think it's something that will propel him to the head of the Reichstag."

Weisband considered letting this madman through. If Chancellor Hendrix was elevated to the Reichstag, it would leave an opening that Weisband was only too ready to fill. But that was not how protocol worked. "Alas, Chancellor Hendrix is kept busy. If you could leave any papers you brought, I will review them."

Seward bit his lip. "That won't work. Perhaps if I could discuss them with you, I might convince you? And then you would go to the chancellor?"

Weisband groaned. Protocol said he didn't have to offer his time. If asked for it, though, he couldn't refuse.

"We can use the Habsburg room. It's old, but should suit our needs. And what are we talking about today?" he asked, leading Seward into the main concourse.

"I have a means of securing the Republic's economic relationship with the Nippon Empire. They will be so beholden, they will have no choice but to take a side in the Cold War."

Weisband missed a step as he walked. He had heard this sales pitch before, but something about the doctor's sincere tone caught him by surprise.

"And how will we do that?" he asked drolly.

"By eliminating the *kaiju* threat for them."

* * *

The chancellor of the fourth republic was a study in contrasts. On weekends, away from the offices and corridors of power, Hendrix spent his time with his wife and their grandchildren. For two days at a time there was only the sound of laughter, the smell of fresh baked breads, and a hearty hearth to settle beside into the night.

When he returned to the city each Monday, he would don his charcoal gray suit and stony face. The task of running a multinational government fell on his shoulders alone.

He stared at Weisband, eyes dull as he sipped his morning *kaffe*. He set the cup down on its saucer, his gaze never wavering.

"You understand it is your duty to act as a deterrent to these people," he said after a long silence. Weisband opened his mouth to respond, then closed it. "If I took the time to listen to every insane petitioner that managed to lie, cheat, and bribe their way into our offices, I would never get any work done. He didn't bribe you, did he? Offer you something you wanted? Money, or a woman perhaps?"

"Of course not," Weisband said hotly, offended. "I have done everything within my powers to dissuade this Dr. Seward from aggravating you."

Chancellor Hendrix eyed his cup, but didn't pick it up again. His morning *kaffe* was a ritual, a sacred time that should have been immune to interruptions. Even the most junior of staff members knew to wait until he had settled in for the day. He glanced at Weisband, noting the thin sheen of nervous sweat on the man's brow as the junior obsessively wrung his hands.

"What did he say to make you let your guard down?"

"He claims to have a means of bringing the Nipponese to our aid. Beholden, even, to quote him."

"Fine," Hendrix said, though it was clear from his tone it wasn't. "I will give him five minutes. Then we must really get back to these reports on the Soviets. I hear they want to build another of their damnable nuclear power plants."

"Another?" Weisband asked, shuffling around the desk to help the chancellor collect his papers.

"This one near the Red Forest. What do they need so much power for, I wonder?"

Weisband followed in the chancellor's wake, a step and a half behind. "Isn't there an amusement park there? Pripyat?"

"You might be right. Find out for me. Also get me the latest figures on *kaiju* attacks. Might as well have numbers as ammunition to argue with this lunatic."

"Of course," Weisband said. He hurried ahead of the chancellor, opening the doors to the Habsburg room.

A large, ornate table filled most of the space. To Weisband's knowledge, the great family had never used the room, the name coming later in memorial of the early casualties in the fear bombings between the Soviets and the Germanic nations of the Republic.

The chancellor sat down across the table, waving a hand in recognition of Dr. Seward.

"You have something to share?" he asked abruptly, shuffling through the stack of papers he had brought with him.

"Y-Y-Yes," Seward said, stuttering. Weisband hid a small smile of satisfaction. The doctor was all bluster until faced with real power.

Seward slid a small portfolio across the table, then folded his hands together. Hendrix arched an eyebrow, glancing up. "What is this?"

"Blood toxicology reports."

"Of *kaiju*?" Hendrix asked with interest. Research into the giants had dwindled when the resources needed to defend and recover had reduced below the cost of research itself.

"Of vampires."

Weisband closed his eyes, listening to the thrumming of his heart. He could feel his career slipping away with each word this man spoke.

"Is this some kind of joke? Weisband?" Hendrix demanded, turning his attention on his adjunct.

"I'm sorry," Weisband said, fingering the silent alarm beneath the table's lip. "He never said anything about this in the pre-interview. Had I known, I would never have let him in."

"Let me explain," Seward said, rising up from his chair. Security guards burst into the room, stunners at the ready. They looked from Seward to the chancellor, then back. Stunners raised, they circled around the table, their aim never wavering.

"You can stop the *kaiju*!" Seward cried out as the guards grabbed him by the shoulders, dragging him toward the door. "The Nipponese will be indebted to you."

"Indebted?" Hendrix said, his interest piqued. The guards hesitated, watching the chancellor for direction. Weisband understood the chancellor's hesitation. To have the Nipponese indebted meant having an ally on the other side of the Soviets. With only the Chinese wastelands between the steppes of the Kremlin and the Empire of the Rising Sun, it could mean an end to the Cold War once and for all. Hendrix made a motion with one hand. The two guards exchanged a glance, releasing Seward before taking a step back. Weisband caught one of the guards fingering the stunner still at his side and gave him a slight nod. Best not to leave too much to chance.

"How?" Hendrix asked.

"If I may?" Seward said, nodding at his satchel on the table.

"Get him his case," Weisband ordered the guards. They retrieved and handed over the leather case. Seward grabbed it and rummaged through it, ignoring the menacing look the nearest guard gave him.

"I have in here something," Steward said, stalling, "that will make up your minds for you." He let out an excited gasp, retrieving a glass vial out and holding it up. The guards tensed, their stunners raised again.

"What is it?" Hendrix asked, oblivious of the threat.

Seward handed over the vial, eyes shining. "Suspended in that glass is the pathogen responsible for turning perfectly normal people into vampires."

"Are you insane?" Weisband hissed, taking a step back. He raised a handkerchief, covering his mouth. The chancellor eyed the vial skeptically.

"It's perfectly inert at the moment," Seward assured him.

"And when it's active?"

"There's enough there to turn an entire population into blood-sucking, sun-fearing vampires."

"Or one *kaiju*," Hendrix said, guessing at Seward's bold plan.

"Or one *kaiju*."

"Why have we not heard of this breakthrough before? While we may have no interest in the *kaiju* epidemic of the Pacific, the threat of rampant vampirism has always been a part of our agenda."

"I felt some discretion was the best course. My neighbors wouldn't take kindly to knowing that the foreigner next door was also capable of destroying their entire village."

"You've approached no one else about this?" the chancellor asked.

"Actually," Seward admitted, a bead of sweat appearing on his brow, "I did."

"Who?"

"The Canadians. Then the Americans."

"They laughed at you, no doubt?"

Seward nodded, face red.

"Because the *kaiju* threat isn't big enough to endanger them. They see maybe one or two attacks a season, and never anything as large as mainland China before its collapse." Hendrix turned to his adjunct. "You ever wonder about that, Weisband?"

"Sir?" Weisband stood still, staring at the vial. Inert or not, it gave him chills thinking how close he was to the substance. His palms itched, his knuckles aching to move his fingers, to sterilize himself and the room. Just being in the presence of the vial he could feel hot chills running down his spine.

"Why do certain size *kaiju* never cross the Pacific to the Americas?" Hendrix droned on, oblivious. "Is it something in the waters? And what were the Chinese doing in '78 that caused the *kaiju* to swarm so far inland that only the Great Wall stopped them?"

"Before my time, sir," Weisband said, slipping a sanitation wipe out of his pocket and rubbing absently at his fingers and palms.

"What about you, Doctor?"

Seward shook his head. "My expertise has been in vampires, Chancellor."

"Well," Hendrix said, handing the vial back with care. "Your idea certainly has tenacity. But why come to us? Why give us this advantage?"

Seward shrugged. "How do you mean?"

"I believe the chancellor is trying to ask what you want in return," Weisband piped up, still wiping at his hands. The deadly virus mocked him, sloshing against the glass walls. Like a few millimeters of hardened glass could hold back a plague. Vampirism might not be as contagious as influenza or polio, but the results were no less mortal. Weisband breathed a sigh of relief as the vial was placed in the cushion of its carrying case and sealed away.

"Vengeance, of course," Seward said.

"Vengeance?"

"My wife," Seward said, the words catching in his throat. "My wife and child were on travel through the Indochina Sea when the *Kaiju Surge* happened."

"I'm sorry for your loss," Hendrix offered, but Seward shook his head.

"That was many, many years ago. I swore to put an end to it, by any means possible. My family," he hesitated again. "My family has a history fighting against the vampire plague. Long before the Great War, we were traveling here and abroad to combat the spread of the plague. When tragedy befell me, it only made sense to combat my own tragic grief with the object of the family tragedy."

"Then let us put an end to tragedy," Chancellor Hendrix said. Weisband watched the two men shake hands, his stomach turning in knots with a terrible foreboding.

* * *

The Emperor of Nippon proved as naive as his former chancellor, now reichchancellor. Weisband stood on the bridge of the airship *von Schleicher*, Doctor Seward at his side. From the observation deck of the dirigible, they could see across the choppy gray waters to where the giant, scaly *kaiju* made its way. Weisband had never paid attention to the classification of the beasts, though the mission report had identified this one as being more temperamental than most.

Seward stood beside him, knuckles white as he leaned over the railing in anticipation, watching the small Nipponese plane thread its way to the monster. Weisband held small, one-man planes in distaste. He preferred a sturdy dirigible, the platform firm and broad beneath your feet. But, he had to admit, the *Tenzan* was a lithe machine for delivering the payload.

"A shame Hendrix couldn't be here to enjoy this moment," Seward said, still raptly watching the *kaiju* approach.

"A shame," Weisband agreed. And a price for promotion, he mused. Seward's plan had propelled both his and the former chancellor's careers up the ladder, but at a terrible price. Now Weisband was required to travel to this remote ocean nation to watch a giant fall. Without even being conscious of it, he slipped a hand into his pocket and squeezed a tube of antibacterial gel into his palm. Traveling meant new experiences, new pathogens to be exposed to. He rubbed the gel between his palms vigorously.

"This better work," he said out loud, his voice low so that only Seward could hear him. If Seward was intimidated, he didn't let it show.

"It will work."

There were no speeches today, only the spectacle. Weisband squinted, watching the plane dwindle until it was almost impossible to spot in front of the behemoth. There was a moment where he thought he saw something drop, and then the plane was looping back toward them.

The *kaiju* didn't take the interference well. With frightening speed an arm shot out, shattering the small bomber in a small puff of fire and smoke. It followed that with a roar that Weisband could feel in the soles of his feet as the deck plating vibrated beneath him.

"You," Weisband called to a porter nearby. "How fast can we get this ship out of range of that thing?"

"There's nothing to fear, Undersecretary," the man reassured him. "The captain can change the course of the *von Schleicher* at a moment's notice. Our top speed may not be comfortable, but it will put enough distance between us and the monster to keep you safe."

"I see," Weisband said, though he didn't feel the least comforted. His companion continued to stare on, a pair of binoculars raised to his eyes. "You will give us warning before making such a course change? I'd hate for my companion to fall," he said.

"There," Seward suddenly interrupted, pointing.

Weisband squinted. "I see nothing."

"Here." Seward handed over his binoculars. Weisband hesitated for a moment, staring at the eyepieces. Were the eyes any less a source of germs? "Hurry," Seward prompted, lifting the glasses to Weisband's face.

Resigned, Weisband adjusted the lenses, not sure what he was expected to see. And then he saw it.

The flesh of the *kaiju* was transforming, metamorphosing. The infection spread like a wave of gray paint over the creature. The flesh died as fast as the vampirism hit it. In the full light of day, the cells burst and burned as fast as they converted.

The *kaiju* stood still for a moment, balanced between life and death. And then it exploded in a cloud of dead flesh. The blood drained in falls of crimson. Huge sections of the beast fell to the water forming small tidal waves. There would be damage on shore, but no one would care.

The *kaiju* had not only been stopped but destroyed for all time to come.

* * *

Seward's promise had come true. The *kaiju* threat seemed to be under control at last, and in exchange Nippon had entered into trade and securities agreements that would forever lock the Soviets out as a world player. Weisband should have been elated, reeling in his rise to power.

Instead, he stood in his now spacious offices in Vienna, listening to the late-night bells ring through the city. It would be midnight before he could return home, but he had no intention of leaving his home in the Vienna Woods for days. The affairs of the world could proceed without him just this once.

"Undersecretary Weisband?" He recognized the fear in the voice of his long-time assistant, Meyer. The woman would never make it in politics if she didn't learn to be more assertive.

"What is it?" he asked without turning. He wanted to take in this reminder of the city at rest, without interruptions or petty paperwork. Budapest, the place of his work, was a lovely city, but in these moments before sunset he felt God himself had dipped low and painted Vienna in the dying light as a testament to the German people.

"It's the news, Undersecretary. You are going to want to turn it on."

Weisband grunted, waving a hand absently at the wall screen controls. The screen snapped into focus, and a wall of fire projected into his office.

All thoughts of his beautiful city abandoned him as he stared at the televised fires. Knees weak, Weisband sat down at his desk.

"How?" he asked.

"*Kaiju*," she said. She clutched a portfolio of overflowing papers to her chest.

"The *kaiju*?" he asked, absently dabbing at the antibacterial hand sanitizer he kept out. Meyer waited for him to complete his ritual before handing over the papers.

"Standard interception. A *kaiju* was spotted headed towards the northern coast of the Korea province."

Weisband flipped through the pictures, absorbing the graphic photographs.

"What happened?"

"A bad storm hit the area while the planes were in the air, delaying delivery."

"And?"

"The delivery was delayed, sir," Meyer repeated as if that said it all.

Weisband frowned. "They delivered after sunset? What kind of fools are they?"

"No," Meyer said. "But the storm blocked what little light there was. The *kaiju* survived."

"Survived." The word hung in the air, filling his mouth. "Aren't there protocols for this? Backup UV light arrays?"

Meyer shook her head. "There was an accident."

"How many accidents can there be?"

"Enough," she said, laying down the next set of photographs. These lacked the polish of the military assessment photographs. They were grainy, and blurry, but they were clear enough. An infected *kaiju*, its skin gray with vampirism, sunk its teeth into a healthy...*kaiju*.

"Tell me there's an end to this nightmare," Weisband said, his throat tight.

"The emperor has already announced an evacuation."

"Of the palace? I thought you said this was near the Korean coastline?"

"Of the Pacific."

Weisband didn't need projections to understand why. Two *kaiju* were a destructive force. Their bloodlust would only make that worse. He shakily pulled out a bottle of whisky and eyed a glass. He unstoppered the bottle and took a shot straight from the bottle. Any germs on the lip of the bottle would be killed by the alcohol.

Two vampire *kaiju*. They would sow a path of destruction in their hunger, and the only way to stave that hunger would be to feed on other *kaiju*, turning them. Someday, the *kaiju* would be destroyed, but until then they would devastate the world.

"Undersecretary?" Meyer asked. He'd forgotten the woman was still standing there. Rather than turn to her, he slumped back in his chair, tipped the bottle back again, and started to weep.

All News, All Day, All the Time

T. M. Starnes

Editor: Honor. Duty. Love. These are more than just words.
Sometimes they require us to fight and sometimes to die.

*"…All active and reserve personnel are required to contact or report
to their nearest base or military liaison contact regardless of their branch of
service…"*

Daniel Cortez paced in the bedroom staring at the photo of his wife
and their daughter. He remembered the trip to the water park. It had
been before he received the Medal of Honor and two years before his wife
was diagnosed with terminal brain cancer. His blonde hair hadn't thinned
yet, or at least not noticeably. D.J. wore her favorite jeans and the blue
top her mom had given her for Christmas. The one she grew out of as she
blossomed, much too quickly for his liking, into adulthood. He removed
the picture from the frame and set it beside him.

*"…after the President signed the executive order excluding citizens past
the age of sixty and under the age of thirteen from participating in the national
lottery. Social security numbers will be…"*

The television droned on in the living room as D.J. spoke on the
phone to her best friend. The previous year had put the world in a constant
state of anxiety. Daniel was used to it, but D.J. hadn't done so well with the
loss of her mom. Even with his limited understanding of young women
and her adult-like patience with his often-wrong advice, D.J. seemed to
muddle through and keep the family together.

*"…contacted by military personnel, or local authorities, or directly by the
lottery board."*

Daniel looked at his sun-weathered hands and the printout from the
lottery board, the confirmation number in large black font across the top
and instructions beneath. The bunker waited only an hour away and the
escort group would be coming soon. He continued preparing himself for
what was to come.

"Families will be divided. Families will not *be kept together. We all
must make a sacrifice.' the president said earlier today before leaving the White
House with the First Family to await the lottery results at their vacation home.*

The president has excluded himself from the lottery with the hopes his family may be picked."

Daniel cringed at the president's words.

D.J. rambled on in the living room on her mobile phone, probably twirling her long, blonde hair in knots or chewing her nails, a habit her mom had tried in vain to break her of.

He picked up the two books he had selected, put the picture from the frame into one of the books, and set them down on the dresser beside the bed.

The lottery rules were specific; how was he going to be able to live without her?

"...riots continue overseas in London with the smallest number of protective bunkers per country..."

Space was limited, families made sacrifices, they needed the strong to survive. The capable, those willing to adapt, overcome, and prevail against adversity.

"...New York state's eighth completed bunker located in Rochester was destroyed by Christian fundamentalist terrorists in the same manner as West Virginia's..."

Fear, justified fear, not the paranoia of the past or fear of the 'other,' gripped the world now. Martial law had been declared throughout the world as the bunkers were built. Mass hiring for construction and development began on the ten per state colossal bunkers over the last year from the United States. It was one of the largest mass efforts of humanity ever endeavored. Other countries created their own bunker systems and populated them as they deemed fit. Some countries were not as rich and the numbers of bunkers were arbitrary per capita depending on the finances, the ruling class, and the local populace.

"...last month when more recent imaging revealed the thousands of objects approaching Earth were not interstellar debris but individual...there's no other way to describe it...spaceships of various..."

Daniel paced the bedroom floor. Aliens. Aliens! He never thought in his lifetime the world would be approached by aliens. Literally thousands of them on their way.

"...trajectory and speed indicated the path of the ships, previously thought of as a storm of comets, continues on a collision course with Earth and the moon. Judging by the grouping, many of the ships will pass by our planet but thousands..."

He examined his Senior Chief dress uniform. His medal sat on the dressing table. He palmed his eyes. D.J. would never forgive him. He hoped she would but he doubted it. The strong have to help the weak... the less strong...all are the less strong now.

"…like killed the dinosaurs."

The doorbell rang and three hard knocks struck the front door.

"…signals sent to the ships but none…"

"Dad! Someone's at the door!"

He picked up the two books but couldn't leave the room. Tears and guilt were striving to take over.

"…no hostile intent imagined due to no noticeable reduction in speed or course change…"

"Dad! Someone's at the door," she yelled as he heard her get up and go to answer it.

"…possibly empty, possibly expired, perhaps not understanding our communications…"

The front door opened and he heard voices. Seconds later, she rapped on the bedroom door.

"…lottery for each of the ten bunkers per state…"

"Dad? Daddy? There's…soldiers here to see you," she said through the door.

He set the books down for a second, scrubbed at his eyes, took a deep breath, picked up the books and hid them behind his back before opening the door.

D.J. wore her oversized tee-shirt with the latest superhero group from the latest blockbuster movie, jeans, and her sneakers. She was beautiful, with his blonde hair and her mother's height and figure. Thank goodness she had her mother's features. As soon as she saw his face, a look of concern crossed hers.

"…no one accepts blame for the attacks on the Israeli or Iranian bunker systems from either country."

"Daddy? What's wrong?" She took his free hand, just like her mom always did when he heard news of fallen friends.

"I…have to talk to them for a minute, sweetie. You stay in your room, okay?"

She frowned. "Daddy? They're not calling you back to duty, are they? You're retired. You served your time." She squeezed his hand.

He released her hand and pushed her toward her room. "You go to your room now, okay? No listening. Need to know authority only. I'll explain in a few minutes."

"…racial strife in the wake…"

"Daddy?" she stared at him and wiped a tear off his cheek.

So much like her mom it made him smile. "Go on now; I'll be right back."

She did as he asked, reluctantly, as she began biting her nails and twirling her hair.

He made his way to the front door, the TV still too loud.

"...*limited occupancy*..."

He took a deep breath before he opened the door, the helmets and uniform outlines visible through the opaque door. He pulled the confirmation letter out of his pocket. Set the books down on the hall table, put on his military bearing and turned the knob.

"...*two hand-sized personal objects per individual*..."

Both of the soldiers straightened; they must know about his medal. They were young, maybe reservists. The younger was a corporal. A second look at the older and taller, a sergeant, and he corrected himself. That kid had seen war. He had the stare.

"Sir? We're looking for Senior Chief Daniel Cortez," they rattled off his serial number and birthdate; he was just shy of his fiftieth birthday.

"That's me. You need something from me?"

He heard D.J.'s door creak open. He stepped out the front door and partially shut the door behind him. She was headstrong; she got it from him.

"...*no pets*..."

The tall sergeant nodded. "Yes, Senior Chief, we need your authorization number and your confirmation number."

Daniel handed them the slip of paper. They scanned it with a blue scanning gun. Checked the results, double-checked their list, and nodded.

"...*months' worth of instructional visual recordings gathered for the inheritors once the danger has passed and the environment will be habitable once more*..."

"I've...got to...say goodbye first," Daniel said.

"...*leaps and bounds with cryogenics freely distributed among the world's nations for reciprocal technologies and advancements*..."

"Understood." The sergeant glanced at the corporal. "Um...we...he and I...we want to thank you for your service. We heard what you did. The Medal of Honor."

"...*poorer countries and less technologically advanced countries will have fewer bunkers available*..."

Daniel nodded and gave a humble acknowledging smile. "Thanks for your services in this difficult time."

"...*corruption reported among some foreign countries: political or economic elite classes regarded the lottery winners. Thousands mass at the offices of the*..."

He heard the floorboards creak in spite of the TV. "Just to let you know. She's a fighter. She's not going to like me doing this. But I've got to. You understand?"

Both of the soldiers nodded. "We understand, sir. But we are on a schedule."

"Understood. No hurry up and wait for the military anymore."

They nodded.

"*…military personnel are ordered…*"

He opened the door to find D.J. halfway down the hall, twisting her hair with both hands. She had been crying. He motioned for her to come to the door.

"*…arson in the Hollywood hills…*"

"Daddy? You're not going back on active duty are you?"

The soldiers turned respectfully away as he pulled her into his arms and fiercely hugged her.

"No, sweetie, I'm not returning to active duty."

She spoke into his chest. "Then why are the soldiers here?"

"*…parties broke out…*"

"They're escorts."

"Escorts for what?" she asked, then she looked over to her left at the side table. "Why are my books out here?"

"*…religious groups in mass prayer today…*"

"Well, you love Harry Potter and Malala's Yousafzai's autobiography. I thought you might like to read them again."

"*…paramilitary groups lashed out…*"

She pulled away. "Why would I want to read them…" She glanced at the TV. "The lottery?" Her eyes widened. "I won the lottery?"

The two soldiers kept silent.

"You did. These men are here to take you to the bunker in Asheville. You'll—"

She began to pull away but Daniel grabbed her hands.

"*…airstrikes continue in Kaesong, North Korea…*"

"No, Daddy! No! I can't go! I've got to stay here! I can't leave you! Who's going to take care of you! I can't go!" She struggled harder, pulling and tugging.

"I'll be fine." He pulled her close as she began to sob and fight him. "You're thirteen now, sweetie, going on forty. You've won the lottery. Someone in our family has to survive."

"*…last minute trips to the Caribbean…*"

"Daddy, I can't leave you." Her tears soaked his shirt. "You're all I have left."

He kissed the top of her head. "You're all I have left too. That's why your mom would want you to live. And me. You're the strong one. You always have been. Do you realize what sort of gift you've been given?"

"*…supplies unavailable to non-sanctioned bunker construction…*"

She squeezed him as one of the soldiers coughed to indicate they needed to go.

After a few more seconds of crying and denial, Daniel finally drew his military bearing and attitude up from within and handed her the books.

"*...committed suicide on the Senate floor in protest to...*"

"Sweetie, these men have a duty. Now I'm going to give you yours." He made her look him in the eyes. Hers were filled with tears; he imagined a panic-filled sailor under his command and he had to get him back in gear. "You, Daniella Jeannette Cortez, are hereby ordered to live, survive what's about to happen, and help those who survive with you. You are going to protect those who need protecting, save those who need saving, and be an example for others. Do you understand these orders?"

"*...jailed for price gouging.*"

She frowned.

"Do you understand these orders?" He gave her the sternest look he could give, which hardly ever worked with her.

"*...utter and complete destruction of many continents...*"

She hugged the books, glancing at the picture of Malala on the cover of her book, and looked back up at him and nodded.

"Yes, Daddy. I understand." She had that look of determination she gave when she had finally set her mind to something.

"*...human life in the billions...*"

Daniel melted inside but kept his bearing. "Save what's left to save, sweetheart."

She rarely kissed him anymore except in private, but this time she stood on her toes and kissed his cheek.

"I will. Just like you would."

He grinned. "Better than me."

"Not possible." She wiped her eyes.

"*...not an invasion, a crash course...*"

Daniel turned to the soldiers. "I think she's ready to go, gentlemen." The younger one stepped aside. "Right this way, ma'am."

She blushed. "I'm not a ma'am."

He grinned. "Yes, ma'am, I'll try to remember that."

"*...continued efforts to make contact...*"

As the corporal led the way after her final goodbye kiss to her father, the sergeant turned to Daniel.

"Are you going to be all right, Senior Chief?"

"She doesn't have to know, does she?"

"*...armed men attacked and freed...*"

"Negative. We won't tell her." He straightened. "It's an honor to have met you, Senior Chief Cortez."

Daniel nodded. "Same to you. Be safe out there. Good luck to you and your family."

The sergeant jogged to join his squad in their Humvee, and D.J. gave a final wave before Daniel shut the door.

Daniel lasted a full thirty seconds before he broke down as the TV droned on in the living room.

"…Family members transferring their win to other family members must adhere to the following restrictions: ages thirteen to sixty are the only authorized ages. Further, the terminally sick, injured, mentally or physically impaired are also…"

13 Signs of the Coming Apocalypse

Stephanie Vance

Editor: Healthy skepticism is good. Some things didn't exactly happen the way history teaches us.

One day, as Jesus sat at his favorite spot on the Mount of Olives, trying to eat his figs in peace, the disciples who followed him EVERYWHERE came unto him.

"Jesus," they asked, "what shall be the signs of thy second coming, and of the end of the world?"

And Jesus sighed and wondered why these people couldn't figure anything out for themselves. He answered onto them, "Since you ask me that ALL THE TIME, I made a list." He pulled a scroll from his linen tunic and handed it to them. "Just read it and let me finish this fig. The list is in no particular order." As he waved them off, the disciples took the scroll in reverence and awe. And on the scroll was written the following:

Stuff My Dad Told Me about the End of the World

1. The sun shall be darkened, the moon shall not give light, the powers of the heavens shall be shaken, and a company named *Microsoft* shall issue forth a new Windows operating system for the tenth time.
2. The antichrist shall come in the form of a woman named *Kim Kardashian.*
3. There shall be earthquakes, pestilences, Starbucks, kale and hipsters.
4. Men shall be disobedient to their parents, and play what will be called *video games* in their mothers' basements for hours instead of getting a job like they said they would.
5. A phenomenon known as *Reality TV* shall appear, in which everyone will deceive his neighbor, and will not speak the truth.
6. Rich men shall cast their gifts into things like *day care for dogs* and *designer salt.*
7. Knowledge of these prophecies shall increase, and many shall look

to a thing called the *Internet* for answers. And in their desperation, they shall pay heed to the deceitful doctrines of false prophets who post their blasphemy on scrolls called *Wikipedia* and *Facebook*. And multitudes shall run to and fro trying to improve their *streaming speeds* and understand their *privacy settings*.

A Few True Things from Revelations
(Dad says most of the rest of it is crap)

8. The vials of the wrath of God shall be poured upon the earth in the form of *gluten-free, 100% organic, wheat grass juice.*

9. Upon partaking of the weed of the tree of life, people called *stoners* shall see three unclean spirits like frogs come out of the mouth of the dragon and hear from the horns of the unicorns that their darlings shall be saved from the power of the dog. And they shall see a leopard having seven heads and ten horns rise from the seas. And they shall have the munchies and head to the nearest purveyor of sustenance known as *microwave burritos.*

10. All the chosen shall receive a mark on their right hand, or on their foreheads, or as a tattoo reading *God is Good* affixed to their rear-ends. Fornicators, idolaters, adulterers, thieves, drunkards, revilers, extortioners, and an evil clan known as *telemarketers* shall have no mark and shall be destroyed.

11. Four horsemen shall be unleashed to bring conquest, war, famine, and death to the world. They shall use something called the *iPhone map app* to get here, and they shall get lost.

12. To seven angels shall be given seven trumpets. And those angels will make the great mistake of giving those trumpets to someone whose demonic symbol means "the artist formerly known as Prince" who shall create such a calamitous noise that no one will ever play the trumpet again.

13. And lions shall lie with lambs, and goats shall lie with horses, and elephants shall lie with dogs, and hundreds of thousands of moving images of these occurrences shall appear nonstop on something called *YouTube.* See pestilence above.

After reading the scroll, the disciples looked up at Jesus in fear and wonder. "Lord," they asked, "when shall this come to pass?"

Jesus spit out the skin of the fig, and picked at his teeth with a toothpick. He looked grave and leaned in as if sharing a great secret.

"Oh, my friends. It shall come to pass soon. Very soon." His face reflected great sorrow. And the disciples *oohed* and *aahed* and began to talk a little too excitedly about the coming rapture.

Then Jesus leaned back and laughed.

"Nah, just kidding. Don't worry about it," he said. "We've got over two thousand years." With a wink, he pulled out his knife and started on another fig.

The Centaur Project

Janice Law

Editor: Sentience is a thin line. Humanity is even thinner. Where does our humanity hide when we choose survival?

Entry 1: Observer John Prichert, August 3, 2010, first word recognition experiment with genetically enhanced subject 4578. This subject is now eight years old and competent in Ameslan, American Sign Language. A modified keyboard that produces audio and visual cues as well as large print characters was employed.

BanAnna. ApLe. Watr. Bred.

* * *

Entry 123: Observer John Prichert, October 13, 2011. One hundred and twenty-third session with computer and genetically enhanced subject 4578.

Kao like banan. 000# Kao want watr. Thnk you Jon. Kao want aple. Has Jon Apple? Give//Aple.

A number of other simple sentences, statements, commands and questions are produced. All generated and used without trainer cues. Subject is now completely confident with machine and keyboard. Genetically enhanced subject 4578 has progressed markedly faster than the control subjects. Use of computer spelling component to improve intelligibility is recommended.

* * *

Entry 235: Observer Paula Gleiss, December 20, 2012. Session with computer trained, genetically enhanced subject 4578. Observers note: all communication for this session was done via computer screen.

Dr. Gleiss: Hello Kao.
Kao: Hello Paula.
Dr. Gleiss: Are you ready to do some work Kao?
Kao: Give Kao a hug.

Dr. Gleiss: All right. Now are you ready?

Kao: Kao write. What?

Dr. Gleiss: Tell me something. Something that happened in the past.

Kao: Happened-past? Kao saw John.

Dr. Gleiss: Yes, that's right. Anything else? Another happened-past?

Kao: Paula and Kao went into wood.

Dr. Gleiss: That's very good.

Kao: Tickle Kao.

Dr. Gleiss: All right.

Kao: Trees tall green. Kao climb swing whooo. Trees swing in the dark like Kao swing. All green and dark. Kao fall into cage.

Dr. Gleiss: That's good. Did you fall when we went for a walk?

At this point subject refuses to answer, appears distressed, session ends. I wonder if this is an authentic memory. John?

* * *

Entry 236: Observer John Prichert, December 22, 2012. Genetically enhanced subject 4578 refused to use the computer during this session. Showed teeth. First sign of unprovoked hostility from this subject. Possible premature sexual maturation?

* * *

Entry 237: Observer Paula Gleiss, January 15, 2013. Computer session with subject 4578, Kao. This is the first session for weeks since subject refusal before Christmas.

Dr. Gleiss: How are you, Kao?

Kao: Kao glad. Paula back.

Dr. Gleiss: Paula is glad to be back. Will you write?

Kao: Kao write. What?

Dr. Gleiss: What does Kao like?

Kao: Bananas apples oranges. Paula. Trees. Walk outside.

Dr. Gleiss: What does Kao not like?

Kao: John baths happened-past.

Dr. Gleiss: Why not?

Kao: Make Kao sad.

Dr. Gleiss: How does John make you sad?

Kao: John is no-sign. 1

Dr. Gleiss: How does happened-past make you sad? 2

Note 1: This is Kao's word for stupid.
Note 2: Subject refused to answer and session ended. This is first session where Kao has indicated strong emotional preferences. I think he undoubtedly possesses memories of a strong and disturbing nature, but lacks the signs and vocabulary to give them shape.

* * *

Memo from John Prichert: Paula, you are anthropomorphizing again. Do not offer interpretations, only observations, please.

* * *

Entry 267: Observer Paula Gleiss, June 12, 2013. Computer time with Kao, #4578. This subject now prefers to work alone.
Night see. Walk with Paula. Trees grass roots. I wanted let go. She took off leash. I ran went tree-walking swung free, never fell. Time to go home she said. Where where I ask. Paula angry. She hides her face on my questions. Come down she said. She is angry. She speaks and signs at once. When I come down she is happy.
John, I think this shows evidence of more abstraction than your last report indicated. Kao is asking a very basic question here.

* * *

Memo to Paula: Please remember to refer to the test subject as Subject 4578. Your tendency to humanize is leading you astray scientifically.

* * *

Entry 287: Observer John Prichert, September 3, 2013. This follows an experiment in socialization for subject 4578. In an effort to develop other facets of subject 4578's psychology, we arranged a visit to the University's main Primate Center. Subject was reluctant and only began to write once observer left. This and other sessions were followed by a remote monitor hooked into the keyboard.
Walk with Paula and John. Big house big outdoor barred house. Apes in trees on swings on bars. All no-sign apes. I jumped

into their tree. They showed teeth. All sad. All frightened. Big house bad smell. Go home I signed. Play said John. No play go home I signed. What will happen to the no-sign apes? Why are they sad? Why can't they sign? What they tell Kao? Paula asked want see them again? I signed no. But when we walk I look in their cage.

This seems an unusually complex and sophisticated production. It is clear that the genetic enhancement experiment has succeeded in producing a specimen with normal health and chimpanzee physique but with a somewhat greater mental endowment than usual. My personal view is that these genetic changes extend only to communication skills…I have questioned Subject 4578 closely about his feelings, but he is unable to put emotional material into words.

* * *

John is always boss boss boss. I not like him in his bone color snow color tooth color. I screamed in the tree and fell to earth into his hands. I cannot tell past pain. Enough in present, Paula is different. She speaks she signs she makes happy. Without her Kao crazy sit in corner beat on bars.

* * *

The no-sign apes die. I smell death at Big House. Paula says no. Paula lies is sad. John lies. Kao lies about computer.

* * *

Entry 302: November 28, 2013. John Prichert report on genetically enhanced subject 4578. Subject is making covert computer entries as well as the official entries for the observers. The regular entries deal strictly with events, answers to questions. The secret entries, some of which we have not been able to recover, express emotional reactions, opinions, what seem to be memories. Subject refuses to discuss any of these which have come to light.

Recommendation to Committee: A structurally heavy keyboard of any PC-compatible type be installed in the subject's quarters. It could be easily hooked to the television monitor already standard recreational equipment for the housing of this group of experimental subjects. Could it be arranged so we get an automatic printout whether material is commanded to be saved or not?

* * *

Committee response: Request of November 28, 2013, approved. Proceed, Prichert.

* * *

John asks questions. Paula is sad. She lies about no-sign apes. They suffer. The trees outside green swinging with wind. The trees inside are dead. Green hands cut off feet lost. No-sign apes are inside trees. Is Kao?

* * *

Something is wrong. Paula and John are jump around. He said I could be kaldup you know. Kaldup is new word. I have no sign for it.

* * *

Entry 320: December 14, 2013, Observer Paula. Report of conversation with Kao, #4578.

Dr. Gleiss: How are you today, Kao?
Kao: Jump around.
Dr. Gleiss: Jump around?
Kao: Yes.
Dr. Gleiss: Nervous? Upset?
Kao: Yes. And Paula how are you?
Dr. Gleiss: All right.
Kao: Paula lie.
Dr. Gleiss: Yes. I'm nervous.
Kao: Is it kaldup?
Dr. Gleiss: I don't understand.
Kao: John may be kaldup. Will you?
Dr. Gleiss: John may have to go away. He may be called up to the army.
Kao: He will fall from his tree.
Dr. Gleiss: Yes.
Kao: And Paula?
Dr. Gleiss: Not yet.
Kao: What's wrong? What is called up? Where is John going.
Dr. Gleiss: There is trouble. A fight.

Kao: John does not like to fight. I show my teeth and he is afraid. I know he is afraid.

Dr. Gleiss: We are all afraid.

Kao: Dont cry Paula. Kao write something nice for you. Something new. Something secret. Dont cry.

Observer unable to continue session. The present situation makes scientific work almost impossible.

* * *

Request, Gleiss to Committee—In present emergency has any provision been made for preservation of the subjects of the genetic enhancement experiment? Might I submit that the most valuable of these be treated as essential personnel?

* * *

I got a Life Tag today. Paula brought it and showed me hers. Don't lose it she said. I tasted. Bitter and cold like bars on cage. Don't she said. If you know the work to get that for you she said. She put it around my neck and took me outside. We went past the no-sign apes house. No Life Tags.

The Life Tag opens door to big hole in ground. Paula made me try. The door opened. Remember, she said. When the Time Comes, use the tag and hide in here she said. God I hope they let you in. Paula says more than she signs. I listen. God I hope you understand she says.

What is Time Comes. You will know says Paula. You will know when Time Comes.

How will I get there?

Paula is upset. I will leave your door open she says. I promise she says.

You leave it open now I sign.

It may never happen she says.

What? I sign.

Time comes.

* * *

Food late. No cleaners. Outside rumble manshout. Dogs bark. I jump around. Paula came with food. What's wrong? I sign. Where cleaner foodman Peter?

He has been called up, she says.
I want to go out I sign. Out.
No, she says.
Out. I jump up and down and show my teeth. Paula closes the door.

* * *

No food today. Manshout in halls. I jump up and down and scream. No answer. Is this Time Comes? Now it is dark. Only screen is light. Nothing in halls. Nothing outside. Kao is frightened. Where is Paula?

* * *

Morning. Manshout, rumble. No food. Where is Paula? Where is Peter? Dogs cry. Afternoon., Rumble rumble outside. Kao is alone. Where is Paula? Big light heat thunder. Building shakes. Roof crumbs fall. Bang. Silence. Dust. Dark. This is Time Comes. And where is Paula. PAULA!!!!

* * *

End of the first print out.

* * *

The no-sign apes mark by pissing on their trees. I mark on this friend machine. Long gone now back. I left it in dark with Paula name on screen. Her light came down corridor all dogs barking. She called Kao Kao. I screamed. Jumped and rattled bars. In dark questions without answer. A shadow through bars, scratch-rattle of keys. Hand wet. Smell of fear.

Come, quick she says. I follow light down corridor. Outside hot dark with smoke red with fire. I smell Time Comes. It smells of fire, of fear. I hear Time Comes. It roars and bangs. Hurry says Paula. I start to hole in ground. No. no. She is crying. You must help she says. I jump cry roll on ground. How well I know that happened-past. And if I forget I look out the window and see what is left after Time Comes.

What we did is this marking my last. We ran over roads sharp with glass. Feel bleed. Buildings burn and howl. Death smell. Fire smell. Bitter smell. At Big House, no-sign apes dead. Trees black. I stopped. Hurry hurry said Paula. Why why I signed. The blast. All killed she said. People? People dead too. She pointed. On road on grass. All dead she said. But some called to her made manshout.

John? I signed.

He is gone she said. She pulled me to building with big door. Kao get in she said. Open door from inside.

Kao frightened.

Stupid ape. We must get away. We will die here. She shook her fist and showed her teeth.

I climbed up tree at side. She found me stone and smash down window sharp glass.

Go in go in she said. Inside high up dark.

The door the door Paula said.

Light dim no shape. Outside fire roar. I jumped into dark. Hard floor. Glass like ice. Paula bang bang on the door. I touched smooth rocks in dark. Found door. Opened.

Good good said Paula. Red light came in. Showed rocks cars trucks. She tried for rumble.

Get in she said. Kao frightened. Car started to move.

Get in. I jumped. Door she said. Bang. Rumble rumble we swung on ground fast faster than tree walk faster than run fast faster than Time Comes ahead of fire ahead of death smell.

We stopped once. Paula ran into building came out with bag came out with sticks came out with boxes. I carried boxes too. What's this? I signed.

Food medicine she said.

What kind of medicine?

Medicine to protect us she said. We got in car and away in night.

* * *

Long night long dark like dark near friend machine I tell. No sun. Black ground clouds hot and dusty. This is from the blasts Paula said. In dark car eyes truck eyes. We will get to the highway and see said Paula. There was manshout. Screams. We cant stop said Paula. We will get help.

On highway cars and trucks lay dead. Manshout smoke and bad smell. Its jammed said Paula. Our car jumped on grass between cars. We left highway. Its no good said Paula. Its no-use. She stopped car and put her face on inside wheel and cried. I opened boxes. No fruit. No lettuce. I jumped around and showed teeth. Then I bit each box. One had hard bread. I ate. There was no-use to ask Paula. Not with Time Comes.

Sun came back small. Everything gray dark. Paula sleep. I climb trees by stream. Leaves dusty. I dropped them in water and ate them. They were not good like lettuce.

Paula woke up and rumble car. We'll just go as far as we can. Maybe we'll find a station open she said.

What is that? I signed.

For gas. Where car eats, Paula said.

We eat, I signed.

We need the car Paula said. We can get away in the car.

Where? I signed.

Somewhere she said.

We found child on third day. This is the third day Paula said. We passed houses but Paula did not stop. Food I signed. Fruit. Lettuce.

No sick said Paula.

Why Why?

Sickness came first Paula said. From our enemies.

Will we be sick I signed.

We have medicine said Paula.

What about Time Comes I signed.

Time Comes because of sickness. The war. The fight. Paula stopped car. Theres a child she said.

It was alone smaller than Kao and crying.

Can you pick it up Paula said.

I got out and child stopped crying. Monkey it said. I put it in the car.

Poor thing said Paula are you hungry?

It ate bread and told happened-past. It was Suzi and lived outside town. Her mother and father were at work and white flash came. They did not come back. She hid in cellar.

That was right Paula said.

We found food for car that day and on day five we saw black place. Dust fire death smell. We must go South said Paula. We cant go into the city. Everyone is dead said Paula. But some men were on the road. There was blood on their faces. They stood in front of the car and shouted. Help us. Get out of the car. Give us food.

We have none Paula said.

Manshout and pound the car. Show teeth and jump around

red fear. They shook car like tree swing.
Kill the money we'll eat it instead,
Paula took stick and showed it to them. Bang flash blood.
Rumble. Fast faster than tree walk fast like Time Comes. Manshout
behind us. They would have killed us Paula said. They would have
killed us for the car and the medicine. They would have eaten Kao
said Suzi. At night Suzi cried for mother and father.

* * *

Friend machine spills words like sick. Like Kao. Like Suzi. Suzi
spitting yellow and red sick. Paula gave her medicine but Suzi
had no Life Tag. The day we had no more bread Suzi died. We
put branches over her. Paula said I am not strong enough to dig
a hole. But a hole in ground is only good before time Comes. So
no-use for Suzi.

We traveled long time until car died of no food. But there
was food for us South. There was food grass in the fields. I found
roots and things to eat. We night walked and day slept in food
grass fields. We walked south all time. Still dark. Always bitter
smell smoke smell death smell. The leaves on trees brown and
food grass turned black.

We must find people who have food said Paula. She was
thin. Grass and leaves I ate make her sick with pains. We have
medicine she said. We can trade it for some food.

We reached first fence one morning. Gray sky not black.
Mansmell. A man on fence had a stick.

No refugees he said. We haven't enough for what weve got
already.

We have some medicine said Paula.

Not enough to do no one good he said. He showed teeth.
We bury more in a day than you and that monkey could tote
drugs for in a week. Unless its coke now or smack always a market
for those he said. He showed his teeth. I showed my teeth jumped
up and down swung arms.

Hey he said and raised his stick.

Quiet down said Paula. Is there no other settlement?
Everywhere can't be fenced.

Naw. Elsewhere they just shoot you. This on the main route
is civilized. He showed his teeth. Ha Ha. Listen he said they are
sneaking into Haiti by boat. Boats to Haiti. Ha ha. And Cuba. Every
sail from Pensacola to the Keys is at sea and the island people are

shooting em out of the water. Ha Ha.

After some more talk and Ha Ha he gave us oranges. Paula gave him medicine.

Try to the west if I was you. Some big camps along the line. That monkey do tricks? Ha Ha. Takes all kinds. His stick went off bang bang over our heads. Dirty no-sign.

Hes crazy said Paula. But now people lived in cages like no-sign apes. Outside people showed teeth. Paulas stick went bad and they stole from us. We ate fruit and Paula got thinner.

In spring we found people with food. They lived in big house. We dont want any more man said.

We need food said Paula. Were not sick. We can work.

Thats a laugh man said. Your a skeleton and thats a monkey. Get out of here.

Paula was tired. She sat down on ground. I jumped up and down and rolled over and over to cheer her up.

Ha Ha said the man. The kids would like that said a woman. Let them come in for a while. It wont hurt cause weve got potatoes left. So tricks and Ha Ha and potatoes. We found a keyboard with no screen and I wrote. Always Ha Ha but food.

Well have a party they said. Before we die. Ha Ha. They burned sticks for light and box made music and board speak with strings. They banged ground with their feet and manshout. Taste this they said. Corn mash. White in head like lightning. Like tree swing. Lets see the monkey dance. Dance swing. Is this a monkey? What does genetically enhanced mean?

It means hes special said Paula. Leave Kao alone.

I think hes more man than monkey know what I mean? Ha Ha. What would you bring him all this way for? Give your friend a kiss fellow. Ha Ha.

Paula jump around. Stop it. Leave Kao alone.

Maybe it would be incest said woman. Eyes white like corn mash. Arm around my neck. Hes not so bad considering.

Leave him alone said Paula. Chimps are very strong. They bite when they're excited.

Havent seen anything male excited since they dropped the bombs. Ha Ha. You tell em. Play that goddamn music. Give Kao a drink. Hey.

Music whirl white light white hands white legs on fur. Ha Ha. Scream. Paula cry. White hands new smell spring smell life smell teeth sharp blood. Manshout. Ha Ha.

Dont hurt him said Paula. It wasnt his fault.

Goddamn ape bit me said woman. Ha Ha.
Run said Paula. Run run for godsake. They have a gun.

* * *

In morning head bang like Time Comes eyes white like corn
mash. A swamp. Paula killed bugs slap slap no eat. I bit my Life
Tag. Groomed her hair. Rolled on the ground. She cried. It was
a terrible thing she said. But it should have been all right. You
would have been a cleverer chimpanzee she said. You would have
been boss of the colony.
What does this mean?
We lived by the swamp. I found roots. Frogs. Snakes. Fish.
Paula ate little. She had Life Tag but she was sick. I made bed of
leaves for her. Go for people I signed. No she said. They would
kill you. She got weak. Too weak to sign too weak to talk. The last
night she said stay here. This place. Its warm safe. Theres plenty
of food. Promise.
I jumped around rolled on ground. She smiled she laughed.
She stopped. Warm sleep? Cold later.
Scream jump tear ground break branches stamp pain. Heart
dead with death smell. I covered Paula with branches. I ate roots
of lilies and put blossoms on her face.
I was lonely in safe swamp. Lonely for Paula. Was Paula lonely
for animals? Was John? I left swamp for north sky dark. No food
grass. In cold I found this friend machine. Pale dying little light
weak friend machine. I sit at it like Paula like John. Manlook hair
thin.
We are left friend machine and Kao. The ones who asked all
dead. I tell anyway to friend machine. I saw No No No. But then
I make my name Kao Kao Kao. I make my mark. I am not dead.

Unnatural Selection

Mike Barretta

Editor: What is a good enough motive for murder on a colossal scale? What about a single murder? Do the morals differ?

Major William "Bill" Whitaker slid his sleeping niche's curtain open and stepped out onto the dirty gray carpet. He felt Martian grit through his thin socks. He blinked his eyes to focus in the dim LED light. He faced the mirror and ran a dirty finger along the inside of his mouth tasting bitter oils and rust. His gums bled and his teeth wobbled in their sockets like tombstones planted in mud. Dark shadows surrounded his sunken eyes and his utility uniform hung from his body like a bedsheet. A dull, throbbing ache wrapped his skull. He jerked open the corrugated fabric curtain that defined his room.

"Bill, you have a private message," said Ammad Suliman, the Pakistani mission geologist. Ammad sat in the dim glow of an LCD computer monitor. The elegant curve of Arabic script scrolled across the monitor.

"Thanks," said Bill.

Ammad's hair was thinning out and he had stopped shaving every day. He had the grizzled look of a man on a four-month alcohol binge.

"I'll take it in the office," said Bill.

Bill climbed the three-story ladder to the office, the cockpit of the ERV, the Earth Return Vehicle. He stopped on the second deck to catch his breath.

Dr. Jessica Harrison sat at her electron microscope.

"Bill, how are you doing?"

"Jess, fine. I got a message. I need to go up. Just taking a breather," said Bill.

As the ship's doctor, she knew exactly how poorly he and the other two crewmembers were doing.

"Are you sure you're feeling okay?" asked Jessica.

"Not as good as you, but all right," he explained.

Other than a little weight loss and pale skin she was the picture of health. He'd slept with her almost a month ago and suspected that she had slept with Ammad and Landon also. He didn't care.

She turned back to her work, looking for proof of life, past or present. Bill didn't care if she found it or not. He was simply the captain of this particular ship of fools and only needed to get them home safe to be successful. If life was discovered she would be the famous one; who remembered Captain Robert Fitzroy, Commander of the *H.M.S. Beagle?* He resumed his climb, entered the ERV, and closed the hatch. He settled into the command chair, tapped the receive icon on the glass panel display with his fingertip, and waited.

"Bill, this is an Eye's Only message, enter your encryption code," said Mitchell Devry, Flight Operations Director.

* * *

Mitchell Devry took a seat in the secure conference room. He tapped his ring against the desktop like a metronome. As he looked at his watch his mouth drew into a frown and the brows of his forehead wrinkled.

The heavy door opened and Gary Schweizer, NASA's administrator, walked in. Two others followed. The first was a severe bureaucrat-type who looked somehow familiar though he couldn't quite place the face. His dark pinstripe suit and a red power tie screamed Washington beltway or professional assassin. The other was a short, balding man in a white button-down shirt that stretched over his paunch. All three men arrayed themselves on the opposite side of the table.

"It's that kind of meeting?" said Mitchell.

"Mitch, it is good to see you again," said Gary.

Gary extended his hand and Mitchell shook it.

"Mitch, this is Mr. Dennis Cole, Director of Homeland Security, and Dr. Howard Nguyen, Centers for Disease Control."

Mitchell reached across the table and shook Dennis Cole's hand. Yes, I do know who he is, thought Mitchell. Seeing the man in person was like finding an alligator in your pool. You know what the creature is, it just takes a moment to squeeze it into context.

He reached to shake Dr. Nguyen's hand, but the man just looked momentarily uncomfortable and nodded his head in acknowledgement. Dennis Cole took a matte black device out of an inside jacket pocket and placed it in the center of the table. A green power indicator light glowed like a reptilian eye.

"A scrambler," said the Homeland Security director. "It's just a precaution."

Mitchell sat down and leaned back into his seat. He kept his face carefully neutral.

Dennis with his power tie began. "How well do you know Dr. Jessica Harrison?"

"Well enough, I imagine. On a professional basis. We've worked quite closely for the last five years since her selection for the mission. She has multiple doctorate degrees. She's a competent pilot, and nationally ranked in Tae Kwon Do," said Mitchell, just a bit surprised where this was starting. "You probably already have her resume if you're asking about her." He thought for a moment. "She is the smartest woman I've ever met, probably the smartest on the planet."

"As I thought," proclaimed Dennis. "That is why she needs to die."

He looked to Gary.

"Really? Gary? What the hell is this about?" said Mitchell.

"Prior to launch did you notice any suspicious behavior?" asked Dennis.

"We don't send suspicious people to Mars," said Mitchell.

"Did you screen everything in her personal allotment?"

"Everything on that ship was inspected, but there is a certain degree of trust among astronauts. It is an exclusive club, once you're in, you're in. She probably wouldn't even need to smuggle anything, she designed the medical and scientific equipment manifests."

"Mitchell is correct, Mr. Director. Beyond mission safety we don't interfere with our people," Gary offered.

"Mr. Devry, Are you familiar with REAPER?" asked Dennis.

Mitchell recognized a code word when he heard one. More than few NASA projects brushed awkwardly against military or intelligence requirements.

"No, I'm not. I am busy managing manned space flight operations," said Mitchell.

"An admirable devotion to duty," said Dennis with equal sarcasm. "What I am going to tell you is code word specific and goes no further than this room."

"Don't you want me to sign something?" asked Mitchell.

"No. Let me explain," said Dennis. "The National Security Administration's REAPER program is a counterterrorism signal intelligence gathering program. It is a decentralized computer network running adaptive pattern recognition software that scans telecommunications for security threats and then forwards suspicious activity to a human analyst for action."

"What does that have to do with my Mars mission?" asked Mitchell, exasperated with the conversation.

"REAPER detected a data compressed email with very sophisticated encryption from Mars. I understand all of your communications are routed to your mission servers and then the astronaut's private correspondence is split off to administrative servers for routing to their ultimate address."

"That's true," Mitchell agreed.

"We've checked your system and you don't scan private email," said Dennis.

"Well, no, they're astronauts. We trust them," said Mitchell.

"Unfortunate," said Dennis. "This email was routed to the Centers for Disease Control from a dedicated channel from your aerospace medical servers. Two weeks later, the process reversed and she received the results of her program. She was able to backdoor your system because she was a trusted user."

"She was doing sanctioned NASA research on advanced cellular senescence in space environments with the CDC's whole human modeling programs," said Mitchell.

"Of course, but in this case, she didn't want you to know what she was doing because she was running these very powerful simulation programs for her own purposes," said Dennis.

"What was she simulating?" asked Mitchell.

"Herself," Dr. Howard Nguyen interjected. "Specifically, she was simulating the effect of an artificially created virus on her own body. We've been briefed on the crew's medical status. When exactly did Dr. Harrison's condition begin improving in relation to the men?"

"I would have to consult the mission flight surgeon for an exact date but about two months ago she spiked a severe fever and then she began to improve dramatically. We had hoped she was just the first to improve, but the men just continued their gradual deterioration," said Mitchell.

"Have you eliminated all Earth-borne pathogens or toxins?" asked Dennis.

"We can't test for everything. Obviously, we were not quite as prepared to go to Mars as we thought," said Mitchell. "We are calling it Mars Syndrome."

"The timing is right. It just might be when she beta tested her virus," said Dr. Nguyen to Dennis.

"Are you telling me she brought a virus to Mars?" snapped Mitchell. "What the hell for?"

Dr. Nguyen looked at Dennis Cole for permission to explain. The potential use of biology for a terrorist attack had grown exponentially and as a result the CDC had virtually become a branch of Homeland Security.

Dennis nodded, granting permission.

"She has created a synthetic anti-agathic, a viral rescriptor that stops cellular senescence."

"Excuse me, Doctor, but I hold three PhDs and I didn't understand what you said," Gary interrupted.

"In short, Administrator Schweizer, Dr. Harrison has invented immortality."

"That's impossible," Mitchell retorted.

"I assure you it is not," said Dr. Nguyen.

"Why go to Mars to test it?"

"Mars is the perfect place. There is no danger of accidentally releasing a flawed virus into the wild; she has ready access to the most powerful computers ever lifted into space for her basic research, and a secure dedicated back channel into the CDC whole human model," said Dr. Nguyen. "I would wager she has been working on this for quite some time and Mars gave her the opportunity to take her research to viable prototype without any of the oversight that she would be subject to in a level five bio-containment facility."

. "Is this virus contagious?" asked Mitchell.

"Our interpretation of her computer modeling shows that in its current form the virus is not contagious. It has to be tailored to the patient and then directly injected," said Dr. Nguyen.

"Which is the only reason we are even having this conversation," said Dennis.

"You should nominate her for the Nobel Prize," said Mitchell. "Imagine what it could do for the entire human race?"

"That is exactly why we are here," replied Dr. Nguyen. "Our simulations of premature human immortality result in total collapse of the biosphere."

Dennis spoke next. "We need to reliably access the resources of the solar system to even have a chance at surviving immortality, and even then it may not be wise."

"Mortal creatures retain the ability to evolve and adapt. They out-compete immortal creatures. Immortality is synonymous with stagnation," said Nguyen. "But of course, that's just theoretical."

"This is too much to process," said Mitchell, "and it still doesn't say how this impacts my mission."

"You don't need to process. That is why I am here," said Cole. "For the sake of argument is it possible for us to terminate the mission without attracting undue attention?"

"What do you mean by 'terminate'?" asked Mitchell.

"Is it possible for us to kill the astronauts while they are on Mars?"

Mitchell looked to his boss.

Gary nodded, indicating to give the Homeland Security director a straight answer.

"Anything is possible, it's just not likely, and we have a small army of very smart people dedicated to bringing them home," said Mitchell.

"What about a software attack?" asked Gary.

Mitchell shook his head. Gary was a smart man, but a political appointee. No one achieved his level of success in government bureaucracy without having a reputation for competence, but his area of expertise was politics. His job ensured that NASA's programs survived congressional space and not outer space.

"The *Beagle* is the most sophisticated and multiply-redundant vehicle ever developed. Its software has been run for tens of millions of virtual hours without a single glitch and its backbone OS is smart enough to defeat any attack we could generate. Even if you worked around those issues, then you would need to manufacture a problem plausible enough to convince Major Whitaker to permit a software update," said Mitchell.

"I see," Dennis mused, his eyes focusing elsewhere.

Mitchell thought otherwise. Dennis Cole probably didn't "see" because it wasn't necessary for him to. Cole was at least three times removed from the tactical level where things got done. Like most high-level bureaucrats, he was a big picture person concerned with the broad sweep of history. He had people to manage people and their people managed the nasty technical details.

"Mr. Devry, my personal preference is to destroy the entire mission and be done with it." He held up his hand, staving off Mitchell's angry rebuttal. "But in this case, my personal preference has been overridden by politics. The president has invested a substantial amount of political capital in the success of the mission, and he wants options. He would like someone to make it back. It's the only reason we are even having this conversation."

"If you want to minimize collateral damage and maximize operational secrecy, then the best way is to convince the other astronauts to kill her. The conspiracy would be limited to us and the three male astronauts," said Mitchell. He was shocked at how easy the words came out of his mouth.

"That just might be a workable solution," said Dennis.

"I imagine you came to that solution before you even stepped into the room," said Mitchell.

"I did. I need your expertise and your cooperation. Major Whitaker will trust you. He won't trust me," said Dennis.

"Both Major Whitaker and myself need a much better reason to commit murder than an unauthorized medical experiment that most would consider a boon to humankind," said Mitchell.

"Boon," said Dennis. He laughed. "If it was just immortality we might have a snowball's chance in hell of surviving immortality, but Dr. Harrison has thrown us a little curve ball."

He looked to Dr. Nguyen.

"I've run the effects of Dr. Harrison's virus on generic male and female modeling platforms and I've concluded that her anti-agathic only works for women; for men it is fatal."

* * *

"Thank you," said the computer after the major had entered his credentials. Mitchell's image formed again. He sat next to the Secretary of Defense and two others that Bill did not immediately recognize.

"Bill, this message is self-erasing. There will be no record of this conversation and it will play once, so please pay attention. You know the Secretary of Defense." Mitchell gestured to his left. "To my right is Mr. Dennis Cole, the Director of Homeland Security, and to his right is Dr. Howard Nguyen, head of the Centers for Disease Control. NSA has intercepted an email message from Doctor Jessica Harrison containing digital data of an artificial virus. The email evaded our scrutiny and was forwarded to the CDC where it was run through a computer modeling process. The results were sent back to her in the body of a personal email. We have a high level of confidence that she has successfully designed, constructed, and tested a virus on herself. Our simulations indicate that her treatment is a grave threat to stability and human civilization. For women her virus produces effective immortality. Her virus doesn't work for men; it will kill you.

"Bill, I'm your friend so I am giving you fair warning. Don't be clever and try to fool me. If you leave the surface of Mars with her onboard there are contingency plans to destroy your ship. You're a military officer and I am going to leave the operational details to you. You have no choice in the matter and there is no option on the table for discussion. I am sure your initial reaction is to be a bit confused, I know mine was. Get over it.

"You are authorized by executive order of the president of the United States to ensure that Dr. Jessica Harrison does not return home and you have full latitude to execute your orders in any manner you deem appropriate. I'm sorry, Bill."

The screen went blank and Bill stared at it for the longest time in disbelief. At first he thought it was a sick joke or a really good hack, but Mitch never joked and the validation codes on the message were correct. He checked the message log. Like a snake that successfully swallowed its tail there was no record that a message had ever existed.

* * *

Bill and Rob Landon, the lander pilot, spent their shift cleaning out the inertial particle separator. Bill pulled his intercom system cord from the tensioned reel and jacked it in Rob Landon's input to bypass the radio intercom which was subject to eavesdropping from the ship.

"What's with the James Bond shit? Radio is working," said Landon. He opened up the access plate for the inertial particle separator. Martian dust clogged it again. The machine sucked in Martian atmosphere and centrifugally separated the dust and ejected it out the exhaust port. The carbon dioxide was mixed with hydrogen in a Sabatier reaction to make methane for the ship's engines. When the tanks were full they could leave.

Bill was tired of Landon's smart mouth and crappy attitude. If they were anywhere but Mars he probably would have gotten a fist in the mouth. He wasn't sure when he started disliking Landon but suspected it correlated with the onset of Mars Syndrome.

"We've got a problem," said Bill.

"No shit, this thing is jammed up again," said Landon. He swept out handfuls of dust as fine as baby powder.

"Will you just shut up for a second and let me talk," said Bill.

Rob plastered on his innocent look and waited.

"I got a call from Mitchell and we have to kill Jess," said Bill.

"Hey, count me in," said Landon sarcastically.

"I'm serious. Haven't you noticed that she doesn't have whatever the hell we have?"

"Yeah," said Landon. "So?"

"She's prototyped a virus that will keep her healthy," said Bill. "Forever."

"She needs to give it to us," said Landon.

"It kills men and makes women immortal. Homeland Security figured it out, and if we don't kill her on Mars then we all die. They won't let us come home," said Bill.

"You're serious, aren't you?" asked Landon. He looked around his commander at the miserable Martian wasteland.

"Deadly," said Bill.

"Does Ammad know?" asked Landon.

"Not yet," said Bill.

"I need confirmation," said Landon.

"You'll get it tomorrow at your scheduled personal time," said Bill. He was stunned at how fast Landon had accepted the idea of murder.

"Fine, I'll talk to Mitchell then. As much as she pisses me off and as much as I'd love to kill any one of you for a decent hamburger, you had better hope you're not screwin' with me."

* * *

"I understand there is a plan in place to deal with the situation," said Dennis Cole from behind another power tie.

"There is. Major Whitaker hasn't informed me of the details. He will tell us when it's done," said Mitchell.

"If he fails, we will kill the vehicle in space."

"I don't think that will be necessary."

Mitchell brimmed with remorse. It was important to him to spare his team and keep them isolated from this ugliness. Every procedure, policy, piece of equipment, and person around him was built to do one thing: bring the astronauts home. Now, no matter how perfectly his organization worked they were going to lose at least one.

"You think we are doing a terrible thing, don't you?" asked Dennis.

"I wonder," said Mitchell.

"You shouldn't," said Dennis. "The absolute best case scenario is a controlled shift of wealth and power to a class of immortal women, provided they survive the destruction of every political, social, and religious power on this planet. We've never been very good at creating the preconditions for a best-case outcome."

"The worst?" asked Mitchell

"The worst?" A crash of the planetary ecosystem after decades of increasing anarchy and warfare," said Dennis.

"How can you be so sure?" asked Mitchell.

"I can't be sure, but imagine fifty percent of the human race becoming immortal and you were in the wrong fifty percent?"

"I've always thought the world would get along without us," said Mitchell.

"In the long run, the Earth abides without us," said Dennis. "In the short run, the violence of our passing and the legacy of our abandoned achievements will have far reaching ecological implications."

Mitchell thought of untended oil wells discharging into the oceans, wind-swept radioactive waste from molten reactor cores and cities turned to toxic cesspools.

"What are the odds someone else could duplicate her research?" asked Mitchell.

"She is a rare talent, in a class by herself. Now that we know what to look for we can suppress lines of research, violently if necessary," said Dennis. "It should buy us some time."

* * *

Bill stood over Jessica. He flexed his aching right hand, the one he'd punched her with. He smiled just before he hit her, and to his surprise she didn't drop. A stunned, confused look seemed to flash across her face and then it turned to something closer to hatred. Without further thought, he punched her two more times till she fell unconscious against her workstation scattering her samples and slides. With help from the other two he dressed her out in her Mars-stained excursion suit and zip-tied her arms and legs together with nylon straps. They lowered her down two levels and dragged her through the airlock into the experimental greenhouse. The translucent fabric of the greenhouse fluttered in the moaning wind. He could smell the withered tomato plants.

"Why," she asked when she woke up.

"What did you do?" asked Bill. "Why won't Homeland Security let us come home unless we kill you?"

"I don't know, Bill. I don't know what you're talking about."

"Why are you so healthy? Why are you back-dooring the CDC with gigabytes of data?" asked Bill. "They know, Jess. It works, doesn't it?"

"Yes," said Jess admitting defeat.

"Do you know what it would do to the world?" said Bill.

"I know exactly what it would do," said Jess.

"They're making me," said Bill as a weak attempt at apology.

He looked at her broken bleeding nose. He had never hit a woman before in his life. He surprised himself with his desperate savagery against a colleague.

"No one's making you do anything, Bill," said Jess. "This is all you."

Bill reached and Ammad handed him the helmet. He put it over her head. The helmet latched with a metallic click and the external LED indicator on her data display indicated twenty-two minutes of oxygen remaining. They had run her suit all night.

"Let's take her outside," said Bill.

"What for?" said Landon. "It doesn't matter where she suffocates."

"I don't want it to happen in our home." As much as he hated the ship he didn't want her to die in it.

They put their helmets on and then Ammad and Landon grabbed Jess by her arms and lifted her from the greenhouse floor. .

"Ammad, Landon, you don't have to do this. Bill, you could just leave me here with the lander. Give me a chance." Her voice was muffled and far away.

He couldn't. She was too clever and their return launch window was two months away. She was capable of anything in that timespan. Bill reached and freed her intercom jack and plugged it into her own port bypassing the suit-to-suit radio. They wouldn't have to listen to any pleading over the radio circuit. They exited the dying greenhouse and took turns dragging her across the frigid Martian sand until the lander was out of sight. Then they dropped her.

"You two go back," said Bill.

Both men left.

Bill knelt in the sand and unplugged her ICS jack and plugged in his own.

"Jess, I'm sorry. I really am."

"Bill, please don't do this."

"I have to Jess. I need to get home," said Bill.

"Bill, it's just the first phase—please, it was easier to make it work for myself. I can make it work for everyone."

"I'm not sure I believe you, and it doesn't matter. They don't want your discovery, and they won't let us come home unless we do this. I'm sorry."

He unplugged his jack and plugged her cord into her Comm system's ICS jack to short the system. No one would have to listen to her die. As he walked away he could hear her screams through the thin Martian air. He suspected it was more out of rage than fear.

* * *

The cold seeped into her Mars excursion suit. She struggled against the nylon straps until her arms and legs burned with lactic acid fatigue. The five-minute warning chimed and the heads-up display icons turned red. She tried to slow her breathing and then gave in to the panic. She ranted and raved and cursed the men in her life: her alcoholic father who had slowly destroyed her mother until she took her own life, the high school boys that had humiliated the awkward teenager, the college professor who published one of her brilliant undergraduate papers under his own name and then groped her while making sweaty promises of repayment, the administrators and fellow scientists that grudgingly recognized her accomplishments, and now her astronaut colleagues that dragged her across the surface of an alien world to die. She measured her life by the men who had terrorized her, which of course was why she created the virus in the first place, to risk destroying the world in order to shatter the patriarchal institutions that had been built on the backs of its women—and if the women were too weak to claim their prize and survive then to hell with them also.

The oxygen counter indexed to zero and her lungs drew upon empty air. Her heart raced and the world dimmed to a gray pinpoint.

* * *

Bill left the ship alone with a shovel. It was nearly six hours since they had dragged her outside to die. He followed his carefully orchestrated script and made the appropriate reports. He followed the drag marks softened by the Martian wind.

She was facedown. Sand had started to drift in the crooks of her arms and legs. Her suit was heavily scuffed and frayed far more than what he would have thought. It was in her nature to fight. He rolled her over and tried to avoid looking in her face. He couldn't.

Her face was dark and mottled gray and dried blood laced her blue lips. Her eyes were sunk beneath gray blankets. He expected them to spring open and accuse him but they didn't. Dr. Jessica Harrison, inventor of female immortality, was dead. He dug a grave until he was overwhelmed with fatigue and dragged her to the edge.

"I'm sorry," he said as he rolled her in. He filled the grave with soft Martian sand and stabbed the shovel in the ground as a marker.

He fled all the way to Earth.

* * *

Washington burned. An orange glow suffused the horizon, brighter in the center and tapering out to darkness. Pillars of smoke rose into the evening sky. He could see the first stars through the smoky haze layer. A siren howled in the distance.

"I should have killed all of you," said Dennis Cole.

"I know," said Bill. "You should have." He took a long pull from his imported beer. There wouldn't be too many of those since international trade had all but collapsed in a futile attempt to stop the spread of immortality. He scratched the label from the bottle with his thumbnail.

"Tell me what you know," said Dennis. He had hired Bill when it became clear that NASA projects would not be funded for the foreseeable future. The man had a keen analytical mind, military-level discipline, and a strong personal interest in the project.

"I am not sure it matters anymore," said Bill.

"Everything matters," said Dennis.

"The virus is airborne and effectively uncontainable, as common as the cold and just as easy to catch. Declining estrogen associated with perimenopause is the apparent trigger for immortality in the female vector with the side benefit of reversing the symptoms of menopause itself. All humans function as natural reservoirs for the pathogen. Male hosts carry the disease as a subclinical infection and remain asymptomatic except for the pheromone lure component of the disease. It is fatal for approximately fourteen percent of males who contract the virus. This accounts for the current geo-political instabilities in the…ah…more traditional nations. We lost Ammad in the Indo-Pak nuclear exchanges."

"Makes pretty sunsets," said Dennis. "Pity about Ammad, but you, Ammad, and Landon are pretty much irrelevant as vectors anymore.

Goddamn that clever bitch. Outsmarted us all and destroyed the world."

Jessica's design, the one fed into the CDC's whole human model, was a prototype, a ruse designed to ensure that even if she didn't make it back, her legacy would. Men who survived the virus did not become immortal, but instead, exuded a pheromone cocktail that was irresistible to an uninfected woman.

"Landon is riding it out in his family's New Hampshire cabin," said Bill. He shifted in the deck chair. The bones in his back crackled. "I need to get home." He was lucky he had one. His wife had forgiven him his long string of affairs after his return and why not? She had forever.

"I think I know why the stars are so quiet," said Bill.

"The world will find a new equilibrium," said Dennis. Billions were being spent to design an equivalent virus for men, but Dr. Jessica Harrison's genius was a once-in-a-generation phenomenon. Under present conditions, the best outcome was a gradual shift of wealth and power to a class of immortal women.

"Maybe this is how it works," said Bill. "My sons will never know what's out there, but maybe my daughters will. That's something at least." He looked up through the roiling clouds to the quiet stars. Something in the distance exploded and the sky flared yet again.

"Doubt it," said Dennis.

"Probably right," said Bill looking at the conflagration. "You are probably right."

Heatwave 1976

Jonathan Cromack

Editor: It is also brightest before the sunset.

Thursday: 86 degrees Fahrenheit.

It was just like this after Davie died. I remember being here beside the orange armchair, but back then, I didn't have my Evel Knievel stunt bike. I love my Evel Knievel; it looks just like the real thing. I used to turn a handle really quickly to rev-up and spin the back wheel, then I'd press a button, which let the bike go and it'd shoot across the kitchen—it's best on the slippery floor in there; but now I just push it around because it's broken—something's snapped inside. When I grow up, I want a motorbike, and I'll have a crash helmet with stars and stripes on it just like Evel Knievel.

Nobody's saying anything. Mum keeps bringing cups of tea and biscuits to Aunty Mable and Uncle Keith, and Dad's staring out of the window with his arms behind his back—his fingers are white and held together. I don't know what he's looking at because it's only the back garden and he knows what that looks like. Maybe he's looking at his roses—he's lived here since before I was born and that was ages ago. I'm seven now.

"I feel there should be something we can do. There must be something," Aunty Mable says as if she's cross about something. She keeps fanning herself with one of Mum's magazines.

"Like what?" my mum says. The armchair creaks beside me as Mum flops down on it. She talks like she does when she's telling me off.

"We just have to sit and wait, and hope. That's all we can do, Mable," says my dad, still staring out of the window.

I can't help but smile as I hear Aunty Mable swallowing her tea noisily. They can't see me here by the chair, otherwise I'd get told off. I can't help it though. There's another spell of nobody saying anything, that's when I'm most likely to laugh, so I put my hand over my mouth and concentrate on the brown zigzags on the wallpaper which can look like 3D if you stare at them in a funny way. Aunty Mable's swallowing seems even louder—like a cartoon frog gobbling up a big fly.

"Martin. Try the TV again," Aunty Mable says to Dad.

Dad turns away from the window and fiddles with the front of the TV set, making pinging noises as the buttons switch in and out.

"I'm sure they interfere with the stations just to keep us in the dark," grumbles Aunty Mable.

Dad shakes his head. "They're probably just working on something and have to shut down the TV wavelengths for some reason."

He goes over to the mantle-piece and switches the radio on, stretching out the aerial, which I'm not allowed to touch. He turns the big silver knob on the top, which makes the sound crackle and then hiss and another station comes on; I hear a song I like. Mum said it's Heatwave—"Boogie Nights." I've seen them on Top of the Pops—I like the singer's dancing and the flame pattern on his jumpsuit; I also hear KC and the Sunshine Band, but the radio crackles again and I'm disappointed because they all just want to listen to a man talking. The man talks about Russians but it's funny because he can't say the word properly but says "Vussians" instead. I keep listening out for that word and every time he says it, it makes me smile. Davie would've laughed at that too if he was here.

"*...it is imperative that Vussian leader Podgorny and the Soviet leadership cease their military support to the MPLA immediately. Since the crises in China and Angola explosively re-ignited earlier in the year, communication between the superpowers has been strained to say the least. There have been speculations that the Soviet Premiere has now rejected all further discourse with the West. The threatening deadline imposed by US President Ford with full backing from United States' allies, however, remains firmly in place, despite the hugely unpopular and potentially unthinkable consequences. An official government speech was expected to have been made to the British media by Prime Minister Jim Callaghan from Downing Street approximately forty-five minutes ago. We are still waiting...*"

I don't understand grown-ups, they don't like to do fun things, and they just sit down, drink tea, and listen to people talking on the radio. I want to go for a wee but I don't want to disturb them by getting up when they're listening; Mum might shout at me if I disturb them now; she's always like that at times like this. I'm best off waiting and keeping out of the way.

I'm bored today; I wish Mum had let me play out with Daniel—he lives opposite—he's older than me by four years and he's got a Raleigh Chopper. It's got gears with a big stick in front of the saddle and everything. I told him that I'm going to ride a motorbike when I'm older and do stunts. Daniel knew my brother Davie, even though Davie was older than him.

Everybody leans forwards as the man on the radio slows down his talking. It goes quiet for a bit and I'm a bit scared—I don't make a sound either. We're all as still as statues.

"The Prime Minister is at the front door here at Downing Street...I can hear him now..."

Just hiss and crackle on the radio. The man's not speaking. I look around the room to see if anyone's moved, but they haven't.

"...Thank God...CODE AMBER. Podgorny has instructed the withdrawal of Soviet assistance to the MPLA in Africa...That's the official word—we are again re-classified at risk zone—CODE AMBER...If you've just tuned in—Britain is at CODE AMBER. Now back to the studio, it's just after three o'clock at BBC Radio..."

Aunty Mable and Uncle Keith lean back into the sofa; they both breathe out loudly. Dad claps his hands together and looks across at Mum who smiles and gets up, takes the tray of tea things, asks if anyone wants another, then she walks past me, brushes my hair as she does. "Orange juice, Jimmy?" she says as she goes to the kitchen.

Aunty Mable and Uncle Keith start to whisper to each other on the sofa and Dad kneels down next to me. He smiles and puts his arms out and says: "Come on, Jimmy, give your dad a hug."

"I've been playing with Evel Knievel," I say. "Dad, when I'm older, will you buy me a motorbike for my birthday?"

As he hugs me, his whiskers, the long ones that grow down in front of his ears, scratch my cheek. "Of course, son," he says. "That's a promise."

Friday: 87 degrees Fahrenheit.
Mum is taking me to school. I was hoping to have another day off, but Mum said I have to go back today "because everything's back to normal, after the scare."

It's already getting hot again this morning and the bright sun hurts my eyes. There're always lots of cars on the road when Mum takes me to school, but today it seems there's more than usual. All the cars are beeping their horns at each other but not nastily like when they get in each other's way at the roundabout; it's friendlier "toot-tooting."

There was music playing from a window of the tall flats that we passed. I asked Mum what it was, and she said it was David Bowie—I've seen pictures of him in a magazine. Some of the boys at school say that he's from outer space—that's why he's got orange hair and his eyes are different colours.

A man is painting a fence; the paint smells nice, like summer. He smiles and says hello as we pass.

We're getting to the school gates and all the mums are in little groups talking to each other waving their arms around. As Mum leads me over the crossing by the lollipop-lady, an old man with a bottle comes around the corner where the shop is. He has short hair and no moustache, not like Dad at all.

He looks at me as Mum stops to get past the other mums who are blocking our way. "Hey, son," he says. "Why're you going to school today? Why're you going to school at all?" He takes a swig from his bottle.

"Piss off," One of the mums says to him.

The man just smiles. "You may as well enjoy yourself an' all, Love," he says to her. "We're all gonna die soon anyway. Have a drink. Fuck."

"Bugger off out of here, drunken sod," someone else says.

The man shrugs and wanders into the road and a blue car has to stop suddenly because the man doesn't wait for the lollipop-lady to let him cross.

I turn to Mum. "Why did that man say we were all going to die, Mum?"

"He's just stupid; don't listen to him."

"Why did he say it though?"

"Because he's stupid and likes trying to frighten people."

"We're not going to die, are we, Mum?"

Mum drags me through the crowd of other mums; someone's shopping bag brushes across my face, cold—a huge Union Jack. There's bare feet, painted nails, stripy tights and sandals, long skirts, and big platform shoes. Patterns, swirls of white, blue, purple, orange, and yellow.

"Mum?"

"Don't be stupid, Jimmy; no one's going to die." She doesn't look at me properly as she says this but hurries me on.

We're at the door of the demountable building, I can see the other kids inside, through the windows; chasing and running around before the teacher arrives and tells everybody to "settle down." Mum gives me a hug and hands me my bag. She gives me a wave and waits for me to go up the three bendy steps to the door; it's cooler in the shade. As I turn around, she smiles at me, waves once and walks away.

For some reason, I want her to stay with me today more than ever.

Later.

I'm playing Clackers in the playground. I didn't eat my dinner today; I wasn't hungry—normally the dinner-ladies would tell me off, but they didn't seem to mind today. They seemed more cheerful than usual.

Nigel Stevens is watching me, he doesn't seem to want to join in with me but he keeps trying to show me his new digital watch. Dad says that they're really expensive and not for little boys, but Nigel Stevens has got one.

"It was nearly the end of the world yesterday," he says.

"Don't be stupid—how can the world end. It goes on forever."

"If the Russians drop bombs on us and the Americans, we'll drop bombs on them and then there'll be so many explosions going off that it'll be the end of the world."

I don't say anything; I don't want him to see that I'm scared, so I carry on swinging the Clackers. The plastic balls click together at the bottom of the limp string, but that's it—I can never get them to work properly, like you see on the TV advert where the balls are supposed to knock into each other at the bottom of *and* above your hand.

"My Dad says that if you look at an atomic bomb go off it's so bright that it'll melt your eyeballs and you'll be blind forever."

"Don't be stupid," I say.

"The explosion is so loud that your ear drums will burst and you'll be deaf as well."

I look up from the swinging Clackers with a horrible picture in my head of not being able to see anything or hear anything.

Nigel carries on: "Then your skin'll melt off your bones and you'll be a walking skeleton. That's if you're lucky."

"Lucky? How do you make that out?" I ask. I'm getting fed up with the Clackers now.

"If you're far enough away to survive all that, then the radiation will get you. You won't notice a thing—houses, roads, cars, shops—it'll all look the same as before, but *everyone* will get ill—*really ill*—and drop dead." He chuckles as if he's said something clever; his fat cheeks wobble.

"Go away if you're going to be silly," I say.

Nigel laughs; he knows he's starting to scare me. I think of the old man I saw on my way to school.

"There'll be nothing left alive on earth, just dust and rubble."

I walk off towards the demountable classroom, leaving Nigel and the Clackers behind. I keep my face away from him so he doesn't see that I'm starting to cry. I can still hear Nigel as I walk away.

"There'll be so many bombs going off that the world will be knocked off balance. My dad says that time and space will alter..."

Saturday: 87 degrees Fahrenheit.

It's so busy today; Mum's taking me round the shops in town and there are people everywhere. I'm clinging on to Mum's hand as she leads me around the grocery store—all the different coloured fruits and vegetables looks fab. People are shoving into each other to get to the produce. I saw a man putting apples and bananas into his bag and then run out of the shop without paying. Nobody seemed to mind, but a big woman with curly hair tutted.

I want to get out of here. My head feels dizzy but I have to keep holding on to my mum because if I get lost in all this, I'll not find her again. Anyway, it's nearly time for us to go to Woolworth's. I want to see the new Steve Austin: Six Million Dollar Man figure. I've seen the advert on the telly—he has a bionic eye that you can hold up to your eye and look through, and if you pull a lever on his back he lifts up an engine block which comes with the set.

We're just outside the grocery store; it's bright and hazy in the street and everyone is standing around on the pavement. I ask Mum what's going on so she takes me to the front by the road. There's a metal fence so that people can't walk into the road. Everybody is watching the road like they're waiting for something. Policemen stand on the other side of the railing, guarding it so no one jumps over. On the other side of the road, behind another fence, there are a group of punks with really bright hair—green, red, and orange. One of them, a man, has his hair pushed up really high in the middle—he looks like the cockerel on the cornflakes packets. Even though it's hot, they all wear black jackets, some with loads of badges on them. Some of the punks have written on their clothes in white paint, not neatly though, so I can't read the words. One of them has a big pin going through his nose. I can't keep my eyes off the pin. I wonder how he got it in there. I wonder if he put it in himself. It must have been agony for him. He sees me looking at him, but just before I manage to look away, he wrinkles his nose at me and spits on the floor, letting it ooze from his mouth in a long stream. I don't know why he doesn't like me, just because I looked at him. They're all drinking from cans and a policeman is talking with them, but they're laughing and joking at him when he's not looking at them.

I look up at my mum and ask her what everyone's waiting for, but before she says anything there's a drum beating down the road. I lean forward as far as I can to see, holding onto the bars with my head on the cold metal. There are people coming slowly along the road, some of them are dressed in white sheets like I did at Halloween when we went trick-or-treating. The two at the front are each beating a drum slowly in time with each other; behind them, others march along holding boards on sticks high above their heads. They're shouting out at the crowds on either side. The cornflake-cockerel and his friends clap and shout out "Oi, oi" and drink from their cans.

The drummers pass right by me and I gaze up to see that they are wearing white masks which look like skulls, you can see the grinning teeth and the black eye-holes. It must be hot in there. I step back. I'm scared—they might reach over and get at me.

One of them shakes his arms and shouts something angrily at one of the policemen; the policeman points his finger at the man to warn him as he walks past. One of the punks with black panda eyes and no sleeves in his jean-jacket to show off his tattoos, is arguing with one of the skeleton men on the other side where some of the railing has fallen down. The punk pushes the man in the chest. He falls back onto the road but gets back up quickly and hits the punk. The two men punch and kick at each other like two dogs I once saw in our street, until three policemen separate them and take them away to their car—the punk is limping and holding his head. I'm glad that Mum's hand is on my shoulder.

More skeleton men pass by, some of them walk quietly, holding their boards up high, others shout out nastily or even, I think, cry behind their masks. I wonder what their faces look like underneath. I can only see their eyes.

"It's not too late," one of them says to me as he goes past. "Stop it now, before it's too late," shouts another.

The huge group gets thinner and thinner and finally just a few of them pass. At the back, one of them is wearing a long black robe with a hood—I can't see his face inside but he carries a long, moon shaped knife on a long pole. He is the scariest of them all and I step back into the crowd again and watch him walk past. I don't want him to notice me.

When they've all gone by, the policemen open the gates and people start to cross the road and go back into the shops, shaking their heads and mumbling to each other. The road seems quieter than it was before.

I don't feel like going to Woolworth's to see the Six Million Dollar Man anymore. I wish Davie was here; he'd know what this is all about. He'd tell me.

I want to go home now.

Sunday: 90 degrees Fahrenheit.
I had a dream about Davie last night; it was just like how it actually happened. I remember waking up; there was a screech of tyres then a smashing sound and a tinkling of broken glass. My pushchair was on its side—I was inside. When I looked out, Davie was lying in the middle of the road with his arm at a funny angle and all the traffic had stopped and people were crowding around. Mum said that he had died straight away and wouldn't have felt a thing. She said that my pushchair had rolled down the bank into the road while she was in the newsagents buying Dad's cigarettes and that Davie had run into the road to save me from getting run over. Only in my dream last night we both died and we lay together in the road; but the funny thing was that we could still talk and joke together, invisible, so nobody else could see us.

I'm lying in bed now. It's so hot that I can't keep still long enough to get to sleep. It's very late because I heard Mum and Dad going to bed—

whispering on the landing, brushing teeth, toilet flushing, then their bedroom door closing quietly, and then silence—and they always go to bed *really* late. Mum and Dad spent all day watching the news on television. They wouldn't even let me see the Muppets tonight.

Mum had one of her "turns" today. She was shouting at Dad in the kitchen and I watched from the upstairs window as she ran into the back garden pulling on her hair. Dad told me afterwards that everybody was frightened at what's happening on the news with the Russians and the Americans and that I shouldn't worry because we weren't close to any big cities. I don't know what he meant by saying that. What's wrong with living near a big city; and what's that got to do with Mum anyway?

The house is really quiet now. I heard lots of cars going past and people talking and walking around outside earlier. Something was happening, but I don't know what.

Now it's just the house creaking and a dog barking in the distance and, every now and then, the drone of big helicopters far, far away.

Monday: 62 degrees Fahrenheit.

It's supposed to be the start of the summer holidays today, but it's not sunny anymore. This summer has been a "heat wave" so my teacher Mrs. Lennox was telling us. But today it's just dull and cold. The wind became really strong late last night, rattling the windows and keeping me awake. Mum wasn't here when I woke up; Dad said she'd gone to see Aunty Mable at her house. He said the heat we've been having was starting to get to people and that now it's gone cooler, things will soon get back to normal. I hope they do. He's listening to the radio again; he said the TV's not working. I asked him why he wasn't at work at the railway yard today and he just laughed as if I'd said something funny and said he was off work for a long time now.

I've got a headache, but I'm still going to go and see Daniel who lives opposite.

Daniel is wearing his Parker with the hood up, so I went back home to get mine. Dad asked me where I was going and when I said that Daniel and I were going to play on the rope-swing at the park, I thought he was going to stop me, but then he smiled and said that I might as well enjoy myself while I could. He told me to be careful. Dad didn't look very well. He had dark circles around his eyes, which were red and puffy, and he looked pale.

The streets are empty as we make our way along the pavements of our estate—past trimmed hedges and front lawns—there are a few leaves blowing around in the breeze, blown down from last night's wind. As we walk, I hear a shrill screaming and a moaning sound muffled behind someone's front window. I look at Daniel who gives me an odd look, but we carry on. We stop and look around Mr. Cooper's brown Datsun 240Z parked in his drive; I like the bucket seats and the big front spoiler. Daniel says that the car will do 125 miles per hour at top speed.

"I'm going to have a motorbike when I'm older," I tell him. "And I'm gonna do stunts like Evel Knievel."

Daniel steps back and looks at me with his head on one side. "You might not grow tall enough to be able to ride a bike," he says, looking down at me. "Anyway, I prefer cars; they're safer if you ever have a crash."

"It didn't stop Evel Knievel," I shout. "He broke his pelvis last year when he tried to jump over thirteen London buses, but he carried on after that and jumped fourteen Greyhound buses in America."

"That's stupid," snorts Daniel. "He'll end up killing himself."

I ignore him and walk onwards. Davie, my brother, wouldn't have said that. He would've been on my side.

"Why's it so quiet, Dan?" I ask when he catches up.

"Everybody thinks that the Russians are going to go to war and bomb us any time soon. Most people aren't even leaving their homes—I had to sneak out of my bedroom window onto the garage roof to get out—they wouldn't have let me go otherwise. Lots of people have left town—didn't you hear it all in the road last night? Haven't you been listening to the news? They're saying that parts of America were hit last night."

"I don't like the news. It's boring," I say.

We round the corner and weave our way through a line of parked cars and then go between the three concrete bollards which lead us into the park—an empty field all to ourselves. Far over to our left is a row of oak trees lining the brook which flows by the side of the field. From one of these trees is where our rope-swing hangs—if it's still there. We head in that direction over the sun-burned yellow grass.

My tummy flutters as the long rope comes into view; a thick, stubby piece of wood—the seat—hangs at the bottom, dangling from a thick branch high up in the leaves. I start to run, heading for the small bare patch of dusty earth below the swing. I can't wait for the thrill that I remember so well.

It's quite hard for me to heave myself upon the rope, but I get comfy on the seat. My legs dangle as I spin around—first one way—faster and faster and then the other way. It makes me laugh as Daniel runs up. He pushes me, slowly at first, then higher and higher. The wind pushes on my face, blowing my hair into my eyes as I hug the rope close. This weightless feeling—it's like flying.

I soar over the brook, with a thrill of danger in knowing that if I was to fall, I'd be head first into the streaming water. I'm so high up at the top, I can see the tops of some of the smaller trees, the narrow tracks me and Davie used to chase along through the woods on the other side of the stream. I spin round and round as I swing and Daniel is standing looking up at me. Every time I twist and turn, I can see him watching me, then I see the brook and then the wood appears in front of me, again and again.

I love this. This is brilliant!

"Do you want your turn, Dan?" I ask.

There's no reply.

I lean back, holding the rope at arm's length, to spin around and see what's keeping him from answering. When he comes back into sight, he's not wearing his Parker coat anymore but a brown tank top and blue shirt with the big collar; the long, wavy blond hair and the worn corduroy flares which I remember so well. He stands tall, arms crossed and with a big smile. He seems to be waiting for my reaction. It's not Daniel, but *this* boy knows me *very* well.

"DAVIE!" I yell.

I'm still swinging high and twisting on the swing, so I can't go to him. "What happened to Dan?" I shout.

"He went home half an hour ago, Junior. You were too busy enjoying yourself to notice." He's still staring at me and smiling.

"Do you remember when you climbed up to tie this rope on—ages ago, when I was little?" I say, my swinging slowing slightly but I'm spinning faster.

Davie chuckles. "We had some fun. You and me, eh?"

It hits me that Davie shouldn't be here. "But you died, Davie. How did you come back?"

He nods his head, still smiling, but this time his eyes look serious. "One minute, I was nowhere and the next moment I was standing at the other side of the field. I saw two figures in the distance, the only people, so I walked over; that's when I recognized you and Dan. I watched you for a while by the trees until Dan went away; that's when I took his place here."

"Where were you, Davie, before? I mean, after the accident?"

"I don't know, Junior. It's as though I were to ask you to remember where you were before you were born."

Davie looks around into the distance, at the trees and then at the sky. "The light's different, sort of blue-ish, more like twilight. Where is everybody?" His voice sounds serious.

I'm confused, my head still hurts; I need to get down so I can talk to him properly—to check that he's actually here and not just another dream. "Can you help me down, Davie?"

He doesn't move but turns back from looking at the sky and stares at me. He nods his head slowly as if he's just realised something new; he's still smiling but his eyes look sad.

"Davie, I'm sorry if it was my fault that you got hit by that car. I didn't want you to die. I've missed you a lot. It hasn't been the same since..."

I need to get down. I feel stupid, up in the air trying to talk to him. "*Please* get me down, Davie."

"There's no time, Junior. I just wanted to have this moment with you. You see, I may have to go away again."

I lift myself off the seat and stretch a leg towards the ground to try and stop the swinging with my foot, but I can't reach, and anyway, most of what's beneath me is the ditch where the brook flows far below; but I have to get down.

"It wasn't your fault, Junior," Davie's voice says. "I missed you too. We had some fun. Remember our last holiday; remember roller-skating on the pier at Bournemouth? Neither of us could stay on our feet."

I laugh, but at the same time I want to cry. I dangle myself from the rope-swing. I get ready to drop, even though I'm still swinging quite high and I'm scared I might break something. I've got to do it though.

There is a sudden white flash which stays in my eyes. I shake my head and squeeze the rope. Did something hit me?

A sudden gust of strong, hot wind stings my right side. The rope snaps and I fall onto the dusty ground. I cry out but I can't hear myself in the roar of the burning wind which seems to get even worse. It hurts to try and breathe but I have to crawl forwards as hot dust scorches my face. The wind gets hotter, stronger still. The hurting on my face gets worse.

I can't bear this...

Behind me, the brook starts to bubble and steam rises from it. Everything's going cloudy and red. I can only see out of one eye, and it hurts really bad, but I can just still see Davie...or is it Daniel standing there...?

There are huge black clouds in the distance, way, way behind the trees at the end of the field. They look really cool, growing so quickly, so massive...

Am I still crawling to him...?

...He's on fire. He's falling over in flames, his face burning black.

"*DAAAVIEEEE...*"

Everything's black but I can taste metal.

There's an *almighty* rumbling and shaking in the ground but I can't hear anything anymore.

OH GOD, THE PAIN!

PLEASE...

JUST GIVE ME...MORE...TIME...

Of Dreams and Song

Filip Wiltgren

*Editor: Too often we turn a blind eye to the apocalypses
that take place every day in our own world.*

In the beginning was the Song. The Song created the waters and the waves. The Song created the dreamers and the air we breathe. And we dreamers heard the Song and joined our dreams to it.

For untold dream-sleeps we chorused, dreaming the pure Song throughout the waters. But amongst us were those who were not content to dream, those who would change and overpower. They were the singers.

It would be comforting to say that the singers were strangers that rose from the depths, but the Song is truth and the truth is that the singers came from amongst us. Remember this, you who will sing and dream after my flesh rots and my bones drop to the silt, remember that the singers came from amongst us and that their sin is ours.

The singers took hold of the Song and changed it. They sung the waters cooler and the krill fatter, and they sung their own greatness and mastery. But like the wind that stirs the water into waves, so, too, did the singers stir the Song. Where there once had been calm there now was storm, and from that storm rose the rocks that kill.

Once the rocks were sung, they could not be unsung, no matter how hard the singers tried, and their singing brought new dangers to the waters. It tore the dreamers into clans, and warped them. Some of the dreamers shrunk, becoming like calves even when adult. Some lost their baleen, feeding with teeth, like sharks. And some became twisted, eating other dreamers. These are the killers in black and white, the eaters of dreams, and when they joined the Song, they ripped it, battering it like a hurricane.

The Song grew shrill, giving the singers power over blood and life, but as even the mightiest wave breaks, the Song broke. It cracked into pieces and from those pieces came the rock-men.

At first the rock-men dwelt upon dry stone and when they ventured into the waters the killers would hunt and eat them. But the rock-men learned to kill from the dream-eaters and soon they killed all that swam.

This is our shame, that the singers would draw such pain and such death into the waters. For the rock-men were deaf to the Song, and their souls were dry. They killed without end, and they filled the waters with the blood of dreamers. Only the dream-eaters did they leave alone, for the eaters of dreams were their kith and kin.

Throughout the waters, the plea and pain of the dreamers flowed, and dreamers and singers alike joined to save the rock-men from the dryness of their souls. We dreamers would swim up to their rock-shells and dream at them, and the singers would sing at them.

The rock-men would not hear the Song, nor heed the dreams. They could but kill, and as we died the Song grew weak. The noise of the rock-men drowned it, pushing it deep under the surface where even the great bone-tooth singers could not dive.

And thus the waters changed. The dreamers died. The singers died. Even the eaters of dreams died, for once the rock-men had tired of killing dreamers they turned on their kin. The singers grew remorseful, and they would swim onto the rocks, trying to dream them back into the ocean, but the Song has grown weak and the singers few. The rocks would not budge.

They are our shame and our punishment, dry teeth growing from the waters. There the rocks will remain until the Song is dreamt by all, dreamers and singers, even the eaters, alike. Then the waters shall return and wash over the world, and the rocks and the rock-men will sink back into the nightmares whence they came. The dreamers shall be united one and all, with no blood or tooth between them, and the waters will lie peaceful and still.

But that day is far off yet, young dreamers, so dream, dream the Song as it was dreamt in the beginning. Dream it to each other over the noise of the rock-men, over the cry of our dying. Dream it, and dream of times to come.

Every Day

Naomi Brett Rourke

Editor: Apocalypses come in all shapes and horrors, some of our own creation.

Chuck found the old neighborhood almost unrecognizable. He had been gone a long time. He stepped carefully over cracked, uneven chunks of broken pavement. Only the brown crabgrass told him that anyone or anything had ever lived on Oak Street. He spent his boyhood here and eventually traded it for manhood.

The sun beat down on his head and sweat trickled down his brow. The trees were brown and sere, no leaves on their branches; and empty, forlorn nests from birds long gone could be spotted here and there. The remains of a tree house, long rotten, perched in the big oak tree in front of his house. He looked at it, rapt, musing at the boy he once was and the man he became. A piece of wood, hanging by a splinter, caught a random bit of wind, separated, and fell to the ground with a muffled thud. *So much for my childhood*, he thought wryly. Chuck Rose fought by nature and by profession, but even he couldn't escape reality. What he'd had here was long gone. He had turned his back on it a long time ago. The world had turned its back as well. Charred cities and toxic earth.

Chuck strode toward the dilapidated house, deliberately crunching the fallen lumber under his boot. He stepped up onto the porch avoiding broken steps and tried the doorknob. It turned in his hand. *Well, why not?* No one had lived here for many, many years. He eased the door open with the music of rusty hinges. He peered into the dark and stepped inside, closing the door behind him. What he had to do was personal; no one could know the reason for his visit.

The silence screamed. There should be something making noise—wind, mice, anything. The stillness pulsed, and to Chuck it seemed like he was underwater with that cool hush that he remembered from boyhood swimming pools and still, glassy lakes. For Chuck, there were no more lakes. They had all dried up. There were no more swimming pools with no one to fill them. There was just silence and loneliness and regret.

He stepped forward, surprised when his feet made no sound. *Perfect.* He strode to the living room. Where intact, the carpet wore a deep stain of mildew. Chuck stared at it in surprise. *That isn't right.* His brow furrowed as he pondered. *There's very little water so why would it be mildewed? Huh.* He circled the carpet and the mouse-gnawed sofa but there were no mice anymore. He looked for tiny corpses but there were none. The tiny rodents must have been eaten long ago when food got scarce. By cats or—

Chuck shook his head with a smile that only touched his mouth. *Who else might have been eating the three blind mice?*

As a boy Chuck had jumped and tried to touch the tall center of the arch to the dining room. He looked up and raised a lazy hand to try again when a whisper touched him from behind.

"Chuck…"

Icy fingers touched his neck as he stopped short and carefully reached his right hand for his Beretta 9 mm. His hand found nothing. *What the—?* He barely held his sphincter in check. He felt the gun's weight instead on his left side. With his left hand he snatched it out and aimed. His weapon pointed at an empty dining room. He pivoted right and backpedaled. No one was in the living room. Slowly, Chuck crept into the dining room, listening, looking. No one. No voices. Hesitantly, he holstered his gun, then he remembered. He was right-handed. He always had his holster on the right side. *What is going on here?* Chuck looked down at his hands, turning them over. He'd felt no awkwardness as he whipped the gun out left-handed. The left hand had felt absolutely normal. He didn't feel right-handed. *Weird.* Chuck turned and continued into the dining room, mulling his change of handedness and the whisper that had almost unmanned him.

In the dining room he almost smelled the turkey and gravy of Thanksgivings past, when his mother had been the best cook on the block. Her holiday dinners had been legendary and for a moment his mouth watered with the flavors of silky, buttery mashed potatoes, tart cranberries, crunchy Brussels sprouts, and green bean casserole with fried onions atop. When he married, his wife, Teresa, made the best pies. Pecan and creamy pumpkin in the winter; apple, cherry, and blueberry in the summer. He remembered taking his children out by the dirt road where blueberries grew, and in the early summer the royal blue of the berries vied with the endless robin's egg blue of the cloudless sky. He and his children—how many were there? Two? Three? *That's odd. I can't remember.* They yanked berries and ate so many, the blue juice staining their mouths, that Chuck swore every time that they'd never eat their dinner but they always did. Teresa's handmade pastries topped even her pies with her signature daffodil cut-out designs on top, slightly brown and steaming from the oven.

As he skirted the remains of the table, he lightly touched his fingers to the dusty top. It invoked even more memories. He snatched his hand up in disgust. *I don't need this. Since when have I been all gooey-like and a family* man. *Never. The job was my family.*

"Chuck…" The whisper came again.

He turned and, as he was expecting, saw no one. *Weird. Weird things are happening. Why?* Spinning back, he exited the dining room and made his way through each of the remaining rooms, barely glancing at broken furniture, threadbare carpet, broken mirrors, and remembering deserted dreams.

He couldn't wait to finish his tour of the house. He went outside to a broken-down shed. Yanking the door open, he found rusted garden implements. He chose a crowbar and a pickaxe and went back inside. His heart beat slowly as he entered the bedroom he had shared with his wife. Chuck steeled himself for what was to come. *Just to make sure…* He knew what he had to do but he didn't relish it. Looking down at the moldering carpet, he found just the right spot, and swung the pick high. He almost toppled forward as the bite of it slicing through the wood was easier than he thought. *Stupid. The wood's rotten, asshole.* He shook his head and raised the pickaxe high again and again and, after a time, chose the crowbar to pry up the floorboards.

When he yanked out the rotten wood, he threw the crowbar away and used his hands, digging, digging, and even this far below the surface it was bone dry. The dust was everywhere, clogging his nose and his mouth. Chuck licked his lips and blew a breath out and when he leaned down again, he felt something soft. *It couldn't be. She would be desiccated, all dried up—a mummy.* He gently moved the dirt off the soft thing which, when uncovered, turned out to be a soft female hand. *Teresa.*

Chuck sat back on his haunches and looked at the hand. That hand had loved him, made him countless dinners, reared his children, and finally had brushed away the tears that just couldn't move her recalcitrant husband to stay with the family. Chuck gazed at it. It was soft. So soft. The times, though, needed hard hands. Hands that knew what to do and didn't pause at doing it. She had been weak.

"No, Chuck." The whisper began and to Chuck's horror, the hand, that soft hand, began to move. "You were weak. You didn't stay with us. You abandoned us. All of us."

The dirt fell off her in sheets as she struggled to sit up in her grave. Other than the dirt on her face, she looked exactly like the last time he had seen her alive.

"What was so important that you couldn't stay with your family? We loved you." Her arms rose up and hands grasped for him. Chuck gasped, pistoning his legs, clods of dirt hitting Teresa on her breast and face, shooting him to the very back of the pit, where he scrabbled in the dirt and climbed out.

"I had to go," he yelled. "I had to go save the world. I had to."

"Is your world saved now?" Teresa asked, tilting her head like a hound. "Is this the world you wanted? Everything's dry, unloved, dead." Putting her hands below her, she pushed herself to a standing position and stood, gazing up at her husband. Her eyes, once blue, now only held cloudy white and gray. Her lips were gray as well. *Other than that*, Chuck thought confusedly, *she looks all right. Except...except that hole in her chest where her heart should have been. That's nasty.* He didn't remember doing that.

"No, you don't understand. It was my job. I had no choice."

"You always had choices!" Teresa suddenly bellowed, and then whispered, "And you had no job." She began to drag herself out of the hole with hands now resembling claws. She never broke eye contact with her husband. Chuck stumbled back.

"You always had choices." Another whisper came from behind and Chuck pivoted and, when he saw his son, a groan came out of his mouth.

Just as dirty, but not looking anywhere near as good as his mother, nine-year-old Tad shuffled forward. Tad's ears and mouth were black craters matching the one in his mother's chest. Worst of all, his hands were blackened and rotted. Chuck remembered those hands throwing balls, making birdhouses, playing his guitar, and he gave a sob.

"Tad..."

"Daddy..." Behind her older brother, Emily shuffled in her faded pink nightdress. *She's five years old*, Chuck thought wildly, *but she's not! She's not!* Intact hands didn't match her blackened and rotted feet. As she shuffled forward, she tottered like a broken doll, reeling and swaying. Her blonde hair was matted and sparse. Chuck remembered brushing her long, golden hair and dancing with her every night before she went to bed. There was another hole in her chest.

"Daddy," Emily whispered. "Daddy, I missed you. Why don't you dance with me. Didn't you like us?" She held her arms us and started toward Chuck, but then started to growl deep in her throat. Tad joined with his own wail.

"Get away from me," Chuck mumbled, taking step after step backward into the hall, grabbing at his Beretta, which suddenly was not on either hip.

"Look what you've done to us," Teresa said, stalking her retreating husband. "Look what we've become. And you're to blame. You took this," Teresa's voice took on a shrill tone as she gestured to her chest, to the hole where her heart had been. "With your apathy. With your absence." The children's cries became louder and keener. "Look at your daughter, your son! Look!" Teresa transformed from regretful memory to terrifying nightmare. She hunted quicker now after her husband, scuttling sideways like some demented crab, but faster and faster, while Chuck retreated in front of her rage.

"Look! Look! Why?" she screeched. She was running now, on vengeful feet, and in a moment she was on him. She clawed his face.

"I'm sorry," Chuck shrieked, "I'm sorry. I didn't mean it." Stepping backward, Chuck lost his footing on a scrap of rug. As he strove to right himself, his howling children threw themselves on him. Together they all bumped down the stairs in a heap. As his leg broke, Chuck shrieked. When his shoulder dislocated, he ground his teeth together so hard one snapped. Over and over he tumbled. The pain blanketed his mind. All pain he'd felt before didn't compare to the agony he felt when he hit the bottom floor with his entire family on top of him.

Chuck groaned; his body was bruised and broken. The children circled him, looking down at him as he writhed on the floor. His wife spoke from her height, head tilted.

"We'll be here with you, darling. Every time you come back to this house. Every time you step foot in this house. And you come back so very often. Every time, every day, every hour, every minute. We'll be here for you just like you weren't here for us." The children keening, kneeled down beside him. Teresa bent down and grasped the hole in her breast and rent it open with an inhuman howl. Then, when the sides of her chest hung open with gobbets of blood and meat hanging down, she cradled his face in her soft, gore-riddled hands. Chuck, eyes wide with horror, opened his mouth for a scream that never came as she placed her mouth over his.

* * *

Lisa's nurse's clogs made shushing sounds as she walked quickly down the path on her way to the elderly man in the wheelchair under the widely spreading oak tree. Dee, the blonde-haired nurse in charge of Chuck, looked up from the book she had been reading.

"Hey, watcha doing?" Dee smiled and patted the seat next to her on the bench.

"Not much. Just here for Mr. Rosenstein's weekly visit. I have to be quick." She held out a pack of cigarettes, looking over her shoulder. Dee took one and plucked her lighter out of her pocket, first lighting hers and then Lisa's.

"Still hiding from Vasquez?"

"Still." Lisa exhaled a plume. "I don't know what her problem is. We're outside."

"A healthy home is a smoke-free home," Dee sing-songed.

"Yeah, well, most everyone in this place isn't going to live out the year anyhow," Lisa sucked on her cigarette, "so I don't think that matters too much. More forced family fun for Charlie, here?" Lisa queried.

"Uh-huh." Dee perched on the edge of the bench as if ready to flee at any moment. "I don't know why they bother," she whispered. "He didn't want to have anything to do with them before, and I'm sure he doesn't want to have anything to do with them now."

"Why are you whispering? It's not like he can hear us or even understand us if he does. What's his problem again?"

"Repetition compulsion," Dee said, plucking on her cigarette. "He relives the same traumatic event over and over. When he first came here—when he wasn't catatonic—he'd be running all over, screaming. He thought he was a spy or something, called himself 'Chuck Rose.' Thought that he killed his family and they were after him. Like zombies or ghosts or something. Brrr. It was spooky."

"But I thought he left them?"

"He did. Again and again."

Lisa ground her cigarette out beneath her heel and scuffed it under some vegetation.

"Was he a spy?"

"No. He used to say he was an undercover whatever but he was just an accountant. He was a miserable human being when he got here. I can't imagine being his family."

Lisa said pensively, "I wonder what he thinks about now."

Dee looked over at Charlie Rosenstein as she pitched her cigarette into the bird feeder. She shrugged with indifference.

Lisa got up and stretched, putting her book in her pocket. "If you're taking him back I'll come with. I'm almost off."

Dee leaned in front of Charlie and said, over-enunciating and loudly, "Charlie, your family is here. Your wife Teresa's here with your kids. Isn't that nice? Let's go see them, shall we?"

Lisa smirked. "You're going to give yourself a hernia yelling that loud. I told you he couldn't hear you."

Dee smiled, turning Charlie's wheelchair around. "I have to try. What are you doing this weekend?"

"Double-date."

As the nurses walked off with Mr. Charles Rosenstein, the birds chirped steadily to insects humming in the flowering stalks. The earth was fecund and moist and alive. Chuck—Charles Rosenstein—lived differently, however. Every day, every hour, and every minute.

Revelation

Matthew Buscemi

Editor: Who have we influenced? Who have we loved? What have we wrought? Whether death comes in a great apocalypse or from long illness, the Ferryman makes each of us take stock in the value of our lives.

apocalypse
from Greek apokalupsis, *meaning "uncover"*

So, this is what it feels like to know you're going to die. Now that I think about it, I always knew that I was going to die. It's just that…the *exactly when* of it felt deferrable. Part of some far-off future not worth bothering over. Ten percent of my salary is about all the care I ever gave that future, and it seems inadequate now.

I wonder if I should have known. If I could have avoided this by simply paying more attention. But if I walk my life back far enough to have not ended up at this place in this time, then I can't imagine the decisions I would have to have made to be rationalizable.

And yet here I am, standing atop this roof, looking down over…I close my eyes. I don't want to look anymore.

People who know they are about to die are supposed to relive their lives in the moments before their death. I've got about ten minutes, give or take. Could I have done any better? Reduced any suffering, affected one more rescue? All the same, I feel guilty. And ashamed.

I remember a small tremor during the meeting with the executive committee. I have no idea if the shaking was related or not. For all I know, it could have been just a tiny earthquake, but it was the first moment that I became aware of something worming its way into my mind, whispering that things were not as they should have been.

At the time, Angela's presentation held all of my attention. She talked about how my team was to prioritize work for Jeff's team—that's the Tooling and Product Support team, TPS—over the work we might do for Rachel's team—that's Data Analytics; no one calls them DA (don't ask me why).

TPS had been late on their last three projects, and each time Angela had confronted Jeff with this uncomfortable fact, he'd attempted to drag my team—that's Central Technology, usually Central Tech, but never CT—down with him. We'd bounced back of course. During such incidents, I would just calmly explain my position, meet all the demands made upon my team and more, and then I'd go back to the meetings, just like this one, and show everyone the numbers. No hysterics, no finger pointing. Just numbers. It's worked well for my team, I think.

Angela stopped speaking only momentarily when the building juddered. Jeff gripped the table and his knuckles turned white. Rachel looked around the room anxiously, as though the walls might collapse inward at any moment. Martin was there too, my team's technical lead. He furrowed his brow momentarily.

I just watched them.

The moment passed. It couldn't have been more than a second or two. Angela just proceeded onward as though nothing had happened. Had it, though? I know it's odd to fixate on such things, especially now, but I find myself wondering if that's a moment we should have been aware of something, some veil being lifted—and I use words like that because as I gaze across the Seattle skyline now, that's what I see. I see a vast revealing, the world's farcical mask being stripped away and its true nature, which was always there, merely coming to the foreground.

I wonder how much pain I'll be in.

But I'm jumping ahead.

I'm the production lead for Central Tech, and if you don't work IT, which you probably won't because from the sound of it there won't be any IT left by the end of the day, then those terms need a bit of unpacking. Unlike Jeff's and Rachel's teams, who work on one thing—a piece of software, or some service—my team works on all the things for the whole company, just not all at the same time. We've got our own engineers, who jump from project to project as need be, making sure that individual teams don't end up reinventing the wheel or going down some technological garden path that someone else has already discovered won't work.

The engineers on my team decide how to build things. Always has been that way, always will be (at least for about ten minutes more). If I took that away from them, I'd be a bad leader. As the production lead, I decide *what* they work on, while leaving them complete autonomy over the *how*. And if you think that sounds important, remember that most of my time is spent in awkward meetings about how to resolve the fact that Jeff and Rachel both want us to work on their respective projects during the same two-month period.

I listen, and I observe. That's most of what my job entails. So I wonder how I missed something as big as this.

After Angela, Jeff, and Rachel had left the exec meeting, it was just me and Martin, my team's "how" authority, sitting there. He asked me if I had a moment, and after Jeff had shut the door, he stared silently at the tabletop.

I wasn't looking out the large wall of windows along the conference room exterior wall—I should have glanced at least, but didn't—I was looking at him, his gaze reticent, his eyes telling me he was thinking something that he wasn't sure he should voice.

"What's on your mind?" I tried.

He finally looked up. "How are you?"

I shrugged. "Fine."

He seemed to allow himself a small smile. "I appreciate you looking out for our team at every turn."

He didn't know the half of it. Central Tech is an easy target. I fended this kind of stuff off two or three times a week, just usually not on the level that would warrant getting exec, and therefore Martin, involved. Production types attached to typical product teams can't help but set their sights on us when they blunder into something unexpected and need a scapegoat. "We're a good team. It's easy to sing our praises." It's true. I've never had to creatively recast our numbers into something that looks better than it is. I can just tell the truth.

"Are you okay?" I asked, wondering if this had been some attempt to deflect some insecurity on his part.

"Yeah," Martin replied easily. "I like the work, and the team is great."

"But?"

He pursed his lips. "It's so great to find enclaves like this one in a company. I've been lucky to find them in the past, and especially lucky here. Everywhere I've worked, the petty politics always seems so much larger and so much more…omnipotent than the healthy enclaves. It's like human systems just aggregate that way. And the only way to keep the healthy enclaves healthy is to fight tooth and nail all the time."

I nodded. "Yeah."

"Yeah?" Martin raised an eyebrow.

"I just want to help good people do good work. It feels empowering to empower others."

Martin blinked at me a few times, then smiled a bit. I remember thinking that I'd outed myself as some kind of unicorn of management—someone who's more interested in doing good work than manipulating the system? Blasphemy!

I changed the subject to our schedule for Rachel's team, then we talked code for a bit. Those details are fuzzy in my memory. Nothing really gets clear again until the roof—but I'm jumping ahead again.

Martin and I left the conference room at some point and went to the elevators. We pressed the buttons, but they didn't light up. In fact, the elevator lobby felt awkwardly, wrongly silent. At any time during the business day, one should be able to hear the little squeaks, rattles, and grinds of the passenger cars ascending and descending, but at that moment—pure silence and dark buttons. Maybe one of the banks could have been out of commission, but all six of them?

I suggested taking the stairs up to the eighth floor, and Martin followed.

What was I thinking as I climbed those stairs? Certainly not yet thoughts of total catastrophe, but something more amiss than normal. A fire drill that had uncovered a broken fire alarm system, perhaps. Or perhaps an elevator system of the same make and model had encountered a design flaw that had resulted in the deaths of a car full of people, and our building's administration had deactivated our elevators in response. I admit that I let a stray thought to the effect of, "thank goodness it wasn't me" pass through my mind before chastising myself for it. The irony of my present situation is not lost on me.

When I got back to my desk, Jones stood over his desk (which is next to mine) looking out the large exterior window wall. He's not a part of my team, but his desk is in our area for some reason known only to facilities. His first name is Kelly, but he hates it. He makes everyone call him Jones. I once asked him what his middle name was, and he replied that he hated it even more than his first. That was the last time I talked names with him. I just called him Jones like everyone else.

He stood there just gazing out the window. I was nearly ready to ask him about what he was looking at—I came so close to finding out right then and there—but Mary, one of our software engineers, who'd seen me return to my desk, jumped out of her chair and began asking me—

You know, I really don't remember. Something to do with priority of some task over such and such another. Something TPS wanted done. It's so odd. That thing we call the backlog, that prioritized list of tasks, that abstract entity so crucial to keeping my team healthy and safe, is now the furthest thing from my mind. Maybe that's because half my team has gone, and I think the other half is on the other side of the rooftop. None of it matters anymore, because the ones I kept safe are safe, and the ones I couldn't aren't, and the backlog had nothing to do with any of it.

But you'd think I'd still be able to recall details regardless.

Anyhow, I helped Mary determine what to work on next, and then Carmine, who's the Quality Assurance lead on TPS, came up and had a question about yet another task I can't remember anything about. When she finally left I slumped down in my seat, took a deep breath, thought about maybe getting coffee. Why can I remember wanting coffee but not the items on my backlog?

Now all I could see was Jones. He was still standing there, looking out the window, catatonic, same as he'd been when I'd first come back to my desk…five minutes before?

"Jones?" I asked.

No reply.

"Jones!"

Still nothing.

"Jones, what's—"

That was it. That was the moment I knew that something was really, truly, very, deeply wrong. More wrong than a small earthquake or an elevator malfunction. I turned my gaze over the desks of Central Tech, half of which lay against the wall-windows that cover our building's exterior.

Sarah stood gaping over her own desk. Nate stood next to her, his hand over his mouth. Their eyes radiated terror.

I scrambled to a window, perhaps even shoving Jones aside in order to do so. Down below, no traffic moved. There were cars in the road, sure, but all crusted over brown and green, as though they'd all molded over. Corpses lay slack behind wheels, human-shaped tufts of fibrous pus. Everything had been engulfed, the roads, the lampposts, the trees, the buildings, all of it turned brown and green, with tiny cilia swaying and glistening with each passing breeze. It spread as far as I could see, down Sixth Avenue, in every direction. A few bodies lay huddled on the sidewalks, consumed, just like the sidewalks and everything else. And most horrifyingly of all, one could see, against the building adjacent to our own, the green-brown mold spreading itself out, unfolding again and again, like a perpetual, biological Jacob's ladder, across the exterior of the building's third floor. It took less than a second for me to conclude that my own building was under just such an attack, and was now only five flights away from my present location.

I shot to my computer, jittery, fingers shaking. I had to try two, maybe three times in order to type my password correctly. Having logged in, I found that nothing would load in my browser. Ethernet and wifi were both out. I slammed the laptop shut and grabbed up my cell phone. I have no family in Seattle, nor a spouse. The woman I'd had two recent dates with didn't register as a concern—my team did. These are people I'd fought for, bled favors for, and will die for.

I opened my mouth to speak, but found no sound ushered forth. My eyes remained fixed on the tiny, green-brown hairs spreading across the building across the street, the buildings beside it, and all the buildings beside them, on and on up Sixth Avenue.

I shut my eyes, blinked and shook my head. "Guys."

No one spoke.

"We have to get to the roof. Let's go."

Jones swung around, his gaze piercing but his voice quavering. His face was flushed red. "How will that help?"

As if to answer his question, helicopter blades sounded overhead, and, just as quickly, retreated into the distance.

"It's preferable to waiting here," I shot back.

Maybe I'm making myself sound braver and nobler than I actually behaved. I remember feeling that he was raving, and I got snarky back at him. Such details of who was more in the right and who was more in the wrong feel so trivial now, even though with Jones—

No. I'm not going to spend my last minutes on piety or self-righteousness. Absolutely not. I'm just as much to blame as anyone else.

I herded my team into the stairwells and we all headed upward.

At some point I called Jonathan. It must have been before the stairwell, because I don't get cell reception in the stairwell, and I don't think the conversation took place on the roof. Jonathan is a member of our team, but he works from his home in Renton, a Seattle suburb, often videoconferencing in for meetings.

"Jonathan?"

"Hey, man." That was Jonathan. If someone put a gun to his head, he'd find a way to still sound chill. "How you guys doing?"

"Not good, Jonathan. How are you?"

"All right for now. Apparently the crazy shit is just downtown for now, but they say it's spreading fast."

"They're not lying. You got Internet?"

"Yup. You should see social media."

"What happened, Jonathan?"

"Don't know. Some people are saying terrorists, but that ain't it, not with this stuff all over the world like it is."

I remember a jolt of shock on par with my seeing the mold for the first time. "It's not just Seattle?"

"No man, it's in all our major cities, all cities in Canada, all cities in Mexico, it's in Rio, and New Delhi, and Beijing, Cairo, Cape Town, Melbourne, Riyadh, Dubai, everywhere. That's not terrorists, man, that's something else. Something way more destructive than terrorists."

"And no one knows where it came from?"

"They're saying all kinds of shit—the cranks are on their usual alien and secret government soapboxes. I even read some guy who thinks that antibiotic resistant microflora finally evolved into something really nasty at random. Who knows? All I know is it sounds like we gotta evacuate every major urban area now."

My mind reeled. All urban centers on Earth. The first thought, I admit, was selfish, not really for me, but for my profession—computers were done. The Internet and cell phones and software engineering: gone.

At some point I regained my focus. "Jonathan, we need a helicopter. Eight of us. Make that two helicopters. 1014 Sixth Avenue. We're going up to the roof."

An awkward silence. "My wife wants me and our daughter out of the house and on the road to her mom's place in Maple Valley ASAP. But I'll do what I can until she tears me away from the computer."

"Thanks, man."

"Oh, hey," Jonathan added. "That monetization platform implementation I was working on? It's coming in pretty late. Definitely not before the end of the sprint. Just sayin'."

I actually chortled at that. "Duly noted." Was that my last smile? I don't think I've smiled since that; there's been nothing to smile about. "I'll adjust the backlog."

"Take care of yourself, man."

"You too, Jonathan."

At the twelfth floor, some guy from another company and I kicked down the roof access door. Other details from along the way: Jessica kept twitching her head and jamming her body into the corners of the stairwell. I had to fall back and pry her out. Nate kept shouting at everyone, and we all shouted back to hurry on upward. A fire alarm erupted mid-ascent and continued blaring; no one paid it any mind.

We flooded onto the roof: myself, my team, others from my company, and employees of other companies in our building. I remember a mass dispersal to the building's periphery. Once there people formed one of two reactions: fixation, like Jones, and also those who shot back toward the building's center, huddling and crumbling inward on themselves, shuddering and sobbing.

I stood in between them. I found myself over time creeping slowly toward the edge, all while random human projectiles shot away from the edge past me. I reached the precipice and gazed, spellbound: all the streets, the whole grid, lay swathed in green-brown fuzz in every direction. That same growth had reached the fifth floor of most buildings. My mind jumped to the possibility that somewhere within a building there could be some chamber or compartment capable of keeping the mold at bay. But just as quickly I realized that such a room would be a coffin of a much more terrible sort.

The mold clung to the base of the Space Needle a few blocks north. Bus-, car-, and truck-shaped clumps of mold dotted the streets, some overturned.

Helicopters buzzed and darted, and from the tops of other buildings, screams for help. It seemed as though commotion erupted on our rooftop later than the others, but I don't trust that memory. In hindsight, that seems unlikely.

Screams erupted from behind me, and I ran to the opposite side of the roof. Sarah dashed past me screaming and bawling, alongside others. I looked down over the edge and immediately felt bile rise in my throat. My vision went white at the edges, but in the center I beheld the roof of the six-story building across the street from our own: mold grew over its top. Where it touched the people who had raced to the supposed safety of its height, it devoured them over the course of many terrifying seconds. They flailed and shrieked. Their bodies hurtled mold pellets of themselves into others, who shouted epithets in return and pushed those already partially consumed into ravenous green and brown.

I retched and crawled away, trailing the others and wiping vomit from my lips. The mold had only reached the eighth floor of the taller building beside us. Four more to go for us.

We grew more silent then, on our roof.

A helicopter passed directly overhead. I wondered if they would stop here. I tried calling my parents, though I was not surprised to find we had no service. They live in the San Fran metropolitan area, and I said a silent prayer that they'd come through this safe…but through to what? Would the mold, or moss, or whatever it was, satisfy itself with only metropolitan areas? Or would it keep spreading? Probably the latter.

At first I wondered if it were an illusion, some kind of mirage. The screaming and waving of the crowd as a whole had become a timeless infinity. How many helicopters had passed us completely by I couldn't say. And then, suddenly helicopters were approaching, slowing, and, apparently, landing on our roof.

The helicopters drew toward us, and some of us drew too close, and others, myself included, pulled people back so the pilots could land their crafts. The metal creatures descended, their landing struts looking thin, wiry and feeble. All around me, shrieking and screaming, people punching, clawing, and drawing blood for just the chance to get in. My voice joined the maelstrom to let Martin, Nate, Sarah, Arthur, Charlie, Carol, and Seth on board. A punch to my gut, and I doubled over, my entreaties reduced to wheezing gasps. I was shoved and pushed away, others fighting to get in. In one final burst of energy, I pulled a man I didn't recognize off the helicopter, grabbed out for Sarah's arm, and pulled her into the helicopter. A blow to my head, and then an image of Jones climbing into the helicopter as it was taking off. The helicopter tilted to one side and wobbled. Some twenty meters above the rooftop, I saw Sarah plummet from the door. Jones leaning over her as she toppled out of the crowded craft. I couldn't decide if he'd pushed her or had been trying to pull her in. In the end it didn't matter much as she slammed into the roof, head first.

My next memory is of the helicopters departing, flying away south and east. I lay, my elbow supporting me, the helicopter buzz diminishing. The screams, shrieks and sobs of those still on the roof erupting at intervals. Sarah lying, shuddering, a pool of blood beneath her. Martin, Nate, Seth, and Arthur stood some ways off, glaring at me. Charlie, Carol, and Seth must have gotten on a helicopter, and I suppose I will never know if I played any part in their escape. I can only hope they will survive into a world that will not be utterly cruel.

Martin, Nate, Seth, and Arthur walked away toward a corner of the roof. I hobbled toward the opposite corner. At that time, the mold was two floors below us.

I stand now, looking out over the ruins of my former city. All its buildings, all its infrastructure, all its power, all its glory, gone. I used to pride myself on being capable of participating in all this. I wonder now whether or not that pride was misplaced. People talk of the things that run through the mind before certain death, the memories of all the things that have come before. I had a happy childhood. I've had girlfriends. I even had a few glancing blows with love. I cling to little things—breakfast at dawn on vacation with Ashley in Cannon Beach—making my first three-point shot in basketball club at the age of eight—the birthday party my parents threw for me when I was twelve at the Milwaukee Zoo—the day I got my first job in tech and felt as though my decade-long journey to be validated as a professional coder had finally come to fruition.

My whole life I have tried to help others, and I wonder whether or not I have really succeeded. I think though, that at least I have tried. I cannot imagine having done otherwise. But I also feel it wasn't enough. For all our technology, for all our social services, for all our bureaucracy, for everything we have built, we are biological creatures susceptible to a biological world too small to be fully understood by any but very a specialized few. Perhaps that applies to more levels of our existence than even biology.

The green-brown draws closer. I'm going to retreat toward the center of the roof now. I will not fight. I will not harm others in some futile defense of myself. Perhaps I can give Sarah some peace in her final moments. I will soon need such comfort myself.

The First Shot Fired

Tom Jolly

Editor: The thirst for knowledge always outpaces our own morality.

"The planet is about twenty-four light-years from Earth. From what we can tell from here, it's got water and free oxygen, and it's in the sun's habitable zone. It's very promising, sir."

"And it's called Gliese?"

"Gliese 667C. The naming committee has tentatively come up with 'Vogt's World,' after one of the scientists who discovered it."

"And you think we should fund a mission to it?"

Henderson shrugged. "A probe. Nothing spectacular. Take some photos, gather a little spectral data, transmit it back. If there's plant life, or even just bacteria growing there, we'll be able to detect it. But it's going to need some leading-edge tech to communicate its findings from twenty-four light-years away. And to get there within our lifetimes."

President Cochran smiled. "Well, my doctor says I'm likely good to one hundred forty, and I'm only seventy now, so that shouldn't be a problem. Twenty-four years isn't that long."

"No, sir, that's twenty-four light-years. It's a distance, not a time. With our best tech, it'll take forty years to get there, without slowing down once we arrive. It'd be a fly-by. And once it gets there, another twenty-four years for any data to return, moving at light-speed."

The president's brow furrowed. "So if I understand you right, that's what? Sixty-four years? That'll be a hard sell to the American public. What sort of cost are we talking about?"

"Maybe ten billion, plus or minus a few billion in pocket change. A big chunk of that is for the modified ground-based lasers stationed around the world that can be reused for other light-sail missions. We've got a top-secret mod to reduce beam divergence to zero, so we can maintain thrust at a half-gee for almost eighteen months, though we won't be telling the public about that. But we can pitch the ground-based installations as an innovative reusable laser-launch system that anyone can use, and develop the long-range light-sail probe on the side. It'll look cheap in comparison."

The president tapped his teeth with a pen, thinking. "Well, let's label it as a defense system so we can sell it to both sides of the aisle," he said. "Do we have the tech we need?"

"The solar sail and the ground-based lasers are proven hardware. As for the rest of it, I've brought Dr. Shamut, here, to explain the new tech required."

President Cochran nodded at the other man seated in the room, and said, "My next meeting is in five minutes, so try to keep it simple for me."

Shamut smiled nervously, running his hand through dark and unruly hair. He clearly wasn't used to visiting anyone but his engineering staff. "Well, to start we have to engineer the solar sail material so it can switch from clear to opaque. This should not be difficult, since such transition materials are commonly used as films on windows, but it will increase the weight of the solar sail. When the probe is very far from here, we select a trajectory that puts it between the Earth and Gliese 667C once a year, thus blocking a small fraction of the light from that sun. Then, we use a tiny bit of power to wink the solar sail on and off, either blocking Gliese's rays, or letting them through. It eliminates the need for a high-powered transmitter. We use the power of Gliese 667C to power our communications."

"Brilliant!" the president exclaimed, eyes glazed like a china doll. "And that will provide communications from twenty-some light-years away?"

Shamut and Henderson exchanged a hesitant glance, which immediately put the president on alert. Shamut clasped his hands together, and said, "Well, not exactly. When we get close enough to gather visual data, the probe will no longer be between the star and us. However, we have a technology loosely based on ferroliquids that will let us disperse a large cloud of ionized particles in space and shape them with a magnetic field. This can be used as a giant low-frequency antenna with which to transmit data back to Earth once the probe arrives."

The president sniffed, as though trying to ferret out a rotten egg. "Okay. So far that doesn't sound too bad. What is it you're not telling me?"

Henderson butted in. "Sir, we need a shaped tactical-nuclear device. If the ferrocloud disperses slowly, the solar winds will trash it before we can shape it and use it. We need to use a very powerful, precisely designed explosive to disperse the particle cloud fast enough and widely enough to be of use to us as a high-gain radio antenna."

President Cochran rolled his eyes. "So what you're actually telling me is that you want part of the probe design to be run as a covert project?"

They both nodded.

The president sat back and drummed his fingers on the desk. He glanced at his watch. "Time for my next meeting. You'll have to excuse me." He stood and shook Shamut's hand. "Generally, Dr. Shamut, I like the idea and I think we can move forward with this. Work out the details with Henderson, and please keep me informed on the status."

* * *

From Vogt's World, locally known as Pru, Vogt-1's solar sail looked like a tiny star headed for their solar system. The pruins had known for forty years that the probe was headed their way; they'd heard about it from Earth broadcasts. And they'd been arguing continuously as to whether they should let the probe arrive or not.

"The humans are not ready to contact the Twelve. Even now, there are six wars continuing on Earth. Their news is rife with murder, conflict, and the destruction of their own ecosystem."

"Well, they do have their downsides, I'll admit. But they had the technology and curiosity to send this probe out."

The pruin snorted, his *loquin* quivering in disdain. "So did the Hive Machines back in 60601, but that did not make it acceptable for them to join the rest of us."

Another *borbolled* in agreement. "The universe would likely be a safer place without the potential threat of the humans."

"You aren't seriously suggesting removing humans from the *shozbat* pool merely because of what they *might* do in the future?"

"Why not? Humans are apparently quite good at killing off imaginary threats before they become actual threats."

"So we should lower our standards to that of humans?"

One pruin, larger than the rest, slapped his *palak* on the table. "This isn't a moral discussion about eliminating humans, we just need to decide whether to destroy their cursed probe or not."

"We will regret letting the humans survive. Mark my words."

The bureaucrats, as many do, continued to rail at each other while postponing any decision or action. The probe entered their solar system and started recording data. They adjourned for their four-hour lunch break. By the time they returned, it would be far too late to do anything about the probe.

* * *

All species harbor a few specimens who are willing to go down to the beach to watch a tidal wave. Lepranik and Varprasil had taken a day-jaunt to Shinpru, one of the moons off Lamuth, a gas giant four orbits out from Pru. The crawling gardens of Shinpru were known throughout the Twelve. But Lepranik had other ideas once they reached space.

"Let's visit that Earthling probe!" he suggested, shading his *labut* to olive-green, indicating a level of excitement mixed with anxiety.

Varprasil curled his *loquin* in disapproval. "The council has not yet decided if the probe should be destroyed or not."

"The council couldn't make a decision in a full orbit, even if it concerned putting out a fire on their moldy gray *labuts*. The probe has passed its closest approach to Pru, and if it hasn't finished taking pictures, I'm sure it's going to very soon." Lepranik shifted the lever on the quantum equivalence relocator and transferred their quantum stats to a nexus near the probe. "Where's the light sail?"

"It detached from the probe shortly after the probe left their heliosphere to reduce interstellar drag. You can see the probe on the monitor, though." Varprasil pointed to a glowing dot hovering in the map-space between them. "It's very small." He peered at the map-space as the glowing dot split apart. "Now there are two pieces. One is drifting away from the other." He leaned back, his *loquin* shaking nervously. "We shouldn't be here," he muttered.

"Pah. Let's get closer. It's only moving at point-seven light." Lepranik flipped on the lightwarper to make sure they appeared invisible to the probe's cameras, then tweaked the control lever again to match vectors. A few gentle adjustments got them within ten meters of the smaller probe section.

"Not much to it," Varprasil said.

"This part of it would fit in our cargo bay, don't you think? We could grab it, pop over to Earth tonight, drop it in their orbit, and be back before *zutch*. Wouldn't they be surprised!"

"I think the council would cut off our *drassils* for such a stunt. You know we're under a strict mandate to avoid contact with humans." He stared at the probe. "Fortunate for us that we haven't used radio waves for over 50,000 years."

"Let's grab it anyway. In a big city like ours, we could get top creds for a human artifact."

Varprasil chuckled. "Well! I do believe you are correct. However, humans may be curious if their probe suddenly stops broadcasting data."

"Pah. It's well past perigee. I'm sure it's done taking data by now. They'll never notice."

∗ ∗ ∗

Molnidoss had a reputation in the alien artifact and fossil business, along with a sideline of contraband living biospecimens. His storefront gaudily displayed the legal half of the business, but they were mostly items that could be had from a dozen such dealers across the city. The advantage of living in the largest city on Pru, despite the competition, was the ready access to a wide base of customers who wanted something unique. Something that the law might frown upon.

Varprasil and Lepranik had business on the marginal side of legal with Molnidoss in the past. They brought the human satellite into Molnidoss's warehouse on a floater and proudly displayed it for him, waiting for an estimate.

"You're in luck," Molnidoss told them. "When you contacted me, I called a client who already has some interest in human artifacts."

"Here in Varsanika?"

"No, hundreds of drik from here," Molnidoss said, evasively. The two of them, he knew, were just the types to try to circumvent him as the middleman. "Let me scan this for pathogens. You'll get less if I have to sterilize it first, and a lot less if it makes me sick with some *polotni* bug."

He grabbed the scanner from a storage shelf and stared at the 3D display that popped up above it, positioning it to see the entire satellite. "Hmm. No biologicals. Plenty of radiation."

Varprasil nodded. "The humans use radioactives with thermal converters to provide long-duration power. They use it whenever they send a probe far from the sun."

Molnidoss pointed at a tube-shaped device. "That explains this bit. What about this cluster over here?"

They leaned forward, peering through the layers of holographic imagery. Molnidoss frowned. "You did disconnect the power before you brought this thing in, didn't you?" They heard something click, and for a very brief moment, watched as a dozen small squibs exploded, driving packets of plutonium together, and Molnidoss used the last fraction of a second of his life to consider how disappointed his customer would be that his Earth artifact was no longer available, and whether he'd complain to the authorities about it.

* * *

Ex-President Cochran sat on the porch in his retirement home in Avila Beach. He was celebrating his 110th birthday, and his old friend Henderson had come to visit.

"Vogt-1 will have started transmitting its first photos back by now," Cochran said.

Henderson nodded. "And all we have to do is wait twenty-four years to see if the planet is habitable. I hope I live long enough to see that day."

They sat and watched the evening sky, celebrating his birthday with thirty-year-old Glenmorangie and comfortable silence stirred by a warm ocean breeze. Stars began to appear, and then more stars, and more stars.

The sky became dense with tiny lights, and then they all began to move.

"Now that's odd," Cochran said.

Henderson stared in disbelief at the sky. Memories from forty years before poured unbidden into his mind, and it only took moments for him to guess what had happened. Momentarily, he thought about what faster-than-light flight could mean for humanity. If any of them were still alive by tomorrow. He bent his head down and closed his eyes, a tear trying to escape from one corner, but he rubbed it away before it could morph into an actual emotion. What use was that now? Sighing, he stood up, picked up the bottle of Scotch and topped off both their glasses, then sat back down to watch the show.

The Fluffpocalypse

Madison Keller

Editor: We are not the only tool user on earth. We are not the only ones to communicate. We are not the only ones to build structures for our purposes. It is only our blind arrogance to believe humans are something special on this planet.

"A summer job as a fire lookout? Really, Mother?" Katie didn't even glance up from her laptop, instead opting to roll her eyes at the screen. "I'm studying to be a wildlife biologist, not a firefighter."

"I know, dear, but you'd have lots of time to study the animals in their native habitats."

"Don't forget free room and board," her father piped up from the other side of the table. "Plus, you'll be saving every dime you make. Not much opportunity to spend money in the middle of the woods."

Katie grimaced and acknowledged the point. "All right, I'll look into it."

Two weeks later Katie pulled her Ford Ranger to a stop in front of a cutesy log-cabin with a tin roof. A green and gold US Forest Service shield decorated the front. Moments after Katie slammed her door shut the cabin's door opened and a blond, well the only word to describe him was hunk, strode out.

"Ah, you must be Katie!" The muscled hunk had a big smile on his face as he held out a hand toward her.

Katie reached out and shook it. "Yes, and you must be Broderick."

"Call me Brody, please."

Katie grinned at her new boss. Summer already looked better. Brody motioned her into the cabin and pointed to an elevation map pinned to one wall. He stabbed a finger down close to one of the highest points. "Now, we've got you assigned to Yaak Mountain. Due to the location you'll have to hike the last few miles up. The tower is equipped with a two-way radio that lets you communicate directly with me here at the station." Brody pointed to a mess of wires and electronics stacked on a rickety-looking table in the corner. "Any questions?"

Are you single? popped into Katie's head but she squashed the voice down. Katie suspected flirting with the boss on the first day wouldn't be appropriate. Instead, she walked over to the radio. "Yeah, how do I use it?"

"No worries, I'll go up to the tower with you and give you a quick rundown. Each tower is also equipped with an instruction manual and emergency procedures."

* * *

Katie stared up, and up, and up at the tiny building perched on stilts high above their head. "I have to live *there* for the entire summer! Are you kidding me?"

Brody cracked a smile and shrugged. "It's not as bad as all that. And the views are spectacular."

"Wanna swap?" Katie said, only half joking.

"Sorry," Brody chuckled. "I gotta keep the ranger station manned so I can keep in contact with all the towers. The radio here isn't set up for that. But I'm not kidding when I say it's not that bad. This was *my* post before I got promoted. The heights bothered me, too, at first. You'll get used to it. Even come to enjoy it."

Katie eyed the cardboard box that Brody held and hefted her own heavy pack higher. "How do I get all these supplies up there?"

"There's a trick to it. Here, you follow me up. I'll help you get settled in before I head back to the station."

Brody lifted the box to one shoulder and climbed up the side of the tower one-handed, only stopping to adjust his grip on the box. Katie watched him in awe, her mouth hanging open as he swiftly ascended. About halfway up he stopped and yelled down at her. "Coming?"

Katie groaned as she put her foot on the bottom rung. How had she let her parents talk her into this again? The pack pulled at her shoulders as she climbed, and her hands and calves were sore and trembling by the time she pulled herself through the door. She found Brody meditating in the center of the room. He let out a deep breath and opened his eyes when Katie dumped her backpack on the floor. He suppressed a smile as she rolled her arms and massaged her collarbone where the straps had dug in.

"Yeah, I know. I'll get used to it," Katie grumbled as Brody stood up.

"Trust me, you will. I saw your resume, you're a future wildlife biologist. You want to be a park ranger?"

Katie nodded, brightening at the approval she heard in Brody's voice.

"Well, when you get your first job as a ranger, you'll be thanking me for putting you up here." Brody winked at her. "You'll be fit as a fiddle and have no fear of heights by the end of the summer."

Katie giggled as Brody moved over to the radio set up in front of one of the room's four picture windows. "Now, here's how you use this bad boy."

For the next thirty minutes Brody ran her through the radios basics and then waited while Katie demonstrated each operation.

"Perfect." He pulled a tattered book out from between the tangle of wires. "If you forget anything you can look it up in here. Don't forget to check in with me several times a day."

"Great."

He set the book down and checked the sky, which had darkened into twilight while they talked. "I need to be getting back to the station. I'll be back in two days with more supplies, unless I hear from you sooner."

A concussive boom drowned out Katie's reply and sucked the air from her lungs. Bright light flooded the room as she staggered for balance. She and Brody rushed over to the window and looked up just as a second boom shook the tower. A light streaked across the sky high above them, a miniature sun moving across the heavens leaving a trail of fire in its wake. Smaller lights branched out off of it at each of several successive explosions. The light disappeared beyond the horizon in the north, the ringing in Katie's ears the only evidence of its passing.

After Brody left, still gushing over the fireball, Katie tried to share the news with her friends. That was when she discovered that her phone didn't get a signal up here. At all. Not even a single measly bar, like she'd had back at Brody's ranger station.

No matter. She still had all her games and apps, and she'd just send out all her texts during her supply runs. That held her over for about a day until her phone got down to less than 10 percent battery life and she discovered that the tower didn't get electricity. Her cries of anguish had sent the crows flying away.

She could get through this, Katie told herself as she paced. The walls of the tower seemed to be closer together on each circuit of the room. A future wildlife biologist would most likely work in conditions like these. After the third time she caught herself pulling out her dead phone, Katie decided she needed a walk to clear her head.

The climb down was easier than the previous day. As she straightened her shirt and checked her shoelaces, she noticed a chipmunk climb out onto a branch next to her. Katie smiled at it and offered it a peanut from her bag of trail mix.

"Here you go, little guy." Katie set the peanut down on a rock and left. While she fed the squirrels and pigeons from the park at home by hand, these were wild animals.

When she returned from her hike an hour later the chipmunk still sat on the branch nibbling on the nut clutched in its little paws. Its eyes tracked her as she walked by. Chipmunks in the park never did that, but perhaps wild animals had different behavior patterns.

Back up in the lookout tower Katie pulled out her textbooks. This, at least, was paper and didn't rely on a charger like her phone or kindle. She'd brought them along to get a jump on the school year. Now she flipped open to the section on order Rodentia.

Chipmunks, she read, always stuffed food in their cheeks and consumed them later in a safe place, like their dens. Katie pulled out a notebook, jotted down the date, time, and a note on the aberrant behavior, and then went to bed.

Over the next few weeks she added field notes to her little notebook, places where she observed species acting in ways that contradicted her textbook. At first she thought she would use these notes to grill her teacher when class started in the fall, but the more she saw the more she wondered. How could everything in the book be wrong?

By the end of the first month her single chipmunk watcher had morphed into a considerable gathering. And it wasn't just chipmunks anymore. Squirrels, rabbits, mice, minks, and even a skunk on several memorable mornings joined the audience. Lonely as she was, Katie came to consider them her friends, prattling on to them in one-sided monologues each time she entered or left the tower. She couldn't explain why, but the talks made her feel better, and it almost felt like they were listening and absorbing her words.

* * *

After months of observations, Katie decided that the animals of Kootenai Forest deserved to be the subject of her graduate paper. She continued recording her notes and even picked up a disposable camera on one of her rare trips down to Bonner's Ferry.

Her lookout tower job would be over at the end of August, just two short weeks away. A light sprinkle of rain muddied the trail while Katie enjoyed her morning walk. As she listened to the birds chirp and enjoyed the way the sunlight sparkled on the wet leaves, she came across a fluffle of bunnies. Not a rare sight, but this group was taking turns sliding down a mud-slicked hill on a large piece of bark.

Katie grinned and pulled out her camera. Now Brody would have to believe her tales about the strange animals around the forest. No one, on seeing these pictures, would say this was natural bunny behavior.

The camera made loud clicks as she cranked the dial between pictures, but the rabbits either didn't care about her presence or were having too much fun on their improvised slide to want to leave. Katie moved in closer; her cheap camera lacked a zoom and the rabbits at play were just too cute.

She stepped off the trail and crouched when something screamed underneath her foot. Katie jumped backwards, revealing a tiny rabbit, no bigger than her thigh. Its mud-caked fur blended in with the ground and she took a moment to see why it screamed. The rabbit's back leg was embedded in Katie's boot print, its leg broken by Katie's boot. The rabbit continued to scream and lifted a front paw, pointing at Katie. Since when did rabbits have fingers on their paws?

A shuffling in front of her drew Katie's attention, and she lifted her eyes. The entire fluffle stopped their play and were hopping her way, every single black eye fixed unblinkingly on Katie.

"I'm sorry, it was an accident!" Katie stuffed her camera in the pocket of her jeans and backed up, but then she wondered what she was doing running from rabbits, for Christ's sake.

The biggest member of the fluffle lifted a paw. It held a long stick, taller than the big rabbit's tall ears, with a sharpened piece of rock tied to the end, looking for all the world like a cartoon caveman spear.

Katie's mouth dropped open, and she stuttered something unintelligible, unable to pull words from the maelstrom of her thoughts. Had she lost her mind? She turned and ran, her boots sliding as she clawed her way back up to the path.

Gotta tell Brody! gotta tell Brody! kept racing through her mind as she sprinted down the trail. Her ever-present fan club wasn't in its usual place in front for which Katie thanked the gods. She wasn't sure if she could handle seeing any more small forest critters right now. She didn't even slow down as she approached the base of the tower; instead she jumped as she got close, saving herself a few feet of climbing. Katie climbed as fast as she dared, eyes fixed on the hole above her that led to her balcony.

A furry squirrel head popped into view, staring down at her through the hole for a moment before disappearing again. Katie's heart beat faster, a bad feeling in the pit of her stomach. A piece of electronic equipment dropped through the hole and Katie stopped climbing to cover her head. The box hit her arm, leaving a nasty gash before bouncing away.

Chittering and crashing sounds came from the hole above her. More debris tumbled down on her, but nothing else as big as the heavy electronic container. Katie climbed inside just in time to see hundreds of fluffy brown tails disappearing over the balcony.

Inside, shards of glass littered the tower from the remains of the windows. Only a few torn wires and a smashed microphone remained of her radio.

Blood dripped from her arm and she grabbed a torn tee-shirt off the mess on the floor, shaking broken glass out before pressing it against her wound. Almost all her clothing seemed to be missing, along with her textbooks, the first aid kit, her dead cell phone, her Kindle, and even her backpack with her car keys. The bed lay disassembled, the metal frame in pieces and the screws strewn about. Her mattress was shredded beyond use—as well as, if the smell was any indication, urinated on.

Her climb back down the tower was uneventful. A few crows circled her before flying off, but their eyes didn't show the malevolent intelligence that marked the fluffle as something other, probably just drawn by the blood on her arm. Probably. But Katie descended faster after seeing them.

Katie sprinted down the trail toward her car and freedom, done with this forest, done with this job. Through the trees twice she spotted a flash of brown fur and once a pair of glowing eyes, but made it down to her car without further incidence.

She was just having a nervous breakdown and her mind playing tricks on her. Her heart rate slowed and as she calmed down the whole thing seemed more and more far-fetched. She'd just been out here alone in the woods too long that was all.

Her Ford Ranger pickup was where she'd left it, untouched, and looking incongruous amongst the ferns and trees. More evidence that the attack was all in her head. Still, her hands shook as she felt around in the wheel-well for her spare key. The magnetic box was right where her father had put it after the third time Katie locked her keys in the car in high school. Moments later Katie slid into the driver's seat, starting the car as she fastened her seatbelt.

As she reached over to put the car into drive a shadow approached from behind. She glanced up into the rear-view mirror and her heart froze. A group of white-tailed deer and pronghorns poured out of the woods behind her. Katie threw the truck into gear and stomped on the gas; the rear tires fishtailed on the leaves before she roared away. A bull-moose jumped out of the trees, joining the deer and pronghorns in the chase.

The moose, hooves pounding on the blacktop as it galloped alongside her speeding car, glared at Katie through the driver's side window. Its mouth moved, and Katie was glad the roar of her engine drowned out whatever sounds came out of it. Katie gripped the steering wheel tighter, her knuckles turning white as she floored it. A standard student beater truck, the engine screamed as the needle passed fifty on the speedometer.

Trees flashed past, and she pulled away from the moose. The bull lunged to the side; antlers scored the camper-top with a screech, shattering the back window and jerking the car to the side. Katie struggled to keep the car pointing forward as they hurtled down the narrow road.

The moose slowed to a trot and disappeared in the distance. Katie didn't dare slow down; the pronghorns and deer were coordinating for an attack, lining up to again ram the side of her car.

On her speedometer the needle edged over fifty-five. The white-tails fell back barely able to stay even with the truck bed, and even the pronghorns were struggling. A burning smell wafted to Katie from the dash, but she ignored it. The truck whipped around another tight corner— Katie would have sworn that two of her wheels left the ground—and then she was alone on the blacktop.

The rear-view showed the animals trotting to a stop gathered in the middle of the road. One stood up on its two rear legs and shook a front hoof at her as she flew around another corner. Katie shuddered and willed the car to go faster.

* * *

The turnoff to Brody's ranger station was somewhere back behind her, missed during her wild flight from the deer, yet she didn't dare turn around. Not with the herd back there waiting for her. Forward was the only option, even though she had no idea where this road led. The paper map in her glove box wouldn't do much good until she spotted a landmark that would tell her where she was.

Her car dinged helpfully and Katie glanced at the dash. Low on gas. Perfect. Katie grimaced. Lost, chased by deranged wildlife, and now almost out of gas in the middle of nowhere.

Ten minutes later Katie despaired of ever escaping these woods. So far she hadn't passed a single sign to indicate where she might be, not a single turn off, nor any sign of a house. A house at least would have a phone, a way for her to call Brody and warn him about the animals.

The road curved and as she came around it the ever-present trees fell away, revealing a grassy meadow. At the far end, just within view, she spotted a tall chain-link fence. Behind that, almost hidden in the shadow of the trees, a house. A dirt road wound its way through the grass parallel to the fence.

Katie chewed her lip. If she stayed on the blacktop, there was the chance of her missing the turnoff, but her only other option was driving through the meadow. Her Ranger wasn't meant for off-road driving, but the field looked flat enough.

The wind howling through her broken window and the dent in her camper-top decided for her. Her truck was already a total loss, and she'd have to abandon it anyway when she ran out of gas. Katie lifted her foot from the pedal and turned off the road, bouncing the truck down a small incline and into the meadow.

From the road the grass looked deceptively short; the tops of the stalks were taller than the roof of her car. Well, the fence was a straight shot off the road. She kept the wheel straight and drove forward. Chain link was visible in flashes as the car bumped along.

Suddenly, the truck shot free of the grass, just feet from the fence, onto the dirt road. Katie stomped the brake and twisted the steering wheel. The tires spun on the mud and the back end of the car fishtailed around, crashing through the fence with a crunch. Katie's head whacked into the steering wheel as the truck jerked to a stop.

* * *

Katie came to slowly. Her head ached and when she reached up, she had a big goose-egg on her forehead. The driver's side door wouldn't open at Katie's fumbling touch and when her bleary eyes focused enough to see it was obvious why. The left side of the truck was wedged against the fence. Katie tried to crawl to the passenger side but something held her in place. Her seatbelt. She unbuckled it and crawled across to the passenger door, falling out into the mud with a groan.

She lay there for a moment, recovering, and then pulled herself to her feet to inspect the damage. The rear left of the pickup's bed had slid through the fence, tearing down the chain link and smashing through a pole, shearing it off. That point slashed the tire and came to rest underneath the truck, holding the back end off the ground. She wasn't going anywhere else in her Ranger now.

Katie looked around, surprised that the crash hadn't drawn the attention of the house's occupants. Or maybe it had. A squirrel stared down at her from atop the barbed wire, its tail twitching.

"Get out of here, human," the squirrel chittered in a rough approximation of human speech.

The words sounded incongruous coming out of the mouth of a cute little forest animal. Katie screamed and fell back on her butt, scrabbling backward away from the thing. This was the first time one of these nightmare animals had spoken; she pushed the moose's moving mouth from her thoughts. Until now she'd been able to write off the aberrant behavior of the animals but the talking squirrel, she had no explanation for.

The chipmunks, mice, and rabbits that had seemed abnormally interested in watching her go about her day had just been curious. Squirrels tearing up the radio in her watchtower had just been hungry and looking for food. The moose, antelope, and deer chasing her had eaten something rotten and become enraged. Now the stress was causing her feverish mind to hallucinate. That had to be it. Hallucination.

Her hands brushed a rock, and she picked it up, chucking it with all her might at the thing from her nightmares. "Leave me alone! I'm not crazy, I'm not!"

The squirrel danced away from her clumsy throw and scampered away down the fence, disappearing into the long grass heading toward the house. Katie jumped to her feet and chased it. The house might have a telephone, or even a map and a car.

She reached the driveway first and turned to run along it. Easier than fumbling her way through the long grass, tripping on unseen obstacles, and she now had her first unobstructed view of the front of the house. The garage door sat open, and inside the setting sun gleamed off the shiny paint of a humongous 4-wheel-drive truck.

Brody had been right about one thing. She was already thanking him for the endurance she'd built up over the summer. She wasn't even breathing hard as she pounded up the front steps although her head and neck still hurt from the car crash and her arm throbbed under her tee-shirt bandage. As she reached the porch, the front door opened and a bloodhound wearing a loose pair of overalls stepped out on two legs to greet her. The dog held a shotgun leveled at her head in his two front paws.

"Stay away," Katie stuttered, falling back a step.

The dog gave a little whuff and lowered the gun. "No hurt you," it barked as it retreated through the door. "Come."

Katie stood still, frozen with indecision. Could she really trust this dog after the events of today?

A growl made her turn. Wolves prowled around the corner of the house, yellow eyes staring at her. All three had what looked to be assault rifles slung over their backs. Although they were on four legs Katie followed the bloodhound into the house.

As soon as she was through the door, the dog slammed it shut behind her and threw the safety bolt. He turned to her, his big tail wagging behind him. Drool hung from one jowled cheek and he licked it back as he propped the shotgun in the corner. Katie backed down the hall as she stared.

"You hurt," he growled in a way that reminded her of Scooby-Doo.

"I'm fine, really. I just got lost, and I crashed my car into the fence." Katie figured she might as well roll with her hallucinations and placate the talking dog.

"Not good."

This voice came from behind her. Katie spun and stifled a scream. A Rottweiler stood there on two legs, naked except for her black fur. She held a plate in one paw, raw bacon piled high on it.

Katie stared at the plate and the dog cocked her head, following her gaze. She held out the plate to Katie. "I share food with master."

"Star, we need to get master out. Remember old masters?" The bloodhound squeezed past Katie in the narrow hallway and pushed the Rottweiler, Star, away into the kitchen. For lack of anything better to do Katie followed them.

All the cupboards were open, the dishes, pots, pans, and silverware spread about the floor. The fridge door lay on the ground and brown paw prints covered the shelves and tracked through the spilled condiments.

"We need to get out of here, the wolves..." Katie shuddered and hugged herself as she sunk down into a chair. "What is going on?"

"Don't know. We try help old masters, but wolf and fox come kill them. Star and Tank alone." The bloodhound's ears drooped, if possible, even more, and he looked at her with his liquid brown eyes.

"Tank, thank you for helping me. But what are we going to do about the wolves?"

"Wolf not get house, house bunker," Tank explained, wagging his tail as he pulled aside a curtain. Thick iron bars laced the window.

Katie closed her eyes and laid her head on the table. "What is going on? Why are dogs and squirrels talking to me?"

Tank leaned over and licked the side of her face. "Tank not know. Just one day Tank understand masters."

"What happened to your masters?"

"Come, we show." Star put down her plate of bacon and grabbed Katie's arm, tugging her to her feet. The dogs led her upstairs to a room overlooking the back of the house. Tank crouched, as did Star, so Katie followed suit. Tank nodded at Star then Katie before lifting the bottom of the curtain. Katie peered up. Small round holes punctured the glass in several places, bullet holes.

Underneath them lines of wolves and foxes milled about, each one with some kind of gun strapped to its back. The pop of gunfire came from somewhere out of her sight. Smaller animals dashed about underfoot of the others, squirrels, rabbits, and mice, carrying ammunition. She saw a group of mice off to the left all gathered around something open on the ground. It looked like a book, but she was too far away to guess more than that.

Both Star and Tank's gaze fixed on something and Katie shifted to see. Three dead humans lay off to the side of the barn, tossed in a pile out of the way of the milling animals. Katie sat back and covered her mouth. No wonder Tank and Star had been so eager to see her.

Tank motioned her away, and they moved into another bedroom.

"Where did all the guns come from?" Katie asked, pacing back and forth.

"Masters," Tank said, licking another big slurp of drool up. "Masters keep for end times. But mice crawl in, take guns, kill masters, and let in wolves."

"Why didn't the wolves kill you two?"

"Wolf want us help them, tell plan to kill other masters. But Tank and Star good boys, not hurt masters. Masters give pets."

"And bacon," Star piped up.

"We need to warn someone." Katie smacked her head. How could she have forgotten her original reason for heading for the house? "Where's the phone?"

Tank and Star took her back downstairs to the living room. But when Katie picked up the old handset nothing but silence greeted her. Not even a dial tone.

"Damn it, they must have figured out where the phone lines are and cut them." Just like her torn up radio. "Or just cut every line they found."

Katie flicked the switch on the living room wall, but nothing happened.

"We can't stay here," Katie said, remembering the empty fridge and the ransacked cupboards. "We need to make a break for Bonner's Ferry. Do you know where the car keys are?"

Star wagged her tail and bounded off, her claws clicking on the hardwood floors. She returned a few moments later, a ring of keys dangling from one paw, which she presented triumphantly to Katie with a big doggy grin. Katie took the keys and had to resist reaching up to pat the big dog on the head.

Katie found a flashlight and went through the house to gather supplies. In the basement she found a pantry as yet untouched by the dogs that contained what looked like years' worth of food. Still, she couldn't just hole up here and hide. She needed to get to town and warn them about the gun-wielding wolves and foxes. Either that or Katie would get to town and check herself into the nearest mental hospital. She still half suspected that the talking animals were a hallucination. Despite them walking on two legs and talking to her, their every action was still very doggy like. Like they would be if they were just regular dogs and her mind played tricks on her. She'd know for sure when she reached Bonner's Ferry. If the townsfolk could see and talk with Tank and Star, then she wasn't crazy. With that in mind, Katie carried upstairs only enough food for that night and the next day, leaving the rest.

In the kitchen, Katie opened a can of chili and out of force of habit from long years feeding her parents' dogs, dumped it into the doggy bowl on the floor.

Tank glared at her. "We like you now. Feed proper."

"Oh, yes, sorry." Katie blushed and opened a new can which she divided up onto three plates, setting them out on the kitchen table, along with forks.

They dined on cold chili and green beans in the light of the flashlight. The dogs used the forks, mostly, although Star needed some prodding from Tank. The implements looked odd in their paws, but it gave her an opportunity to study them. It appeared the dog's dewclaws, the vestigial fifth claw on their legs, had grown longer, giving them a proto-thumb.

Between the bump on her head and the throbbing gash on her arm Katie had little appetite, but she forced herself to eat. Occasionally a wolf howled outside.

"We'll leave in the morning," Katie announced when they finished eating.

Her head needed a chance to rest, and she wanted to search the house for a first aid box to clean and bind her arm. A household like this must have one around here somewhere. Plus, wolves and foxes were nocturnal hunters. Despite the changes she'd seen in Tank, Star, and the other animals, their base nature hadn't changed, so she suspected early morning hours would be their best chance to escape. Tank insisted she should take the masters' room upstairs. She understood why, when after she'd changed into a pair of pajamas borrowed from the dresser and crawled under the covers, Tank and Star both curled up in the bed with her.

* * *

During the night Star crawled onto Katie, pinning her to the bed with her massive Rottweiler body. So when Star got up as the sun rose, she woke Katie. Outside birds sang, and the sun shone. A normal day, and a perfect one at that, until Katie, unthinking, pulled aside the curtains. A wolf walked by below on two legs, a pistol held in its paws. Its ear twitched, and it looked up at her. Katie gulped and pulled the curtain closed again.

Breakfast consisted of cold franks and beans with Tank and Star. Tank still wore the overalls and Katie debated if she should ask Star to put on clothes too. After several minutes of watching the dogs eat, Tank with a fork and Star by licking things directly off the plate, she decided not to. If she *was* crazy, there was no need to buy more into the hallucination, and if she wasn't then it was Star's choice whether to dress like a human or not.

Katie changed into a clean pair of clothes from the dresser upstairs. They were a little big for her, but much better than her mud-and-blood-splattered ranger uniform. When she was ready, she gathered Tank and Star by the locked door to the garage. Katie gave Tank the backpack filled with food.

"Tank, your job is to get this backpack, you, and Star, into the back of the pickup truck."

Tank licked his jowls and nodded, setting his long ears flapping.

Star gave Katie a doggie smile. "What I do?"

"You follow Tank and hold on," Katie said, holding up the keys. The pickup truck had an automatic lock which meant no fumbling around with the door trying to get inside. "I'll drive. Tank, you sure you can give me directions to Bonner's Ferry?"

"Bonn Fair, yes, yes. We go with masters many times. Tank good dog."

Katie sighed. If Tank was a product of her hallucinating mind, she was in big trouble, but since she hadn't found a map, he was her only option. "All right, on three."

The two dogs looked serious while Katie grabbed the bolt. "One, two, three." Katie twisted the bolt and flung open the door. The two dogs raced past her, claws squealing on the linoleum. Katie dashed after them, not bothering to close the door behind her. She pushed the unlock button on the truck's key-fob and the driver's side door clicked. Tank tossed in the backpack then pushed up Star as Katie reached the door. The truck was so big that she couldn't even reach the door handle without standing on the door runner.

The door opened smoothly at her touch. Katie slid inside and jammed the key into the place. A howl rose up from the driveway, but she ignored it and slammed the door shut as the truck roared to life. In the rear-view she watched Tank climb over the truck bed, and as soon as he was inside she threw the truck into gear.

As they shot forward a group of wolves moved into the driveway, leveling weapons at the truck. Katie slammed down on the gas, flooring it straight at them. A few shots whizzed by the truck; one slammed through the windshield and shattered the rear-view mirror. Katie flinched away from the broken glass and plastic shards, but kept the truck heading steady. At the last second the wolves scrambled out of the way, and the truck barreled through where they'd just been standing.

Katie sped up as they approached the closed gate. The big truck hit with a scream of metal, tearing the chain-link right from its moorings and crushing the remains without even slowing down. The tires squealed for purchase as they swung out onto the blacktop and sped away. Tank crawled forward and stuck his head through the back window; his drooping ears flopped onto the back of the seat next to Katie as he gave her directions.

Several hours later they chugged into Bonner's Ferry and straight into a war zone. Dead deer, raccoons, rats, wolves, and more littered the streets, rotting in the summer sun. From the smell they hadn't been there more than a day. Bullet holes pockmarked the buildings and smoke wisped up from somewhere farther up the street. Here and there through the wreckage she could see a hand, or shoes sticking out. She hadn't been hallucinating after all, but it was too late. Katie averted her eyes and drove, looking for any signs of life.

Look for the next installment of our post-apocalyptic anthologies in Enter the Aftermath available September of 2017.

Author Biographies

Nick Barton

Nick Barton is a speculative fiction writer living in Somerset, England. His horror short story, THE LAST RESORT can be found in Wicked Tales anthology, 'Muffled Scream: Corner of the Eye.' If Nick has gone missing, chances are high he is living as a wood elf in Skyrim, dancing to The Beatles or watching The Lord of the Rings, again. Visit him at nickbartonauthor. co.uk or on Twitter @NickBarton101.

Matthew Buscemi

Matthew Buscemi is a speculative fiction author and founder of Fuzzy Hedgehog Press. He grew up in Illinois, but left to explore the world. He has taught English in Japan and Thailand, and has studied linguistics in Hawaii.

Nowadays he lives with his husband in Seattle, Washington, where he types code by day and prose by night. He dreams of exploring the multiverse himself, but until humanity gets around to inventing a means of inter-dimensional travel, his imagination will suffice.

Jessica Conoley

Jessica Conoley was raised on 80's action films, *Jem and the Holograms*, *X-Men*, and big-brother mandated *Star Wars*. Sitting in the back of class she never felt like she fit in with the other kids and escaped reality by reading. Three decades later she started writing fantasy novels, flash fiction, and essays to help other readers escape their own realities. In 2012, she became the Managing Editor of Kansas City Voices arts and literary magazine. In 2016, her short piece "I Am Descended From Giants" was awarded 1st place in creative nonfiction by the Writers Alliance of Gainesville. Get a free sneak peek of her work at http://jessicaconoley.com/

Lana Cooper

Philadelphia-based writer Lana Cooper doesn't usually talk about herself in the first person, but makes an exception when writing an author bio. In 2014, she published her first novel, Bad Taste In Men, a humorous coming-of-age tale for awkward teens who grew up in the '90s. Her work has appeared in several anthologies, with her short stories steeped in horror-humor and urban fantasy. Cooper has written extensively on a variety of pop culture topics for PopMatters and her own blog, DelightfullyDysfunctional.com. She enjoys communicating with stuffed animals and avoiding eye-contact with strangers on public transportation.

Lisha Goldberg

Lisha Goldberg started her professional career as a technical writer, then switched to teaching science to elementary children. She enjoys writing short stories and poems. Her hobbies include playing piano and creating artwork with mosaic tiles. Her short stories have appeared in Mad Scientist Journal, The Blotter, and Chicken Soup for the Soul.

Bruce Golden

Bruce Golden's short stories have been published more than a 150 times across 20 countries and a score of anthologies. Asimov's Science Fiction described his second novel, "If Mickey Spillane had collaborated with both Frederik Pohl and Philip K. Dick, he might have produced Golden's Better Than Chocolate"--and about his novel Evergreen, "If you can imagine Ursula Le Guin channeling H. Rider Haggard, you'll have the barest conception of this stirring book, which centers around a mysterious artifact and the people in its thrall." You can read more of Golden's stories in his new collection Tales of My Ancestors, which has been described as "The Twilight Zone meets Ancestry.com." http://goldentales.tripod.com

Russell Hemmell

Russell Hemmell is a statistician and social scientist from the U.K, passionate about astrophysics and speculative fiction. Recent stories in *Not One of Us*, *PerihelionSF*, *SQ Mag*, and elsewhere.

Tom Jolly

Tom Jolly is a retired astronautical / electrical engineer who now spends much of his time writing SF and fantasy, designing board games (such as Wiz-War, Drakon, and Manhattan Project: Energy Empire), and creating obnoxious puzzles. He lives with his wife Penny in Santa Maria, California, in a place where mountain lions and black bears still visit. You can find more of his stories at www.silcom.com/~tomjolly/tomjolly2.htm.

Madison Keller

When she was young, MADISON KELLER wanted to be one of the X-Men. While that dream never came true, her dream of writing did. Now she is the author of several epic fantasy novels and a plethora of short stories spanning multiple genres. When not writing she can often be found bicycling around the woods of the Pacific Northwest or at the dog park with the original Kerka, her adorable Chihuahua mix. More of Madison Keller's work can be found on her website, www.flowersfang.com

Simon Kewin

Simon Kewin is the author of over 100 published short stories. His works have appeared in Nature, Daily Science Fiction, Abyss & Apex and many more. He lives in England with his wife and their daughters. His cyberpunk novel The Genehunter and his Cloven Land fantasy trilogy were recently published. Find him at simonkewin.co.uk.

E.E. King

E.E. King is a performer, writer, biologist and painter. Ray Bradbury calls her stories "marvelously inventive, wildly funny and deeply thought provoking. I cannot recommend them highly enough."

Her books are; Dirk Quigby's Guide to the Afterlife, Real Conversations with Imaginary Friends, and Another Happy Ending.

She has won numerous awards and received grants in writing, painting and biology and has been published widely, most recently in Bram Stoker Nominee anthology, Darke Phantastique, Three Flatiron Anthologies, in Gemini as winner of the $1,000 Flash Fiction Award, "Now Write! (Science fiction)" (Tarcher/Penguin) and "Next Stop Hollywood" (St. Martin's Press).

She has worked with children in Bosnia, crocodiles in Mexico, frogs in Puerto Rico, egrets in Bali, mushrooms in Montana, archaeologists in

Spain, butterflies in South Central Los Angeles and lectured on island evolution and marine biology on cruise ships in the South Pacific and Caribbean.

Her art has been collected internationally and she's painted murals in Los Angeles and Spain.

Check out paintings writing and musings at www.elizabetheveking.com

Janice Law

Janice Law is an Edgar nominated novelist who also writes short stories and award winning non-fiction. Her most recent novels are Nights in Berlin, the start of a new trilogy featuring the gay, alcoholic painter, Francis Bacon (mysteriouspress.com), and Homeward Dove (Wildside Press). Earlier work includes the Anna Peters novels from Houghton Mifflin, Walker and St. Martins, and several contemporary novels from Forge Books. She regularly publishes short mystery fiction in Alfred Hitchcock Mystery Magazine and other mystery publications.

She lives with her sportswriter husband, Jerry, in Eastern Connecticut. www.janicelaw.com

Katrina Nicholson

Katrina Nicholson has a degree in history, a diploma in writing for film and television, and a horrified obsession with infectious diseases. Two of her short films have been produced in Toronto and fourteen of her short stories have been published in anthologies such as Tesseracts Fifteen, Futuredaze, The Future Embodied, Kisses by Clockwork, and the upcoming Schoolbooks and Sorcery. She lives in Nova Scotia, but you can visit her online at www.katrinanicholson.com.

Naomi Brett Rourke

Naomi Brett Rourke is an author and teacher living near the beach in Los Angeles. When not writing, she can be found with a book in her hand, with horror, crime, and mystery being her favorites. Naomi is an up-and-coming writer with stories published in the anthologies *Life on the Rez, Brewed Awakenings 2*, and in magazines such as London's *Morpheus Tales*, *The Mature Years*, and the *Young Adult Journal Refractions*. Coming out in 2017 are stories in the anthologies *100 Voices, Volume 3, Tragedy Queens: Stories Inspired by Lana del Rey and Sylvia Plath*, and *Straight Outta Tombstone*. You can see her work online at www.culturedvultures.

com and www.triggerwarningshortfiction. com. Her novella *Devil's Night* will be published by Frith Books in Great Britain. She is a member of Horror Writers Association, Mystery Writers of America, and Sisters in Crime. Visit her on her website at www.naomibrettrourke.com, on her facebook page at www.facebook.com/naomibrettrourke, Instagram at naomibrettrourke or Twitter at @NaomiBRourke.

Jacalyn Schnelle

Jacalyn Schnelle is a 26-year-old queer writer living in Tucson, Az. Her horror is influenced by the desert she was raised in, her queerness, and her struggles with mood disorders, including anxiety. More of her work can be found at https://jacalynschnelle.tumblr.com/ and the webcomic Springs Falls.

Jay Seate

After Jay read a few stories to his parents, they booted him out of the house. Undaunted, he continues to write everything from humor to the erotic to the macabre, and is especially keen on transcending genre pigeonholing. His tales span the gulf from Horror Novel Review's Best Short Fiction Award to Chicken Soup for the Soul. They may be told with hardcore realism or fantasy, bringing to life the most quirky of characters. See longer works at www.melange-books.com. Website: www.troyseateauthor.webs. com.

T.M. Starnes

T. M. Starnes has lived and traveled in the South Pacific, Hawaii, and Australia, discovering a deep love and respect for the people of the region and the varied cultures.

T. M. has been writing since the fourth grade and single-finger typed his way through his first short story before the sixth grade. His half-century mark recently arrived and the quality of his work has greatly improved since then.

He prefers writing in the horror, science fiction and, occasionally, romance genre.

His favorite authors include Clive Barker, Patricia Briggs, Dean Koontz, and Edgar Rice Burroughs.

Samples of his random writings can be found at TMStarnes2013. wordpress.com

Aaron Vlek

Aaron Vlek is a storyteller whose work focuses on the trickster mythos in its role as transformer, bringer of delight and proponent of disquieting humors. Some of her stories, involve the jinn, and of a universal imagining of the Native American character, Coyote. She indulges from time to time in the reimagining of classic themes of horror and the occult.

Hark, the Herald! appeared on The Wicked Library Christmassacre on December 24, 2016. Pickman's Daughter appears on Creeparoni YouTube channel December 2016. 13 appeared in The Wicked Library Live Halloween Special, October 31, 2016. The Accursed Lineage appears in the Alban Lake anthology Miskatonic Dreams, The Summer of the Amazing Mr. Fig appeared on Creeparoni YouTube Channel December 2016.

John Walters

John Walters is an American writer, a Clarion West graduate and member of Science Fiction Writers of America, who recently returned to the United States after living abroad for many years in India, Bangladesh, Italy, and Greece. He writes science fiction and fantasy, thrillers, mainstream fiction, and memoirs of his wanderings around the world. You can find his website/ blog at: www.johnwalterswriter.com.

Filip Wiltgren

Filip Wiltgren is a writer and tabletop game designer based in Sweden. A member of Codex and the Ubergroup, Filip has published in markets such as Daily SF, Grimdark and Nature Futures, as well as a number of anthologies and semi-pro markets. In his day life, he's worked as a journalist, copywriter and communications officer, and when he isn't writing, he spends time with his wife and kids. He can be found at: www. wiltgren.com

Brigitte Winter

Brigitte Winter is a storyteller, a jewelry-maker, a convener of artists and art lovers, and the executive director of Young Playwrights' Theater (yptdc. org), a Washington, DC, nonprofit that inspires young people to realize the power of their voices through creative writing. In 2014, Brigitte and her partner Dustin Blottenberger co-founded No Discipline Arts Collective, an artist-led initiative committed to producing cross-disciplinary work that breaks down traditional boundaries between creators and consumers. No Discipline regularly hosts art-a-thons, artist socials, museum crawls, writing critiques, figure drawing classes, and pop-up shows benefiting charities. Hang out with Brigitte at brigittewinter.com, and stay tuned for her latest project: a pre-apocalyptic coming-of-age adventure novel.

Other works from TANSTAAFL Press

Novels by Stephanie Weippert from TANSTAAFL Press

Sweet Secrets

At seven, Michael gets into trouble no more than any other boy his age, but he does have a sweet tooth. When the mailman brings a package from a candy company, he has to sneak just one. As he eats the chocolate, his home, stepfather, and everything he knows melts around him and disappears. Suddenly, he is in a dreamlike world. He is taken as an orphan, tested, and before he knows it, he's a student in the premier magic school on the planet. His fellow students can make cookies that fly and chocolate turtles that actually walk. Michael is told he has more power than any of them.

Brad, Michael's stepdad, had been charged with watching his stepson for the first time. When the boy disappears before his eyes, Brad panics. Within hours he is on an adventure tracking his son alongside his neighbor, an enigmatic chef and former graduate of the magic school. Always one step behind his son, Brad soon finds that Michael is being used as a pawn between the two most powerful chefs on the crazy planet. Worse, he has to get Michael home before his mother finds out he's gone or there is going to be hell to pay.

Road to Chaos

Robert Thompson is a vain, egotistical actor bent on making his mark on Hollywood. On his way to an important audition that may make his career, another car crashes into his. The other car is totaled but his land yacht is barely dented. The other driver, in a fit of lunacy, insists that they get in his car and drive away before the chaos mathamagic police find them. Robert scoffs. Magic is for rubes and what in this crazy man's delusions does chaos or math have to do with it?

Robert clings to his beliefs until he finds out that the other driver is his long-lost cousin, the magic police tries to kill them both, and his cousin Eric teleports them to Tibet. Robert finds himself bounced around the globe on a mixed attempt to both evade the brutal mathamagic goon squad and clear Eric's name, all the while hoping that he can return to salvage his real life of movies.

Novels by Tom Gondolfi
from TANSTAAFL Press

An Eighty Percent Solution—CorpGov Chronicles: Book One

In a world where corporations suborn governments as a part of good business practice and unregistered humans can be killed without penalty, Tony Sammis, a midlevel corporate functionary, finds himself unwittingly a pawn in a guerilla war between a powerful cabal of business leaders and an elusive but deadly underground movement. His final solution to the biological terror unleashed mirrors Tony's own twisted sense of justice.

Thinking Outside the Box—CorpGov Chronicles: Book Two

Winning one war doesn't seem to be enough. Tony Sammis and the Green Action Militia are once again thrust into the center of a conflict that will change the lives of everyone in the solar system. This time they are allies with the fledgling CorpGov and even the United States government against the ravages of the corrupt Metropolitan Police force. The GAM and their allies are fighting a losing war with few soldiers and even fewer weapons. Behind the scenes, a humble and unsuspected power block lurks with its own axe to grind.

Self-interest, romance, freedom, and a lust for power simmer together in this chaotic soup of tension, intrigue, assassination, and war.

The Bleeding Edge—CorpGov Chronicles: Book Three

Tony Sammis and Nanogate lead a patchwork alliance that includes the nascent CorpGov, Green Action Militia, the president of the United States, the Pacific Northwest Mob, most of the megacorps and the United Brotherhood of Bodyguards. The war the CorpGov alliance knows they can't win has begun, but they are no longer fighting to win. Tony and Nanogate know they may not survive, but they intend to deliver the most grievous wounds they can. The most dangerous animal is one with no hope.

Toy Wars

Flung to a remote world, a semi-sentient group of robotic mining factories arrive with their programming hashed. They can only create animated toys instead of normal mining and fighting machines. One of these factories, pushed to the edge of extinction by the fratricidal conflict, attempts a desperate gamble. Infusing one of its toys with the power of sentience begins the quest of a 2-meter-tall purple teddy bear and his pink polka-dotted elephant companion. They must cross an alien world to find and enlist the aid of mortal enemies to end the genocide before Toy Wars claims their family—all while asking the immortal question, "Why am I?"

Toy Reservations

Isp, toyanity's religious zealot, returns at the head of a massive new Army of the Humans. He openly announces his intent to replace President Quixote's government with a theocracy. With most of his toys modified to peacetime purposes, Don Quixote must make a horrific decision for the very soul of his people.

Novels by Bruce Graw
from TANSTAAFL Press

The Faerie of Central Park

The last of her kind in New York City, Tillianita tends the land and beasts as best she can, reluctantly obeying her departed father's warning to avoid humans at all costs. A freak accident casts her out of the relative safety of Central Park. Lost and alone with a broken wing, she wonders if she'll ever see her home again.

On his own for the first time in his life, college freshman Dave Thompson isn't sure he'll ever fit in. When he stumbles upon an extremely realistic fairy doll, he thinks perhaps it might make a good present for a future date until he discovers that it's not a doll at all. His find turns not only his life upside down but also expands his narrow view of the world.

Lady Hornet

Elizabeth Fontaine is a lonely, ordinary young woman in a world where superheroes struggle daily against evil. To fill the empty void within her soul, she becomes a hero fangirl, following every super's event, subscribing to multiple fanzines, and never missing the daily superhero talk shows... until one day, fate grants her the opportunity to leave behind her boring, dreary life and become what she's always dreamed of...a superheroine!

Elizabeth learns the hard way the meaning of the phrase, "Caveat Emptor!"—let the buyer beware!

Demon Holiday

Torval, Demon Third Class, Layer Four Hundred Twelve of the Eighth Circle of Hell, has been in the business of chastising sinners longer than he can remember. Delivering punishment is the only job he's ever known—the only job he's ever wanted. After Torval witnesses something unexpected, his demonic Overseer demands that he take time off to resolve this personal crisis. And so, Torval, the demon, finds himself sent on vacation...to Earth, the proving ground of souls!

Demon Ascendant

Torval, Demon Third Class, Layer Four Hundred Twelve of the Eighth Circle of Hell, on vacation to Earth has managed to find another demon, dated a woman, and inadvertently explored some of the sins of humankind: greed, gluttony, and lust. Through all this, his biggest struggle involves deciding if he wants his holiday to end or to continue forever.